DREAMQUAKE

BOOK TWO OF THE
DREAMHUNTER DUET

Elizabeth Knox

SQUARE
FISH

Farrar, Straus and Giroux
New York

To Margaret, with affection and admiration

✧ ✧ ✧

SQUARE
FISH
An Imprint of Macmillan

DREAMQUAKE. Copyright © 2007 by Elizabeth Knox. All rights reserved.
Printed in September 2009 in the United States of America
by R.R. Donnelley & Sons Company, Harrisonburg, Virginia.
For information, address Square Fish, 175 Fifth Avenue, New York, NY 10010.

Square Fish and the Square Fish logo are trademarks of Macmillan
and are used by Farrar, Straus and Giroux under license from Macmillan.

Library of Congress Cataloging-in-Publication Data
Knox, Elizabeth.
Dreamquake : book two of the Dreamhunter duet / Elizabeth Knox.
    p.   cm.
Summary: Aided by her family and her creation, Nown, Laura investigates the
powerful Regulatory Body's involvement in mysterious disappearances and activities
and learns, in the process, the true nature of the Place in which dreams are found.
    ISBN: 978-0-312-58147-3
[1. Dreams—Fiction.   2. Family life—Fiction.   3. Fantasy.]   I. Title.

PZ7.K7707 Dre 2007
[Fic]—dc22

                                                            2006048109

Originally published in the United Kingdom by Faber & Faber
First published in the United States by Farrar, Straus and Giroux
Square Fish logo designed by Filomena Tuosto
Designed by Irene Metaxatos
First Square Fish Edition: 2009
10 9 8 7 6 5 4 3 2 1
www.squarefishbooks.com

Contents

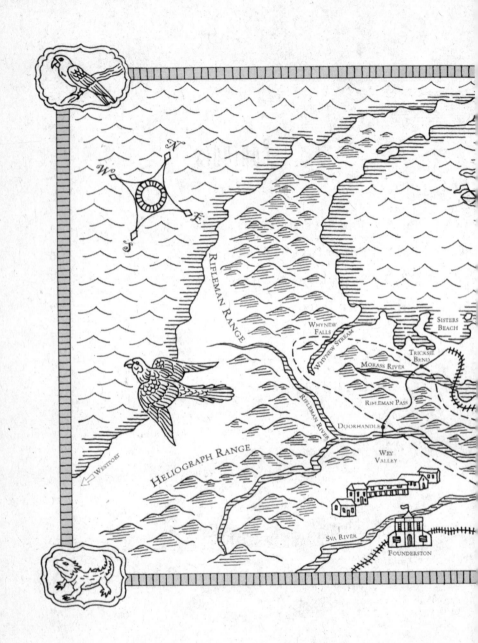

N

W

E

S

RIFLEMAN RANGE

WHYNEW
FALLS

WHYNEW STREAM

SISTERS
BEACH

MORASS RIVER

TRICKSIE
BEND

RIFLEMAN PASS

DOORHANDLE

RIFLEMAN RIVER

HELIOGRAPH RANGE

WESTPORT

WEY
VALLEY

SVA RIVER

FOUNDERSTON

LIGHTHOUSE

So Long Spit

Coal Bay

Road

Railway

Border of Place

Rivers and Streams

Awa Inlet

Mt Kahaugh

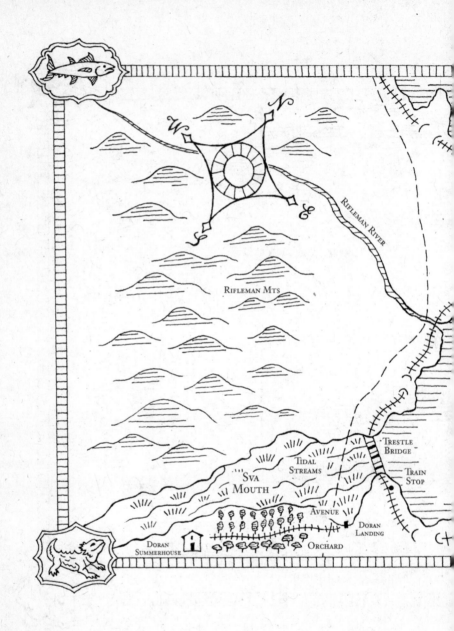

Coal Bay

Awa
Inlet

Mt
Kahaugh

Railway

Border of Place

Rivers and Streams

Road

Marshes

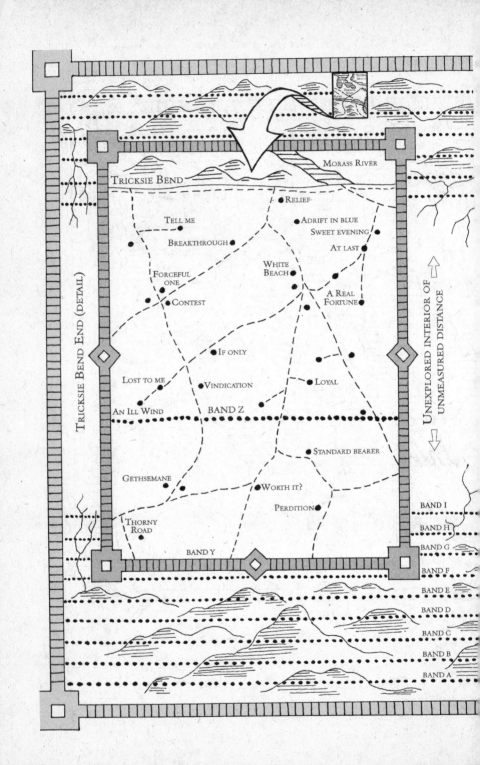

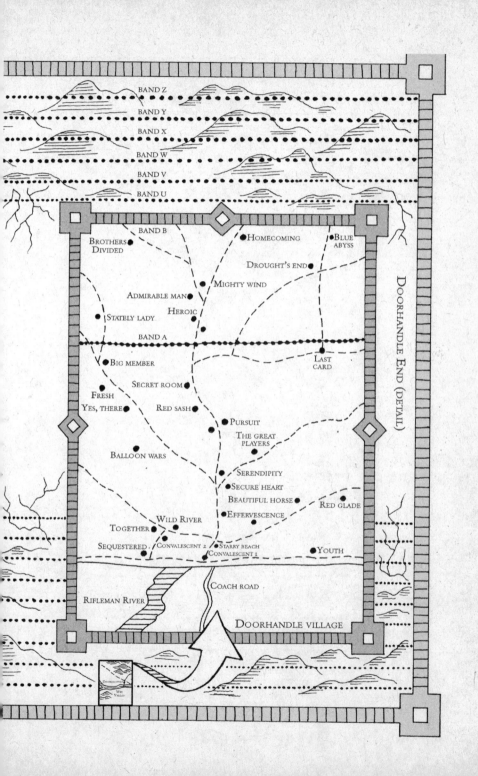

I

The Isle of the Temple

1

✧ ✧ ✧

*O*N ST. LAZARUS'S EVE IN 1906, OVER
ONE THOUSAND PEOPLE WERE AT THE
RAINBOW OPERA TO SHARE A TRADITIONAL
feast day dream. A dream named Homecoming, performed
by the dreamhunter Grace Tiebold.

Grace had told the Opera's manager that she'd been having
trouble falling asleep, and that it wouldn't do to keep her audience awake and staring at the ceilings of their bedchambers.
She'd arranged for another dreamhunter, George Mason, to
lie in with her. He had caught Homecoming too and so would
boost her already famously powerful performance. Also, Mason was a Soporif. He often worked in hospitals, enhancing
the effects of anesthetics. He would enter the operating room
before the surgeons and their assistants, and lie down near
the prepared patient—for anyone who was close to the Soporif
when he fell asleep would fall asleep with him.

At ten that evening, Grace and George Mason were settled
head-to-feet in the dreamer's bed, a silk-upholstered platform at the top of the dais in the center of the Rainbow
Opera's huge auditorium. The Opera had a full house.
Founderston's fashionable people—magnates, generals, politicians, and the President himself—were all in attendance.
The manager was happy and, at the time, looked on the

dreamhunter's change in the evening's arrangements as a good thing.

By midnight the Opera's four tiers of balconies were empty, waiters had collected the cups, liqueur glasses, and bonbon trays from the little tables and ottomans around each balcony. The padded doors to the bedchambers were fastened shut. Everyone—all but the President's and Secretary of the Interior's bodyguards, and the men from the fire watch, who were either patrolling balconies and back stairs in their soft-soled shoes or at their post in the window of the Rainbow Opera's control room—was in bed. The men from the fire watch were awake and vigilant. The building was secure and peaceful. A stage was set in the thousand drowsy heads of the Opera's patrons.

✧ ✧ ✧

Grace Tiebold lay under the thick, down-filled quilt of the dreamer's bed. She could hear Mason breathing quietly. She waited to fall through the trapdoor of his sleep into their shared dream. It was nice at least not to have to worry about when she'd drop off.

Instead, Grace worried about her husband, Chorley. Chorley had packed a bag and left the house a week before, and hadn't told her where he was going. Grace worried about her daughter, Rose, who had been boarding for two terms at Founderston Girls' Academy, a school that was less than a mile from her home. She worried that Rose, having been sent away by her parents, wouldn't want to come back and live with them again. Grace wanted to do something to reassure her daughter that they were interested in her. Perhaps she should arrange for Rose to come out at the next Presentation Ball, instead of having to wait another year and a half.

Grace worried about her dreamhunter niece, Laura. Since Laura's father, Tziga, had disappeared earlier in the year, she had been quite distant from her family. But at lunch that afternoon Laura had behaved beautifully. She'd been polite and affectionate. She had even remembered to bring her aunt and cousin St. Lazarus's Day gifts—the kind of nice gesture that was usually beyond her. Not that Laura *wasn't* nice—only that she was solemn and wrapped up in herself. At lunch Grace had watched Laura smiling as Rose opened her present, a box of musk creams from Farry's, the family's favorite confectioner. Grace had thought, "She's finally growing up." Rose, even biting into a musk cream and moaning loudly in delight, didn't give her mother a moment's doubt about *her* maturity.

As Grace waited to fall asleep, she mused on that lunch. She fretted. True, Laura had bought gifts and behaved herself, but, as Grace gazed into her memory and studied the face across the restaurant table, she could see that Laura had a look in her eyes, a dangerous look—like that her dreamhunter father had often worn—a kind of dark haze made of desperation and determination and power.

Lying in the white cloud of bed at the pinnacle of the Opera's dais, Grace thought, "What is Laura planning?" She turned her head and looked over at the second-story balcony, and the doors to the Hame and Tiebold suites, where Laura and Rose were sleeping. Firmly fastened, the quilted doors gave Grace no clues.

A moment later she was drifting. Something passed through her mind, a proud happiness about her home, her city, her country, the golden age in which she was living, the fine people she'd chosen to manage her world. The thought pleased her—and amused her too, since it was so unlike her. Why should she be thinking of President Wilkinson when she had so much on her mind?

Then Grace saw the crisp brown, late-summer leaves of oaks in a grove by the road that would take her *home*. George Mason had fallen asleep and had dropped her into her dream.

And then—suddenly—she wasn't at home. She was in a coffin, and under the ground, and she could not get out.

✦ ✦ ✦

Sandy Mason's bed at the Opera was one tier above and across the auditorium from the Hame and Tiebold suites. Sandy lay, his eyes fixed on the unadorned ceiling of his standard-sized room, and thought about Laura Hame.

When Laura saw him that evening, she had seized his hands and said his name, as if he was really something to her, more than a friend. Her hands were shaking, and Sandy was sure she'd been chewing Wakeful, the drug dreamhunters used to ensure they didn't sleep till they were ready to broadcast the dreams they'd caught. But if Laura had a dream, she shouldn't have been at the Opera. A dream would interfere with the sleep of people in rooms near her, and possibly contaminate the dream her aunt Grace would perform. Laura had made excuses, she'd said that her mouth was stained from sucking lollipops, not chewing Wakeful, but Sandy was sure that she was lying.

Laura had lied to him, but she had grabbed his hands and pulled him close, and gazed up into his face as if looking for salvation.

Sandy sat up abruptly, pounded his pillow a few times, then flopped back down again. He decided that he'd rather stop thinking about Laura Hame. She was too difficult, a sad and secretive girl. And despite the fact that they were both dreamhunters, had first entered the Place at last autumn's

Try, earned their licenses only months apart, despite all they shared, they were from very different worlds. Laura was wealthy. When her father, the famous dreamhunter Tziga Hame, had disappeared into the arid and silent interior of the Place, he was missed by dream palace patrons and *mourned* by all the invalids he had helped to better health. Laura's aunt was on the dreamer's dais and about to deliver a vivid and perfectly clear print of Homecoming to the audience of a dream palace that had been built for her. Even Laura's non-dreamhunter uncle, Chorley Tiebold, was famous—a figure of fashion and a talented hobby inventor. Laura was *somebody* by pedigree, while Sandy—Sandy was the middle child of seven, whose family lived in the provinces and whose father was the shop steward in a factory that made flax matting. Sandy's father thought that dreamhunting was fortune hunting. He'd said to his son, "Most dreamhunters wind up like wizened, squinty-eyed old gold prospectors, and the rest are corrupt or crazy." Sandy's father saw himself as the salt of the earth. He scorned his dreamhunter brother and was disgusted that any son of his should want to take up the trade, "if you can call lying around in a stupor in silk sheets a trade," he'd said. Sandy's father saw dreamhunting the way much of the population of Southland did—those too far from the Place for dreams to travel and keep fresh. The majority of Southlanders thought that dreams were a luxury, a drug of idleness. And though Sandy wanted more than anything to become a great and famous dreamhunter, a star like Grace Tiebold, or a magician like Tziga Hame, part of him felt his father's squeamish mistrust of dreamhunters.

Sandy bashed his pillow some more and told himself sternly that he was *not* falling for Laura Hame. He was only starstruck and infatuated with the idea of her family.

Sandy felt his Soporif uncle fall asleep and for a moment

resisted the cozy wave of weakness; breathed through it as though it were a spasm of pain. He held to his memory of Laura Hame's pale face and dark eyes, her stained lips and the mauve cave of her stained mouth. Then he felt himself slipping, and then he was asleep.

✧ ✧ ✧

. . . he woke, an invalid, weak and encumbered in sheets, wrapped in smooth cloth. Why was it so dark? He took a deep breath and sucked in a bubble of lily-scented satin.

A shroud was covering his mouth.

He flung out his hands. They hit the soft quilting that lined the sides of the casket, beneath which he felt the hard wood of the box itself. The box—narrow, and irresistible, and dark . . .

✧ ✧ ✧

The Rainbow Opera was oval. One of its longer curves faced the Sva River, the other a paved, crescent-shaped plaza. The building and plaza were enclosed by a high fence, built to keep out anyone hoping to get near enough to the auditorium to pilfer dreams. But the Opera patron's chauffeurs and coachmen parked overnight in the plaza could go to sleep if they needed to, for dreams very rarely spilled beyond the Opera's walls.

A dreamhunter's projection zone was known as his or her "penumbra"—a term borrowed from astronomy, where "penumbra" describes the partial shadow the moon casts on the face of the earth during a total eclipse. (The "umbra," or totality, was the dreamhunter himself or herself, asleep and haloed by the shade of a dream.) Grace Tiebold's three-hundred-and-seventy-five-yard penumbra could comfortably fill all the Opera's rooms and spill only a little beyond its walls. If one of the Opera's security men, patrolling between fence and walls, did happen to hunker down and doze off, he might well find himself involved in one of Grace Tiebold's dreams. Grace's brother-in-law, the great dreamhunter Tziga Hame, had had a four-hundred-and-fifty-yard penumbra. Dozing guards or chauffeurs could find themselves immersed in any dream Tziga Hame performed at the Opera. However, city ordinances and cautious supervision by the Dream Regulatory Body had, for years, guaranteed that none of the households above shops in the streets surrounding the Opera would *ever* feel the faintest bit of color from any of the Opera's performances.

That was until the early hours of St. Lazarus's Day 1906, when sleepers in those houses found themselves snagged by the rim of a great, screeching wheel of nightmare. Only its edge—and although they woke with their hearts pounding, and gasping for breath, their distress quickly passed, to be replaced by something else. Fear. They sat up in bed and strained to hear. Some ran to their windows and threw them open and looked toward the festively lit Opera, from which came the sound of screams—a hellish howling that filled the still, chilly spring night.

✦ ✦ ✦

Grace Tiebold knew that she was caught in a nightmare and wasn't really in her coffin. She was a skilled and experienced dreamhunter who'd had to free herself from nightmares before. She fought to be free from this one. At first she fought it on its own terms—she struggled with the shroud, tore at the padded satin lining of the coffin, and finally with its undressed wood. She made the futile repeated movements—the clawing, thrashing, hammering—of the person she was in the dream. *In the dream*, she reminded herself, and kept in mind, as the spark of her experience, her mastery of other dreams, brought her back to herself.

Grace finally burst right out of the battered limbs and welter of blood and filth—out of that miserable, suffering self. She jumped like a specter out of the trapped body, the grave, the dream. For a moment she was paralyzed by sleep, then she struggled free from the silk quilt, panting, and found that her face and fingertips were torn and slick with blood.

She fell off the bed, got up, and looked around the auditorium.

The balconies were empty. Electric candles around the walls of each tier, and the unsteady glow of the gas jets beyond the stained-glass dome, showed Grace her beautiful Rainbow Opera—just as it always was, but as though turned inside out. Its beauty looked ghastly. The men of the fire watch looked monstrous. George, lying rigid, his face contorted, mouth alternately straining open and snapping shut, looked monstrous too.

Grace shouted at the fire watch to sound the alarm bells. She could barely hear her own voice over the storm of screaming that came from the closed bedchambers.

A door was open on the second tier, the door to the Tiebold suite. Grace saw her daughter, Rose, lean over the balcony, her hands gripping its rail. Grace felt herself swoop toward her daughter. She nearly jumped from the dais, stopping herself just in time. As Rose's face came into focus, Grace saw that her daughter was pale and confused, but not bloodied or maddened.

Grace turned back to George Mason. She picked up the water jug and tipped it out over him. Then, for good measure, she slammed the jug itself down onto his chest. The

Soporif woke, then rolled onto his side to spit out blood and a piece of cracked tooth.

Grace turned back to Rose, who wasn't looking at her. Grace followed her daughter's gaze and saw someone running toward the fire watch control room.

It was a man in a long coat and broad-brimmed hat. He moved fast but as though he was skating, his limbs seeming to stretch and blur. He jumped into the control room, among the fire watch.

Then, it seemed, Grace momentarily lost her grip on wakefulness, and the dream came back to change the shape and sense of events she was trying so hard to follow. She saw the coat and hat float to the control room floor. Had the ceiling collapsed? The men of the fire watch appeared to have been knocked flat and were struggling under something that had fallen on them—something dark and heavy. Then one body got to its feet, although it seemed to be covered from head to foot in some crumbling substance, as if it had been in the ground and had emerged contaminated by earth. The body moved toward the power board, put out a hand, and was suddenly caught in a cascade of blue sparks. The control room went dark. The bells didn't sound.

Mason was still struggling to get up, but kept flopping back as if stunned. Grace didn't wait for him to recover. She left the dais. The turns in the spiral stairs forced her to lose sight of her daughter several times as she descended. When she was only halfway down, she felt the dream leave the building. It didn't disperse but departed all at once, like a flock of birds breaking from a stand of trees.

Grace reached the bottom of the dais, located the nearest staircase, and scrambled up it. From above her came the sound of timber splintering.

Halfway up the stairs, Grace was knocked back against the

wall by a phalanx of men—the President's bodyguards. They were carrying President Garth Wilkinson on their shoulders, like a body on a bier. Bloody foam spilled from Wilkinson's gaping mouth.

Grace Tiebold was used to being treated with respect, to being *somebody*. It was years since she had been shunted aside by anyone. These men did just that—shoved her aside. Worse, she *was* noticed by the last man, the one following those who carried the President. He was rushing too, but he stepped aside to avoid bowling Grace down the stairs. Then he recognized her, his face filled with disgust, and he struck her across the mouth. It was an open-handed slap, but it knocked her down. She clung to the handrail, her ears ringing. She thought: "He thinks the nightmare was me."

Once she'd had this thought, another followed it: "If it wasn't me, then who was it?"

Then, *"Laura,"* Grace thought, though she couldn't think where her niece might have gone to catch a nightmare like that. It was like something from the "shadow belt"—a region in Band X, four days' walk into the lifeless desert of the Place. Grace knew that an eight-day walk In and out again was beyond Laura's stamina, that her niece was simply too small and weak to carry enough water for a journey of that length. So where had the nightmare come from? How had Laura managed to catch it? And *why* would Laura bring a dreadful thing like that to the Rainbow Opera on St. Lazarus's Eve?

Grace collected herself and went on. She reached the top of the stairs and saw her daughter. Rose's jaw went slack, and she took a step back, apparently appalled at her mother's appearance. Grace ran to Rose, took her hands, and scanned her face. Rose was unhurt—her lips were mauve, but, Grace recalled, that was only the stain of the musk creams she had been nibbling since lunch.

The terrible howling had stopped. Behind the Opera's doors, people had begun to call out for help—a sane, human clamor. A few started to spill out onto the balconies.

The door of the Hame Suite opened, and Laura emerged, her face white and mouth bloody. She was clumsily unwinding bandages from her hands.

Grace called to her. Laura looked at her aunt, her expression closed and remote.

There was a loud crash from the auditorium. Grace turned and saw that George Mason was in trouble. A group of men were making their way up the spiral stairs with murder in their eyes. Mason had hurled his own water jug at them. For a moment they fell back, shielding their faces with their hands, then they continued on up.

The control room was dark, but the power board was cascading sparks, by the light of which Grace could see several men from the fire watch leaning across the sill of the window that looked out over the auditorium. They appeared stunned and battered.

Grace ignored the sounds behind her—of breaking glass, and her niece calling to someone—and shouted across the auditorium to the fire watch. "Please help him!" She gestured toward Mason.

A long moment went by. The Opera's rooms disgorged retching, staggering people. Grace yelled some more. She still had hold of her daughter, who was trying to pull away from her. Grace hung on to Rose but kept her attention on the control room and the dithering fire watchmen. She urged them to do something. In another moment George Mason would be overwhelmed. The staircase was so packed now that Grace imagined she could see the dais swaying. Finally the fire watchmen seemed to see what she wanted, and, lit by blue flashes, they began to move and act.

Grace turned back to her daughter as Rose broke away and rushed to the stairs that led to the dreamer's door. Rose stopped, clinging to the doorframe, and peered down into the dark. The lights seemed to have failed in the stairwell. "Rose!" Grace called, and her daughter turned and came back. "Are those stairs clear?" Grace asked—she was thinking how they might avoid the angry crowd.

"No. Laura went down there. *It* took her," Rose said. She was stammering with shock. "Did you see it?"

Grace frowned at Rose and touched her forehead, as though testing for a fever. "Darling, we have to hide," Grace said gently. Then she grabbed Rose and propelled her toward the balcony of the Presidential Suite. These balconies were usually locked, but Grace was hoping that, since the President had been carried to safety, his bodyguards hadn't bothered to close the door behind them when they fled.

The first door was not only open but broken and hanging from one hinge. The balcony was empty except for an overturned chair. Grace hustled her daughter into the suite. She pulled the door closed and bolted it.

For the next five minutes Rose and Grace hid; they cowered as an enraged crowd beat on the bolted door. Then they heard police whistles.

Rose tried to talk in stops and starts. She said to her mother, "Did you see it? What was it? Why did Laura want *that*? Why was she calling it to her?"

And to these incoherent questions Grace could only reply, "It was a dream, darling, just a dream. It must have seemed like that to Laura too. Just a dream. She's not like you and me."

✦ ✦ ✦

When he was finally able to drag himself free from the nightmare, Sandy staggered out of bed and into his room's cramped bathroom. He ran the cold tap and rinsed his mouth. Ribbons of blood spiraled down the drain in pink-tinged water. It was only once he'd stopped running the water that he became aware of the racket coming from the balcony beyond his door. He went out to look.

The doors of rooms around the third tier were flung open. It seemed that many people had come out only in search of a less confined space. Near Sandy two women in torn silk pajamas were leaned over the balcony rail, one gasping for air, the other scrubbing her lacerated face with blood-slick palms.

People were heading toward the stairs. Some wept and staggered as they went, others were more purposeful, pushing their way through, their faces injured and contorted, but wrathful too.

Sandy looked at himself. There was blood under his fingernails. His pajama top was open, its buttons gone or dangling by threads.

From below came sounds of a melee, crashes, shouting, and police whistles. Sandy went to the rail, leaned over, and saw his uncle. George Mason was at the top of the dreamer's dais, facedown on churned-up bedding. Two men had hold of him by his legs and were trying to drag him into a crowd of enraged people who were fighting for space on the spiral stairs. Sandy saw a few members of the Opera's fire watch among the crowd and, at the foot of the stairs, a bunch of police officers fighting their way up, swinging their truncheons.

Sandy stood frozen, gripping the rail, till the police managed to reach his uncle and wrap both a quilt and their uniformed bodies around him.

Another clutch of police came into sight in the main auditorium. They fought their way through the crowd toward the main exit. Grace Tiebold was in their midst, the train of her opulent gown in tatters, her cheeks and throat smeared with blood.

Reinforcements arrived. Police poured onto the auditorium floor. Sandy heard a gunshot and saw glass rain down from a hole punched in the Opera's stained-glass dome. He flinched back from the rail and joined the crowd pouring down the nearest staircase.

There was a press of people on the stairs. Sandy was surrounded by the sound of weeping. For a brief moment he was snagged in a group of men in suits who seemed to be trying to decide whether to continue up or turn and follow the crowd back down. Sandy caught snatches of their talk.

"The police have her already . . ."

"But was it her? I think that nightmare was Hame's Buried Alive . . ."

Someone elbowed Sandy in the ribs, and the men slipped ahead of him. He followed, stumbling over a dropped bowler hat.

Outside, in the Crescent Plaza, there were more bowler-hatted Regulatory Body officials. Most of them stood in little groups, turned away from the throngs of distressed people. There were ambulances and paddy wagons in the plaza, and a fire truck, the firemen passing out blankets.

Suddenly Sandy spotted a head of unmistakable bright hair. He ran toward Rose Tiebold, calling her name. He couldn't see Laura with her. Rose turned to him. Her face was pale but unmarked. Someone grabbed Sandy by the collar of his pajamas and held him. Sandy grappled with the hand but concentrated on Rose. "Where's Laura?"

Beside him a voice said, "This boy is a dreamhunter. You should make sure to catch any who were here."

Sandy looked around. The man who held him was a police

captain. The other man, the one issuing instructions, was the Secretary of the Interior, Cas Doran. Doran had his hand under Rose's elbow, to comfort rather than detain her it seemed. His lips were bitten and bleeding. He didn't look calm, but he did have an air of command, of mastery and self-mastery.

Sandy heard Doran tell the police captain that any dreamhunters who had been at the Opera would be reproducing the nightmare when they next slept.

It hadn't occurred to Sandy that he'd taken a print of the nightmare, but now that he knew, he thought he could feel it inside him, a capsule of terror and airless darkness. He moaned.

Rose touched his hand. "Sandy, your uncle is with my mother at the city barracks," she said.

"But where is Laura?"

Rose glanced at the man beside her. "Laura ran off. She was scared. I had bare feet, and there was glass on the stairs— or else I'd have followed her."

Cas Doran released Rose to lay both his hands on Sandy's shoulders. He shook him. "Who was Laura Hame with?" Doran demanded.

Sandy was puzzled—hadn't Doran heard what Rose had said, or did he not believe her? "She was with Miss Tiebold," Sandy said, then added, insolent, "That's why I'm asking Miss Tiebold where she is."

"Laura was in bed with me," Rose said. "We didn't sleep. We were talking. When the screaming started, Laura got scared and bolted down the stairs to the dreamer's door." Rose looked from Doran to Sandy, her expression earnest and, beneath that, very alert.

Sandy wanted to find Laura. He gazed around at the people in blankets. He saw one he recognized, bundled up and shivering, Maze Plasir's apprentice, Gavin Pinkney. Sandy noticed the odd, imploring way that Gavin stared at Secretary Doran, then dismissed it as irrelevant. He had to find Laura.

Rose was plucking at Secretary Doran's arm. She said she wanted to go home. Her cousin would have run there. Doran shook his head. Rose was his daughter Mamie's best friend, she must come home with him, he said. "I'll send some people to your house to find your cousin." Then the Secretary turned to Sandy. "As for you, Mr. Mason. The police and Regulatory Body officials are gathering exposed dream-hunters . . ."

Sandy was so startled that the Secretary of the Interior knew who he was that he missed the next few things the man said. Something about public safety, and a quarantine for those affected.

Doran called over one of the Dream Regulatory Body officials. Sandy thought to himself that whenever they showed up en masse like this, the officials did rather have the appearance of a private army. Doran's private army.

"I have a dreamhunter here," the Secretary said, and laid his heavy hand on Sandy's shoulder once more. "And Maze Plasir's apprentice is standing just over there. Also, Miss Tiebold tells me that her cousin, the dreamhunter Laura Hame, will have run home."

The official gave a curt nod.

"She didn't sleep," Rose said, urgent. "We were talking." Then she gave a choked laugh.

The official took hold of Sandy and walked him away. They collected Gavin Pinkney as they went. The official said, "We'll find you some clean clothes. Then we'll take you straight In and see if you can't overwrite the nightmare before you have to have it again."

Sandy realized the "clean clothes" remark was directed at

Gavin, who stank of urine. The poor boy had wet himself.

Sandy craned back over his shoulder at Rose Tiebold, hoping for some communication, some sign. But she was speaking to Doran, standing with her head erect and a haughty expression on her face, as though she was somehow above even her own worries.

Sandy turned away, trudged on, and fumed. For a moment he reverted to his earlier resentful thoughts about the rich and famous Tiebolds and Hames. Then he remembered how Rose had insisted *"We didn't sleep."*

It was clear that *she* hadn't, because her cheeks and mouth weren't marked by her own fingernails. But Laura was another matter. What if the truth was the opposite of Rose's story? What if the girls were not together, were not talking, were not both awake?

Sandy stumbled. The official made an impatient noise and jerked him upright. "Leave me alone!" Sandy said, and drove his shoulder into the man's side. The man wheezed, then, "You're not about to give me trouble, Mason, are you?"

Sandy glowered but let himself be led on. His head was spinning—in fact, the whole of him seemed to be spinning, speeding up, draining away down some great, dark whirlpool. For he knew Laura *had* been chewing Wakeful. She'd taken the drug and walked some distance out of the Place carrying a nightmare. She'd kept her nightmare fresh and had delivered it, overpowering her aunt, and Sandy's uncle, and Sandy, and every other sleeping soul in the Opera that night.

✦ ✦ ✦

When the Mason boy had left them, Doran asked Rose, "Is that your cousin's beau?"

The girl replied, "I'm sure *I* wouldn't know," every inch a

Founderston Girls' Academy senior asserting her sense of what was proper.

Cas Doran realized with a small shock that he knew very well what Rose's life was like. She had the kind of agile spirit to be found in those who straddled very different worlds. She attended a fashionable school, had all the manners of a nice young lady—in other words, she prickled with barbed boundaries—but she was also from a dreamhunting family and party to the daily phantasmagoria of life with dreamhunters, to their frequent exhaustion and feverish wildness.

These dreamhunters—they were *his*. His responsibility, his study, his stock-in-trade. But Cas Doran was not a dreamhunter, nor was anyone in his family. He lived a regular domestic life in a household run by a refined woman—herself a graduate of the Girls' Academy. And that was how he knew what Rose Tiebold's life was like, how contradictory it must be. Because, even given the differences in their ages and occupations, this girl was in some ways *like* him.

✤ ✤ ✤

Secretary Doran's car came through the crowd. The chauffeur stood up and called to his employer.

"Come," said Doran to Rose, his tone gentle but managing.

Rose went with him. He spoke soothingly. He said that everything would be all right. He helped her into the car. Its interior smelled pleasantly of new leather. Rose realized that there had been some terrible smells, as well as terrible sights, in the plaza.

The car began to move again, easing its way through the thronging people. There were seething shadows on the plaza,

interrupting the lights from streets and houses. Rose stared at
Doran's profile. In the light ghosting over his face, Doran
looked grim and intent, like someone getting ready for a
fight. Then he turned and smiled at her.

Rose knew she'd do everything she could to keep people
from guessing that it was her cousin's nightmare. Before too
long she'd speak to Laura, then she'd know why her cousin
had done it. There would be a reason, some kind of sense.
Rose suspected it had something to do with the letter Laura
had torn up, a last letter from her missing father.

The letter had, for some reason unfathomable at the time,
been partly buried in a large amount of sand in Laura's bedroom at Summerfort. Laura had been into the Place illicitly,
looking for clues to why her father had disappeared. She was
back in Summerfort when Rose and Rose's father, Chorley,
had found her. Laura had kept them out of her bedroom;
then, when she had finally opened the door, they'd found her
standing up to her ankles in a pile of sand. The envelope that
held the letter was sticking out of it.

Sand!

When, that very night—St. Lazarus's Eve—the howls of terror had wound down, Rose had seen her cousin emerge from
the Hame Suite and stand for a moment unwinding bandages
from her hands. Laura had looked up at Rose, then seemed to
dismiss her. She began to call. What she shouted sounded like
nonsense, but it was a name. At her call a monster had come
running. A great statue in the shape of a man—a beautifully
muscled, nobly serene man. A man apparently made of sand.
The monster had swept Laura up in his arms and run to the
stairs down to the dreamer's door. Rose had tried to break
away from her mother to follow them. But Rose's mother had
kept a firm hold on her. Then Rose, straining after Laura,

had seen something. She saw the name Laura had called scored in the sand on the back of the monster's neck. Four letters: N O W N.

Rose was trembling. Secretary Doran touched her arm and said, "How are you, Rose?" Then, "We're nearly home."

There was no one in the world Rose was closer to than Laura, but Rose had known nothing of any of this—the nightmare or the monster. She felt herself shrinking. She didn't *know* anything. All her schoolmates thought she was a bit of a hero, but she wasn't. She was baffled, and in the dark.

2

✧ ✧ ✧

LAURA'S SANDMAN CARRIED HER ALL
NIGHT. HE WALKED FOR TWENTY
MILES, FOLLOWING THE RAIL LINE SOUTH-
west from Founderston, traveling along the railbed with long,
rocking strides. Laura was careful to keep her eyes open. She
was afraid of waking up in her dream again, of opening her
eyes on blackness and the chilly embrace of a satin shroud.

They left the tracks at the small train stop near Marta
Hame's house. They didn't follow the road, for it was getting
light, a dull twilight rinsed by drizzle.

As Nown clambered up a hillside, Laura heard sheep pattering away from them. She saw the flock pour down a slope
together and flow into the groove of a gully, like raindrops on
a large leaf spilling to pool at the stem.

Nown pressed down the top wire of a fence, and the whole
thing strained, twanging along its length. He stepped over it.

At the edge of Aunt Marta's yard, Laura told Nown to stop.
She slid from his arms, and he steadied her till she found her
footing. She said, "You hide yourself. But stay near." Then
she recalled that she had set him free.

Nown had helped her do what her father had asked in the
letter he left for her. Laura had hated having to catch Buried
Alive and overdream her unsuspecting Aunt Grace. As she
had gone about it, she had come to understand that her sand-

man had doubts about what she was doing. When he'd tried to speak to her, she had silenced him.

She had *made him*; he was her servant, bound to obey her by rules she knew she didn't fully understand. But she did understand the most simple rules of the spell that had made him. She knew that if she erased the W in his name, made it NON instead of NOWN, he would fall apart, as her father's sandman had. And she knew that if, instead, she erased the first N in his name, he'd be his own—free. With Nown's help, Laura had completed the task her father had set her. Then she found that what she wanted next wasn't obedience but guidance and wisdom—and to be cherished.

So it was that, a few hours before, in the dark of night, when frost was forming on the timber ties of the rail line they walked along, Laura had leaned over her sandman's shoulder and scratched out one letter on the back of his neck, the first N in his name. She'd freed him. And he didn't leave her (as her father had). Instead he gathered her close and kept on walking.

"You hide yourself but stay near," she told him, then stood for a moment stupefied by the thought that since she'd freed him he didn't need to obey her. Then, "I'm soaking wet," she said. "I must go in. *Will* you wait for me?"

"Yes," said Nown.

Laura approached the house. She went up the stairs to the porch. As soon as her foot touched the top step, barking erupted from within. It was Downright, her aunt's dog. She heard the dog coming till he was on the other side of the door, his nails clicking on the wooden floor as he danced around.

Laura called through the door, "It's me, Laura!"

Downright paused to listen, then began to bark again.

The stained-glass border around the door lit up as a lamp

was carried to it. It was Mr. Bridges, one of Aunt Marta's elderly servants. Laura heard the man speak sharply to Downright. Then Marta joined him, calming her dog with praise. "There's a good boy, settle down now." The bolt rattled, the door opened, and two people and the dog all stared at Laura.

Downright surged forward, and his collar jerked free from Marta's grip. He brushed past Laura, ran outside, and began to track back and forth across the lawn with his nose down. He reached the long grass at the edge of the mown area and stood, stiff-legged, silent, pointing. Then his ears went back, and he hunkered down on his haunches, made a tight turn, and scuttled back across the lawn. He pushed past the people in the doorway and vanished into the dark dead end below the main staircase, where he cowered, whimpering.

Marta looked after her dog, frowned, then drew Laura indoors. She released her niece and looked at her wet hands. "What is this?" she said. "Where have you come from? And what on earth are you wearing?"

"I walked here. I'm wet through," Laura said.

Marta made a small sound between a grunt and a gasp, more exasperated than shocked. She took hold of Laura and hustled her up the stairs, issuing instructions over her shoulder about breakfast.

Marta's bedroom was warm, last night's fire smoking still. She gave her niece a nightgown and told her to change out of her wet clothes and get under the covers. Marta poked at the fire, put on more coal. Laura stripped off her silk pajamas, which weren't evenly soaked—no, her back and seat and one shoulder were dry, for they had lain against the shelter of Nown's body. Laura could see that the pattern was incongruous, so she crumpled the silk into a wad so that the dry patches blotted the wet ones. She dropped the bundled pajamas and put on her aunt's nightgown. Her bare feet tingled with the blood coming back into them. She climbed into her aunt's bed but remained sitting. "I mustn't sleep," she said.

Marta got up from the hearth and stared at her niece. "What have you done?" she said.

"I showed them." Laura shivered.

Marta put on her dressing gown and stood at the mirror to brush out her braid. She wound her hair into a coil and pinned it. She was silent throughout, and it was as though she hadn't heard Laura. But then, without turning, she met her niece's gaze in the mirror and asked, "*What* did you show them, Laura?"

"What happens," Laura said. She opened her mouth again to add, "The dreams they take to the prisons," but something inside her interrupted. It wasn't like being interrupted by her own thoughts. She recognized it as different from her, a fragment of planted intelligence, something that had come to her with the dream. It seemed to say: "What *has* happened," to warn: "What *will* happen."

"Laura." Aunt Marta was sitting on the bed beside her, hands gripping her shoulders. "Lie back, girl, you're faint. Your face is completely white. You can sleep if you need to. No one in this house is about to go back to bed." Marta began to muse. "Though, really, if your dream is that dire, I will have to have you moved elsewhere."

Laura put her head back on the pillow. Her shivering began to subside. She closed her eyes. A moment later she felt her aunt lift the covers. Marta said, "You weren't wearing any shoes, but your feet are clean. Who brought you here? Who else knows you're here?"

"No one," Laura said. "I came on my own." In her mind she saw the three remaining letters on the back of Nown's neck. She flicked her thumb against her forefinger and felt the sand packed under her fingernail.

Her aunt said, "Why did you choose to come here?"

"I haven't anywhere else to go. Everyone will be mad at me," she said, and thought, "And it was raining."

She had been wet and cold. But if when the day came the sun had appeared too, then she might have asked Nown to keep on walking, to carry her away somewhere, as if a spell held her together, instead of all her regular needs—food and shelter, clothes and money.

The bedroom door closed. Aunt Marta had gone out. Laura opened her eyes and looked at the plaster decorations on the ceiling, the white ropes of leaves and flowers gathered at the four corners of the room by big bows borne by birds in flight.

Once she was warm, Laura got out of bed and stood at the window. It was a gray morning, not much lighter than the dawn had been. Laura saw Mr. Bridges hurrying off down the road, patting one pocket as he went.

The bedroom door opened. "Get back into bed," Marta said. "I've sent Mr. Bridges to the telegraph office at the station. I feel the need of some advice. You were always an honest girl, Laura, and open—without having picked up that habit the Tiebolds have of broadcasting constant reports on their mental weather . . ."

Laura got back into bed, remained sitting, but drew the covers up to her chin. She listened to her aunt mutter about the shortcomings of the rest of her family. Marta was opening drawers and rattling hangers in her wardrobe as she spoke. "You were honest, but now I see you're heading down the same path your father took. You have to understand that you shouldn't abuse your gift for any reason. Not for any reason."

"I'm not. You'll see."

Marta shook her head, bundled her clothes in her arms, and went out of the bedroom again.

Half an hour went by. Mrs. Bridges came in with breakfast on a tray. She too told Laura that her husband had gone to the station's telegraph office. "Miss Marta has asked her friend the Grand Patriarch to send a car—'immediately' is what she wrote."

It appeared that Laura had come all this way only to be carried back to Founderston.

Mrs. Bridges shoveled more coal into the grate, then said, "You should eat up, dear. You must be famished. Here, let me take the top off that egg." The woman came and did that and then stood making soothing noises over Laura as she ate. "That's right. Get that down you," she said, and, "Have some more toast. My quince jelly turned out particularly well this year."

When Mrs. Bridges finally left, Laura eased the tray off her legs and got out of bed. She posted herself at the window and waited. Mr. Bridges came back along the road and turned in at the gate. Once he was indoors, Laura pushed up the window and thrust her head out. It was dull, full daylight outside, but she couldn't see where Nown might have hidden himself. She called his name—in a loud whisper.

Behind her, the bedroom door opened. "Get away from that window!" commanded Aunt Marta.

Laura took her knee off the sill and shuffled back to the bed. Her aunt's nightgown was too long for her.

Marta closed her wardrobe doors. She turned the key in the lock, removed it, and put it in her pocket. "I have nothing that would fit you anyway. You'd be swimming in all my dresses," Aunt Marta said. "And this way you won't think of setting out cross-country again."

"Mrs. Bridges told me you asked the Grand Patriarch to send a car."

"That's right. Upon reflection I've decided that I can't turn the Bridgeses out of their beds just because you're carrying a nightmare."

Laura's aunt stood straight-backed, with one hand pressed flat to her pocket as though she thought the key might leap out of it. Her face was stern and full of suspicion. "While I am pleased that you think you can come to me, Laura," she said, "I'm afraid that this is all a bit beyond me."

When Laura had last visited Marta, she'd had her aunt teach her "The Measures." Laura had told her aunt that she had been talking with her father about "The Measures" and other old Hame songs the last times she saw him, at Summerfort, and at Sisters Beach Station before the special train carried him away. She'd told her aunt that her father said the songs were his only real family legacy, and that she should know them. Marta Hame had, till recently, been the choir mistress at the Temple in Founderston. She was a musician, a music teacher, and a Hame—the ideal person for Laura to ask about the family music. But Laura hadn't been collecting songs to remember her father by—no—she had wanted to learn "The Measures" because it was a spell, a recipe for making a servant out of earth. Now, looking at her aunt, Laura wondered how Marta could know the chant and not know what it could do.

Laura's aunt said, "Erasmus will tell me how to handle you."

Laura laughed and shook her head, partly out of a sense of absurdity—her aunt had such faith in her friend and spiritual guide, the Grand Patriarch of the Southern Orthodox Church. But the Grand Patriarch was always speaking out against dreamhunters and dream palaces. According to him, the Rainbow Opera was a place where people indulged in "a secondhand education of the senses" and "acts without consequences." What kind of advice could the Grand Patriarch

offer a lawbreaking dreamhunter? All he believed in was ab-
stinence. Besides, Laura hadn't wanted advice, she'd only
wanted to *get the job done*.

Marta pulled the window closed before she left the room.
For a long time Laura didn't dare to stir. She was sure that her
aunt was just beyond the door, listening for movement. Laura
waited. She became drowsy, and it was her drowsiness that
frightened her out of the warm bed and across the room. For
a minute she stood pressed against the window—her face
turned to the door. There was a light in the hall, a candle
perhaps, its wavering radiance lancing through the keyhole.
Laura watched it, and the strain of watching was so great, and
she so still, that everything seemed to come to life around
her; the bedroom furniture, the plaster garlands carried by
plaster birds, the patterns on the carpet—everything became
animated and seemed to watch her back. Laura felt like a wild
animal; she ached for escape.

After a long time she turned back to the window.

Nown was standing on the lawn looking up at her.

Laura pushed the window open and swung her legs over the
sill. She stepped out onto the cold, corrugated iron of the
veranda roof. She walked as far as she could, to where the
curve began to plunge down to the gutter.

Nown stalked nearer, till he stood at the veranda rail, directly beneath her.

Laura looked down into his black-banded, statuesque eyes
and thought that it wasn't really any wonder she'd imagined
the bedroom furniture had come to life. Nown was made of
inanimate matter, sand all the way through—and yet here he
was, waiting to hear what she wanted. She said, "My aunt has
sent for a car. She's taking me back to Founderston. Not to
the authorities, though, I think."

Nown didn't move, show surprise, nod to acknowledge

he'd heard, or make any noise to encourage her to go on speaking.

Laura looked around the misty farmland. She saw a pine plantation—trees black in the mist—growing on the curve of the nearest hill like the neatly cropped mane of a cavalry horse. She pointed. "Wait for me there, in that forest. Can you do that? I'll be back as soon as I'm able. I don't want anyone to see you."

Nown didn't reply—he didn't say "I'll do that."

"Please," she said.

He lifted his arms and held them out. He didn't say anything, but the gesture meant, "Jump!" It meant, "Jump, and I'll catch you."

From the room behind her Laura heard her aunt, shocked, shouting, "Laura! What are you doing out there? Come back inside this instant!"

Laura took one last look at her sandman's open arms, his black-banded, brilliant eyes, then turned and made her way carefully back to the open window and stepped into the warm bedroom.

3

❖ ❖ ❖

ONLY THE DAY BEFORE—ST. LAZARUS'S
EVE—WHEN LAURA'S OVERNIGHT
TRAIN HAD ARRIVED IN FOUNDERSTON AT
nine-thirty in the morning, she had pushed three envelopes
into the mailbox on the concourse of the station.

The letters were collected and sorted at the Central Post
Office. None made the ten-thirty delivery. All three went out
at noon.

One landed at twelve-forty in the basket of the assistant to
the Director of the Regulatory Body. It was still lying there
unopened when the man put on his coat and hat at one
p.m.—the beginning of his half-day holiday—and went out to
meet his wife at the People's Gardens.

The second letter was delivered to the Temple at noon,
but the Temple was always busy over the feast of St. Lazarus,
and the letter didn't find its way into the hands of Father Roy,
the Grand Patriarch's secretary, until seven the following
morning. When the Grand Patriarch returned to the vestry
after the celebration of early mass, he was met by Father Roy,
with the letter and a telegraph from his friend Marta Hame
asking him to send a car to her house. The Grand Patriarch
read Marta's message and dispatched a car. He read the letter,
then handed it back to Father Roy and said, "Perhaps this explains the crowd at mass. Much more than the usual St.

Lazarus's Day throng. There were people wrapped in blankets standing at the back and lining the aisles. They looked like they'd wandered in from the site of a disaster."

The Grand Patriarch went back to his apartments and sat down to breakfast and the morning paper. The paper carried a red "Stop Press" report of the riot at the Rainbow Opera.

The third letter found its way to the mailroom of the *Founderston Herald* shortly after one on St. Lazarus's Eve, then languished among dozens of other letters to the editor since the paper was being put to bed early that day—printers working overtime to get out the holiday edition, a paper full of advertisements, announcements of engagements, and the Ladies' Supplement's thoughts on hats and tango heels. A paper very light on actual news. At midnight on St. Lazarus's Eve, the skinny, seedy little man whose job it was to sift through letters to the editor burst out of the nearly deserted *Herald* offices and into the street to jog several blocks and over a bridge to the Isle of the Temple. He arrived in time to see bloodied people spilling out of the Rainbow Opera and the first constables pushing their away in. Despite his protests, he was turned away from the Crescent Plaza by the police. It was hours before he managed to find the *Herald*'s editor, who was at home by then, cleaned up but still gray-faced, and with fresh scabs on his scalp from where he'd torn at his own hair. The skinny, seedy man handed the letter to his editor, who peered at the elongated, backward-sloping handwriting and read:

Dear Sir,

Please publish this letter. It has come to our attention that the Dream Regulatory Body has been using nightmares to terrorize and subdue the inmates of this nation's prisons in order to guarantee a cooperative labor force to work in mines and factories and on road and rail projects.

The accusation was all in one long, mad, bad sentence. The editor frowned and read on:

> *The public may already be aware that dreams are used for education and rehabilitation in prisons. But the public does not know that, instead of sharing dreams about the wages of their sins, the prisoners are forced to endure frightful nightmares from which no one could learn anything.*

"The author of this letter has a large vocabulary but is semiliterate in my opinion," said the editor.

> *The nightmare broadcast in the Rainbow Opera on St. Lazarus's Eve is one such dream. We have overdreamed Grace Tiebold's Homecoming so that the public will know that this is what it is like for those prisoners. We did it in order to wake the public conscience.*
> *Stop the torture!*
>
> *Lazarus*

"I'll deal with this," said the editor to his assistant. He saw the man to the door, then sat down to compose a note to his friend Cas Doran, the Secretary of the Interior.

✧ ✧ ✧

The police handwriting expert peered at the two letters, the one that began "Dear Sir, Please publish this letter" and the other beginning "The time has come for the Regulatory Body to submit to judgment . . ." He said that the writer was left-handed, and secretive. "Look at those backward-sloping letters." He said that the stationery was the same for both letters but that one page was more yellowed than the other, was perhaps the top sheet of a pad that had sat around in sunlight

for some time. It was export-quality linen paper, manufac-
tured in a certain paper mill in the south. The letters had
probably been written at a desk equipped with a writing set,
because the ink was blotted with sand. The handwriting was
highly distinctive, fluent, and not—the expert thought—a dis-
guised hand. "But, it seems to me that the handwriting is
more mature than the composition of the letter—the bad
grammar and poor punctuation."

Having given his opinion, the handwriting expert was
shown from the room. Cas Doran, the Detective Inspector
from Founderston Barracks; and the Director of the Regulatory Body were left alone.

The Detective Inspector said, "Before we ask Grace
Tiebold in here, we should think about charges."

Doran closed his eyes, saw darkness, winced, and opened
them again. His mouth and jaw were sore. It hurt him to
speak. "What can she or Mason be charged with? There is no
crime called 'grievous mental harm.' "

"Perhaps there should be."

"Certainly not," said Doran. "We'd then have this Lazarus
and his allies bringing criminal charges against the Regulatory
Body and the Department of Corrections."

At this the Detective Inspector merely cleared his throat.
Then he said, "So, you believe this Lazarus has allies?"

"Yes. The letter says, 'We have overdreamed' and 'It has
come to our attention.' But I doubt that 'we' is George Mason
and Grace Tiebold."

"Mason and Tiebold could be charged with disturbing the
peace," said the Detective Inspector.

Doran shook his head. "There are regulations that cover
safe practices in dream palaces, just as there are regulations
that govern how many fire escapes any new building must

have. But the regulations haven't thought to ban Soporifs from sleeping in dream palaces. Though—believe me—that's about to change."

The Detective Inspector sighed. He would have been much happier if he were closer to an arrest.

The Director of the Regulatory Body said, "Shall we speak to these dreamhunters now? Mason first, I think."

✦ ✦ ✦

George Mason was cooperative—and no real help at all. He spent only half an hour in Doran's office, then was sent to join the dozen other dreamhunters who had been at the Opera. They had all taken prints of Buried Alive. They were to be transported to Doorhandle and then into the Place so that they could attempt to overwrite the nightmare with something harmless.

The Place was where the dreams came from. It was a territory infinitely more vast than the hundred or so square miles of the mountain range it encompassed. A limitless, lifeless place, a landscape of plains and rolling hills covered in white grass and scrub, where leathery leaves still hung on bone-dry trees but fell if touched; a silent, windless, waterless landscape, where time had apparently stopped. Only a very few people could actually enter the Place. Most, on approaching its invisible borders, would only find themselves going on up into the temperate rain forest of the Rifleman Mountains. Perhaps one person in three hundred was able to pass through into the Place, and of those, only a very few were any good at catching the dreams they found there. These became dreamhunters and made their livings—or their fortunes—from dreams caught, and carried out, and shared with others.

When she was shown into Cas Doran's office, Grace

Tiebold was still wearing her dreamhunter's finery, though the peacock-print train of her gown had been trodden to tatters by both the police and the people the police had protected her from. Doran saw that Grace had a bruise on her jaw, as well as the now familiar self-inflicted scratches on her cheeks. And, of course, it hurt her to speak.

The first thing Doran did was push one of the letters across the desk and under her nose. "Is this *your* schoolgirlish false officialese?" he asked. Then, in mocking imitation, " 'It has come to our attention . . .' " He waited, then said, "I believe you left school at twelve to work in your father's tobacco shop?"

The dreamhunter's eyes flicked up to his face. She showed fright. Then she stared at the letter and looked puzzled. "I don't recognize the handwriting," she said. She seemed surprised.

"Should you?" asked the Detective Inspector.

She hesitated. Then, "No," she said, finally.

"And how does this letter strike you?"

"It's demented, fantastical," Grace said. "The writer is defending an act of terror. An act of spectral terror. But apparently, according to the letter, you people all deal in terror too."

"You *know* what we do," Doran said. "There's nothing you don't know about what we do."

Grace looked into his eyes. She was exhausted, bleak, but she seemed to have recovered from her moment of fright. She said, "I doubt that."

"The Intangible Resources Act provides for the use of certain sorts of dreams, including nightmares—punishments that cause pain but not injury—'for the public good.' I'm sure we can agree that this is something you already know."

"I know it," Grace said. She gestured at her own nail-marked cheeks, then at Doran's injured mouth. "But—is *this* pain without injury?"

"There were no precautions. No restraints."

"So you strap your prisoners down, then give them nightmares?"

Doran leaned back in his chair. "Mrs. Tiebold, are you defending yourself? You seem to be saying that inflicting a virulent nightmare on the general public is no different from the controlled use of nightmares on convicted criminals."

"It wasn't my nightmare!" Grace Tiebold's eyes blazed. "This Lazarus used me! Me *and* George."

The Director of the Regulatory Body spoke up then. "Why did you ask the Soporif George Mason to lie in with you?"

"I've been having difficulty falling asleep. George went In with me to catch Homecoming. We even have a witness. Jerome Tilley was at the site with us, catching it too. Jerome had a booking in Westport for a feast day performance at the Second Skin Theater. George and I walked back to Doorhandle with him, and George drove us all to Founderston. He dropped Jerome at the station and me at my house. Three hours later I met my daughter and niece for lunch, then we went home, changed, and came out to the Opera. I'm sure George can account for all *his* movements that afternoon too. We didn't hike back In—*days* In—and catch that nightmare. We are not Lazarus. I'm very sorry that this person chose to spill his nightmare out on my penumbra. And I'm sure George is very sorry that he made it difficult for everyone to wake up."

Doran made a steeple of his hands and gave Grace Tiebold a little pinched smile over the top of them. "That wasn't your penumbra—it was Lazarus's. Perhaps five hundred yards. Lazarus wanted your *audience*, Mrs. Tiebold, not your powers of amplification. Lazarus is very probably a more powerful dreamhunter than you."

"Where has he been hiding himself all this time?" Grace said.

"*Has* he been hiding himself?" Doran said, as though she knew who they were talking about.

"Tziga's dead," Grace said, and dropped her gaze. "I'm tired, Mr. Doran. I don't know anything more. I want to go In and erase this, if I can. And first I want to go home to wash and change and check on Rose and Laura."

"Rose is spending today in the company of my wife and Mamie," Doran said. "The girls go back to school tomorrow."

Grace glared at him. "You might have mentioned that first. And if Rose is with Mamie, where is Laura?"

Doran spread his hands and shrugged. "I thought you might know."

"Laura will have the nightmare too. She might not realize it until she falls asleep."

"Your daughter told me that Laura didn't sleep. But we are looking for her," Doran said.

"Good," said Grace, and turned her face away.

"That will be all for now," said the Director of the Regulatory Body. "Some of my people will escort you to your house, then take you on to Doorhandle."

"Thank you." Grace Tiebold got up and nodded to the Detective Inspector, who said that he'd like her to come and see him once she was back. At the door the dreamhunter turned and asked, "How is President Wilkinson?"

"He is recovering well," Doran said.

"I'm glad to hear it. We need him," Grace said.

Doran smiled again, his mouth performing a kind of spasm of involuntary glee that opened the wounds on his lips. Here was evidence that, despite the nightmare, Plasir's apprentice Gavin Pinkney's little bit of "coloring" had been absorbed and remembered. Doran risked saying, "Yes, we do need Wilkinson, and it's such a pity his term is nearly up."

"Yes." Grace hovered in the doorway, frowning. "Eight years does seem far too short a term for such a constructive President. Or, at least, that's what *I* think."

✢ ✢ ✢

Grace was feeling very foggy when she left Cas Doran's office, but once she was out in the cold morning air, she remembered something she'd noticed while she was there. Something much more important than what a shame it was that Garth Wilkinson was shortly to retire. She had recognized the stationery on which Lazarus's letter was written. The paper was expensive, and probably plenty of well-off, or very particular, people liked to use it. It was expensive and elegant, like everything of Chorley's—for it was Chorley's. Grace's husband wasn't much of a letter writer and tended to make all his plans on drawing paper in his workshop. So the stationery sat in a boxed block on the desk of Summerfort's library, in full sunlight, often for weeks—and for months once the family packed up at the end of summer and went back to Founderston. The paper of the letter had been yellowed, and printed with a paler mark, a star shape, where Chorley's fossilized starfish paperweight had sat while the sun shone and turned the page yellow around it.

"*Laura,*" Grace thought, again. For the letter showed her niece's lack of punctuation and, as Doran had so descriptively put it, her "schoolgirlish false officialese."

But the handwriting was not Laura's.

4

✧✧✧

𝐼T WAS AFTERNOON WHEN THE CAR SENT FOR LAURA AND HER AUNT MARTA REACHED ITS DESTINATION. IT passed through an open arch into the courtyard of the Grand Patriarch's palace. Laura had a glimpse of Temple Square—of sunshine on damp cobblestones and people strolling about in their feast day finery. She could hear the music of an accordion coming from one of the cafés in the square. These signs of life came to her through a hot mist of fever and exhaustion.

The running boards of the car were slick with mud from country roads. Laura climbed out carefully. She had slippers on her feet and one of her aunt's coats over the borrowed nightgown.

There was a priest waiting to meet them. Aunt Marta called him Father Roy. Marta and the priest fell into step, their heads together. As they were climbing the steps to the side entrance to the palace, Father Roy turned and gave Laura a sharp, wry look. Laura was led into a chilly room with dark wood-paneled walls and ceiling. Father Roy asked her to wait. He and Marta went out. A few minutes went by, then Laura heard several people hurrying back along the passage. Father Roy returned with a couple of black-clad religious sisters.

They got Laura up and conducted her out. Aunt Marta was nowhere in sight.

Laura was marched up several flights of stairs, along corridors, then out a door onto a rooftop walkway, which crossed from the roof of the palace to that of the Temple, and to a small door beneath the deep masonry lintel around the base of the dome. One of the sisters behind Laura tapped her back to urge her forward. Laura stooped and went on. The door led into a short tunnel, at the end of which Laura glimpsed a grille and, beyond that, a place she recognized, the gallery that ran around the inside of the dome, which was as far up as she'd ever been on visits to the Temple with her schoolmates. The sister behind Laura seized her arm and turned her in the narrow space to face a dark opening in the wall of the tunnel. "Wait," the woman said. Laura heard a match struck. The sister edged past Laura, carrying a candle, and stepped up into darkness. She was standing on a stone staircase that disappeared upward in a tight spiral. She gestured for Laura to follow her.

The dome of Founderston's Temple was eggshell smooth but was set into a four-tiered crown of decorated masonry, topped by an ornate turret. The turret had blind arches, window-shaped recesses filled with mortared stone. The stone was coated with gold leaf.

Like every other child in Founderston, Laura had wished she was allowed to climb high enough to stand on one of the little iron balconies below the dome. She had occasionally caught sight of someone up that high. And she—like every other child in the city—had noticed that a ladder ascended from one of the balconies to the golden turret on its top.

Laura remembered her childish wondering when she emerged from the long climb up the spiral staircase and found herself on the balcony below that ladder. The balcony wasn't big enough to hold four people, so one sister lingered at the top of the stairs while Father Roy edged around Laura and stepped onto the ladder. "Please follow me," he said.

The dome was like a horizon. Laura felt that she was nestled up to the moon. Below, the accordion music and the metallic slither and clanging of a streetcar sounded far away. All noise was sucked up into the blue air surrounding them.

"It's completely safe," said the sister behind Laura. "Just go carefully."

Metal loops enclosed the ladder at every fourth rung. Laura saw that she would be inside this protective spine of iron. She began to climb. Father Roy's black coat flapped and crackled above her. The ladder vibrated. They ascended the curve till they weren't climbing but crawling.

Laura put her head down and watched her hands. The more shallow the slope became, the more precarious she felt. When the curve had been steeper, gravity had seemed to hold her on the ladder; now it seemed all too easy to slip through the protection of the bars beside her and slide away down the smooth marble skin of the dome. Laura stopped. She clutched the ladder and closed her eyes.

"Come on, you're nearly there," the woman behind her said.

"What's the holdup?" said the sister bringing up the rear; she sounded anxious.

"Lift your head, Laura," said Father Roy.

Laura raised her head and opened her eyes. She saw that Father Roy had emerged from the ribbed tube and was standing at a doorway in the gold wall. There was light in the room behind him. A room! An enclosed space. Safety.

Laura scrambled toward him. He gripped her by the collar of her coat and drew her into the room. There was a step down, and Laura stumbled and caught herself on the edge of a big round table. The sisters piled in behind her, the second with a basket on her back filled with bundles, blankets, candles. The woman heaved the basket off her back and tipped it out onto the table, then lunged to catch the candles as they rolled toward its center.

In the little bit of light coming through the door, Laura saw that the table was about ten feet in diameter, so big that it nearly filled the round room. Its surface was concave, so anything set on it slid into the middle.

The sister sorted some candles from the pile of blankets. She placed them on the ledge above the door and lit one. Then she began to arrange the blankets into a bed on top of the concave table.

Father Roy faced Laura. "You'll be safe here, and sufficiently removed that other people should be safe from you."

Laura looked out the door at the blue air, then down at the floor, as if it were transparent and she could measure the distance between this isolated, elevated room and the nave of the cathedral below. She considered how far she'd climbed but still wasn't sure if it was far enough.

Father Roy said, "Someone will come to wake you before everyone else's usual bedtime. Any parishioners nodding off during the sermon will just have to take their chances." The priest studied Laura's face. "We can't warn them," he said, then, "His Eminence has spoken to your aunt and has read your letter. It *is* your letter, isn't it? Anyway—we know what dream you have."

The nuns were waiting at the door, flanking it like black sentinels, their hands concealed in the folds of their habits.

"Sleep now," said Father Roy.

"Don't lock me in," Laura said.

He nodded and went out, followed by the sisters. The door was closed. Laura walked around and checked it—it gave when she pushed the latch. She fastened it again, then peered around the cylindrical chamber. There was a mirror suspended in one corner of the room, high on the wall, angled down, a round mirror about forty inches in diameter. Beside the mirror was a handle and meshed cogs and wheels.

Laura went closer to inspect this machine and experimentally pushed the handle. It was stiff but slid half a turn. She heard a rolling noise of machinery moving in the ceiling and thought she saw a colored shadow swimming on the surface of the mirror. She leapt back. The whirring stopped, and the mirror showed her only the tabletop and the blot of her makeshift bed.

Laura took her aunt's coat off and added it to the bedding. Then she pushed down the rolled sleeves of Marta's nightgown. The sleeves dangled from the ends of her arms; they would do to trap her hands and save her face from scratches. Laura pulled the nightgown off, knotted the ends of the sleeves, then put it back on. Then she clambered onto the table, burrowed into the blankets, and closed her eyes.

Before long she was drowsy. She could sense the nightmare suspended in her sleep like a monstrous fish hanging motionless beneath the surface of a dark pool. It wanted to swallow her. She was afraid but so worn out that she simply gave in and went under.

✣ ✣ ✣

Laura struggled up in pain. Her tongue hurt, and the roots of her nails, which she'd bent back by clawing at the tabletop. She lay still. There was salty blood in her mouth. She opened her eyes. The room was filled with bright light. By the light she saw first the small tears in the sleeves of her nightgown, and her fingers hooked through the cloth, nail tips split and nail beds white with prolonged pressure. She closed her hands, hid her abused fingertips in her palms. Then Laura saw that the sleeves of her nightgown were covered in color—blurred scales in warm terra cotta—and that there was movement in the color, a tiny, flapping splash of vivid red and shapes that crawled in a grid of brown and gray, through which—*within which*—she could see the shape of her own arm.

She felt dizzy. She felt that she had woken up to find herself lying on a window. She was in a big wheel of light, in which she could see tiled rooftops, a silver river split by streets, and one familiar roof, oval, with a jeweled dome—the Rainbow Opera.

Laura sat up. She found that she was sitting within a circular image of the Isle of the Temple. It was a projection. She turned to the source of the light and looked up into the mirror. Through its dazzle she thought she saw the island, impossibly bright, impossibly compressed.

The candle above the door had gone out.

Laura climbed off the table and pulled the door open. She looked back at the table. The image had disappeared. When she closed the door again, sealing out the light, the image came back.

Laura pushed her blankets off the table and looked down on the round bird's-eye view of the Isle. She made out the movement of vehicles in streets, pedestrians in the square, the quick alteration of sunlight across the face of the river, the streaming speed of a flock of birds passing over the rooftops. She gazed at this small circle of the world surrounded by darkness. She was turned inward but looking out. She watched without being seen. It was eerie and wonderful. And, as she circled, peering down, the image very gradually grew darker. The windows of the Isle bristled with gold light, then the streetscape and river turned ghostly, and, finally, the chamber went black.

Laura felt her way to the door and opened it on a square of dark blue twilight air. She fumbled around on the ledge above the door and found the other candle and a box of matches. She lit the candle, set it upright, and sat on the floor to wait.

Later there was noise and vibration from the ladder, and one of the sisters reappeared, a basket on her back. Laura gave the sister a hand and helped her into the room.

The nun unpacked food and drink. She said, "I'm here to feed you and prevent you from sleeping." And, "Here," she passed Laura a chamber pot and a bottle of water.

"Thank you," said Laura. "Where's my aunt?"

"I won't answer questions. Would you like to make yourself comfortable now, then replace the lid, rinse your hands, and have something to eat."

Laura did as she was told. She emptied her bladder and washed her hands. The nun had found two seats under the table. She set food before one and watched as Laura ate. Then she lit several more candles, got out some darning, and passed Laura a Bible. She asked that Laura read to her as she plied her needle. Acts. Then the Gospel of St. Thomas. "His disciples said to him: On what day will the Kingdom come? Jesus said: It cometh not with observation. They will not say, Lo here! Or Lo, there! The kingdom of the Father is spread out upon the earth, and men do not see it."

Sometime during the night Laura picked up a blanket and wrapped it around herself. And sometime during the night the nun gave her a lesson with needle and yarn and darning egg. Laura hadn't darned before—nor had she ever worn a darned stocking. She was clumsy; her hands were sore. The sister read to her while she worked.

When they heard the bells in the bell tower ringing, the sister stopped reading. "Matins," she said. "I'll go now. I was told you could be safely left by morning. I suggest you push that chamber pot well under the table so that you won't risk knocking it over with your foot." She gathered her darning and the remains of the meal, leaving Laura several apples, a bottle of water, and the Bible.

Laura left the door open. She reassembled her bedding, knotted the sleeves of her nightgown again, and lay down. She made no attempt to fight sleep. She'd managed perhaps five hours in all—five hours in five days. The nightmare didn't let her stay asleep. She'd had it three times now—when she'd first caught it, then at the Rainbow Opera, then in the late afternoon of the day before. Each time she'd fought her way out, fought as the buried man strained to escape his coffin.

This time her body's need for sleep anchored her in the dream. Her struggle was horribly prolonged. When she was finally able to free herself, she could scarcely move. She lay in her twisted bedding and howled with shock and despair.

Once her shuddering had subsided to shivers, Laura's eyes kept trying to shut themselves again, so she got up and went to sit on the sill of the low doorway in the cold morning air. From there she watched the Isle come to life, its bridges fill with cars, carts, and pedestrians. She watched the men at work on telegraph poles, putting up wires for the new phone system that was slowly spreading its way around the city. She watched the smoke of trains passing across the two bridges that linked the west bank to the Isle, and the Isle to the east. This was a commuter line; it came in from Founderston's western suburbs through villas and parks, then past Founderston Girls' Academy. It passed through the district that held the museums, galleries, libraries, and government buildings, after which it crossed the river, went through a tunnel built under the wide plaza before the tower of the Regulatory Body, and left the Isle by a bridge to the east. The line then passed through the Old Town and terminated at Founderston Central Station, with its rail yards, warehouses, station hotels, circling cabs, and rail lines on to long-distance destinations. Laura watched all the traffic, and birds passing above and below her. The sun came out of the clouds and warmed her where she sat. She ate an apple.

Midmorning she felt the vibrations on the ladder, and shortly afterward a head appeared over the horizon of the dome. It was Father Roy. He was followed by a man in a white robe, with a golden beard and a square, brimless white hat.

5

✦ ✦ ✦

FATHER ROY REMAINED BY THE DOOR, AND THE GRAND PATRIARCH, ERASMUS TIEBOLD, ADVANCED AROUND THE CONCAVE table—the screen for his camera obscura—till he realized that the girl would continue to drift away from him, trailing her damaged fingertips around the rim of the tabletop like someone house-proud checking for dust. He came to a standstill and started to talk. He spoke softly. "I thought I would give you some time to reflect," he said.

Laura Hame had reached a point equidistant between Father Roy and himself. She stopped and looked at him. "Where's Aunt Marta?"

"She is at home with Downright and the estimable Mr. and Mrs. Bridges."

"So, she left me to you."

"Yes. You do know that we are kin, Laura. Your Tiebold grandfather was my cousin."

The girl nodded.

"And when you sent me a letter, you gave me a certain amount of responsibility for you." The Grand Patriarch produced the letter and laid it on the tabletop. Then he told Father Roy to close the door. Laura stumbled against the wall away from them, but once the door was sealed and the image from the twenty-four-inch lens and forty-inch mirror of the camera obscura flowed in full, brilliant color, the girl came back and stood staring at him, her face lit from below. The Grand Patriarch pointed at the camera housing. "Can you reach that handle above your head?" he said.

She put her hand on it.

"Give it a turn."

She had to use both hands and hang her weight on the handle to bring it down. The camera moved with a hollow, rolling noise. The image swam, and the east bank of the Sva swung into the light as the bridges to the west slid away into darkness. Laura stopped winding and looked down on a slightly different slice of the city.

"Does it make you feel godlike?" the Grand Patriarch asked. "Like a hidden and disembodied witness?"

"No," said the girl.

The Grand Patriarch touched the image on the tabletop. "Why did you write to me?"

"I wrote to the Director of the Regulatory Body and the editor of the *Founderston Herald* as well."

"And none of the letters were signed with your name?"

"No. They are all signed 'Lazarus,' and I had someone else copy them out for me."

"Why disown what you chose to do?"

"I did what my father asked me to do. It was his idea. There wasn't any other way."

The Grand Patriarch made a gesture—putting that aside for now. "I can't question your father about his motives, but perhaps you can answer for him."

"I want to *go!*" Laura said, plaintive. "I need to go In and overwrite this nightmare. I'm so tired my heart won't slow down. What will happen when I can't make myself wake up? I don't know what happens in the *end*. But the man in the coffin never gets out. He dies in there. He takes a long time to die. I don't want to go on and dream that."

"So—is that what you caught? A man trapped in a coffin until he dies?"

Laura blinked at him. She looked surprised and momentarily relieved. "No. I didn't catch the nightmare to its end. I woke up before I got there."

"Then I don't see how you can dream a death you didn't catch," the Grand Patriarch said, practical. "Laura, I want to talk to you about what you've done."

The girl sighed and shrugged. "My letter explains it."

"Well then, according to your letter, you wanted to gain support for people who were being terrorized?"

Laura nodded.

"And in order to do that you chose to terrorize people?"

She stared at him, sullen. "What other way was there to show them? How else could I prove it? I didn't have any evidence. I couldn't take *photographs* of what was happening."

The Grand Patriarch paced back and forth for a moment, thinking. He ran his hand along the table through rooftops and courtyards, streets, flights of steps, waterways, hurrying people. "In my grandparents' day, no one was taking photographs. Do you think that the people back then believed that testimony—to any crime—needed photographic evidence to support it? Are people now any less inclined to listen to testimony? To listen in good faith?"

"You would say 'faith,' " the girl said, insolent but without any great energy.

"Faith doesn't just mean faith in God, Laura. It means faith in people, in the truth, in truth-telling. Faith in your own ability to make yourself heard. Faith that people will understand what you take the time to explain to them. Faith that people don't need to be tricked, or *sold* the truth."

"I wanted to do what Da told me to. He left me a letter asking me to do what I did. I followed his wishes. I kept faith with him."

The Grand Patriarch studied the girl before him. "Do you think you did the right thing?"

"I was *asked*. And it wasn't just Da. I kept catching dreams about convicts. Why would I dream about convicts unless the Place wanted me to help them too?"

"You caught dreams about convicts?"

"I found convicts in dreams. Sometimes it seemed they *found me*. I did what I could. I could only think to do what Da asked me to." Laura sounded quite desperate. She pressed her forearms into her stomach so hard that she stooped. She seemed to be trying to hold herself together. Then she took a deep, shuddering breath, straightened up, and said, "Besides, if you could do something that no one else could, wouldn't you have to find your own way of acting in the world?"

"I can't think what you might mean," said the Grand Patriarch. "Unless you're boasting—as dreamhunters do—about the size of your penumbra." He shook his head and saw that she was echoing his gesture. "Tell me, how does finding a new way match up with just doing what your father asked you to do?"

"Maybe I found a new father," she said, and gave a little, wild laugh.

⸸ ⸸ ⸸

The Grand Patriarch's assessing stare was so prolonged and intent that Laura dropped her gaze. Then she heard Father

Roy shuffling his feet. When the Grand Patriarch resumed his questions, his tone was careful, almost gentle. "Your aunt says that the letter you sent me was not in your own hand. Did you therefore mean to get away with it?"

Laura nodded.

"And you involved someone else in your plans."

"Someone copied the letters for me."

"Your cousin?"

"No!" Laura was horrified. "I wouldn't do that to Rose! This was my responsibility. But I've done enough now, and I don't want to do any more. Everyone knows now. Someone else can figure out what to do next." She stamped her foot, in petulance and frustration and weary misery.

The Grand Patriarch told her to calm herself. Father Roy approached and handed her a handkerchief. She took it, spread it open, and held it against her face. The wounds on her lips had reopened, and they printed the white cotton with bright red blotches.

"There are dreamhunters who get on the wrong side of the Regulatory Body," the Grand Patriarch told her. "And I've tried to help them. They've confided in me—misgivings, fears, rumors."

Laura removed the handkerchief and licked her bleeding lips.

The Grand Patriarch said, "Have you ever heard of a dream named Contentment?"

She shook her head. "It doesn't sound like a nightmare."

"No, it doesn't. Have you heard of the Depot?"

"That's a funny name for a dream," she said. "Dream names tend to be descriptive."

"I don't know that it *is* a dream." The man regarded her steadily. Laura could see he was weighing something in his mind. He said, "Do you know what a master dream is?"

"No, not really."

"You may have 'done enough,' Laura, but you don't *know* enough." The Grand Patriarch shook his head. "The Regulatory Body sends you off into the Place with signal whistles but without a full education!"

✦ ✦ ✦

The Grand Patriarch watched the Hame girl, feeling vexed and sad. He found her lack of shame deeply offensive. The sullen set of her battered mouth, the stubborn ego looking out of her eyes.

But when she answered back, he was less offended than surprised by her coldness. "This isn't about what I know," she said. "What I did at the Opera will open a public discussion. We will all soon know more." She spoke as though she were an angel guarding the gates to Eden.

The Grand Patriarch took a deep breath and began to rethink his approach. He wanted to help this girl more than he wanted simply to ease her misery. She had been left—orphaned and formidably gifted—to find her own way. She had gone off the rails—as the saying went—but in her own peculiar way. She might have gone looking for love and ended up in some unsuitable entanglement. She might have gone looking to forget and drugged herself with dreams or drink. Instead she'd found refuge in this hard, self-righteous autonomy. Though she was clearly suffering, in a way her heart had stopped. To Erasmus Tiebold it was clear that he must find some way to start her heart up again. And he must do it before he sent her to her father. Hame could help his daughter just by turning out to be alive. Finding her father should restore the girl's faith in the general shape of her life. But right now, looking at Laura, Erasmus felt that he was watching water set into ice. There were forces at work, altering her soul—the nightmare itself, the act of sharing it, and her obvious terrible loneliness.

The Grand Patriarch had an inspiration then. He said, "Laura, you haven't injured me. But I'd like you to explain to someone you have injured why you felt you had to do what you did."

"I'm sure I couldn't do any worse than I already have," Laura said, brisk and unfeeling.

The Grand Patriarch retrieved the letter. He turned away, touched Father Roy's arm, and conducted him out through the small door at the base of the dome. Once they were down the stairwell, Erasmus Tiebold said to his secretary, "She'll need clothes for her journey. Let's have her cousin deliver them to her."

6

✦ ✦ ✦

THE DREAMHUNTERS WERE HUDDLED IN A DISPIRITED GROUP AT ONE CORNER OF THE PORCH OF THE RANGERS' STATION AT Doorhandle. No one was standing anywhere near them. Around their feet were their dust-covered packs and bedrolls. They had been In to get Beautiful Horse. But none of them had been able to catch it.

Buried Alive *was*—it turned out—a master dream and could not be overwritten. It had to be endured for six to eight nights at least. The dreamhunters were waiting to be escorted out to the Regulatory Body's dream retreats—cabins on the near slopes of the Rifleman Mountains. They were "guests of the Body," detained and guarded by rangers.

The Chief Ranger appeared to explain the delay. He was having trouble finding volunteers. Rangers were not normally so skittish, but the combination of newspaper reports on the riot and the sight of these dreamhunters emerging from the Place with freshly bleeding mouths had proved a little too much for some. "They're behaving like novice dreamhunters with superstitious tales of fatally indelible dreams." He spread his hands, made a gesture of helplessness. "I'm sure you'd rather *not* be escorted by men I had to force."

Grace asked if she'd have time to send another wire.

"Certainly, Mrs. Tiebold."

Sandy asked if he could go with Grace to the telegraph office, then said, as he fell into step with her, "I want a word with you in private."

Grace pulled a paper from the pocket of her long silk coat and handed it to him. It was a message she'd received earlier. Sandy smoothed the paper out against his chest. He read, LAURA IN MARTAS CARE STOP SHE DID NOT SLEEP STOP ONLY FRIGHTENED STOP ROSE.

Sandy read the telegram twice, then hurried to catch up with Grace. "Where is Mr. Tiebold?"

"I don't know," Grace said. "And Rose didn't bother to tell me where *she* is—though I'm told she's back at school. Still, that is what you wanted to know, isn't it? Where Laura is?"

"When I found Rose outside the Opera, I could see she hadn't slept. She said Laura hadn't either. I guess they were talking."

The telegraph office was brightly lit. There was one key man and two clerks in the booth. Grace stood at a counter in the center of the room and wrote her message. "Do you have any money on you?" she asked Sandy.

"Yes."

"Have you wired your parents? They might be worried. They'll have seen your uncle George's name in the papers."

Sandy shrugged. He said, "I'm reluctant to wire my parents. My father's attitude will be that, since I've decided to take up a 'frivolous and unproductive' life, I deserve any difficulties my decision brings me."

"He'd really say that?"

"Probably."

"We'll be detained for a week," Grace said. "Or, at least, *you* will." She went up to the cage and pushed her message and money under the bars. Then she and Sandy trailed back to the others.

Maze Plasir's apprentice was sitting on the steps, rocking back and forth, his face wet with tears. George Mason leaned toward Grace and said, "If I was Plasir, I'd be on my way here already to protect my investment." He nodded at the weeping boy.

"Plasir seems to go through apprentices pretty quickly."

"Do you think he will come?" said Mason.

"I've offered him a lot of money," said Grace.

"For what?" Sandy was bemused.

His uncle said, "Several of Plasir's dreams are master dreams. He can catch—say—Secret Room and overwrite this nightmare. Would you like me to send him on to you, Alexander? I'm splitting Plasir's fee with Mrs. Tiebold, though obviously she's first in line."

"Plasir might not agree," said Grace.

"Well, if he does decide to, you'd better make sure our guards know to direct him to us," said Mason.

Grace nodded and went indoors in search of the Chief Ranger.

"I can't contribute anything toward Plasir's fee," Sandy said. The idea of being alone in the forest with Maze Plasir made him feel queasy.

Plasir was a Gifter—he could take his own memories of real people's faces and manners and graft them onto the characters in the dreams he caught. He was often employed by people who wanted what they couldn't have, and his dream repertoire included dreams that weren't at all respectable. Plasir wasn't respectable, though he did have powerful friends.

Sandy said to his uncle, "I'd better just tough it out."

"It's your funeral," said Mason, and chuckled at his own black humor.

Grace returned, followed by a group of grim-faced

rangers. One clapped his hands to get their attention. The
drooping, hollow-eyed dreamhunters started with fright.
"Get up!" the ranger ordered. His men scooped up their
packs and bedrolls. They were led away from the station and
out of the village. Five rangers walked before the dreamhunters, setting the pace, and five brought up the rear.

Sandy felt herded and corralled. But he was the son of a
shop steward in a factory that made flax matting. He had been
raised in a house with strong views on the rights of working
people. "You know what we need?" he whispered to his uncle
as they tramped along. "We need a union."

7

✦ ✦ ✦

ROSE CAME IN ALONE WITH LAURA'S BAG AND PULLED THE LITTLE DOOR CLOSED BEHIND HER, AS IF SHE DIDN'T want what she had to say to get out into the open air. She at once began to speak, commencing an attack. A few moments later Laura, thinking she would confound her cousin, wet her finger and thumb, and closed them on the wick of the room's single candle.

"Laura!" Rose was enraged. And then she looked down into the light on the table, the world in miniature, perfect but for the distortion at its edges. Laura monitored her cousin's face, waiting for Rose's set, righteous look to soften in amazement.

Rose stared at the streets, beetling traffic, and brushstrokes of flocking pigeons. She continued to look grim, staring through the world as though it were an apparition. She said, "To think I believed that you were telling me everything. That you'd let me in on what you were planning. But all you told me was what you were *feeling*. If we are friends, do you imagine that our friendship is just made up of shared feelings?"

"I didn't talk to you about my dreamhunting. I thought it was better not to speak about what you'd missed out on."

"Do you think that's what I'm talking about? You sparing my feelings by not tantalizing me with dreamhunter stories?

Are you listening to me? I'm not even talking about what you chose to do—you may have had very good, considered reasons for bringing that nightmare to the Opera. But, Laura, I can't believe that you didn't tell me about that—that *thing*!"

Laura thought it was better to pretend she didn't know what Rose was talking about. She knitted her brow. "Thing?"

"The monster. The statue. The thing that carried you off."

"That was the nightmare. Part of the horrible dream."

"I didn't sleep, Laura! You made *sure* I didn't sleep. You put Wakeful in my musk creams. I was awake, and I know what I saw."

"Do you? You have to realize, Rose, that my talent has made me different from you," Laura said. "I'm not as susceptible to—"

"Lots of people have talent. Lots of people have things that make them different. But, you know, even if we shared every aspect of our lives, the difference between you and me was still going to be huge, not because you're *talented* but because you believe our differences are more important than what we have in common."

Laura looked at Rose and wondered whether her cousin was going to cry. Rose was so worked up. She, Laura, had always been the weepy one. Now she felt dry, deadened, and suspended.

"So—I don't want to hear about your God-given talent. Especially since you are just going to stand there lying to me!"

Laura stood, silent, thinking about the Hame inheritance, "The Measures," her servant. She fought her urge to explain and, fighting it, realized that she wasn't finished, that there was more to do. After a while she said, "When I go to the Place, I feel that I might be able to catch a dream that will make sense of my whole life. Not of other people's lives. Just my own. It isn't that I think I'm different. It's that I have to deal with actually *being* different—with things that have changed me."

"Listen to you," Rose said. "Even now all you're doing is talking about your bloody feelings."

Laura shook her head. She was too tired to properly understand what Rose was saying to her. She doggedly went back to her explanation. Why wouldn't her cousin just let her get this said?

"Try to imagine it was you. Try to imagine that your ma and da disappeared and all you were left with was a letter saying what you were expected to do. Try to imagine that you did something you knew was impossible—but it felt right. It felt like gravity. Not like a mystery and a terror, but like a secret wrapped around its own solution. Rose, I *know* I can be impulsive. But I couldn't see to do anything other than what Da told me to. And setting out to do it was like crossing a narrow bridge over a chasm—I couldn't stop, I couldn't look down. And I had to think my gift came to me because *someone* thought I should have it. That it was God-given." Laura was aware that Rose did not believe in God. All her life Laura had wavered between her cousin's and uncle's atheism, and her father's faith. Now she was firmly in her father's camp. If "The Measures" had not come from God, where had they come from?

Rose said, "You think you've stolen fire from Heaven."

Laura waited. Then she nodded. She nodded to say she accepted that Rose's view was fair and may well have been right.

Rose just looked at her, bleak. "Laura, you haven't told me anything. You don't trust me. Clearly you're not the person I thought you were. Or you're not the person you once were."

Laura said, weakly, "People change."

But Rose had raised a hand to stop her speaking. "The point is—honestly—that I don't know whether I trust you anymore. Or even *like* you."

Laura's face clenched, and two cold tears slid down her cheeks. "I don't believe you, Rose."

"You'd better believe me." Her cousin pushed the bag across the table. "Have a safe journey," she said, then left the turret room.

8

✧ ✧ ✧

CHORLEY TIEBOLD FOUND HIS DAUGHTER AT HER SCHOOL. HE MET HER IN THE PRINCIPAL'S OFFICE AND WALKED HER OUT into the quad, where they stood under a peach tree whose buds had just cracked to show tight, spotless tips of pink blossom. Rose stood a little way from him and slipped her hands under the bib of her pleated pinafore to warm them. She wouldn't meet his eyes. "You're going to ask me where Laura is. You know, if I had a dollar for everyone who's asked me that, I'd be rolling in money."

"I know where Laura is. I've been to the Temple. Father Roy told me that, at his request, you delivered some of her clothes."

Rose was looking at him now. It was a careful, self-contained look, and very grown-up. "For her journey," she said.

"Yes. They're sending her off somewhere safe. To join her father—who I've seen."

"Oh," said Rose. She blinked. She stretched out the toe of one highly polished shoe and pushed it through a puddle to make ripples. "Laura didn't know about *that* when I saw her."

"They plan to tell her when she's well on her way. They're worried about her state of mind, and I think it suits them to keep her subdued."

"Yes, I can see that."

"Darling?" Chorley said. He felt as if he had dropped a stone down a well and hadn't heard either a clatter or a splash.

"So Uncle Tziga's alive?" Rose said; then she looked into her father's face, her expression open and wondering. Chorley reached for her and drew her to him. His earlobe brushed across the top of her head, and he realized she'd grown since he'd last held her. She was hugging him now—hard—so that his breathing was a little constricted. "I've been worried that Ma will be really angry with you," Rose said. "And with Laura."

"I doubt your mother will be angry with me when I tell her I've found Tziga. I'd have come home sooner, except where I was they get five days' worth of newspapers only every five days. When Tziga read about the riot and nightmare, he said, 'It's Laura.' And I shouted at him."

A sharp gust of wind swept over the roofs around the quad and altered the air pressure in the enclosed space. The peach tree seemed to throw up its branches in surprise, and drops of water rained down on father and daughter.

Chorley said, "Tziga has a head injury. He has fits. It doesn't do to upset him."

Rose drew back and looked into his face. "How did he hurt his head?"

Chorley looked away. He couldn't meet his daughter's eyes. He tried to control his face and his feelings.

"Da?"

"I don't expect your mother back for several days yet."

"Da?"

"No," said Chorley. "I'll tell you when I understand more."

"Uncle Tziga is hiding from the Body," Rose said. "The

Body supplies the Department of Corrections with night-mares."

Chorley was startled. "How do you know that?"

"Maze Plasir told Laura and me. We went to see him. That letter Laura tore up suggested she talk to Plasir. And it told her to do what she did—to catch a nightmare and overdream Ma at the Rainbow Opera. It was Uncle Tziga's idea. But—Da—Laura *lied* to me." Rose's voice went high and tight. "She lied to me," she said again. Her father could see she was fight-ing tears. "She didn't trust me enough to tell me what she meant to do. She mixed Wakeful into my Farry's musk creams so that I wouldn't sleep. She thought she was doing me a big favor, but she kept me out of everything, and when I con-fronted her she lied. *To me!* And I can't even talk about it properly till I have proof about what she's hiding. It's like I have to lie too, or look crazy."

"The Hames—" Chorley began, trying to organize his thoughts about the Hames, the three he knew anyway—morbid, dramatic, closemouthed, and apt at times to act like divinely appointed judges. "You can't be too angry at Laura. Her father left her and wrote a letter saying do this and do that. It was as if he'd told her she'd failed him somehow and had to make it up to him. She can't have wanted any of this."

"I don't know. I didn't have the nightmare. It made every-one crazy, but Uncle Tziga could always hold big, forceful, awesome dreams in his head without going out of his mind. For all we know, Laura might *not* have hated it."

"Rose, Tziga *did* go out of his mind." Chorley touched her arm. He wanted to reassure her. And he didn't want to tell her that her uncle had tried to kill himself. "Besides," he said, "it wasn't just that Laura's father told her what to do; it was also a matter of her conscience. What the Regulatory Body and the Department of Corrections are doing is *wrong*. Within the letter of the law, but wrong. And there's more to it. They must be up to illegal things as well—more than just forging Tziga's signature in the Doorhandle intentions book. I'm hoping the Grand Patriarch will eventually trust me enough to let me know all he suspects."

Rose shuffled her feet and scowled at her father. "Those bloody pledge takers," she said. She was talking about the swelling ranks of those who, inspired by the preaching of the Temple, had sworn off sharing dreams.

"The Grand Patriarch calls them his Ark."

"So we'll all be drowned and they'll be saved?" Rose was exasperated. "The Grand Patriarch thinks sharing dreams is sinful and we'll all be punished one day for doing it—struck down by a righteous God. The Regulatory Body may be up to no good, but there's nothing wrong with Ma or Mr. Mason or the Rainbow Opera. *I'm* not throwing the baby out with the bathwater because I'm told to by some bearded, fasting ninny!"

Chorley burst out laughing.

Rose glared at him. "Truth and justice are scarcely *ever* the property of religion!" she snapped. "You taught me that! And if a pack of mangy convicts needs our help, let's help them because it's the right thing to do, not because God loves them!"

The school principal, a tiny woman, rushed with brisk little steps into the quad. "Rose Tiebold! I hope you are not shouting at your father. Academy girls *do not* take that tone with their elders."

"Bearded ninny," Chorley muttered, sniggering. "Mangy convicts."

"I'm sorry, ma'am," said Rose. Then, irrepressible, "But he's a sore trial to me."

"That's enough of that, my girl!" The principal shot the sniggering Chorley a quelling look. She said to him, "It would be far better for Rose if, when she's rude, she wasn't so confident that she's also amusing."

"Yes, I see." Chorley wiped his eyes.

"Is this interview over?" the principal inquired, tartly.

"Yes," said Chorley. "I have to go home and burn my Darwin."

"Da!" Rose squeaked, and they both started giggling again.

"Rose! Mr. Tiebold! Please!"

Chorley took the principal's hand and shook it. "Thank you for your time, and your concern," he said. He gazed into her eyes.

"Well—er—yes," the principal said, then stood blushing and flustered as Chorley turned and left them.

9

✢ ✢ ✢

THE MAN IN THE CHAIR BEFORE CAS
DORAN'S DESK WAS TIRED OF AN-
SWERING THE SAME QUESTIONS, OF GIVING
answers that couldn't satisfy anyone, even himself.

"The assailant smashed the lights and broke the doors," he
said. "He was wearing a mask. Or he had dirt on his face and
a black mask tied across his eyes. He was wrapped up in something thick and squishy. His body felt soft when he knocked
me down. He was there one moment, then gone the next. It
was dark all along the second tier. Mrs. Tiebold was shouting
at us because a mob was after Mr. Mason. I sent my men
down to see what they could do for Mason—then, shortly after
that, the police arrived. I didn't see where our assailant went."

Secretary Doran was silent for so long that the former head
of the Rainbow Opera's fire watch finally raised his face.

"Whoever he was, he was awake before the dream ended,"
Doran said. "Or he hadn't slept at all."

The man nodded.

"A coat, a hat, padded clothes, well-built, masked, perhaps
six and a half feet in height, you say?"

"Yes. And he was gritty, as though he'd been lying on the
ground."

"The doors were hanging off their hinges. The doorframes
were splintered."

"Yes, I saw that later," the man said. He looked miserable. "I should have ordered the alarm bells rung as soon as the screaming started. We just watched Mrs. Tiebold fighting it— the nightmare. We couldn't understand at first that everyone was doing the same thing. I've never seen a dreamhunter with a nightmare." The man made claws of his hands and touched his pallid, unmarked cheeks.

Cas Doran's hand went to his own face and the stiff rows of adhesive bandages.

"It was an emergency. We weren't meant to stand by amazed," the man said. Then, "Will I be prosecuted?"

"That's up to your manager, and the police."

✦ ✦ ✦

Grace arrived home earlier than Chorley expected, battered and dirty. He was able to tell her that Laura was no longer at her aunt Marta's but was safe, and Rose was back at school.

"I'll want to talk to Laura," Grace said.

Chorley opened his mouth to explain that that might be difficult, and why, but his wife interrupted him. "I'm going to have a bath," she said.

Half an hour later, Chorley carried a tray upstairs—soup in a cup, buttered toast, coffee. He put a stool by the tub and set the tray on it.

Grace said, "I'm going to catch the express to Sisters Beach tonight. I've got a copy of Secret Room. It's somewhat spicy, so I'd better not give it to our neighbors. Summerfort is far enough from other houses. The dream isn't at my full size— something to do with Plasir's eensy-teensy penumbra, which I might say may be tiny but is as black and deep as a well."

"You slept with Plasir?"

"Yes, dear. Out in the woods too."

Chorley took deep breaths.

"Only a master dream can erase a master dream," Grace said. "I was lucky. Plasir already had Secret Room. He went In on St. Lazarus's Eve, apparently. He told me that St. Lazarus's Day is a good day for him to go dreamhunting since no one wants his performances on family holidays." Grace smirked. "Anyway, I checked the intentions book before I caught the coach from Doorhandle. Plasir did go In shortly before midnight, almost as though he wanted an alibi."

"You can't seriously think Plasir had anything to do with the nightmare? With his parlor-sized penumbra?"

"I don't know what I think." Grace emptied the soup cup and started on the toast and coffee. She told Chorley she wanted him to come to Summerfort with her. "You'll enjoy Secret Room." She looked at him, cool. "You should be grateful that I want you to come. You must know I'm angry with you."

Chorley nodded. Then he smiled. And it was a smile not of gratitude or reassurance but of plain happiness. "And I bet you could do with some really good news," he said.

10

✢ ✢ ✢

*L*AURA LEFT THE TEMPLE AFTER FIVE DAYS. SHE PROMISED NOT TO SLEEP ON THE TRAIN. SHE WAS ACCOMPANIED BY the nuns who had looked after her, and by Father Roy, who said—once they'd boarded the train and closed the door of their compartment—that they were going with her only as far as Westport.

"This is an express, isn't it?" Laura said. "I had hoped we'd stop at Aunt Marta's."

"Your aunt has been included in every decision made on your behalf," said Father Roy. "She knows where you're going." He watched the girl withdraw into a corner of the seat, then into the folds of her black winter coat. She looked like some animal backing into its burrow.

Shortly before the express passed Marta Hame's stop, Laura got up and went out into the corridor.

Father Roy observed her.

She stood, her cheek laid on the window, and watched the stop come up. Her eyes were fixed on a hill near Marta Hame's house, a hill with a crest of black pines. Laura stared as the hill loomed, then flicked a glance at the compartment. Her eyes were bright and furtive. She left the window and hurried away along the jostling carriage.

Father Roy jumped up, threw open the compartment door,

and ran after her. She was at the end of the carriage, hauling with her whole weight on the red-painted handle of the emergency brake—which, fortunately, had not been designed with a child's strength in mind.

Father Roy threw himself at Laura and tore her away from the handle. She turned on him, hitting him with her fists.

The sisters appeared and helped him subdue her as gently as they could. As they hustled her back into the compartment, her head turned to follow the sight of that hill, sliding from window to window, then retreating along the track.

They closed the compartment door and sat her down.

"I have to see him," she said.

"You will be allowed to write to your friends. So long as you're careful what you say," Father Roy told her. He thought, "And we will read your letters. And perhaps discover who is in this with you. Whose strength you're looking to now. Who the *real* Lazarus is."

II
Foreigner's North

1

✢ ✢ ✢

*F*OUR WEEKS AFTER THE RAINBOW
OPERA RIOT, SANDY MASON RECEIVED
A LETTER. ITS ENVELOPE WAS POSTMARKED
"Westport Central Post Office." The letter was sent care of
Mrs. Lilley at Sandy's boardinghouse in Doorhandle, and he
had to retrieve it under the watchful eye of his landlady's
daughters.

The Lilley girls had a constant parade of young and home-
sick dreamhunters pass under their noses. They were choosy
about whom they would pay special attention to, offer treats,
and flirt with. Alexander Mason, at nineteen, already had one
good dream registered in his name. He had good prospects,
and the Lilley girls were determined to cultivate him. When
the letter arrived, the sisters at once got their hands on it.
They had a look at the handwriting on the envelope and decided that it was from "that Hame girl"—that sullen, flat-
chested thing whom Sandy Mason, for some unfathomable
reason, admired. The Lilley girls didn't hide Laura's letter,
for they were principled schemers. But they did make sure
they were present when Sandy retrieved it from the stack of
mail on the hall table so that they could watch his reaction.

Sandy Mason was big but sure-footed. And yet, the moment he glanced at the envelope, he stumbled and knocked
his knee on the newel post. He stood frozen at the foot of the

stairs and gazed at what he held in his hand. Then he tore the
envelope open while bounding on up the steps. A second envelope dropped out on the landing, and he stooped to pick it
up, then straightened slowly, staring at its address. Then he
began to read the other pages while still stopped on the landing. His hand trembled. He walked slowly out of the Lilley
girls' sight.

The girls' mother came out of her sitting room. "Was that
Mr. Mason? Did he get his letter?"

"Yes, Mother."

Mrs. Lilley regarded her daughters sharply. They were at
their most refined when dealing with—or even thinking
about—Alexander Mason. She wasn't sure which one of them
had decided to snare him, or whether they were still working
it out.

"Mother?" said one. "Are Miss Hame's aunt and uncle still
paying for her room?"

The letter was from Miss Hame, of course. Mrs. Lilley had
recognized Laura's handwriting. "Yes. And that's their business—but I must say that girl's had the slowest start of any
dreamhunter I've ever lodged." Mrs. Lilley went into her
kitchen, leaving her girls in peace, and smirking at each
other.

✦ ✦ ✦

Laura's letter was careful, coded, and chatty.

Dear Sandy,

  *I'm sorry I didn't have more to say to you last time we met. I just
hadn't expected to see you there. I'm sorry for the trouble, and for any
worry I caused you.*

I am mostly quite contented just now. It is very peaceful here. And I keep myself busy. Today, for instance, we all took a cart out along the shore to pick up the seaweed that came up with the king tide on the last full moon. It's had a week now to dry and reduce. The men bale it up and store it all summer under the houses. It sits between the house piles in stiff tangles with shiny glass fishing buoys here and there among it. They use seaweed here as kindling and burn coal all winter. There's hardly any firewood.

I helped gather seaweed, but it was more my job to keep an eye on these two little girls—six and eight. They really know more than I do about (for example) the quicksand one should never walk on, or how one should never get between a sea lion and the sea. (There are sea lions resting up along the coast here. Sick or injured ones among them. We saw one seal yesterday with huge gashes from a shark, or a killer whale.)

There's a big boy here too—actually, he's about my age but seems younger. He applauds diving gannets as if they are performing for him. He is a little odd and wrapped up in himself. He talks and talks and never seems to know when anyone has had enough. On the seaweed expedition, we girls were supposed to be having a nap under the cart, but he kept us awake telling us that this was why motorcars were no good and how Southland could never have been settled at all if people on the plains hadn't been able to take shelter under their wagons. He reminds me a little of you in that he is so full of information. But you are far better at imparting it!

I will write to Rose too, and Aunt Grace, but it is you I have chosen to trust with a task. I want you to do one thing for me. I want you to take the enclosed letter to a certain place. You must catch a train going out toward Westport and get off at the little station at Glass Eye Creek. Then walk up the road past my aunt Marta's house. As you come past the house, you will see a hill with a pine plantation on it. I want you to climb up to the forest and go a short way into the pines and leave the letter lying on the ground. Then go away immediately.

Will you do that? It would mean the world to me.
I promise that I will see you again before too long.
You are my dear and trusted friend.

Laura

Sandy read the letter several times. He realized Laura had given him enough clues for him to guess that she might well be at the lighthouse on So Long Spit. But was she giving him directions? Did she want him to visit her?

As he stood reading, a blush of pleasure had crept through him, heating his skin and robbing his legs of strength. He sat down on his bed and turned his attention to the sealed envelope, which was addressed simply: "From Laura."

Sandy stared at the white square, the two black-inked words. *From Laura*—as if Laura was the only real attachment the intended recipient of the letter had in all the world.

Sandy thought, "Someone walks up to the wood every day to check for a message from Laura." But surely not Marta Hame, whom, after all, Laura had mentioned in her instructions for the letter's delivery.

Sandy's skin began to cool. He seemed to cool and congeal all over. He went sour, sitting there.

Eventually he got up, stuffed the unopened letter into his pocket, and went down to the kitchen, where he was fed tidbits by Mrs. Lilley and courted by her daughters, and where he helped peel potatoes till, finally, he was left alone with the steaming kettle.

Sandy held the envelope in the steam from the kettle's spout until the already dimpled paper dimpled more, and its glue softened. He unsealed the flap of the envelope, then fled upstairs, shut himself in his room, drew out the single sheet of paper, and unfolded it with hands shaking so violently that the Lilley girls would have been amazed by it—and frightened of him.

He read:

I'm sorry to take so long to get word to you. They carried me away. Please come to me. I am where the boy on the shore was in the dream I told you about. My first dream.

I want you to come at once. I feel I must say "please" and call you "my dear" because you will no longer take orders from me.

My dear. Mine still. Please.

I should have gone with you. I should have listened to you on the train. I should have let you look after me. Without you I'm afraid of everything. I think I have put my heart outside of my body.

Partway through reading the letter, Sandy went cold, and his gorge rose, and he had to press his hand to his mouth. He tried to control himself but couldn't. A moment later he was groveling under his bed after his chamber pot, which he never used and which was covered in dust. He vomited into it. He stayed on his hands and knees till the retching had passed. Then he began to cry, dropping clear tears into the mess of regurgitated tea and toast. He hadn't cried in years, so he did it perilously, like a busted machine whose cogs no longer meshed; painfully, straining his scalded throat; help-lessly, because his feelings had him completely—grief, and jealousy as burning and bitter as acid.

2

✧ ✧ ✧

THE TROUBLEMAKER WAS TAKEN ON A LONG TRAIN JOURNEY FROM HIS PRISON IN CANNING TO ANOTHER, A PRISON at the end of a long pier. He knew he was in the north because it was warmer. Westport was where they sent all the hard men. Westport and the government mine.

The prison governor took a look at him, then he was left in his shackles, sitting before a desk in a locked room. After a time a man joined him: a man in a suit and bowler hat with one of those gold fraternity pins winking in his lapel. The man took off his hat, sat down, and studied the papers in the file he carried with him. Then he closed the file, folded his hands, fixed the troublemaking convict with the clouded jellies of his eyes, and began to talk. He talked about "the rehabilitation of an ailing character"; he talked about "criminality" and "being tempted to take shortcuts to prosperity." He talked about "the cleansing sweat of honest work." He said, "You have shown an antisocial resistance to what, however *demanding*, amounted to a course of treatment. And so your treatment must be more aggressive, and tailored to your particular difficulties."

The troublemaker's particular difficulty was that he didn't understand why this person was talking to him. Was the man a warden, or a doctor?

The man put his hat back on, gathered his papers, and left the room. The wardens returned and took the troublemaker to another solitary cell. This one had a barred window, a covered bucket, a table and chair—dinner already there, lukewarm but plenty of it—and a bed with a rolled mattress.

The convict ate. His tray was removed. Just before the lights went out, a warden came by and told him he could now unroll his mattress and go to bed. The convict liked the look of the mattress, it was thicker than any he'd had before, and they had given him an extra blanket, though it was the warmest night he'd felt in a long time.

He lay down. Whatever was to come next, the coal mine, or more puzzling talk, it wouldn't come till tomorrow.

The Lifer was part of a work gang that was building a bridge. For twenty years he had labored on the roads, in the coal mine at Westport, and at the copper mines on Shackle Island. He had worked till he couldn't straighten his fingers anymore. Now he was among men on lesser sentences—the odd character who had strangled all his neighbor's hens, a light-fingered storekeeper, and a young man who had smashed the window of a pawnbroker's shop in order to steal his own hocked violin. He was a murderer among milder men, but old and harmless now, and on easy work. The others laughed when he told them this. One asked, "What easy work is there these days even for free men—with convicts building all the roads and bridges? I started my sentence picking fruit. So who would pay wages to fruit pickers?"

There was something in this. When the Lifer had worked in the coal mine, the only free men were skilled labor engineers and those who set explosives. He told his fellow convicts this. Then they were all talking about the savings a mine owner made and profit pouring back into the penal system. "The whole country's a prison," said the violin thief. "I didn't know that before. But I won't forget it again."

The violin thief was a month from the end of his sentence. The guards trusted him. He was the one who got to work in the tent in the water meadow by the bridge site. They even trusted him to sharpen the mason's chisels. The thief was fresh that afternoon because he'd been in the mason's tent and out of the worst of the heat. (When he'd come back to the bridge he'd stood smiling at the Lifer while the guards reattached his shackles. The smile really wasn't for anyone, but only seemed to say, "Nearly now. I'm nearly free, nearly home.")

The Lifer was faint with the heat. It was April, and the farmers in the valley had been burning stubble and the stumps of trees in fields freshly cut from the forest. Smoke hung over the valley and magnified the sun rather than filtered it. The Lifer asked for water. A guard brought the dipper. The water had a tang of burned blackwood. The old man tried to take his time but the dipper was snatched out of his hands. Half the water splashed onto the ground.

"Get on with it," the guard said, and gave him a shove. The Lifer went back to work. He and the violin thief lifted another shaped block from a stack, checked its number, and carried it to the balustrade, to the gap it was made to fit.

"Are you all right?" the young thief said.

And that was when it happened. The Lifer's head was swimming in the heat; his cramped hands were slippery with sweat and spilled water. His grip on the chiseled sandstone failed and instead of easing the stone into its slot, he let it go so that it slammed down on one corner. The thief's hands lost it too, and it teetered, then tipped over the rail and into the river. It disappeared into the weeds that grew on the river bottom. Weeds that flowed like combed hair in the channel and, nearer the bank, pressed against the surface of the water like hair bundled into a hairnet.

The guards heard the splash and came to look. They craned over the rail. "Where did it fall?" one asked.

"How do you suppose you are going to fetch that up out of there?" said another.

The guards pushed the Lifer and the thief, jostled them about between their fists and feet and rifle butts.

The mason appeared to inspect the damage. The stone beside the gap was cracked. "The one in the water is probably chipped too," he said. "They'll both have to be replaced."

"Do you hear that?" a guard said, and shoved the thief again. "You'll both have to be replaced."

"The stones," the mason said, dogged and irritated. "I meant the stones."

"We could have this scum wade in from the riverbank to get it out," said the overseer.

"Yes. I would like to take a look at it," the mason said.

"But if you're sure it's ruined . . ." the thief began, and was struck in the mouth. He was quiet for a while after that, his top lip skewered by a broken tooth.

The guards turned on the Lifer and pushed him along the bridge and onto the road. He scuttled, pursued by blows, down the bank to the river's edge. He protected his head with his arms, then fell to his knees on the soggy ground and stared at the water. Its shallows were thick with curdled weeds. The thief dropped down beside him. The young man's chin and throat were coated red. Over their heads a guard said, "Which of you dropped the block?"

"It was him," said the young thief. "Look at his hands. He can't keep a firm hold on anything." He sounded desperate.

"All right, old man. Get in there." The guard put his boot in the small of the Lifer's back.

"Remove his shackles, for God's sake!" the young man pleaded.

"Fine," said a guard, "You can go, since you're so concerned for his well-being." The guard kicked the thief, who splashed into the water's edge and caught himself on his hands. Black mud oozed up between his fingers till his hands were buried. The young man turned to the guards, eyes glimmering with fear. He edged around so that his feet and shackled ankles entered the water first. He crept backward, his hands groping and slithering on the sopping turf. He was looking into the Lifer's eyes, and his gaze said, "No. Not now. Not when I'm nearly free."

When he was up to his hips in the weeds, his feet slipped. His eyes flared with terror and he sank his fingers into the turf. He heaved and grappled his way back up the bank, clawing the thick coating of moss from the ground. He came out wallowing in mud, his front coated and face dappled. He lay on the bank, gasping, his hands still full of gobs of mud. He stared at what was in his hands, his

face quite mad for a moment, both horrified and exultant, as though he'd discovered them full of human flesh or the makings of a dreadful weapon.

The Lifer could see the thief's face, and his expression, but the guards
couldn't. They were laughing, staggering with mirth, their feet slipping in the
mire the thief had made. When they stopped laughing, they turned their attention to him. "Let's see how he does." They didn't even put it to him. Only agreed
among themselves that it was his turn. Then they began to kick at him, not hard,
only coaxing, but they didn't stop till he turned to try backing into the water.

"No!" The thief came to life, gave up nursing his handfuls of mud, shook his
hands empty to reach—but was struck down.

The Lifer edged back into the river. The water was warmed by the sun, and by
the vegetation. He went carefully, searching for safe footings. He went down in a
fresh place, not in the muddy slot the thief had made in the bank. He looked over
his shoulder and saw water textured by floating weeds, then, beyond that,
smooth, its skin twitching only where touched by pond skimmers. He glanced up
at the guards, who were quiet now, and at the bridge, the still forms of all the
staring convicts, the beautiful carvings, the lucent scales of sunlit water reflected
on the underside of the sandstone arch. He looked around, and then he slipped,
slithered back, his hands tearing at the weeds. He saw the thief lunge forward
and splash onto his belly, hands stretched out.

The weeds came loose in the Lifer's grasp. He was holding on to them, but
they had let go at the root. There was nothing behind his feet. The weeds parted
and he went back into the water, his eyes open. Billowing clouds of mud followed
him and he lost sight of the surface for a moment. Then it was back, as brackets of black ripples on a hot blue sky. His shackles drew him down into the
channel, and the weeds closed over his head. He was engulfed in caressing green
gloom.

He held his breath. He stretched his arms up. He felt the cool lightness of air
on his knuckles, so he opened his hands, forced his gnarled fingers straight up
into the air. He waited for a grip, a rope, a breath—

The green light turned red, the still water turbulent. His lungs ached, then
opened. He sucked in water. There was nothing behind it, or beyond it. No air.

In a room beside the troublemaker's cell, someone pushed back a down comforter. Maze Plasir turned up the flame of the lamp by the bed. The light was like a reprieve. The dreamhunter leaned back on his pillows and breathed deeply. He felt weak with gratitude just for waking up. It was absurd to feel that way, and Plasir waited patiently for the feeling to fade. While he waited, he hurried his recovery by saying to himself, "It is my nightmare, and so I am the river."

Once the force of the nightmare's end had faded, Plasir again began to feel dissatisfied with it. It wasn't particularly strong, as far as nightmares went. But the Department of Corrections had chosen it from its description in the Regulatory Body's Dream Almanac. The man next door, the troublemaker, had done something that Corrections thought would best be treated with a nightmare in which submersion and the weight of iron figured heavily. Plasir had no idea what the man had done. He just had to suppose that Corrections knew what *they* were doing.

The dreamhunter picked absentmindedly at a loose thread on the silk cord trim of his bolster. In a moment he'd lie down again and begin another cycle of the dream. He caught himself holding his breath as he strained to hear sounds on the other side of the wall. He remembered that there had been one subject who, for some reason unable to wake up, had stopped breathing.

The dream, Sunken, did end with a death. It was one of only a very few dreams that did so. Hame's nightmare Buried Alive was so terrible that it was said no dreamhunter would be able to stay asleep long enough to see its end. Plasir wondered what would happen if an unconscious dreamhunter was set down on the site of Buried Alive. That would be an interesting experiment. But, sadly, no one could experiment with the nightmare since no one knew where it was to be found. Tziga Hame had concealed the dream's site, and Lazarus—whoever the hell *he* was—wasn't volunteering information to anybody.

Plasir liked to experiment with dreams. He had learned to like this process as he became more experienced, and as he began to notice how much some dreams changed.

Second Sentence, for instance, was a split dream. For years Plasir had caught it but hadn't known it was a split dream. Then the Body had had Jerome Tilley, one of the rare "Novelists" (as those who caught split dreams were called), take a good look at all its most effective "Think Again" dreams. The Body had wanted to check that—for instance—a dream Plasir had been catching, about the young woman attacked in her home, might not also have something from the point of view of the husband who discovered her bleeding body at the dream's conclusion. It turned out that it did have, and the dream Violated became Violated and The Husband's Horror. The Body then had all its dreamhunters with Corrections contracts catch the dream till they found one who could reliably catch only The Husband's Horror. Jerome Tilley's experiments were all part of the Body's plan to develop more "targeted treatments" for hardened offenders.

Noting Tilley's experiments, Plasir had begun to wonder about his own specialty dreams. After a time, just wondering seemed to make it possible for him to open some of them up. He never did catch a split dream—he wasn't a Novelist—but he found that a few dreams he knew suddenly switched their point of view. And so it was that Second Sentence had thrown up the nightmare Plasir named, simply, Sunken. Sunken had the same setting as Second Sentence—a bridge under construction in a country town, on a hot day after harvesttime.

Maze Plasir stopped pulling threads on the bolster and held his breath again. He had realized something. That

Alexander Mason's Water Diviner was *also* set in that place and at that time—the country town and valley full of the haze of smoke. Plasir concentrated; he looked very hard at his memory of the country town. It wasn't anywhere he knew in life, and there was something about its reality that was off-kilter. There was the whittled elegance of the women's skirts—skirts with higher hems than those women were wearing. There was the lack of jitters in the sleek motorcars. The town seemed real and not real at the same time (though, of course, all the dreams were *factual*, none had monsters, or unassisted flight, or any of the things true human dreams had). The country town of The Water Diviner, Sunken, and Second Sentence was strange to Plasir, yet, if he squinted through the brown haze at its distances, he thought he could see familiar hills, hills he'd seen somewhere he'd been as a child.

Plasir concentrated. He strained to know. Then he gave up, sighed, settled himself down on the bed, and went back to his first train of thought.

Sunken may have been set in the same place as Second Sentence, but it was very different. It showed the same events from a different point of view. The Lifer's eyes lingered on everything because his thoughts dithered and doubled back on themselves. The man had gotten to the end of his life and seemed still to be trying to put his life together—like two plus two—to *make something of it*.

Second Sentence, however, was from the point of view of the violin thief. The young man began the dream happy, because his sentence was nearly up, and because he'd been working with the mason, a man whose skill he admired. The heat wasn't draining the young thief dry; he had his health, and hope. He had learned his lesson. He was full of a resolve to stay out of trouble, to spend the rest of his life out of the power of the law. The smoke-stained skies made him think of music; the slow, green, waving weed made him think of music. Second Sentence was a constructive, reforming dream. It had lessons to teach, such as "Stick to your resolve" and "Keep your temper." After the old Lifer drowned, straining up into the air, straightening his crippled fingers, the young man stared for a few seconds at his mud-caked hands and a thought flashed through his mind—or more a feeling than a thought, for the dreamhunter Plasir had never been able to make much sense of it. It was a thought about a belief or a story, and, like most of the thief's thoughts, it had a kind of tune to it, a musical chant. "I'm not helpless," the thief thought—as people in desperation do sometimes think the exact opposite of what is true and being proved to them. And then, in the dream, the young man lost his temper and surged up, took hold of a rifle in the hands of the nearest guard, the one standing slack-jawed and sated with cruelty. He tore the rifle away from the man, swung it, clubbing and clubbing, till other guards hauled him off. The guard had a broken skull, and the young thief, only weeks away from freedom, was then looking at years, at a second sentence.

Second Sentence was very effective, less a nightmare than a dream with a nasty, sobering turn at its end. But now that he was catching its other aspect, the dream seemed a lot less useful and positive to Plasir. The old man of Sunken had next to no experience of pity, yet how desperately he looked around him for it. He looked into all the faces. What he saw was what he already knew about the world—that it didn't make any difference if you kept your temper or stuck to your good resolve, for there was malice, always close, and always ready to lend its icy hand.

Second Sentence showed a way out of trouble—though the young man didn't take it. Sunken showed that it didn't matter what you did, because accidents happened, and accidents were opportunities for evil. Second Sentence was a warning dream. Sunken was a nightmare. Taken together, they were horribly incompatible, and Plasir couldn't help but wonder what a Novelist like Grace Tiebold would make of the dream—for it was *one* dream, and Grace Tiebold would catch it intact, the old man and the young together. She'd catch both the terror and despair of one, and the rage and crushed hope of the other.

Maze Plasir closed his eyes. He would go back to sleep. He would give the troublemaker in the next room another dose. And he'd try to take a better look at the other thing about the dream that troubled him.

Plasir had *been* the thief, on and off, for years. He'd seen everything through his eyes. The thief knew his own past, of course, but he wasn't really thinking about it on that morning. For instance, Plasir had known from Second Sentence that the thief played the violin, but only learned from Sunken that he had stolen his own instrument from a pawnshop. Plasir knew about the thief only what he'd managed to gather from the young man's thoughts on that afternoon at the bridge. Then, when he first caught Sunken, the old Lifer had shown Plasir the *face* of the person through whose eyes he'd formerly seen everything.

There was something about that face. Something familiar. The thief looked healthy and happy, and wary and furtive—none of this strange in a criminal on light duty and near the end of his time. But when the stone fell into the river, and the guards turned their spite into sport, and the two convicts were driven to the river's edge, and the old Lifer gazed into the young thief's face and saw fear and pity—

"*I know that person,*" Plasir thought. "I've seen that sensitive, stubborn mouth before. Not in a dream." He pictured the mouth and the eyes. Eyes full of sadness and shame and resignation and, behind all that, power: pitiless, cold power.

3

✧ ✧ ✧

CHORLEY TOLD GRACE THAT HE'D PROM-
ISED THE GRAND PATRIARCH HIS HELP
WITH "THE CAUSE."

"What cause is this?" Grace asked. "Tziga's? Laura's? The
cause of stirring up trouble between dreamhunters and their
public?"

"The Grand Patriarch offers refuge to renegade dreamhunters. He thinks the Body is up to no good. Tziga's ideas
and Laura's actions have nothing to do with him. You can't
blame him."

Grace glared at her husband. "Am I allowed to blame anyone? Or is it best for me to just bite my lip?"

"Better than biting me, dear. It's not my fault that Laura
and Tziga are out of reach."

"No, but it is the fault of Erasmus Tiebold."

Chorley gave a sigh of put-upon patience, kissed his wife
on top of her head, and went out.

✧ ✧ ✧

The Grand Patriarch thanked Chorley for his visit and
told him that, since no one expected him to denounce
dreamhunting, did he think he could investigate the Place?

"Rangers go there and make maps and call it exploration,"

the Grand Patriarch said. "Philosophers muse about it as
a phenomenon and call that—rightly in some ways—*thinking*
about it. But none of us are getting any nearer to knowing
what the Place really is. You've been close to the subject for
years; you are familiar with all the distracting facts already.
You have a reputation as something of a scientific mind, and
an independent thinker. So please, Mr. Tiebold, look into it
for me."

Chorley had gone away, and for days he hadn't been able to
imagine where to start. He reread some of those philosophers
and was struck again by how they all seemed to talk about the
Place as if, by coming up with the right metaphor for it, they
might be able to say what it was. He found that he liked Dr.
King's account in *A History of Southland*. King's approach to the
Place seemed practical; he tried to find evidence of its earliest
appearance. Chorley mused on Dr. King's speculation that
the dreams might be memories of people who had lived in its
geographic vicinity. And on his own idea that the Place was
like a mirage. Chorley considered all this—as, no doubt, the
Grand Patriarch already had.

And then he remembered the telegraph line that had once
run through the Rifleman Pass, from Doorhandle to Sisters
Beach. A line that was long ago abandoned. The wire, though
intact and visible along its entire length, was finally deemed
hopelessly unreliable. Signals were lost, and there were
strange interferences, both a patterned tapping that didn't
match any known telegraphic code and bits of code that could
be deciphered but that gave the key man on the receiving end
bad, mad messages.

And so it was that, several days after remembering the
abandoned telegraph line, Chorley found himself waiting in
a poky room beneath the mosaic floor of the Founderston
Central Post Office. The man Chorley waited with didn't

have much to say, but he stood at his desk sorting through a bunch of keys on a string. The room was dingy. There were windows only at the top of one wall. Through them Chorley could see people—or their feet at least—passing on the street, scuffed shoes and polished ones, the wheels of a pram, a woman in a hobble skirt, and the lower legs of a small girl in flimsy blue sandals.

"It's summer already," he thought.

A second clerk, a man with a coat and a complexion the color of manila cardboard, shuffled into the room. The first clerk stopped sorting his keys and tossed them back into an open drawer. He said, "I was just telling Mr. Tiebold here that if any of the bad transcriptions from the Wry-Valley-to-Sisters-Beach line had been kept, you would know where to find them." He turned to Chorley and said, "Mr. Nevis was a key man at Doorhandle twenty years ago, when the trouble started." Then—to Mr. Nevis, "Can you help Mr. Tiebold?"

Mr. Nevis nodded and held the door open.

As they descended into the cold subterranean corridors beneath the Central Post Office, Mr. Nevis told Chorley that—yes—he had been a key man in Doorhandle. He had sent and deciphered messages to and from Sisters Beach. In fact, he had been at his post in the telegraph office on the evening that the Doorhandle innkeeper came in to wire for a surgeon from Sisters Beach. "For the boy with the broken leg—who later became your brother-in-law, Mr. Hame," Mr. Nevis said. "The line had been complete then for three years. It was working well, except when the road washed out once and took half a dozen poles with it. The weather in the Rifleman Pass was a challenge, but we hadn't yet encountered the problem that closed us down. That problem started after Tziga Hame's fall."

Mr. Nevis opened a steel door, located a light switch, and

let Chorley into a room with long avenues of shelves filled with files. The air was chilly and undisturbed.

"We kept those messages separate," said Mr. Nevis. "We had a special file for them—several by the time the Post Office abandoned the line, which they didn't do, despite the problems, till the Founderston to Sisters Beach Railway opened, and the new telegraphic line with it. Those files had red tape on their spines. I remember making up a new one myself."

"How many were there?"

"Mad messages? Hundreds. We had to have a special short key code for 'Corrupt. Send again.'"

Mr. Nevis made a noise of discovery and dropped into a crouch, his knees creaking. He pulled files from a shelf, bundled them into his arms, and got up with Chorley's help.

At the back wall, there was a bench under a light, a bare bulb in a wire cage. "I'm afraid you won't be very comfortable, Mr. Tiebold. My manager doesn't really like anything brought up from underground. But I'm sure you'll find you won't need to look far for a good example. For nonsense of a special kind."

"Is it formless nonsense? Or nonsense only in the context of the message?" Chorley asked. He longed to edge the man aside and look himself.

Mr. Nevis was patting the pile of files, tidying and talking. "I never thought madness terribly interesting myself, whether it was Lady Macbeth wringing her hands or Lucia di Lammermoor wafting around in her bloodied bridal gown. I never looked at the corrupt messages with any real attention."

Chorley stepped up beside the elderly clerk, seized the stack, and slid it along the bench till it was under his own nose. "Has anyone ever gone through these looking for a pattern?"

"What kind of pattern? All the Post Office did was try to

fix the problem. It even had men camping out nights under every tenth pole in order to catch the pranksters."

"And all this happened before the Regulatory Body was formed?"

"Yes. Otherwise it would have been their problem. The Post Office blamed us key men at first, said it was our mischief. *We* blamed the fellows on the other end. But it was the Place. That telegraph line was unbroken from Doorhandle to Tricksie Bend; it ran outside, not Inside—but the Place used it to try to talk to us. Look!" Mr. Nevis snatched one file, flipped pages, and found a message: MOTHER FAILING STOP DOCTOR SAYS ONLY MATTER OF DAYS STOP PLEASE RISE UP I SAID RISE UP COME AT ONCE STOP ANDREW.

"That's more or less typical. That 'Rise up' stuff." Mr. Nevis sounded triumphant. He peered at Chorley, waiting for a reaction.

Small hairs were bristling on Chorley's nape, his whole scalp tightening. The "interruption" in the telegram was a plea, like the cry of a king besieged on a battlefield. He licked his dry lips. "Does this sort of thing turn up often?"

"'Rise up' you mean? Yes. We got that one all the time. Come to think of it, perhaps that's the pattern you're asking about?"

"Yes."

Mr. Nevis sighed. "I suppose then that you'll want to read through all of these?"

"I will." Chorley was engrossed already, leafing through the first file.

"Shall I see if I can find you something to sit on?"

"Thank you."

✢ ✢ ✢

On the afternoon of the last day of classes, Rose brought Mamie home with her so that Mamie could help her choose what she should take on her proposed four-week visit with the Doran family at their summerhouse in the Awa Inlet. Rose and Mamie came in with the Dorans' chauffeur and Rose's school trunk.

"You can put it down here, thank you," Rose said to the man. "Mamie will stay for dinner, and someone will take her home later."

"Have you even checked that anyone is home?" Mamie said. "Or are you too busy being decisive?"

Rose ignored her friend, thanked her friend's chauffeur, and sent him off. "I could spend hours choosing what to take," she said. "I think I've exhausted my decisiveness."

"Well then, while you're weak and easy to influence, shall we start by deciding what you'll take to read?"

They went to the library, where they met Rose's father, who was standing in the doorway with a notebook held open on the top of his head like a small pitched roof. "Girls!" he said, in a tone of happy discovery. "You know your poetry, don't you?"

Mamie said, "Yes, poetry is the proper province of girls."

Rose said, "Mamie is here to help me choose what to pack. I'm going away on Monday. You won't see me again till Christmas. You have taken that in?"

"Yes, darling, and we mean to spend the weekend at your beck and call. Your mother is coming home tonight. And there's a letter from Laura on your dresser."

Mamie looked at Rose, curious. Rose hadn't mentioned her cousin for ages. "Where *is* Laura?"

"Staying with relatives," said Rose and her father simultaneously.

Chorley wandered over to his cluttered desk and moved books and papers around to find something. Rose came and

peered over his shoulder at a notebook. She read: HOME FRI-
DAY 9:15 STOP SHE IS COMING MY OWN MY SWEET CAN YOU
MEET ME AT STATION STOP PHILLIP. And: OFFER ACCEPTABLE
STOP SHE IS COMING MY OWN MY SWEET WERE IT EVER SO AIRY
A TREAD SETTLE TODAY STOP YOU HAVE MY FULL CONFIDENCE
STOP WELLES.

"She is coming, my own, my sweet; were it ever so airy a
tread," Chorley quoted.

"Yes—that *is* poetry," said Rose. "Almost certainly poetry."

"It's Maud," said Mamie. "Maud: A Monodrama, by Tennyson. We did it last year. You remember, Rose, you kept saying: 'Come into the garden, Maud, the black bat, night, has
flown,' whenever you wanted a word with someone in private." Rose had always been with Laura then, and Mamie was
not her friend. Mamie had watched Rose's joking intimacy,
amused and a little envious of Rose's many 'Mauds.'

Rose went to the bookshelf to look for Tennyson. "What
do you want it for, Da?"

Chorley glanced at Mamie, then said, "I'm writing a scientific article, and I thought I'd give it some polish by adding a
little verse."

Mamie couldn't conceal her look of scorn.

Rose found the collected works of Tennyson and passed it
to her friend. Mamie could find the right lines far more
quickly than she. Rose went to look over her father's shoulder
at his notes again. He flipped the book to show her its first
page, and his title: "Bad Code from the Obsolete Founderston–
Sisters Beach Telegraph Line, 1886–1893."

Mamie said, "It is 'Maud'—chapter twenty-two, stanza
eleven." She read it out loud:

> *She is coming, my own, my sweet*
> *Were it ever so airy a tread,*

My heart would hear her and beat,
Were it earth in an earthy bed;
My dust would hear her and beat;
Had I lain for a century dead;
Would start and tremble under her feet,
And blossom in purple and red.

"That's so strange," Rose said. "What do you make of it, Da?"

"I think that's the least strange bit of the whole over-wrought poem," said Mamie, who didn't know what they were talking about. She shut the book with a snap.

"I'm still working on it," Chorley said to Rose.

4

✦ ✦ ✦

ANDY CAUGHT CONVALESCENT TWO AND took it to St. Thomas's Lung Hospital. But his dream was of a very poor quality, his copy of it somehow murky and strained. He was sent away again. He returned to Doorhandle and Mrs. Lilley's house and tried to pull himself together—he felt scattered, jumpy, and lumpish at the same time. He couldn't seem to fix himself. He thought about Laura all the time. Laura and her unknown suitor. Her letter to him was folded small and tucked into the lining of his wallet. As for the other one—the same night he'd opened it, Sandy had torn it into tiny pieces and thrown it out his bedroom window. It was gone, so he couldn't now decide to be honorable after all and just deliver it.

Sandy's room in Doorhandle was his only home. When he was in Founderston, he was working, and had a bed at one of the hospitals. But at Mrs. Lilley's, he didn't have much in the way of privacy. He couldn't just be alone and nurse his broken heart, or his bad conscience—he wasn't actually sure which was troubling him more. Mrs. Lilley's other young tenants were in and out and kept asking him about Laura. "Where is she? Is she coming back?" And the Lilley girls, seeing him silent and morose, would try to cheer him up with kind little attentions. Sandy was sure his linen was changed more than his rental contract stipulated (and he was someone who read and remembered every clause of any contract he signed). The younger girl kept waylaying him in the hall, darting out of the kitchen perhaps with a stirring spoon for him to lick—the sort of treat he'd once begged his mother for. He got clean linen, food, flattery, flirtation.

And, on a Saturday night when Mrs. Lilley's bed of outrageously pink carnations had all turned modest and furled for the night, the elder girl came and sat beside Sandy on the back steps. She said, "What a shame it is, Alexander, that you can't take up a pipe. A pipe is a peaceful, manly sort of habit, I think. My father enjoyed a pipe. But of course I know dreamhunters don't bother to smoke since they can't keep a pipe alight when they're In the Place." She was showing concern, and what she knew. She leaned forward at the waist and tried to look into his lowered face. "Still, I would like to see you light up, Alexander."

"Why carry around another craving?" Sandy said, brooding.

The Lilley girl laid a hand on his back.

And Sandy turned his head and kissed her, because she wanted him to, and because she wasn't Laura.

5

✦ ✦ ✦

*S*O LONG SPIT'S "BLINKING BOB" WAS NOT ONE OF THOSE LIGHTHOUSES THAT PEOPLE LIVED IN, A TOWER OF MORTARED stone, containing a series of cylindrical rooms and topped with a room holding the lamp. All there was to Blinking Bob was four steel legs, four long flights of steps going up in the center, and a square room with glass around the top half of all four walls. The room housed only the lamp, the mechanism that made the lamp revolve, and several cans of benzene. The lighthouse keepers and their families lived in three weatherboard and corrugated iron houses that stood around the tower. The houses were in a windbreak, the tower on a slight rise, its legs anchored in concrete. Blinking Bob was the second tower built on the Spit; the first had been wrecked by drifting sand.

One day, a few weeks before the summer solstice, Laura sat with her back to the rivet-studded wall of the lamp room at the top of the lighthouse.

Her father, Tziga, was cleaning smoke stains from the lamp. The lamp was bigger than her father's torso, a structure of cut crystals in a copper frame, four bull's-eyes surrounded by curved ribs of crystal. The whole thing was shaped like a glittering bishop's miter.

Laura's father's hands were gloved with rags. He was run-

ning them back and forth between the crystal ribs. It was
rather like trying to clean the blades of an eggbeater without
first immersing it in water. He worked with the sun behind
him, so as not to be dazzled by the light shining through the
lamp. And in that light his scars seemed nothing but the
shadows his hair threw across his face, his smeared eyebrow
only the blurring obscurity of shadow.

Laura had been with her father, sleeping and waking, almost every minute since she'd arrived six weeks before. She
was beginning to be used to the changes in him.

She had been warned, as well. A priest called Father Paul
had taken charge of Laura at Westport and had brought her
to So Long Spit. She hadn't crossed paths with her uncle
Chorley—he'd left several days before she arrived. Chorley
had apparently been there when Tziga read the newspaper accounts of the riot at the Rainbow Opera. He had witnessed
Tziga's fit. He had talked to Father Paul about Tziga's frailty,
and Father Paul had prepared Laura.

It was only when they boarded the schooner *Morningstar* at
Westport that Father Paul had told Laura who was waiting for
her at the lighthouse. Her *father*—who she'd been allowed to
think was dead. Who had been kept from her, and on whose
behalf she'd acted, hurting Aunt Grace and Sandy, infuriat-
ing Rose and earning her cold shoulder. If only she'd known
her father was alive. If only someone had told her. Laura had
said all this to Father Paul—raging at him, at first too resentful to feel relief or happiness.

And Father Paul had patiently explained some things to
her.

He told her that, over the last few years, a handful of
dreamhunters had come to the Church—the institution most
loudly critical of dreamhunting—to express their worries
about some of the Regulatory Body's uses for dreams. "We

lost touch with a few of these persons," Father Paul said. "They disappeared. Too many dreamhunters do disappear. So, Laura, when your father turned up, his famous face swollen beyond recognition, at the Magdalene Charity Hospital in Westport, in what doctors call a 'coma' but still able to infect other patients sleeping near him with terror, we thought it best to report him dead and spirit him away. It was cruel to his family, but after the other disappearances, the Grand Patriarch deemed it necessary. When we heard that Tziga Hame was supposed to have vanished while attempting a crossing of the Place, we knew he had to *stay* hidden."

The other thing Father Paul had said to Laura, just before they climbed down the rope ladder from the deck of the *Morningstar* to the platform by the lighthouse, was that her father's health was very fragile and that she must take care not to upset him.

Laura had been forewarned, and she hadn't upset him. She'd treated him tenderly, waited on him, and, whenever he just sat staring into space, would sit pressed up against him. Her uncle Chorley had dispatched a doctor to the light-house—and paid a fortune to keep him quiet about where he was going and whom he was treating. The doctor prescribed Laura's father drugs that did help reduce the intensity of his seizures, if not their frequency.

Father Paul had stopped by only the day before with letters for Laura and Tziga. He told them that Chorley wanted them both back at Summerfort by Christmas. (Christmas was three weeks away, a few days after the solstice.) "The Grand Patriarch says that now that the government has set up its Commission of Inquiry into the riot, if the Regulatory Body wants to speak to either of you—to question you, or call you to account—then, equally, the *Commission* might subpoena you. The

Grand Patriarch thinks that the Body will think twice about doing anything to call Tziga Hame's existence to the Commission's attention."

Of all this, Laura's father had seemed to take in only that he'd be back at Summerfort by Christmas. He appeared baffled by anything beyond immediate practicalities. For him it seemed there was only ever the task at hand—the crystal clouded by smoke coming clean under his cloth. He'd become slow and remote. There were people to smile at, or listen to with somber attention. There were things that must be remembered—for instance, he was always reminding Laura not to go out in the sun without her hat. But there was no larger world for him anymore, no public life, or any matter of real consequence.

Laura stood up and looked through the lighthouse window. The tide was out along the Spit, and the few patches of scrub in the dunes showed as black flaws on the horizon, wobbling in the heat haze. Scarves of dry sand blew along the surface of the wet. There was sand high in the wind, for Laura could hear the whisper of its grains in the gusts buffeting the windowpanes.

"Da?" she said.

Her father looked at her, then rotated the lamp on its housing so that the cleaned crystals spun scintillating in the sunlight.

"Do you remember I told you about Sandy?"

"Your friend? You mention him often. Did you tell me something particular about him?" Laura's father frowned at her, anxious that he'd forgotten something she'd said.

"No."

"I liked his uncle, George Mason. As a singer, I mean. Marta and I often went to the opera. We would sit up in the top balcony cheap seats with all the other students. Mason was about twenty-five when I was sixteen. He was young, but he had this big bass voice, like the father of all fathers."

Laura laughed at this story, because it was something new, and related to Sandy. And because her father seemed so collected in speaking about his past—his past before the Place.

"Lots of the early dreamhunters were musical. I don't know if that was ever noted as a tendency. No one would think to notice now, since there aren't too many distinguished musicians at fifteen. When George Mason became a dreamhunter, it really was a loss to music in Founderston." Laura's father knelt to gather the cleaning rags into a bucket, and she noted that once he'd simply have stooped to perform this task. She could see that he was actually concentrating on grasping, lifting, and releasing. But he did keep talking, his memory of twenty years ago exact, even if his movements were not. Laura had wanted to hear his thoughts on Sandy—on Sandy's bewildering prickliness—but she didn't want to interrupt his remembering. He was usually so quiet now.

"What about you, Da? How good were you?"

"Marta was a better musician than I was. So it was probably just as well it was me and not her who fell." He hauled himself up, gripping the housing of the light. Then he turned to Laura, and she was forced again to regard the ruin of his face, and that frightening look in his eyes—a kind of tremulous pulling together of his attention. He said, "Laura, you know I wasn't in my right mind when I wrote you that letter."

Was this an apology? she wondered. "That letter was all I had left of you," she said. "Of course I took it seriously."

He touched his scarred forehead. Then he reached for Laura, put an arm around her, and held her.

She closed her eyes and simply basked in being held. She shouldn't ask any more than this. He couldn't answer—wasn't answerable anymore. When she looked into his eyes now, she saw watchfulness and uncertainty. His love for her was intact—but his understanding wasn't.

Laura's father released her.

She said, "Here, let me give you a hand," and took the bucket from him. They left the lighthouse. Partway down from the tower, Laura stopped. She had spotted something. She shaded her eyes and squinted into the wavering air.

There was someone out there, standing still and straight on the bared beach. The figure was far off, but Laura felt that he or she was looking at her.

Laura clattered down after her father, checking now and then on that watching figure. At the foot of the steps, she returned the bucket to her father, then took a few bounding steps backward, making excuses. "I'm just going for a walk, Da—" Then she was off, running barefoot on the springy stems of beach grass, under the pines, then onto the sand. She ran in a long curve, for the watching figure was moving off the beach and into the dunes, and she had to alter her course in order to intercept him.

As she came closer, Laura could see only bright skin, no clothes. It was Nown, and he was waiting for her, just leading her in among the dunes where they wouldn't be seen. As she closed the distance between them, she could see that his head was lifted and that he was checking the lines of sight between himself and the top of the lighthouse.

Laura came to a skidding stop before him. She staggered, panting, then folded over a stitch in her side. For a moment all she could hear was her own breathing. Then she heard the sea, and a tern crying as it flew along the line of low breakers. She straightened up and faced her sandman. He held out his arms to her.

She looked over her shoulder at the lighthouse.

"There must be things you want to say," he said.

She went to him and let him pick her up.

He stooped over her and hurried away, skirting the base of the dunes till they were screened from the lighthouse, and from the sound of waves on the western shore.

Nown stopped within the shade of a high, crescent-shaped dune. Below the dune was a salt pan, and when he set Laura down, her feet cracked its crusted surface and she found herself standing in a shallow trench surrounded by sliding, dirty-white plates of salt.

Nown stood watching her and waiting for her to speak.

She said, "You got my note?"

"No."

"I sent a note enclosed in a letter to Sandy. I asked him to leave it in the forest."

"I left the forest when you moved west. I followed you."

"How did you know where I was?"

"You made me, Laura. You are my compass."

Laura sat down abruptly in a patch of smashed salt crust. The air was uncomfortably hot nearer the ground, but she wasn't able to get up again. She had thought of something, and her thought had taken the strength from her legs.

Nown was speaking, volunteering his story—something he didn't do before she freed him.

"There were many rivers to cross," he said. "I followed the foothills of the Rifleman Mountains and struck only tributary streams. Sometimes I crossed over into the Place, but the distances there are too great. And at the coal mine beside the river—I don't know its name, Laura—there were miners, and barges coming and going, and a river ford with a ferry on a rope. I had to wait till it was dark and disguise myself under a blanket. I had to steal the blanket. The ferryman was drunk. There was one threatening deluge on my journey—and I had

to burrow in under a bank. It took time, but I got here without getting my feet wet."

"Your literal feet," Laura said.

"The feet you gave me."

For some reason this sounded like an accusation. Laura
couldn't tell whether she was being blamed for the shortcomings of Nown's feet or for failing to respect them *as* feet.
"Nown," she said. "If you knew where I was because I made
you, does that mean that you—I mean the eighth you—knew
where my *father* was when he was missing?"

"Yes."

She took several deep breaths before asking, "Why didn't
you tell me?"

"I did tell you that since *I* was, then he was still alive. And
you strode ahead of me smiling and crying. You didn't ask me
where he was."

In the shelter of the dune, the salt filled the still air with its
dry fumes. Laura was having difficulty thinking. She got up
and kept walking. Her sandman followed her. His weighty
steps made wider circles of cracks in the crusted salt.

After a time she asked, "Does anything I say matter to you
the way it did before you were free?"

"I don't yet know."

"But you followed me here."

"Yes."

She led him out onto the beach again. The tide was coming
in, and, as she looked back between the gap in the dunes,
Laura could see that it was making more progress on the western shore than where they were, so that the sea seemed to pile
up against the barricade of the Spit.

She was more comfortable in the open air. Nown had
come close to her until she was standing in his shadow. She
was sure he'd done it deliberately—had noticed that she was

panting and that she'd put up a hand to shade her eyes. Without looking at him, she pressed her hand against his side, his gritty skin and mock ribs and ridges of muscle. She said, "From now on, could you please tell me anything you think I might need to know?"

He was silent.

"Nown?"

Laura could have sworn she heard him sigh. She glanced at him, but his face had no expression, or none she could interpret. Perhaps she had only expected to hear a sigh. He was looking at a bank of cloud closing in on the Spit faster than the light sea breeze. Or at least he seemed to be looking at it. She asked, "Can you see that?"

"There are layers of wind. One is warmer," he said. Then, "Laura—my experience of freedom is limited. So, therefore, is my experience of making judgments. I cannot yet know what I will have to consider each time I am considering what you need to know. My knowledge of your needs has been guided by your instructions. At times I have tried to imagine, without guidance from you, what you might need. I have made mistakes. After you caught the nightmare, you were weeping, and I picked you up to rock the tears out of you—I had seen that done. You did stop crying, but you didn't approve of my action. I cannot trust the sympathy I have for you to guide me. We are too different, you and I. If you ask me to take care of all your needs, are you then giving me *your* freedom? Why would you free me only to hand over your own freedom?"

"Nown!" Laura had to stop him. He was retreating into a thicket of philosophical complications, and she was sure that it was a deeper and thornier thicket than either of them could imagine. She stepped onto one of his feet in order to stretch up and cover his mouth with her hand. "Shh," she said. "That's enough."

He pulled her hand away. "Besides," he said, "if you ask me to tell you anything you might need to know—to remember to tell you from now on anything you might need to know—are you asking me to *promise*? I think a promise must be like a law. I understand laws. They are what I've lived by. If a promise is like law, then, even free, I think I might do whatever I promised. Come what may."

"But—no—I released you," Laura said. "You're free."

"I'm free to promise," Nown said. "And if I choose to make promises, I'll honor them."

"Don't promise then! *Don't* tell me what I might need to know."

Nown's eyes blackened and glittered. "Don't say that."

"You can't possibly still be susceptible to my orders."

"I find I am. I still want to do what you want."

"Well—stop!" Laura ordered, exasperated.

"No," Nown said.

She started to laugh, stood laughing, turned into the wind and the sunlight, which was fiercely hot, concentrated by the encroaching cloud. She felt happy, in a crazy way. Nown was a fearful responsibility, but when she was with him, the feeling she had of being trapped and baffled just disappeared. He was so contradictory—scrupulous and untamed at the same time—that in his presence all the things that had hemmed her in seemed to melt away. Her father was broken and beyond reproach, Rose was right to hate her, and she had been wrong to keep her own promises. But Nown made her feel like God on the first Sabbath; he was a great responsibility, but he was *good*, like the world, and being with him made Laura sleepy with happiness.

✦ ✦ ✦

They kept wandering along the Spit, away from the sentinel lighthouse and Laura's human company. They didn't talk. It seemed that Nown had nothing further to tell Laura, and she, finding herself so content with him, stopped thinking altogether.

The massed gray clouds closed in on them, and a wind came up, a constant, cool, gritty wind. It scalped the dunes and scattered sand into the waters of Coal Bay. As the tide came in, and the waves grew bigger and steeper, water began to percolate through the Spit itself, so that the dunes grew damp and gave differently behind each step they took. Nown hiked up to the spine of the dunes and walked there. Laura followed him with difficulty, till he picked her up again and went along with her, rocking her as he swayed.

"Can you see the sea at all?" she asked.

"No."

"Is it like walking on a bridge, then? A bridge over nothingness?"

"But there are birds," Nown said.

Laura looked where she supposed he was looking and saw the diminishing dunes and bleak, choppy sea and, at the very end of the Spit, flashes of white, not foam on whitecaps but the myriad bodies of roosting gannets. Even in the stiff wind there were gannets out over the sea, weaving back and forth, scanning the water for prey. Hard-pressed and hopeful now, for it couldn't be easy for the birds to spot fish under the agitated waves. Still, every few seconds one of the great, gliding creatures would pause, and close its wings, and fall, an accelerating white dart, into the water. The bird would disappear and would surface sometime later, shaking itself off, clutching at the air till the air shouldered its weight, and flying up to rejoin the rest of the hungry patrol.

Laura asked Nown to set her on her feet. She leaned

against him, sheltered from the worst of the wind, and
watched the gannets fish. She felt she should applaud these
dives as the lighthouse keeper's son did.

They stayed watching for a long time, till it was too cold
and gray, and the birds became hard to see because the day
was coming to a close. Then Laura put up her arms, and
Nown picked her up and set off along the narrow backbone of
the Spit toward the pale streak of the distant lighthouse.

✧ ✧ ✧

Laura had her sandman crawl in under the keeper's house,
where tangles of harvested seaweed were drying among the
timber piles. She told him to stay still and hidden.

In the early hours of the morning, when the dependable
westerly had dropped again, she climbed out of her bed—a
mattress on the floor beside her father's—and crept out of
their hut and under the keeper's house. She found Nown by
touch. She lay down with her back against his body and drew
his arms around her. Then she went back to sleep again, cradled in a nest of shaped sand and snarls of seaweed.

✧ ✧ ✧

At dawn Tziga woke and let his arm drape off the side of
his bed to feel for his daughter's head on her pillow. He
couldn't find it. He ran his palm over the cold, empty dent
where her warm curls should have been and then leaned up
on an elbow to look at her bed.

Tziga put on his patched fisherman's jersey and went out to
find her. He looked on the outer shore and found only a
flock of terns standing by the tide line turned in to the
breeze. Then, as he was crossing the windbreak to look on

the Coal Bay shore, Tziga noticed a smear of pallor between the piles of the keeper's cottage. As he got closer, he recognized Laura's white nightgown. He steadied himself against the wall of the cottage and stooped to look.

Laura was asleep, but the sandman's eyes were open—always open, made that way—and looking at him.

Tziga felt himself recognized. He felt the sandman's calm, alien interest. He saw how the thing's arms enfolded Laura's slight body, how her head was pillowed on its shoulder. The thing looked nothing like his own roughly made and rather grotesque servant.

Laura had been late for dinner, pink with cold and exertion, and very happy. Now here she was, asleep in these inhuman arms. The sight was terrifying to Tziga. He wanted to crawl in among the seaweed and haul her out. He wanted to make the thing disappear.

She didn't need it anymore.

Tziga looked for the letters of its name and saw an unmarked brow, and below the brow the eyes, watchful, but with no sign of concern or challenge in them. The thing was simply waiting for him to go away. It seemed to know that he wouldn't want to wake Laura, and to understand that he wouldn't want her to find out that he'd seen it.

✥ ✥ ✥

Laura woke up when she heard stirring above her, the keeper's wife opening the stove top to drop kindling in on the embers of last night's fire. She turned to Nown. "My uncle Chorley is sending a boat to take me and Da to Summerfort. For Christmas—so soon. I'll want you there, Nown. I'm sorry to have to send you off, but if you're going to get there in time, you'll have to start walking. I know you do most of your walking by night, and the nights are getting shorter."

"Yes."

"What are you saying yes to?"

"The nights are shorter. You'll want me. I should start walking to meet you there. I believe you are sorry. I'm saying yes to all that. And, yes, I will go now, I will do what you ask."

Laura extracted herself from the accommodating hollow he'd made in his body. She said thank you. She crawled out from under the keeper's cottage, picked stiff fragments of seaweed from her nightgown, and crept back to her cold bed.

✣ ✣ ✣

At breakfast Laura's father asked her whether she'd written again to her friend Sandy.

"He didn't reply to my letter. It wasn't much of a letter, I'm afraid. I'm no good at writing them."

"Have you written again to Rose?"

"She's given up on me, Da."

"Don't be silly, Laura."

She scowled at her plate of oatmeal.

"You're just nursing a grudge," said her father. "Rose told you off. A telling-off isn't a real breach, darling."

"But I can't say what I need to say to Rose in a letter." Laura knew there was nothing she had to say to Rose before showing Nown to her. He'd still be her secret, even if she showed him to Rose. Rose was Rose. The only reason she hadn't told Rose everything was that she wasn't *telling herself* either.

Her father was saying, "I may be an invalid, but you're not. You aren't even a fugitive. No one can prove you had anything to do with—with anything. You can take up dreamhunting again. You can catch new and useful dreams, build a career, team up with your friend Sandy, boost each other and play the bigger venues. You're still in the world, Laura. You belong to the world. You don't belong with an invalid. You can't stay sequestered. You should be with *people*."

Laura nodded. "All right," she said. She gave his hand a squeeze. "But until I see Rose, I won't know what to say to her. And Sandy—Sandy prefers to tell people what to do rather than take suggestions."

"Fine. But you can be a dreamhunter. You can have friends. You can have a pretty dress made and go to the Presentation Ball with your cousin."

"And you can be poked and prodded by Uncle Chorley's expensive physicians.".

6

✦ ✦ ✦

*G*RACE WAS BUYING A NEW PACK AT AN
OUTFITTER'S ON THE ISLE OF THE
TEMPLE WHEN SHE RAN INTO SANDY MASON.
He was picking up and putting down sale-price water bottles,
working his way along a shelf. None of the bottles seemed to
pass his inspection. He looked dubious and sour, as though
he was suffering from indigestion.

"Hello," said Grace. "How are you?" She wasn't just being
polite, she really wanted to know. She was sure that Sandy had
suffered some kind of trouble after taking a print of Buried
Alive. She had. Her own suffering had taken the form of a
marked dip in the popularity of her performances. She had
been forced to catch old favorites and to travel with them to
some of the smaller provincial dream palaces: The Beholder
at Sisters Beach—before the summer season had filled it with
its big audiences—and The Second Skin in Westport. She'd
even sat up on an overnight train to the first sizable town
south of The Corridor. Eventually Grace had returned to the
Rainbow Opera for a performance at reduced rates; the
Opera was paid but she wasn't. It had taken her weeks, and
cost her money, but she had finally worked her way back into
public confidence. Her audience had forgiven her.

Though Grace had recovered her old virtuosity, she found
that she couldn't relax. When she was busy wooing back the

public, she'd been able to put other thoughts and feelings out of her mind. Now these suppressed feelings had returned in force.

It had been written in newspapers: "Grace Tiebold should be ashamed of herself." She had read it, and imagined other people reading it—her neighbors, the workers at her favorite bakery, the man who trimmed her hair. She'd gone around with her eyes cast down for fear of finding herself looked at—not by those she had offended or disappointed but by people who had only heard it said: "Grace Tiebold should be ashamed of herself." She was afraid she'd see those people looking at her to discover how she was taking it.

Grace had done the hard work, had shown humility, and was back in favor. But now she wondered if she'd ever again feel her former happy confidence in her power to please people. And if she'd ever be able to forget the *relish* she'd sensed in her public scolding.

So when she asked Sandy Mason how he was, Grace wasn't just being polite but was genuinely concerned.

Sandy only grunted in reply. Then he looked guilty and tried again. "I'm fine now. There was a short period when I was catching poor quality dreams. St. Thomas's turned me away. I nearly had to give up my room, though Mrs. Lilley was good about waiting for my rent. All the other lodgers kept asking me about Laura, as though she was mine." Sandy had begun his account in a brisk, no-nonsense voice but ended sounding bitter. He was frowning at Grace. "Laura's room just stands there empty," he said.

"I can get a message to her, if you have one," Grace offered.

Sandy's frown deepened, he shuffled his feet. "I mean—it's *wasteful* to keep a room empty week after week."

"Never mind that," Grace said. She was puzzled by his be-

havior. He'd been so concerned about Laura after the riot.
"I'm sure Laura would be interested to hear about your union
plans," she said.

"Oh, that." Sandy sounded disgusted. "There was a meeting. We should have been talking about a charter and how
to collect dues. Instead, it was an orgy of whining, dreamhunters slighting dream parlor managers, or complaining
about the state of the dream trails. I saw how much had to be
done. And I saw that, if I wanted it done, I was going to have
to do it all myself. Besides"—Sandy paused—"I want to be a
great dreamhunter. And I've got only seven months of my exclusive left on The Water Diviner. I don't have time to waste."

"Fair enough," said Grace. Then she persisted. "You could
give me a letter and I'd pass it on to Laura. I'm going to see
her at Christmas."

"I know where she is," Sandy said, so blunt he was almost
brutal. "Not that she really meant to let me know." He em-
phasized the "me."

"Oh—well," Grace said. She picked up the pack and
hoisted it onto her shoulder to test its empty weight.

Sandy seemed to be struggling with himself. Grace thought
he might have realized that it was against his self-interest to be
rude to the most famous dreamhunter. He began to talk
again, stiff and expressionless. "I did set out to visit her. I
caught a lift on a barge from Tarry Cove—you know, the last
stop on the Sisters Beach line?"

"Where the fishing fleet anchors."

"And coal barges. I caught a lift on a barge going to Debt
River, the mine at the base of So Long Spit."

"And?"

"And I thought about it as I went."

"You thought about going to see Laura?"

"I thought about whether I really wanted to see her."

"Oh, Sandy, what did she do to you? I mean, apart from—" Grace stopped, not wanting to talk out loud about Laura and the nightmare. She put her hand on his arm. "Was it you who copied out the letters for her?"

Sandy was startled. "What are you talking about? What letters? Laura sent *me* a letter—she wanted me to pass it on to some other person."

"Who?"

"The letter didn't say who. I was supposed to leave it somewhere. I didn't do it." Sandy was struggling to hold back the fury in his face and voice. He ended up looking prim. "She was trying to get me to be her go-between."

Grace looked around them. The outfitter's wasn't busy. They had an aisle to themselves. She lowered her voice, trying to encourage him to do so too. "Where is this letter now?"

"I tore it up. Shreds of it are still plastered to the gutter outside my bedroom window. A nice reminder of Laura, and my limited usefulness to her."

Grace touched his arm again, tentative. "Sandy, I want to apologize for Laura if she—"

"She's just a *child*," he said. "Self-centered, feckless, and childish."

Grace shook her head. She had once thought that way about Laura, but Laura had changed.

"Anyway," Sandy said, "at least I didn't totally waste my time. When I got to Debt River, I met a ranger who was walking the border from Tricksie Bend, mostly on the outside, ducking In only at those earth ramps they use as lookouts. Do you know what I mean?"

Grace nodded. She'd seen the ramps on the border the few times she'd gone along it rather than heading straight In. They were ten to fifteen feet high and made of piled earth tamped down by spadework. Each ramp was a vantage point over the surrounding country.

"The ranger told me about a dream on Foreigner's North," Sandy said.

Grace knew that Foreigner's North was a landmark on maps of the Place. It was on the farthest western border, just Inside. It was in the north as well as the west—possibly also the farthest northern point of the invisible territory—she would have to check a map of Coal Bay to be sure. She had always presumed that it was a compass reference of some kind.

"The dream, Quake, is something only a few dream-hunters can catch. The ranger told me that it was alarming but not exactly a nightmare. No one has claimed it, because it isn't commercial—supposedly." Sandy looked smug. "Though I think I've uncovered its commercial potential." He laughed. "I saw that, Mrs. Tiebold, your eyes lit up."

"I'm intrigued," Grace said. "How can a dream be 'not exactly a nightmare'?"

"Well—if something alarming happens in it but the person whose point of view it is isn't alarmed. Quake is from the point of view of a child, like The Water Diviner. I'm wondering whether that's my affinity—dreams in which the audience gets to be a child again. The boy in The Water Diviner is about ten. This is a much younger child, maybe four or five."

"That's very unusual."

"Perhaps you'd like to come to my performance tonight? I've spent the last two days chewing Wakeful and getting together an audience—mostly scientists from the University. Geologists and so forth. I've rented a whole floor of a hotel here on the Isle. Eight bedrooms. I'm charging twenty dollars a head."

Grace was a little embarrassed for Sandy—standing in the

aisle of an outfitter's and advertising his prices. But she still asked for the name and address of the hotel, and at what time the doors closed before the performance.

"Will you come?" Sandy said, eager to impress her.

Grace considered. She closed one eye. She very much wanted to come and try Sandy's Quake. She hadn't been four or five since she was four or five, and she couldn't remember it very clearly. She'd been to a performance of The Water Diviner and had thought that, although Sandy's penumbra was still quite tight, his dream was very clear, and exact in all its details. He was promising, and he was catching new things, which the majority of dreamhunters didn't even try to do. She said, "If I attend, you'll be boosted."

"Then perhaps you could come at a reduced price."

"Reduced?" Grace didn't believe her ears. He was so brazen. He'd even folded his arms and tilted his head back. He was bargaining. He wasn't going to be flattered by her interest. She said, "A discount then, for me and my husband."

"Done," said Sandy.

"We're fashionable people, you know," Grace said.

"Yes, I do know. And I know I'm supposed to fawn upon all the fashionable people."

He was thinking of Laura, Grace thought. What *had* the girl done to him? What was in that letter he tore to pieces? She said, "We'll see you tonight then. I'm looking forward to it." She patted his arm and took her new pack up to the counter.

✧ ✧ ✧

"A letter! And he destroyed it?" said Chorley. "Was it a letter to some man?"

"He didn't say it was to a man. You're jumping to conclusions—the conclusions you're always jumping to these days.

One moment you're fretting about Laura and Sandy Mason, the next you're fretting about Sandy's supposed rival. Honestly, Chorley!"

"Young men can't be trusted with girls."

"This is the voice of experience, I suppose?"

"Rather remote experience, but still."

"You're turning into such a reactionary. It's that old man with the beard—your new best friend."

There was a scorched silence from Chorley. He put his coat on over his silk robe. He put boots on over his tasseled slippers. He fumed. "The Grand Patriarch is not a replacement for Tziga," he said.

"I'm sorry, dear. But you can be so silly about Laura. She's no more likely to be seduced than Rose is. Less likely, since she's sequestered on So Long Spit. Conveniently," Grace added. "Till I cool off."

Chorley ignored this remark. "Laura doesn't have many barriers left in her behavior. That seems to be something dreams do to some dreamhunters. And—let me remind you— I was *right* to worry about Tziga."

"You weren't worried that he'd be *seduced*."

"I was worried that none of us, and nothing he had, would ever be enough for him."

"I'm like that too," Grace said.

"No, you're not."

"Yes, I am. The only difference between me and Tziga is that I love all the dreams I catch. I love them. And without them I'd be nothing. I'd be a withered apple on a windowsill." Grace pulled her image from a dream, one of her sad ones, in which a widow returned home after her husband's funeral, and a short time staying in the houses of relatives, to find nothing much changed, but her house empty and stale, and her stored apples withered.

Grace said, "I love being borne up by my big audiences—everyone breathing together, breathing in time with my breathing. It's not just that I enjoy what I do, or that I'm proud of how good at it I am. It's this—when I'm carried up on the high tide of a full house at the Rainbow Opera, when I'm *not myself*, that's when I'm most fully alive."

Chorley put his arms around his wife and kissed her. He said, "Dear, none of that is under threat. Your audience fell off for a time, but you got them back again. You had a bad patch, but it's over."

They quietly held each other. Then Grace said, "Shall we go see what this boy has, then?"

✦ ✦ ✦

Sandy's twelve guests gathered in the larger suite to have a drink before they retired. They pulled dining chairs into the space before the hearth, around the sofa and armchairs already there. A waiter wheeled in a trolley with hot chocolate and cakes, port and brandy.

It fell to Grace to play hostess—she was the only woman present, and the collection of crusty geologists was clearly used to being waited on. She poured hot chocolate, handed around cups and glasses, and spooned cream onto slices of cake. Then she gathered her white silk robe around her bright yellow silk pajamas and sat down with her own cup of chocolate.

Sandy stood with one arm on the mantelpiece and one foot up on the hearth. He was giving an account of his journey. He seemed to be enjoying himself, speaking well and with a natural authority.

Chorley leaned toward his wife to whisper. "How old is he?"

"Eighteen or nineteen, I believe—he Tried late."

Chorley nodded and continued his haughty scrutiny of the boy Rose referred to, jokingly, as "Laura's suitor."

"The farther west I went, the poorer the land was. When we think of Coal Bay, we think about Sisters Beach or the dairy flats around Whynew Stream. But beyond Whynew Stream there are only wet paddocks rusty with dock leaf. I slept where it was dry, just Inside the border. But I didn't walk along on the Inside. It's pointless to do that."

"Yes!" One geologist removed his pipe from his teeth with a loud clack. "I read about those experiments. The ratio of Inside to outside is miles to yards, I gather. He put his pipe back in his mouth with another punctuating clack of tooth enamel on polished walnut. "It's simply incredible."

Sandy said, "Because the Place is so vast, its explorers have tried to make landmarks, as well as record the landmarks they find. One of the first explorers was a legendary figure—legendary among rangers at least—a man known as the Foreigner."

"He was French," said Grace.

"He tried to walk the border before anyone else," said Sandy. "The first mapmakers kept finding his marks. Foreigner's North is a landmark. A compass mark on the border, at the point farthest north and west, though I understand his west is somewhere else."

Grace said, "It's because of his west that they suppose he's a foreigner—west is 'ouest' in French."

Sandy said, "A ranger took me to Foreigner's North. The dream Quake is right on top of it. The compass mark—a big N—looks like it's been hit by a quake too. It's cracked all the way across."

"There was a sizable earthquake in Coal Bay in 1886," a geologist said. "That's what first uncovered the coal at Debt

River. Lumps of it washed downstream and began to turn up on the tide. The forest is very thick in the northwest, but prospectors went in and found the slip, and the seam of coal. Of course folks had already found coal at Whynew Stream over a hundred years before. But that seam was soon exhausted. However, that's where the name—Coal Bay—comes from."

"The quake was twenty years ago?" asked Chorley.

The geologist nodded, then turned to Sandy and asked, "Is the quake in the dream a good-sized one?"

Sandy straightened and took his arm off the mantelpiece. "Shall we go and see?"

The boy was practicing his violin on the porch of the cottage when he saw something pouring out of the dead tree trunk in the yard. He put down his violin—his child's violin, a fine thing, as precious and clever as he was himself—and brushed his itching jaw against his shoulder. The rosin made a mark on his shirt. He stepped off the porch and wandered across the yard to look at the flood of— what? Sap?

From far away the substance looked like chocolate sauce from one of his ma's self-saucing puddings. (His ma used to say that she was a "self-saucing pudding," which was a joke about how in their family there was no "Da" like other families had.)

The boy squatted to look at the brown substance. The air was hot nearer the ground, as though the ground was cooking something.

He saw that the oozing mass was ants, thousands of them, flowing in a twisting, glistening brown rope down the grooved tree trunk. He could actually hear them. The ants were making a noise like bursting bubbles in sea foam—except much quieter. The boy could hear them only because the sounds of the world had dropped away. Even the birds in the bushes were silent.

His mother came to the cottage door to ask what he was doing. She was wiping her hands on her apron. He wanted to say to her that the ants were leaving their nest. But he didn't get to say it. He saw her hands grow still, though she continued to hold her apron gathered before her.

They both listened. The boy wondered why the horses in the paddock behind the house had decided, all at once, to gallop down to the back fence.

But the thunder wasn't horses.

The ground began to move; it lurched sideways, and then jolted up in shudders. The boy fell onto his hands and knees. He heard his mother shout. He saw her rush across the porch. At the same time the cottage chimney slammed down onto the corrugated iron roof, then came apart and slid—bricks and boulder-sized chunks of mortar and brick—down the curve of the roof and off its edge. The boy's mother rushed out among the falling bricks. None of them struck her.

She staggered across the yard and picked him up, then stumbled under the yard's one tree, a cabbage tree partly smothered with honeysuckle. The honeysuckle was in flower, and as they stood—he in her arms—the tree dropped honeysuckle blossoms and a thick veil of floral scent down over them. His mother spread one hand over the crown of the boy's head and held him sheltered in the curve of her body. She leaned back against the tree trunk and struggled to keep her footing.

There were crashes and thumps from the cottage—scarcely audible in the thunder from everywhere. And there were high-pitched sounds, the squawk of nails pulled loose from timber, and the painted weatherboards splitting with a sound like gunfire.

Water was jumping out of the puddles and into the air.

Then the heaving and juddering stopped. The yard went quiet, though the air seemed to torque and rustle.

The boy's mother held him tight. Her heart was beating so hard the boy could feel it pushing against him, fierce and powerful. Her heart was strong—the boy thought—but not nearly as strong as the ground, the angry ground.

Grace was shaken awake by the bed heaving. Beside her, Chorley was sitting up. She heard him fumbling around on the nightstand. He lit a candle.

Grace made a muffled noise of irritation. The bedsheets were uncomfortably starchy, and the room was stuffy. She remembered that she was in a hotel—the sort of hotel young Sandy Mason could afford to rent for his performance.

"That was Verity," Chorley said to his wife.

Grace's next annoyed grunt had, at its end, a mild tone of inquiry. Verity was Chorley's dead sister, Laura's mother.

"The woman on the porch," said Chorley.

"Sandy isn't a Gifter," Grace said. She was waking up, reluctantly. She could feel herself shrinking away from something.

Maze Plasir was a Gifter (or, impolitely, a Grafter). He could graft the bodies of real people onto the characters in his dreams. That was why he was in demand by the sorts of men who would send him out to watch—say—their daughters' school friends and then have those school friends stand in for the obligingly friendly females of Plasir's specialty dreams. Gifting was a very rare talent. Some dreamhunters, at certain times in their lives, did make their own substitutions. As a young woman, Grace had found herself replacing the anonymous handsome faces of her dreams' heroes with Chorley Tiebold's after she first saw him at a ball. It just happened, and was beyond her control.

"But why would Sandy think of *Verity*?" Chorley asked, bemused. "Where would he *get* her from?"

"Laura."

"How could he get her from Laura?"

"No. It *was* Laura." Grace sat up so quickly she threw the covers off them. "It wasn't Verity; it was Laura."

Chorley screwed up his face. "Why would Sandy want to imagine himself as a child and Laura as his mother?"

Grace put her hands over her face. She was very confused, appalled, and, at the same time, deeply moved.

"It's perverse," Chorley was saying, his voice strained.

Grace put a hand on his arm. She was worried he might leap out of bed, wake up Sandy Mason, and start demanding explanations. "Calm down," she said, though she was far from calm herself.

"It's so perverse I can't even imagine what kind of perversity it is!" Chorley said. Then, "Why are you laughing?"

"You're funny."

"Grace, Sandy Mason finds he's an angelic, violin-playing little boy so he immediately supplies himself with my niece as his mother. And you're laughing. I'm a liberal man. I have an abundance of tolerance for dreamhunters and their peculiarities. But this is going too far."

Grace wiped her eyes. "Shhh," she said.

Chorley shut his mouth and only radiated indignation.

Grace took his hand and met his eyes. "That was Laura. She wasn't tall or fair like Verity, but she had Verity's sweet, queenly face. Sandy Mason isn't a Gifter. And if he recognizes the woman in his dream, he'll be very upset and angry with himself and suppose it's because he can't get Laura out of his head." Grace kissed her husband's hand. Her own heart was pounding as hard as the heart of the woman in Sandy's dream, but she tried to be calm for her husband's sake. "Listen, love," she said. "The convict in Laura's first dream remembered being a boy racing a schooner along the shore of So Long Spit, and you saw the lighthouse keeper's boy doing just that. The dreams are set in the future. And that was Laura, grown-up, and with a little boy of her own."

III
Summer and Christmas

1

✢ ✢ ✢

WHEN SHE WAS ON VACATION IN THE AWA INLET, MAMIE PREFERRED TO SPEND AS LITTLE TIME AS POSSIBLE WITH her brother, Ru, and his friends. She told Rose that the boys were boring. Right after breakfast she and Rose would often walk up the stream and into the beech forest, or set out along the hot mud track through the reedbeds at the eastern end of the Inlet. Mamie would tell anyone who was listening that they were going to gather shells on the sandbar. Or she'd say they were going swimming and then *would* go to gather shells. Ru had once confronted Mamie about it. "You told us you'd be down by the rocks," he said, aggrieved.

"So?" said Mamie. "Why do you suddenly want *my* company?"

Ru had blushed and hadn't complained again.

Mamie was, in her own brutal way, trying to look after Rose, who had discovered that it wasn't at all fun to be admired by someone she didn't like, especially someone you had to share a roof with. When Ru Doran looked at her, Rose felt at odds with her own body. She felt that there was something wrong with her. She didn't want Ru to think she was beautiful. She felt she should be able somehow to show him that he wasn't allowed to have opinions about her appearance—or, at

least, that he wasn't allowed to show them. Being openly admired by someone she found unattractive made Rose feel that
her beauty didn't belong to her, was in fact something tricky,
a demon hiding inside her, prompting, and making offers,
and emitting strange odors when she'd rather just go about
being her usual self.

Mamie and Rose's favorite beach in the Inlet was toward
the western end, quite a distance from the Doran house.

On a day two weeks into Rose's visit, the weather was very
hot, and the girls had swum for more than an hour, jumping
from the rocks over and over until their ears began to ache.
Then they lay on the sand. Salt prickled on their warming
bodies as their skin grew dry and tight.

"How long can we stay away?" Rose asked her friend. Her
room got the afternoon sun and would be too stuffy to retire to.

"I'm going to have to have a word with Ru, aren't I?"
Mamie said.

Rose shrugged, her shoulders rasping on the sand.

Mamie picked up Rose's skirt and fished in its pocket for
the letter her friend received that morning.

"Hey!" Rose said, but didn't move.

"It's only Patty—Patty is a weakness we share, Rose." Mamie
frowned, then quoted their classmate's letter: "I am deprived
of society here in the South. I see no one I like." She laughed.
"But see, a paragraph later she's dancing the military two-
step with her cousin. You know, I think they're all cousins in
the South. Which is a shame, since poor Patty is one of those
girls who is longing to be able to say to someone things like
'An introduction for the purposes of a dance does not constitute an acquaintance.' But she knows absolutely everyone. And, Rose! It says here she already has the pattern for
her Presentation Ball gown. Hasn't she got *any* other interests?"

"Making fun of what other people are thinking doesn't actually constitute 'an interest,' Mamie," Rose said.

Mamie tossed the letter down. "Let's go back," she said.
"I'm not going to be kept from the house by my brother and
his tedious admiration."

Rose got up and dressed while Mamie tried to think of a
plan to discourage Ru. "You could propose marriage—that
ought to sober him up."

"I could start scratching myself all the time, so he thinks
I'm infested."

"Or you could clear your throat every thirty seconds, like
Miss Toop at the Academy."

"I could make a three-pronged attack, clearing my throat,
scratching, and proposing," Rose said.

"Or you could just attack his three prongs!"

"Mamie!"

Shrieks of laughter.

✦ ✦ ✦

That night, in the early hours of the morning, Rose woke
and lay listening. She heard a disturbed bird twittering in a
tree near her window. Perhaps its calls had hooked her out of
sleep, or perhaps she'd been roused by the same thing that
made the bird cry in alarm. She felt that something remarkable had happened only a moment before. The curtains in
Rose's room were thick, the room black, and the birdcalls
were bright in the darkness.

She got out of bed and shuffled to the window, slid the
curtains open, and squinted into brilliant moonlight.

Outside, all the colors of day were present under a smoky
filter. It was late, and a dewfall had softened and silvered the
grass.

Rose decided to go out. She left her room and crept down the stairs. She went out by the French doors in the dining room. They were locked, but the key was in the lock.

She set off down the flagstone steps of the terrace, then veered away through the orchard and headed for the best path to the sea, the bed of the narrow-gauge railway that ran from the shore to the house.

The Doran summerhouse was on a slope at the back of the Inlet. It was grand and solid, built of blond sandstone, its roof tiled with slate. It had been a big project, in a remote spot, and had presented its builders with some challenges. Labor wasn't a problem, for the hill had been terraced and the foundations laid by convict workers. The difficulty was in getting the materials from the shore to the site across the boggy paddocks of the former farm. The farm already had a rough road that ran, plumb straight, from the shore to the foot of the hill, along an avenue of mature plane trees. Cas Doran's solution to the transportation problem was to have a narrow-gauge railway built along the road. A small engine ran on the line. In many trips, over many months, the engine hauled stone and timber, marble and parquet flooring, roof tiles, window glass, and finally furniture.

When Rose had first arrived at the Awa Inlet, the train she was on made a special stop at the end of the trestle bridge that crossed the mouth of the Sva River. Rose then got into a small boat and was rowed up a broad tidal channel, through the reedbeds, to the Doran jetty. There she was greeted by the sight of a butler sitting in the cab of a little engine. A footman stowed her bags in the single truck the engine was pulling. Then she climbed into the engine behind its driver and rode up to the house.

The engine had been stoked up several times during her visit—to pick up Ru's guests and their luggage, and to carry supplies: baskets of fruit and vegetables; sides of pork and beef; cages of live chickens; blocks of ice; and hampers of dry goods, preserves, cheese, and wine.

Rose emerged from the orchard and went into the avenue of old trees. She patted the engine, which was sitting in its shelter, cool, still, and breathless.

In the daytime the avenue was a shady tunnel; at night it was like a cathedral, a ruin with a broken roof. Rose walked beside the tracks, her face turned up to the moonlight that fell, almost warm, through gaps in the foliage high overhead. She glanced down only now and then to step over tree roots that snaked almost all the way up to the rails.

Rose intended to go to the shore. The tide would be out, and she wanted to see what the bare sands of the Inlet looked like by the light of the moon. But as she came near the two stacks of rails left over from the time the line was laid, Rose saw something that made her stop, and then slink off the track and behind a tree trunk.

She stepped up onto a tree root and peered around the trunk—yes, she *had* seen a light. There was a lamp sitting unattended beside the pile of surplus rails. Nothing moved in the circle of its vaporous white light. And then a moth appeared and began a colliding orbit.

Rose, craning around the trunk of the plane tree, saw four rangers appear. The men flickered into existence beside the pallets and their loads. The rangers were working in pairs, picking up several rails each and carrying them out of sight, Into the Place.

For two weeks Rose had walked by the stacked rails—and, for that matter, the pile of surplus timber ties a few paces away, concealed in a patch of fennel. She had walked past them and hadn't wondered how Doran's builders had made such a huge overestimation when buying for what was, after all, less than a mile of line. Nor had she wondered why the rails, after sitting there for years, lacked even the faintest freckle of rust.

Now she knew. The piled rails never rusted because they were replaced, new ones were landed on the shore—probably when the house was empty—and were carried by engine to this spot, then, by rangers, into the Place.

Rose knew nothing about the country In from the Awa Inlet, but she knew that she'd never heard *anything* about a railway in the Place. Where would a rail line go? And what would run on it, if a flame couldn't be kindled and put to coal to heat a boiler and make steam? If there could be no spark in the valves of a combustion engine, if only muscle could move things?

As Rose considered all this, the rangers came and went, and the stacks of rails were gradually reduced. She remained where she was till she worked out, from snatches of talk and the rangers' gestures, that next they meant to start transporting the timber ties from the fennel patch to the border.

Rose realized that she couldn't keep edging around the tree in order to stay out of sight. She'd have to make a run for it. She'd have to wait till they were all In, then break cover and run as far from the lamplight as she could. She hoped the light had formed a kind of capsule and sealed the rangers into it, so that they would be as blinded as people coming from a bright outdoors into a dark room. She hoped the moonlight would seem weak to their dazzled eyes and they would miss her running form, her pale hair and white nightgown.

Rose waited till all four rangers were out of sight, then sprinted flat-out for the next tree. She slid behind it before they reappeared. Again she waited, ducked out, dashed on, scrambled under cover. When she was five trees farther up the

avenue, she looked back to see the lamp moving, then passing into the fennel, casting giant, feathery shadows on the
smooth trunks of the nearest plane trees. The shadows leapt
to engulf the trees as the lamp was lowered to the ground.

Rose sprinted through the orchard and up the steps to the
house. Her feet and the hem of her nightgown were wet with
dew, the cloth clinging to her ankles. She didn't pause to
catch her breath but headed straight for the unlocked dining
room doors.

Then she stopped dead.

Ru Doran was standing on the veranda beside the only
unlocked door. He looked at Rose, then past her at the lamplight along the rail line. He craned his neck and came forward. Rose edged away a little, so he stopped. "What was it?"
he said.

"Rangers," said Rose.

He regarded her. "You know—most girls would be more
cautious about wandering at night."

Rose shrugged. She met his eyes, but only briefly.

"But you aren't like most girls, are you, Rose?"

"What do you mean?" Rose said. She felt uneasy. Ru was
standing between her and the door.

"Well—your mother is a dreamhunter. And so you've been
exposed." His tone was insinuating.

Rose tossed her head, snorted, and started forward briskly.

Ru intercepted her. He put his shoulder against her,
backed her into the wall, and caught hold of her wrist.

"Please let me go," she said.

"You're still whispering." He sounded amused. "Very sensible. It would be a shame to be caught. Out of your bed.
Snooping."

"Let go of me," Rose said, angry but ineffectual. She found

that she was feeling more indignant than frightened, though she knew fear was probably the sensible response to being cornered and threatened.

Ru Doran *was* threatening her. She knew that he had decided she was a certain kind of girl. A girl somehow spoiled by "exposure" to freedoms and excitements most girls hadn't had. He'd decided she was fair game. And he was laughing at her, chuckling in a superior, indulgent way and shaking his head. How dare he be so comfortable about making her uncomfortable. "Let go of me," she said, "or I'll get my father to take care of you—or, better, I'll get *your* father to do it!"

Ru's face went hard with anger and, immediately following the anger, spite. He put his free hand to her face, perhaps to press it over her mouth. But Rose had had enough. She moved toward him and let herself fall forward. One of her feet thumped onto his instep, and her wrist wrenched free from his grip. She plunged through the gap between his body and the wall of the house, caught herself on her hands, sprang up, ran to the door. She jerked the door open and rushed inside.

Rose hurried back to her room, closed the door, and locked it. She climbed into bed and lay fuming and shivering till the birds started up, legitimately this time, to greet the dawn.

2

✧ ✧ ✧

THE FOLLOWING DAY, SHORTLY AFTER LUNCH, CAS DORAN WAS IN THE LIBRARY, HAVING A FINE TIME MARKING different-sized circles on a map of Founderston, when he heard raised voices in the hallway. His wife's voice, and his daughter's. He opened the door and put his head out to hear.

"You're not doing anything, Mother! I'm sorry I lost my temper at breakfast, but as far as I can tell the day's just humming along as usual."

"Be quiet and go back upstairs, Mamie."

Doran went out to investigate.

As soon as she saw him, Mamie hurled herself at him, though stopping short of actual contact. "Father, Rose is going to go home!"

"What on earth is going on?" Doran demanded.

"Ru assaulted Rose!" Mamie said.

There was a moment of blank, burning silence.

Doran looked at his wife. She appeared pained and put out. "Mamie," she said, coldly, and pointed at the stairs. "Please go, before you do any more damage."

Mamie looked at her father and clasped her hands together to make a gesture of pleading. "I don't see why Mother must believe Ru!" she said.

Doran held up his hand. "I don't see any point in you offering your opinion, Mamie. I'll wait to hear from your friend."

Mamie started to cry. "Don't do that," she said. "Don't do that thing where you start talking about someone not using their name but only their relation to some other person or thing—"

"Mamie, you're being oddly abstract," said her father. He wasn't used to seeing her cry—in fact, he hadn't seen her shed a tear since she was quite small.

"She's Rose, not 'your friend,' " Mamie said. She turned around and stomped back upstairs, wiping her eyes on her sleeve—mottled, stout, ugly, angry.

Doran asked his wife to step into the library. He held the door open for her and closed it firmly after them.

Mrs. Doran told him that Mamie had been in her room since breakfast, after tipping a plate of black pudding and grilled tomato into her brother's lap.

"What did Ru have to say?"

Mrs. Doran folded her hands into one of the pleats at the front of her lace tea gown and looked trustingly and calmly at her husband. She waited for him to take charge.

"Yes, I suppose I should ask him myself," said Doran. "Will you fetch him for me? And I'll want to speak to Rose too. Perhaps you should dispatch Mamie to find her."

Mrs. Doran said, "It's my opinion that, since making friends with Rose, Mamie is showing signs of becoming a rather passionate and dramatic girl."

"So you think Mamie is exaggerating?"

"Yes, I do."

Doran said, "Please send Ru to me."

✦ ✦ ✦

Ru looked astonished when his father asked him what he'd done to upset Rose.

"Sometime last night?" said Doran, prompting.

"Oh." Ru touched his forehead, tapped himself several times between the eyebrows. His father knew this gesture—Ru was organizing his thoughts. "I thought Mother had this all under control. Very well. Last night I couldn't go to sleep," he said. "So I went out onto the terrace to have a cigarette. I'm sorry, Father, I know you don't like me to smoke." He looked contrite. "While I was there, I noticed a light on the avenue. A lamp of some sort. I was about to go and see what it was when I saw Rose hurrying back up the lawn. I guessed that she'd been meeting someone—perhaps her cousin—since the light was just about where the border is." Ru looked earnestly at his father. "Whatever she was up to, I caught her at it."

Doran nodded.

"When she saw me, she wasn't pleased. She tried to push past me. I grabbed her wrist and asked what she was doing. Then she stepped on my foot—I can show you the bruise if you like. She rushed off inside, and the lamp went out a few moments later."

"And that's all there was to it?"

"Yes, Father. Rose was startled because I caught her up to something. It's my fault if she's upset. But I was only having a bit of fun with her, pretending to want to interrogate her."

Doran nodded. "Thank you, Ru. You may go now."

Ru gave his father a tight little smile and left.

✧ ✧ ✧

Rose had her dress back on over her wet bathing suit. Her hair was dull and full-bodied with salt. She was walking back along the railway when Mamie met her. "Good God, Mamie!

Have you been crying?" Rose asked. She reached out for her friend, then thought better of it and only gave Mamie her shoes to carry. They fell into step, Rose still occasionally mounting a rail, her toes curled to grip, swaying as she balanced along it. She told Mamie she'd gone out to get away from everyone. "You were so upset when I said I'd be leaving. I thought I should cool down and think about it. Anyway, I've given it some more thought, and I think the sensible thing *is* to cut my visit short." Rose gave her friend a careful look.

There wasn't much Mamie could say to Rose's plans. She did say, "Father wants to speak to you."

"Did you tell him?"

"No, I—" Mamie's mouth worked, then she smiled. "I tipped Ru's breakfast on him. I mean, on Ru, not on Father. Then I had to explain to Mother. Then Mother spoke to Ru. Then she spoke to Father. I've spent most of the day shut in my room."

"Oh, hell," said Rose. She came to a stop, and her foot slipped off the rail. She tumbled and barely caught herself, then stood rubbing the knee of the leg she'd landed on awkwardly.

Mamie said, "I'm supposed to deliver you to Father in the library." Then, "For goodness' sake, Rose, can't you walk and think at the same time?"

Rose started walking again. She said, "I may have to go home, but you should come stay at Summerfort. Make a return visit. Do you think your parents will let you?"

"One minute you're upset, the next you're arranging your social calendar."

"So?"

"You don't nurse grudges, do you?"

"Mamie, I'm not going to let my feelings about Ru contaminate our friendship. I'd like you to come to Sisters Beach in the new year. We can visit a dressmaker together. We can pick patterns for our Presentation Ball gowns."

"Oh, I can see that happening—after your father has chastised my brother."

"My father doesn't need to know a thing—if *your* father knows his business." With that Rose strode off toward the house holding her head high.

✦ ✦ ✦

Mrs. Doran came into the library. "I have Rose Tiebold," she said.

"I asked Mamie to fetch her," said Doran.

"And Mamie did so. Then she went back to her room. I can't have her creating scenes at the breakfast table, even in defense of her friend's honor."

"Very well," said Doran. "Mamie can remain in her room. But only until this evening."

"That Tiebold girl likes attention," Mrs. Doran said, in a warning tone. She opened the door, ushered Rose into the library, and left, closing the door after her.

Doran got up and gestured the girl to a seat near the window. She sat, and he remained standing, his back to the bright sunlight. "Well, Rose," he began, "you want to leave us early?"

"I think I must," she said.

"Mamie tells me that you're upset."

Rose began to fiddle with her hair—picking up the ends and inspecting them. "Um. Not so much now," she said. "Now I'm feeling fairly resolute."

"May I ask what you mean by 'fairly resolute'? Do you mean that you're approximating resolution? Or that you're being fair?"

"Mamie gets it from you," Rose said.

"Gets what?"

"Hairsplitting." Rose was frowning at the ends of her hair. She dropped the crackling golden mass and looked up at him. She began to tell the story—her side of it. "I went for a walk last night and saw some rangers shifting the surplus rails and ties. I wondered what was In from the Awa Inlet and why you were building a railroad there."

"I see." Doran blinked and rubbed his jaw. He felt his scalp prickle as blood pumped up into his head. He said, "To put you right on that score—directly In from here are The Pinnacles, a range of steep, crumbling hills. They are by far the most extensive known barrier in the Place. Last year a group of rangers built a gate to block the entrance of the only pass through The Pinnacles. They did all the welding here, on the shore; then they carried the gate In and set it up. The gate is often locked because the pass through The Pinnacles is unstable and unsafe. Rangers struggle to keep it in reasonable repair. Lately the Body has had rangers building retaining walls on the worst cliff faces in the pass. As it happened, I had surplus rails and timber, and thought they might like to make use of them." Doran spread his hands. "So there you go," he said.

Rose had listened, but toward the end of his speech her face had gone taut with watchfulness. She looked ten years older and superbly intelligent. Cas Doran regarded her with wonder. He thought, "What on earth is she thinking?" He began to check his story for faults. In a moment he had it. Of course, there were new rails all the time, the pile almost always refreshed the moment a load was removed. The rails never sat there long—so they didn't rust. Rose Tiebold could guess he was lying—but Doran didn't feel in the least uncomfortable. He only felt very alert. He had a strange urge to ask her what she thought of his explanation, and an even stranger desire to know what she'd think of his whole plan. He put these odd ideas aside and prompted her. "You were watching the rangers and . . ."

"And when I came back to the house, I met Ru, and he said I shouldn't be wandering around at night."

"And you shouldn't."

Rose frowned at this interruption and went on in a rush. "And then he said I was different from other girls, and that it was because my mother was a dreamhunter and I'd been exposed. That was his word—'exposed.' Then he squashed me into the wall and grabbed my wrist. I told him to let go. He was laughing. Then I told him that Da would take care of him, and then that *you* would. He got a mean look—so I stomped on his foot and got away."

Doran was as intrigued by the similarities in Rose's and Ru's stories as by the differences.

The sun had moved, and Rose's eyes were now no longer in a strip of shade formed by the window frame. They were watering. She got up and stepped out of the patch of sunlight. She remained standing. "I hope you believe me," she said, dignified.

"Ru has a very different story."

"I'm amazed he feels he needs a story."

"Do you think it's at all possible that you're taking this too seriously?" Doran asked.

"I've been thinking about that. When I talked to Mamie this morning, I was very angry. Then I took a step back. Now my head tells me it wasn't really serious, I wasn't in any danger, I was just being nervous. He did keep laughing as if he hoped I'd get the joke."

"Well, I'm relieved to hear you say that."

"Wait," Rose said. She held up her hand. "Ru made me feel bad. My head may say that I'm being oversensitive. But my

head is timid. It wants to hide itself in the sand. My gut tells
me that Ru might have taken his teasing as far as he wanted,
even if he thought of it as only teasing."

Doran listened, nodding.

"I hope you believe me," Rose said again.

Doran turned away from her and thought—disconnected
thoughts. He thought that his son must learn how to behave.
Ru must not break the law. No child of his could be a criminal. Then he thought that he'd send Rose back to her home.
His wife had said the girl was a troublemaker. It was better
simply to remove her. "I'll have Ru apologize to you," he said,
after a silence.

"Must I be embarrassed further?"

Doran looked at Rose sharply. "You haven't mentioned
embarrassment before. And—Rose—when you told Mamie
your story, she caused a scene. You must have known she'd do
something. You say, 'I hope you believe me,' but really you're
asking me to *do* something. You want to exercise your power,
but only up to a point, apparently. You don't want to be embarrassed. But I think that you are obliged to hear my son's
apology."

He watched her grow pale.

"Rose, I think I can rely on you to be reasonable."

Rose burst into tears and sank to her knees. She pressed
her face into the seat of the chair she had been sitting in. She
wept, totally abandoned—as if in an ecstasy of misery.

Doran was startled. "Come now," he said, hovering inef-
fectually over her. Then, "Do you want me to fetch my wife?"

"No!" Rose howled. Then, "Why do *I* always have to be
reasonable?"

"Well, think how you'd feel if I'd said I depended on you to
be unreasonable," said Doran. He was gratified by the result
of this remark. Rose stopped crying to think, as tantrum-

throwing tots will if some imaginative effort has been made to distract them. He added, "It's a compliment, you know."

Rose wiped her eyes and hiccuped. "People are always trying to control me with compliments."

"I'm not trying to control you. I'm trying to do right by you. I'll have Ru apologize, and you'll hear his apology. It might do him some good to see how upset you are. You will listen to what he has to say, then I'll arrange for you to get home."

"Can Mamie come and stay with me after Christmas? Even if her mother is angry at me?"

"I'm sure that can be arranged."

"Thank you."

"And I'll deal with Ru. I'm sure you're right that he doesn't really see how he troubled you. But I'll make him see."

Rose muttered something that Doran didn't catch. He told her to dry her eyes and compose herself. "I won't be too long," he said, and left her.

✦ ✦ ✦

Alone in the library, Rose considered blowing her nose on the curtain—its nice brocade. It was a spiteful thought. As she considered it, Rose thought of Mamie's mother's rich skirts and imagined the curtain was the hem of Mrs. Doran's skirt. She seethed with fury till she felt she was breathing smoke. Her nostrils were pricking and stinging.

Rose got up and paced. She laughed at herself, at what she'd nearly said said aloud when Cas Doran had said of Ru "I'll make him see." "Yes—I bet there's a nightmare for that," she'd muttered. Thank God Doran hadn't heard her.

Rose was annoyed with herself for crying. But she'd wanted to go home without having to see Ru Doran again. She longed to be with her family at Summerfort. They would all be there for Christmas. Uncle Tziga too. Rose wanted so much to put her arms around them all—Uncle Tziga, Laura, her ma and da—that she could almost smell them, the different smells of their clothes and hair. She felt like an animal—simple, and crazy with homesickness.

In her agitated pacing, Rose had stopped before the desk. She stood awhile in a trance, then happened to notice what she was staring at. In the angling sunlight, she could see that the leather inset surface of the desk was printed with different-sized circles. Many circles, like raindrops in a puddle, except only some of them were overlapping. And, as she had only a short while earlier, listening to Doran's story about the use of steel rails for retaining walls, listening and thinking "That's plausible" and also "But why is there no *rust* on the rails?" Rose found herself of two minds. One—the mind on top—was uncomfortable and unhappy and worried about having to face Ru Doran. The other mind, the one underneath, was shouting like a siren, "Look! Circles!"

There were other things on the desk: piles of papers, folders, an inkwell, and a jumble of pens, pencils, geometry instruments. There was also a large rolled canvas. Rose saw that the roll was embossed with curved lines, like scales, marks that showed clearly in the low sun.

She swooped on it, unfastened the string that kept it closed, and let it fall open.

It was a map of Founderston. A detailed map, with a scale of six inches to a mile. Rose saw that the central city was covered in circles, some drawn in pencil, some in ink. In the middle of each circle, in neat, particular handwriting, was a street address. Rose read, "121 Courtesy Street; 15 Fuller Grove . . ." Some of the circles with street names and numbers also had surnames. Some of these names seemed vaguely familiar to Rose.

As her eyes roamed over the map, she heard footsteps in the hallway. She hurriedly rolled the map, twisted its string around it several times, and set it back at the side of the desk. Then the door opened and she spun around to put her back to the desktop and her face to the window.

The setting sun was hot on her cheeks. She heard Cas Doran say, "Rose?" and turned around, her face burning, to peer blindly through a fog of green, the afterimage of the bright window. In her head she was reciting the few facts she'd gathered. "121 Courtesy Street. 15 Fuller Grove." And the names, "Langdon, Polish, Swindon, Pinkney."

"Ru," said Doran, cuing his son.

Rose saw a shadow step forward. She could scarcely see Ru through the haze of afterimage. He looked like a monster floating in a jar of brightly colored spirits—methanol stained by the monster color leached into it. Rose continued to recite silently, "121 Courtesy Street, 15 Fuller Grove . . ."

Ru said, "I'm very sorry I frightened you, Rose. It wasn't my intention to cause you any distress by my clumsy teasing."

"Rose?" Doran said, as if he wanted her to make an argument or ask something. He was prepared to let Ru make light of what had happened, but he was still offering her a chance to put up a fight.

Ru said, "It was only supposed to be a bit of fun. It was thoughtless of me."

"All right," Rose said. She wanted to get out of the room. Her sight was clearing. She'd felt concealed by her temporary blindness. Now she could see Ru's smirking, false humility, and his father's searching stare.

Rose realized that the names—Langdon, Polish, Swindon,

Pinkney—were those of dreamhunters; she was sure of it. Gavin Pinkney was Maze Plasir's apprentice. And she was sure that the circles represented penumbras. Overlapping penumbras, covering much of central Founderston.

"May I go now?" she said.

"Yes, of course," Doran said. But as she walked by him, he put out a hand and touched her arm. "Thank you for hearing him."

Rose shrank back involuntarily. Then she gave a stiff nod and went out.

✧ ✧ ✧

The following morning, at low tide, Rose and Mamie and several of the Doran household's numerous all-purpose servants walked to the train stop by the trestle bridge over the mouth of the Sva. The men set out the flag for the westbound local, then put Rose's trunk on it when it came. Rose kissed Mamie goodbye and got on the train.

At Sisters Beach Station, she left her trunk with the stationmaster and walked around the waterfront and up the hill to Summerfort. She found her mother and father sitting on the wicker chairs on the veranda, in their robes and with damp hair, though it was past noon.

"Hello, Rosy," said her da. "Is it next Friday already?"

"What happened, darling?" asked Grace.

Rose opened her drawstring purse and passed her father Cas Doran's letter. "I'd like to read that after you," she said.

Grace got up and read over Chorley's shoulder. Partway through she took a deep breath and puffed up all over like an angry cat. Chorley handed the letter to Rose and ran his hands through his hair.

Rose read,

My dear Mr. Tiebold,

 Your daughter cut short her visit, though I understand from both her and Mamie that there is some plan for a reciprocal visit sometime after Christmas. I will leave it to you to decide whether or not that should be permitted.

 Rose asked to leave because she had some trouble with my son, Richard. I questioned Rose and Richard, and, unfortunately, received differing accounts of the incident. I do intend to press my son further and deal with him as I find he deserves. For now, I am very sorry for Rose's distress, and I hope she will soon be comfortable and cheerful again.

Yours sincerely,

Cas Doran

"What did the boy do, darling?" Grace asked.

"Nothing much. I did think he might hurt me. Though it could have been only a nasty sort of teasing. He grabbed me and kept hold of me even when I told him to let go. I had to tread on his foot."

Rose looked into their concerned faces. She remembered how, when she had gotten up the morning after her scene with Ru, she had checked for a bruise on her wrist and was disappointed not to find one. Then she recalled the bruises encircling Laura's wrists, black bands of bruising, marks she'd noticed as her cousin stood, unbinding her hands, on the balcony of the Rainbow Opera the night of the riot. "Oh, Laura," she thought again.

She said to her parents, "I wish I knew for sure that I was in danger."

"You *did* know." Grace put her arms around her daughter.

"I was more angry than scared, Ma. It doesn't seem right to cause so much trouble out of anger."

"The boy deserves trouble," Chorley said. "You can't go around grabbing girls."

"Yes, Professor," said Grace.

"I'll follow it up," Chorley said. "I'll make sure Doran does deal with him."

Grace frowned at Chorley and gave a small shake of her head.

"My trunk is at the station," Rose said.

"I'll go get it," her father said, and stepped off the porch before remembering he was still in his robe.

As her mother led her indoors, Rose asked, "Is Laura really coming home for Christmas?"

"Yes. Everyone will be here," said Grace. "The whole family —just the same as last year." She smiled at Rose. "Isn't that amazing?"

3

✧ ✧ ✧

BY MIDAFTERNOON ON THE DAY LAURA AND TZIGA WERE DUE AT SUMMER-FORT, ROSE HAD COMPLETED ALMOST ALL her tasks. She'd been to Farry's to buy cakes. She'd purchased colored crepe paper to make paper chains. She'd sorted through the boxes of old Christmas decorations for whatever was salvageable. Since the family wasn't going to have a tree that year, Rose rejected the glass balls and birds. She was glad she wouldn't have to sit around with a white soap bar and cheese grater making snow to sprinkle on the branches. Rose's ma had always liked to dress the tree. Grace also liked roast goose and brandy-soaked puddings. But Rose's da had put his foot down several years ago about the midwinter menu, and Summerfort's cook would now roast a couple of ducks the day before and spend her own Christmas at home while the family dined on cold meat, salads, and fresh berries with cream.

"It'll be just like last year," Rose thought as she hung paper lanterns. "Only without a tree." She rather missed the tree, which always smelled lovely, though it had seemed like some magnificent and neglected altar, glittering in the dark indoors, ghostly with its soap snow, and at many removes both from what it commemorated, Christ's birthday, and where it was, a beach house at the height of summer.

After she had hung the decorations, Rose tried to settle down and read a book. Not only was she unable to concentrate but she found it impossible to sit still. She wandered around the house till her mother told her to either sit down or go outside. Rose went out and ambled around Summerfort's grounds, circling the house at the edge of the lawns. When the sun had set, she lit the lanterns. Then she ran down to the beach and stood at the water's edge, looking out over the smooth bay for a boat. There were several lit masts. Some were moving across the water—fishing vessels heading into Tarry Cove—and some were apparently stationary, though any of those might actually have been headed toward their end of Sisters Beach. Rose strained her eyes. Then the dusk-loving sandflies found her and she had to move again.

She left the beach and walked around the base of the headland to the lagoon. The tide was out. When Rose stepped onto the sand, it bubbled as small basking crabs scuttled back down their water-filled holes. She strolled out into the quiet arena of damp sand. There was no traffic on the road beyond the lagoon, or the rail line farther away against the base of the hills. The night seemed enormous. Rose wasn't used to being alone—she was often alone in a room reading and, now that she was grown, almost always alone in bed, but not in a landscape. As she paced out into that space, her bare feet on warm silt and rotted shells, she felt that she was taking a little look at the lives of some of the people nearest to her—Laura, her uncle Tziga, her own mother. "How far away they must be," she thought, "whenever they take one of their walks."

When she and Laura were children and complaining that they were bored, Rose's da would say: "Don't you have any internal resources?" Having "internal resources" meant having a lively mind, interests, appetite. It meant that you should go and get a book or draw a picture. It meant "entertain your-

selves"—preferably quietly. Rose had always been able to entertain herself, and to entertain Laura too. Laura wasn't as avid
a reader, and she was less inclined to think up projects
or start a new game. "Given an audience, I expand," Rose
thought, "but given space, I shrink." Yet Laura—Laura had
found space because she wasn't always with noisy, definite
Rose, and because she'd left school and become a dreamhunter, and because her father had disappeared. "She's grown
so much," Rose thought. Then, "Will I *ever* catch up with her?"

Rose turned around and tried to find the break in the trees
where the track went up behind the headland. She couldn't
see it at all. She walked to the trees and went along beside
them, stumbling sometimes and skinning her ankles on driftwood, till she found it. Its soft, sandy surface was cold now.
There was dew on the trees flanking the path, and dew on the
lawns of Summerfort. All the lanterns were still alight, but
several of their candles were guttering. The glass doors were
closed on the rapidly cooling air.

Rose went in and ran upstairs. There was a light in Laura's
room. Rose pushed the door open.

Laura was standing at her bureau patting one of the furred,
silvery lamb's-lugs in Rose's flower arrangement. She was
wearing a darned jersey; it was too big for her. She also had
on heavy cotton trousers and rope-soled sandals. Her hair
had grown, so that its uneven lengths made a wide black halo
around her face.

"Hello," Rose said. Then, "The flowers were Ma's idea,"
for some reason finding herself unwilling to admit to all the
trouble she'd taken.

"Doesn't your ma usually just cram them in a vase and leave
it at that?"

"Your hair looks nice. You should let it grow," Rose said,
then immediately regretted her bossiness.

Laura wandered over to the window and eased it up a few inches. She looked out into the blackness. Her look was expectant and yearning. Without turning around, she asked, "How was it at the Doran summerhouse?"

Rose plonked herself down onto the bed. She began to talk breathlessly about the map she'd spotted in Cas Doran's library, its circles representing penumbras, and how, in some of the circles, there were names of dreamhunters who had disappeared. "Or dreamhunters who were supposed to have taken 'early retirement,' " she added. "Gone back to their towns south of The Corridor, or gone abroad. There weren't any big earners among them, no one really distinguished. Da and Ma looked up the names I'd managed to memorize. Ma tried to find them by tracking down their friends and relatives. She'd show up supposedly to return something she'd borrowed. And Da's planning to reconnoiter one of the properties. He wants to see who is in residence. I'd like to do it. I could throw my schoolbag over the wall of 121 Courtesy Street and then sneak in, and if someone caught me I could say that one of my friends tossed my bag over the wall. Da can't do that. What's he going to say? 'I'm sorry, but my silly friend Mr. Brown threw my umbrella into your garden'?"

"Do you think Cas Doran wants to get a whole lot of dreamhunters coloring Founderston's dreams?" Laura asked, frowning. "I thought Colorists were rare, not just because coloring is illegal but because it's difficult to do."

"We have no idea what he means to do. But whatever it is, he's got coverage of practically the whole central city."

Laura came and sat on the bed too. Rose smiled but didn't pause in her talk. She felt that she was trying to lure some shy animal. She told Laura about the constantly replenished piles of narrow-gauge railway materials beside the border. "Ma immediately decided to take a trip to The Pinnacles, but when she made inquiries at the Tricksie Bend rangers' station about the pass, she was told it was closed for repairs."

"Which would support Cas Doran's story about the rails being used to reinforce collapsing banks."

"Except he said the rails were leftovers. That there was just one lot. In which case, they've been sitting there for two years without rusting."

Laura nodded.

"Taken together with the circles on the map, the rails just seem—"

"Yes—there's a rail line." Laura seemed certain. "A rail line Inland. But why? And when the pass is closed, is there just a sign saying 'Danger. Closed for Repairs'?"

"There's a locked gate, apparently. A big, spiked iron gate."

The girls looked at each other, wide-eyed. Rose was so curious about this theoretical railway that she was practically urging Laura to go check it out *right now*.

"I'll go after Christmas," Laura pronounced, as if she was reading her cousin's mind. "I'll take Nown with me, to see how he manages the gate."

Rose's hands went numb, then her feet followed. For a moment she thought she might faint. She stared at her cousin, dumb. "Noun" was the word Laura had yelled at the Rainbow Opera. A monster had come running in answer to Laura's call and had carried her away. The monster had NOWN inscribed on the back of its neck.

After a moment Laura seemed to realize what she'd said. She glanced at Rose's face. She looked startled and sly.

"Your monster," Rose said. "Whose name is Nown."

"He's not a monster. He's a—" Laura paused and pondered. "He's a soul called into different bodies, time and again, throughout history. Bodies made of earth, or fired clay. And once of ash—or so he tells me."

Rose sat with her mouth hanging open. She wanted to ask why Laura was telling her this now when she'd denied it before, at the risk of Rose's great resentment. She said, tentative, "Why did you—?"

Laura didn't let her finish. She seemed eager to talk, eager now to tell. "Why did I make him?"

This wasn't what Rose had intended to ask, but she was distracted by the question. "You *made* him?"

"Yes. That's how he comes to exist. He's made. I *said* that. He's made of sand, or earth, or fired clay, and once of ash. And I think whoever makes him has to need him very badly. And they have to give something up. When Da got on the special train last summer, and I learned he wouldn't be at my Try, I just gave up some of my faith in him. I think I understood that, even without knowing it himself, Da meant to leave me. He meant not to be there for me, at my Try, and then not at all."

"Wait. What do you mean?"

"Da jumped off the pier at Westport. Didn't anyone tell you that?"

"I thought it was an accident." Rose was horrified.

Laura shook her head. "No. And I think I knew. I thought he was letting me down, but I *felt* he was leaving me. I gave up my faith in him. Or rather, my faith left me. But it didn't just blow away like smoke. I saw that rock on the railbed, the rock I just had to pick up. I think I put my lost faith into it, without knowing what it was for. And without knowing what wanting to do that was for. What being *able* to do that was for. Then, much later, I put the rock into Nown's chest when I made him."

"Oh my God!" said Rose. To her eyes it seemed that her cousin was framed by brackets of blue light. Then black patches bloomed on Laura's face and obliterated it altogether.

Rose bent and pressed her face into the coverlet. She felt nothing—for a moment saw and heard nothing. Then her sense of touch came back, and the texture of the embroidery under her cheek. Laura was stroking the back of her neck. "Oh my God!" Rose said again, muffled.

Laura reminded her cousin that she was an atheist.

Rose wriggled violently, like an infant trying to avoid being dressed. Then she sat up. "So your monster doesn't just smash things and run off with girls?"

Laura smiled. It was one of her rare very happy smiles, which, having reached its physical limits in terms of crinkling eyes and curving lips, then seemed to go on to pump light into the air around her. She said, "No. Mostly he just does what I say, but all the time noticing the world in a way that's entirely his own."

Rose opened her mouth to ask something further but was disturbed by a knock on Laura's door. Rose's ma put her head around it. "Rose," Grace said, "you should come say hello to your uncle Tziga. He has to go to bed right after we've had dinner."

Rose clapped her hands to her face. She felt the heat come into her cheeks. She got up and ran downstairs. Laura and Grace came after her, talking—Rose caught snatches of their exchange. "You've grown an inch or so," Grace said. "You'll need new shirts and trousers."

Rose's da and her uncle were sitting in armchairs by the window of the lightless living room. The moon was coming up over the headland at the eastern end of the beach. Rose went to kiss her uncle and first saw the changes in his appearance by moonlight—which made them somehow less terrible. She crouched by his feet, and he took her hands in his.

Chorley said, "We've just been discussing Doran's map and surplus rails."

"Us too," Rose said. She glanced at Laura. "That's what we were talking about."

"That's nice," said Grace, droll. "Now you two pairs of conspirators can get together in a pack. I almost feel sorry for Secretary Doran."

4

✦ ✦ ✦

THE FAMILY HAD SEVERAL DAYS DURING
WHICH, IN THE SPIRIT OF THE SEA-
SON, THEY WERE VERY CAREFUL WITH ONE
another. Rose was now keeping Laura's secret and already felt
she wouldn't have much trouble doing so. She was hardly
likely to talk about something she had such difficulty even
thinking about. When she thought about Laura saying "He's
not a monster, he's a soul," Rose would get dizzy with aston-
ishment.

On Boxing Day the cousins ambled along the seafront to
Farry's. They sat at their favorite table, looking out on Main
Street and its traffic of vacationers in summer finery, ladies
in new hats or gowns, men either dutifully or proudly wearing Christmas present ties and tie pins. The children had new
toys, dolls and dolls' carriages, bats and balls and sailboats,
but they were blotchy and fretful, still recovering from
Christmas Eve sleeplessness.

The cousins ate white chocolate and cardamom ice cream,
and Rose told Laura about what she was now referring to as
her "run-in with Ru Doran." She said, "I don't want to exag-
gerate how upset I was. Especially not with Mamie coming in
a few days."

"I would have been upset too, if it was me," Laura said.

"I keep feeling I should have known how to handle him better. And I shouldn't have complained to Mamie. It was Mamie who made a fuss. She's very loyal to me." Rose touched the high collar of her shirtwaist dress. "Anyway, the whole thing has me dressing differently."

"There are nice boys, Rose. You might want one of the nice ones to notice your figure."

"Maybe nice boys don't notice those things," Rose said.

"Huh!" Laura said. "What's the first thing you notice about a boy?"

Rose scanned the room. The only young men in Farry's that day were the waiters. One caught Rose's eye and came over. "Can I get you ladies anything more?"

"Manners," said Rose to Laura, answering her question.

"Manners are off today, I'm afraid," the waiter said.

The cousins giggled. Laura asked the waiter to bring them some lemonade.

Rose looked sly. She asked Laura, "Do you think Sandy Mason notices your figure?"

Laura said, "I wrote to Sandy, and he didn't write back." She sighed. "I hoped at least he'd get angry at me about the nightmare. I'm sure he must have known it was me. Your ma hasn't said anything yet either."

"Perhaps *you* should say something."

"I can't say sorry without making excuses."

"Yes, I know, you were only doing what your father told you to do."

"Yes." Laura laced and unlaced her fingers. "That's my excuse. I followed my father's instructions. But I wanted what came with his instructions. The spell. I wanted to make myself a sandman."

Rose touched her brow. She could feel it coming—the dizziness, chills, a clench of disgust. It was as if her whole body wanted to shrink away from the altered reality of the world she found herself living in.

Laura studied Rose's face, then turned her eyes down to the tabletop. "I don't have a figure," she said, reverting to their earlier subject. "I think Sandy liked me only because I come from a famous family."

"No, Laura, he really liked you." Rose remembered Sandy Mason's fiery blush, the intensity of his attention when he looked at her cousin. "You should write to him again. You could ask him to visit us at Summerfort. You need all your friends, Laura."

Laura studied her cousin, then said, "I need people." Cool and bland.

"Yes," Rose said, innocent of her own meaning, and of the fact that Laura had understood her meaning—that she needed people rather than her monster.

The lemonade arrived, and they drank it and went back to their traditional summertime occupation of watching the world go by Farry's big bay windows.

✦ ✦ ✦

That evening Grace surprised her family by announcing over tea that it was time they all heard what she had to say. Chorley was possibly the most startled of all of them. He stared at his wife with the white-eyed look of a shying horse but kept his seat.

"Pass your father the sugar bowl," Grace said to Rose.

Rose handed the sugar to Chorley, who helped himself to five lumps and sat back, stirring his cup. The sugar lumps thunked, and the spoon rattled sharply.

Laura got up, went to sit on the footstool beside her father. She took his hand and faced her aunt.

"All right," said Grace. Then she set her cup down and stood up.

"Are you making a public announcement?" Rose said.

"Hush," Grace said to Rose. She looked at her brother-in-law. "Tziga, now that you're not catching those horrible, distorting nightmares, you must be thinking more clearly."

"Yes," Tziga said. "Though sometimes I forget what it is I've thought clearly."

"I know that. But my point is, you must be able to see now that your plan, such as it was, wasn't a very good one."

"The papers didn't publish Lazarus's letters," Chorley said, defending Tziga.

Grace stamped her foot. "I don't want to hear any of you refer to 'Lazarus' *ever* again. I might have to maintain that silly fiction in public, but I refuse to do so in my own home!"

Laura said, "I'm sorry I overdreamed you. It's not Da's fault."

Tziga squeezed Laura's hand. "It *is* my fault. I wasn't thinking straight."

"But it's also wrong to give a nightmare like Buried Alive to convicts to make them behave, and slave away in the Westport mine," Laura said.

"Yes, Laura, but is giving the St. Lazarus's Eve patrons a nightmare about being buried alive any way to change that?" Grace said.

"I think you're being naïve, Ma," Rose said.

Grace flushed. She glared at her daughter.

"Think of Doran's map," Rose said. "Think of what he's planning to do."

"What *is* he planning to do?" Grace set her hands on her hips.

"Use your imagination."

Grace rounded on Chorley. "Are you going to let your daughter talk to me like that?"

"Rose, please be more polite to your mother."

"And you—" Grace went on, speaking to her husband now. "You could ask your good friend the Grand Patriarch what *he's* planning to do about Doran and the Regulatory Body. Except, of course, it isn't the Body the Grand Patriarch dislikes, it's dreamhunters."

"That's not true," Tziga said, softly.

"The Regulatory Body has been around for a little over ten years," Chorley said. "Have you ever heard of any institution becoming as powerful as the Body has within such a short time? Even Christianity didn't manage it."

"Napoleon?" said Rose, as though she were doing a quiz. She was ignored.

"That's beside the point," Grace said. "You seem to think Doran has a plan. And you also think—rather trustingly—that the Grand Patriarch has a plan."

"He has vigorous suspicion," Chorley said. "He acts on his suspicions. He hides dreamhunters who come to him for help."

"And how many of those 'disappearing' dreamhunters that you and Rose have been talking about have been disappeared by the Church rather than the Regulatory Body?" Grace said. "After all, the Church didn't tell us where Tziga was."

"They weren't sure I'd recover," Tziga said. "And the Body didn't tell you what had happened to me either."

"True," said Grace. "And the Church did help you. I understand that you feel you owe the Grand Patriarch. And I know you're a churchgoer—a believer. It *is* different for you, Tziga. But Chorley thinks he's doing research for the Grand Patriarch. He's taking it all very seriously. When really it's just another one of his bloody hobbies!"

There was a moment of silence; then Chorley dropped his teacup into its saucer, got up, and walked out.

"Ma!" Rose said.

Grace's eyes glazed over with tears. "Why doesn't anyone ever listen to me?"

"Please don't cry, Ma," Rose said, distressed.

"You're going to start trespassing on properties in Founderston looking for clues," Grace said to Rose, and began to sob. "Your father has got you thinking that it's all right to break the law if it's for a good cause."

Rose went to her mother and hugged her. "Well, I won't, Ma. I'll let Da do it."

"You all act as though you've been appointed to save the world," Grace said, still sobbing.

"I was only trying to mend my mistakes—mistakenly," Tziga said, sadly.

Laura just sat, wearing a dazzled, radiant expression.

"There, there," Rose said to her mother.

"What's so wrong with our lives anyway?" Grace said, querulous. "Why do you all have to be such damn rebels?"

"I'm not," said Rose.

"It does," said Laura. "The world does need saving. Or, at least, I *think* it's the world."

Everyone looked at her. Then Chorley came back into the room, and everyone looked at him instead. He was carrying one of his notebooks and a pen, so vigorously dipped in ink that the fingers of his right hand were tipped brilliant scarlet. He gave the notebook to Grace and said, "If you will, dear, could you please read aloud the passages I have underlined?"

Grace gave him a look of dread but did as she was told. She spoke softly, stammered once or twice, but read: "Rise up! Rise up! I said to rise! Crush them! Rise up and overturn everything! Find your feet and get up! Shake them all off! I said, Get up! I said, Rise up now!"

Chorley said, "I found those within only seventy pages of bad messages from the abandoned Founderston-to-Sisters-Beach telegraph line. Sometimes there's just the odd, plaintive 'crush' or 'rise' or 'shake.' 'Plaintive' is the right word. These are complaints, angry complaints."

"What about the poetry?" Rose said.

"It seems there are two voices," Chorley said. "One complains, the other seems to be in an ecstasy of anticipation."

Grace held the notebook out, and her husband took it. "Dear," he said, "I do feel that I'm blundering around in the dark. I do feel like a dim-witted dilettante. But I don't think I'm wasting my time."

Tziga added, hesitantly, "What Laura did to you, Grace, and to the rest of the Rainbow Opera's patrons, she did because I told her to when I wasn't in my right mind. I don't trust my judgment anymore, but I do trust Chorley's."

"It may all really matter, Ma," Rose said. "What we choose to do might make a big difference."

Chorley kept his eyes on his wife's face. "I promised the Grand Patriarch my time in exchange for his telling me where Tziga was. I'm honoring a promise."

"Marta knew too, and she chose not to tell you," Tziga said. "They thought I might not live. And they thought I knew more about the Body and Doran than I did, that I was in deeper with the Body than I was. And they supposed I knew more about the Place, as though it was a deity and I was its prophet. An evil deity, with an evil prophet," Tziga added, then put a hand over his face.

Chorley started and hurried to him.

"It's all right, Da," Laura said.

Chorley said, "You should be resting, Tziga." They helped him up and walked him slowly from the room. For a time they could be heard making soothing sounds as they helped him up the stairs.

Rose and Grace looked at each other.

"You do know I'm not siding with Da against you," Rose said. "Ma, you're determined we stop snooping only because you're afraid we'll get into trouble. You're just as sure as we are that the Body is up to no good."

"But why does it have to be our problem?" Grace asked.

"Because we know about it."

5

✦ ✦ ✦

*J*UST THREE DAYS LATER GRACE FOUND
HERSELF PRESIDING OVER A VERY DIF-
FERENT HOUSEHOLD.

Chorley came in with an armload of parcels while the girls
were having their breakfast. He turned back the cloth at one
end of the table and put the parcels down, and Grace laughed
as Rose practically climbed over Mamie to grab one and tear it
open. Dress patterns and samples of cloth spilled out onto
the tabletop, some of the swatches of silk crepe so light that
they seemed to skate on cushions of air, speeding across the
polished table and onto the floor. Mamie and Rose snatched
and tussled. Laura gathered up the dropped swatches and
started to hand over the pearls, and pure whites, and oysters,
and creams.

"I'll look awful in all of these," Mamie said, with no hint of
her usual aloof sarcasm.

"Oh no, let's see, there must be something suitable." Grace
got up to join them.

"I'm going to choose a plain design." Rose was sorting
through the patterns. "Something only I can wear." She drew
herself up to her full five foot ten. "And I am *not* going to
show off my bosom."

"At least you have a choice about that," said Mamie, and

crossed her arms over her large breasts, as though hoping to push them back into her body.

Rose shuffled patterns. "I'm sure we can find something pretty and becoming for you."

"But am I becoming?" Mamie raised an eyebrow.

Grace and Rose nodded earnestly.

Mamie looked away. "I'm becoming bored."

Laura, who had been standing stock-still and staring out the glass doors of the dining room, spun around and said, "Excuse me, Mamie. Could I borrow Rose for a moment?"

"She's not mine to lend," Mamie said.

Laura grabbed her cousin's hand and opened the doors.

"Come into the garden, Maud," muttered Mamie as the other two went out.

❖ ❖ ❖

"What is it?" said Rose, then found herself performing a little hop to avoid tripping over some stones—five of them— that had been laid, in a neat row, on the bottom step of the veranda.

Laura let go of Rose to push the stones under the step.

"What?" Rose demanded.

"I'm sure that's a sign," Laura said. She took hold of Rose, led her to the edge of the lawn, and began stooping to peer under bushes.

"What are we looking for?" Rose said, and began to search too—pausing once to dive into a bush and retrieve a croquet ball.

Laura continued to work her way around the house. Then she started down the track to the lagoon. She said, over her shoulder, "He won't be too near the water."

A moment later Laura had to double back for Rose, who had stopped following.

Her cousin pulled at her, but Rose stood firm.

"Don't be scared," said Laura. "He won't hurt you."

"No. No. No," Rose said, and wriggled to shake off Laura's grip. But she didn't make any move to go back up to the house.

Laura let go and faced Rose. "You wanted to know. This is the only way you are ever going to come near to knowing."

Rose said, "I've seen it. I can believe my eyes."

"You should *meet* him."

Rose could feel the blood in her head—indignation, fear, and fury. She told her cousin, "People don't meet monsters. No one offers introductions to monsters."

"Aren't you even curious?"

Rose was quiet, thinking about that. Laura waited, looking so anxious for approval that Rose wanted to smack her. Rose began down the path again. Laura gave a little gasp of relief and darted on ahead, searching the trees. Rose felt she was out walking a silly young dog.

Laura's monster was hiding in the filmy gloom under a tall weeping willow. At first it was hard to see, utterly still, and of a dun shade similar to the tree trunk. But when Laura flung the willow fronds aside, it stirred, and the light scintillated on its sandy skin. Rose saw Laura take one of its hands, her fist closing around a big thumb. She drew the monster out.

Rose backed away as it approached. Laura was between them, her face glowing with love, but the monster was so huge, so competent in its movements, so uncanny, that Rose could not hold her ground.

"This is Rose," Laura said to her monster, who continued

to look down on the top of Laura's head, then into her face as she turned back and *glowed* up at it.

"She looks so proud of me you'd think she'd made me too," Rose said. She heard how steady her voice was and felt a little braver.

Laura laughed. She said to her monster, "Were the rivers and streams a problem on your way back?"

"It hasn't rained, and they are smaller," the monster replied.

Rose thought that no one could ever mistake that voice for human. It was too dry. There was no moisture, no *flesh*, involved in it. The sound wasn't even animal—yet those were words. Rose shivered but continued to stand her ground.

"Let your cousin go back to the house," the monster said. "You must have things you need to tell me, Laura."

Laura looked disappointed, as if she'd hoped they would all sit down together and have a conversation. She looked at Rose, then back up at her monster. "But the things I have to tell you are about discoveries *Rose* has made. We think that the Regulatory Body has built a rail line into the Place. We thought that you and I should go look at it, and see where it goes."

The monster did not move its eyes. It didn't glance up at Rose for confirmation, as any person would have. It hadn't looked at her at all, she was sure. The only indication she had that it knew she was there was that it had spoken to Laura about her. It wasn't as though the monster was being rude; Rose didn't feel snubbed, as she would have if a person had treated her this way. She just felt that she wasn't the monster's business—that she was *so* not its business that her existence was minimal to it. "Laura," she said, "you talk. You make plans."

"Am I to set out somewhere?" the monster said, to Laura.

"Tonight will be safer than today. Where shall we meet?"

Laura clutched the monster's arm and pulled. It didn't lean into her. It was immovable. Her feet slid on the gritty ground till she was pressed against its side. "Don't go right away," she said. "You just came."

"I said tonight, not today."

"You must be tired."

"Now you are being silly, Laura."

Laura laughed again. She sounded very happy.

Rose said to her cousin, "I will leave you to give your—sandman—directions." Then, "He does follow orders, doesn't he?"

"Oh," Laura said, and laughed some more. Then she collected herself and said, "Well, obviously. He's here, isn't he?"

"Here," thought Rose, "and shouldn't be. Shouldn't exist." But she said, "I'll leave you to talk." She backed away from the willow. She kept backing, kept the monster in sight for a time before turning and hurrying up the hill to the house.

IV
The Depot

1

✦ ✦ ✦

*T*EN DAYS LATER, LAURA MADE HER
RENDEZVOUS WITH NOWN A LITTLE
EAST OF THE LAST REGULAR TRAIN STOP AT
Morass River. They began their journey, weaving In and out
across the border. Inside, they tramped through dry but un-
touched and upstanding meadows, Nown going before Laura
and treading the stalks down. The going was easy. Every few
minutes they would stop and listen for signs of other travelers. The trail was deserted.

As they went, Laura gazed Inland, across the grasslands to a
line of low hills, all in graduated shades of beige. Sometimes
she turned her eyes toward what she could see beyond the
border, an endless haze of meadow that faded away to a
creamy sky. Laura knew that if she walked in that direction she would cross back into the green world. But, as she
gazed, she began to imagine facing a second kind of Try, in
which she would find that the reliable border had vanished,
and she'd never be able to get out again. She saw this so
clearly that she had to check, to walk toward the border—

—where she found herself on a path that ran along a bluff
above one of the many brilliant blue coves in Coal Bay's
notched curve. The sun was hot and had raised all the perfume of the forest.

Nown stepped out beside her. Almost onto her, since she

hadn't moved to make room for him. She teetered, and he caught and steadied her.

A light wind was hissing through the scrub and flax between the track and the coast. The sea was calm, the waves idle and sleepy. But it seemed noisy after the Place. Laura said, "We won't hear anyone coming along this track. We'll be caught. And your eyesight is better in there, isn't it?" She said all this but didn't really want to go back In.

"It's only because there's less to see that people are highly visible there," Nown said. "Laura, we'll make better progress on this side of the border. And if I carry you, then you can listen while I walk."

Of course Laura went to sleep in Nown's arms and didn't wake till his gait changed. He was stepping from boulder to boulder along a beach heaped with stones ranging from fist-sized to elephantine. "I think I'll stay where I am for now," Laura said, and tightened her arms around his neck. "Don't drop me." She knew he wouldn't, said it only to savor how safe she felt.

Nown said, "I want to beat the tide. To get around that headland before the sea comes up."

Laura wondered what it was like for him, stalking along the edge of a sea that was invisible to him except as a hole in the world, a void that gradually came up to engulf the path on which he made his way. She asked, "Does the sea frighten you?"

"The tide is reliable. And none of these bluffs is too steep to climb."

"But doesn't it unnerve you? Don't you feel threatened? Don't you think, 'What if a big wave comes?' "

"No," Nown said. "I don't know that I have an imagination." He gripped Laura firmly and vaulted up a rocky spur in several strides, launching himself across gaps lined with kelp and thickly beaded with green-lipped mussels. A high swell pushed into a gap and, white with trapped air, lunged at Nown's legs. Laura squeezed her eyes closed and pressed her face against his gritty neck.

✦ ✦ ✦

By late afternoon they had rounded the headland at the western end of the Awa Inlet. The tide was still high, and they faced a wide sweep of water. Far away across the Inlet was the lacework of a railway trestle across a river. Beyond that they could see the thick forest in the rain shadow at the back of the Inlet and, against the dark hills, the blond stone of the Doran summer house, shining in the low sun.

"We should go as far as that long bridge over the river mouth, then turn back In," Laura said. "If I sleep soon, I can be up again before midnight. And I'm sure we can get from the bridge to the house between four and dawn, at your speed."

Nown pointed at the water directly below them, at a channel, blue between two submerged sandbars. "What is that?"

"I don't know what you mean," Laura said, looking at it. Then she realized. "Oh, damn—there are *two* rivers. That's the Sva going out through the reedbeds way over there. The Rifleman must be hidden behind this headland. I've gone past here in the train dozens of times, but it all looks different." She could see that the water in the channel was moving very fast. Even if they waited for the tide to go all the way out, the river would still be there, pushing against the cliff on the far side of the headland.

"The channel is a colder nothingness," Nown said, to explain how he'd picked out the river from the surrounding seawater. "It is even more nothing."

Laura said, "The rail line is in a tunnel here. After the tunnel it runs along a ledge above the river and turns onto a bridge." She pointed at the hill they stood on. "The tunnel runs through this hill, and the bridge must be just beyond it."

She knew the view out the train windows very well, the long curve of graded track that passed down a channel of rock roughly formed by dynamite, then chiseled out by the pick-axes of—she now knew—convict laborers. The bridge over the Rifleman was iron, and very strong. It had to be. The Rifle-man was a short river, fed by streams draining from a range of rainy mountains. It arrived at the sea swift, chilly, and full. Ten miles farther along the rail line was the other, bleached-ironwood structure, which picked its way across the braided channels and low sandbanks of the Sva mouth. The Sva where it reached the sea was a much gentler river than the Rifleman, its stream hastened only a little as its valley narrowed between the foothills and solitary Mount Kahaugh.

Laura said, "Put me down."

Nown lowered her to the ground, and she leaned against him and stretched and shook her legs to get her blood moving again. Then she took his hand to encourage him and began to scramble up the hill through the scrub, grabbing at the slen-der trunks of Hebes and brilliant waxed sea laurel. She let go of Nown to haul herself up the steepest part of the slope. She could hear him following her, the foliage making a flinty scraping against his hardened body.

Laura reached the top of the hill and went on carefully af-ter that, peering till she saw where the scrub abruptly came to an end. She crept forward and arrived at a drop. She craned over and saw the brick buttresses of the tunnel mouth and the railway line twenty-five feet below.

She turned to Nown. "If we climb down beside the tunnel,

we can go along the track and cross the bridge. It's the quickest route." Then, "Can you see in the dark?"

"I don't know dark, Laura. 'Dark' is what you say to explain not being able to see."

"Oh," said Laura. She lay down on her stomach, unscrewed the copper cap of her water bottle, and held the bottle under a steadily dripping fringe of moss. Her arm tired, but she managed to get a drink.

"I have water," Nown said, and shook one of the two big skins he carried.

"I'll need that later, when we go In."

Laura rolled back from the bluff and onto her sandman's feet. She pulled at his arm to let him know she wanted him to sit. He folded himself carefully into the little space there was, branches snapping as he lowered himself onto them. "I'm going to sleep for a while," Laura said. "Please make sure I don't roll off the drop."

He lifted one leg and placed it, crooked, over her body. She rearranged herself, her back to the drop and her head pillowed on his other foot. She said, sleepy, "You know to stay still, don't you?"

"Yes, Laura."

She closed her eyes and let herself drift off.

✣ ✣ ✣

Laura slept for a few hours and woke up, stiff and cold. The sun had gone, and Nown was nearly the same temperature as the air. It was summer, but she had let herself fall asleep on the ground without wrapping herself in her bedroll.

Though all the sunset color had gone, the sky in the west

had a pithy pallor, and there was still enough light for Nown
and Laura to climb safely down the bluff onto the track.

The tunnel mouth breathed at their backs, smelling of wet
brick and coal smoke.

They began on down the long, shallow incline of the track.
Both were walking as far from the drop as they could, Laura
leading and Nown following. They stepped from tie to tie and
built up quite a rhythm, hurrying, only sometimes steadying
themselves against a pickax-pockmarked rock of the cliff face.

They reached the place where the track turned away from
the cliff. It ran onto an iron trestle that curved to join the
span of the rail bridge. There was nowhere to pause and step
off the track. Still, Laura put her hand back to halt Nown. He
stopped instantly at her touch, didn't blunder into her as
most people would have. She glanced back and saw him
frozen with one foot raised. He looked like a photograph of
himself.

Laura listened to the night. She couldn't hear the river.
The tide was high, slack, and silent. She heard one of the little rain-forest owls giving its two-note cry. She heard oyster-
catchers out over the Inlet. She didn't hear any trains.

Laura stepped onto the bridge. It wasn't a very long span,
probably no more than fifty yards. It was easier to walk on
than the track by the cliff had been; there were girders under
the timber ties of the bridge, a firm skin of rivet-studded
iron. It was a good surface, and Laura hurried.

Then she stopped again to listen. The headland behind
them was booming. Laura looked back at Nown, her eyes
wide.

An engine burst from the tunnel, braked on the incline,
and came sliding and panting down the track toward them.

Laura took off. She closed the distance between herself and
safety—but then her foot slipped and she sprawled across the

tracks, slamming her elbow hard. Her arm lost all feeling, then seemed to fizzle back into existence as if it was breaking out of a numbing foam.

Nown reached her, scooped her up, and ran with her. She saw the train over his shoulder, looming onto the bridge, its light sweeping an engine length ahead of its long cowcatcher. Laura screamed. Nown swerved off the tracks and pushed her through two crisscrossed girders onto the outside of the bridge. He stretched up and over one girder to lower her onto another that jutted from the plane of the bridge. Laura's feet touched the girder, then took her weight. She stood balanced. She tried to pull herself free from Nown's grip. Her arms were stretched over her head, wrists closed together in one of his hands. She could see his face through a gap in the bridge structure, close to her own and sidelit by the growing yellow light of the train. She shouted at him. "Get off the bridge!" She couldn't hear hear own voice over the thunder of the train.

Nown released her arms, and she folded up into a crouch, her palms and boot soles clinging to the girder. The bridge was jolting under her.

Nown stooped and began to ooze through the gap below the one he had rolled her through. Laura saw his head and arms emerge whole and shapely, then his chest and hips follow, extruded like icing piped through a square nozzle.

Laura closed her eyes against the glare of the engine. The train sounded its whistle, then blasted past. She was sprayed with sand. The train's violent jolting dislodged her from the girder. She slipped, scrabbled for a hold, then dropped off. She opened her eyes as she fell, glimpsed the underside of the bridge and a cloud of sand fanning out into the air and already drawing back in thickening eddies toward the shadow that was Nown.

Laura fell into the river. It was cold and salty. Her eardrums stabbed with pain, and her back felt slapped red even through her jacket and shirt. Her pack and bedroll were pulling her down, so she wriggled out of the straps, let her pack go, and kicked up to the surface. She blinked the water out of her eyes and looked back at the bridge.

Nown was visible, in silhouette, backlit by the flashing yellow squares of carriage windows and the straight, sweeping shadows of the bridge structure. He seemed to be poised, looking her way, as if about to jump into the water after her.

She opened her mouth and shouted at him. "No!" Then she realized as she shouted that Nown might imagine she was calling for help. She trod water for a moment longer, then turned and struck out at an angle for the far bank. She headed away from the middle of the stream and—she could tell by the solid power of the water—the current pushing by the bluff and out to sea, even against the full tide.

The train had passed over the bridge. Its thunder diminished. Laura stopped swimming and looked back again. Nown was still there, leaning out over the water, looking after her. Laura swam on.

Suddenly there was a solid shelf under her hands; her hands first, her feet couldn't seem to find it, as if it really was a ledge rather than the bank. It couldn't be the bank anyway—Laura could see the bank, still some twenty yards from where she was, a pale beach scalloped by the river and tide and topped by a tangle of driftwood. But there was *something* under her hands, something solid and strangely furry, like thick dust. She heaved and scrambled up onto it. The crown of her head was touched by heat, then she tumbled out into the bright, diffuse light of the Place. She was soaking, and water ran from her hair and clothes and made thick fawn mud of the dusty ground she lay on.

Laura stood up. She started to laugh. She stood, dripping and hiccuping with mirth. Of course she had known that the bridge was built as far upriver as it could be without crossing the border, but she hadn't imagined that the train line she had traveled on so many times, back and forth to Summerfort, was only yards from that border.

She gave herself a good shake. She wondered how far she'd have to walk along the border to clear the river. She made an arbitrary decision—an hour would do it. Before she set out, she held her watch to her ear and was relieved to hear it making its usual sharp, dry tick—it hadn't been damaged by its dunking.

*L*AURA STAYED IN LONG ENOUGH TO DRY OFF. SHE FINALLY EMERGED ABOVE THE BEACH BY THE RIVER. THE TIDE had dropped and the moon come up. Laura could see the river's current muscled in the moonlight.

Nown unfolded from the beach, shedding sand that wasn't his. As he came toward her, Laura saw at once that he was a little shorter and more slender than before. "Did the train hit you?" she asked.

"My feet," he said. "I lost some of them." He spoke as though he were a centipede and had plenty to spare. "The train carried part of my feet away with it. When I continued along the track, I found some sand—but I couldn't persuade it that it was me anymore."

"You look younger," Laura said.

Nown's head reared back with surprise. "How?"

"Less bulky, I suppose." Laura ran a hand down his arm. She stepped close to him to measure herself against him. The top of her head had formerly come to his sternum; now it came to his collarbone.

Nown said, "I saw you disappear. But I was sure that you didn't go under—then certain of it when I went on."

"Went on *where*?"

"Went on existing, Laura. I waited not to exist—though I

did think you had gone into the Place, not under the river. Then, when I did go on existing, I went on walking too, along the bridge to look for the rest of my feet."

Laura shook her head. They were always having these strange conversations. She asked him, "Do you still have the water skins?"

Nown pointed at a single skin on the ground nearby. "When the train came, I flung them over onto the far shore. One burst."

"Damn."

"And you've lost your pack and bedroll, Laura."

"Yes."

"Then shouldn't we go back?"

"Oh, no! Let's go on to the Doran property. Rose said there was an orchard. I can steal some fruit. We should at least take a look In to see where those rails have gone."

Nown picked up the surviving water skin, then Laura, and began to make his way around the shore of the Inlet.

✣ ✣ ✣

Near dawn they crossed the ironwood trestle over the braided channels of the Sva mouth—without encountering another train. Then they turned toward the back of the Inlet, walking on the hard-packed sand beside a channel through reedbeds, where the warmth of the previous day was still trapped in the thick fur of stalks.

At sunup they found the Dorans' jetty, and the beginning of the narrow-gauge railway. A little while later Laura spotted the orchard. She asked Nown to put her down and sprinted toward the trees. She could see clusters of apricots and black plums with a white bloom on them.

But before she reached the orchard, she ran through the

border and into the Place. She swore. Her voice came back at her instantly, a single flat reverberation, from a mass of crumbling gray landforms that rose abruptly about a quarter mile from the hummocky meadow where she stood.

The Pinnacles—eroded, crooked spikes—stretched out along the horizon, a barrier made, apparently, from heaps of sculpted ash. The peaks looked as fragile as piles of old leaf litter held together by spiderwebs.

Behind her Nown said, "I can't climb that."

Rose had said there was a gate. Laura guessed that she and Nown had come In beyond where it was, simply by turning off toward the orchard rather than continuing up the avenue of plane trees. She asked, "How much water do we have?"

Nown handed her the water skin, and she weighed it—it was several days' ration. But she was without food.

Laura fished in her pockets and found only a tin of Farry's Extra-Strong Licorice Pellets (Recommended for Regularity). "Oh, great," she muttered. Why couldn't she have been carrying mints or barley sugar? She said, "I'll have another nap here, then see how far we can get on this much water and without food." Laura stared at Nown, her finer-limbed and slightly less overbearing sandman. "And I suppose I could send you on farther to take a look *for* me."

"You could," he said.

"We'll see."

"Yes, we will see what you decide," he said.

Laura hadn't expected him to respond at all. And she was even more surprised when he expanded. "You are the one who needs to eat, Laura. And you are the one who needs to know."

Perhaps he was chastising her for saying "we"—saying it and not meaning it, because she was the one with a mission, and he only had to look after her. She said, "Are you angry with me?"

"I'm never angry."

"Then I don't understand what you're trying to say."

Nown was silent, and Laura knew he was thinking because the iron sand gathered in his eye sockets and on his brow. After a time he said, "If you send me to look, you may not be satisfied with my report. You and I see everything differently."

Laura nodded. She was only partly paying attention while casting around her for a bit of ground without bumps, somewhere to bed down. The grass was in very bad condition, not just flattened but shredded. As she scuffed at the humps on the ground, Laura listened to Nown once more giving examples of things he saw. Because she was listening with only half an ear, it took her a while to realize that he was almost singing. Singing without a tune.

"You are a web of light," he said. "You are the shape you are. Trees stream upward, grasses lance, fire billows and makes a flaw of light. The sea is where there isn't anything, but gannets go like spears into it, and fly up again from nothing—"

"You made a poem!" Laura said.

"—sometimes with a fish," Nown concluded, less poetically.

Laura chose a relatively even patch of bare ground. She asked for the water skin, swallowed a few mouthfuls, and lay down. She yawned till her jaw joints cracked. She tried to remember the poems she'd learned for examinations in elocution lessons, and those she'd learned at school. She lay with her eyes closed and recited the few fragments she knew by heart. "A slumber did my spirit seal; / I had no human fears . . ." And "She is coming, my own, my sweet; / Were it ever so airy a tread . . ." Then, as she drifted off to sleep, she heard Nown repeating it all back to her, word perfect. And she thought, "He really does remember everything I say."

✧ ✧ ✧

Laura woke later, in the Place's unchanging light. Nown was standing sentinel beside her, facing west, the direction from which people could most likely be expected to appear. She got up, said, "Stay here," and wandered off to find a bush to squat behind.

Instead, she found a grave.

It was a long, low mound, of the same size and shape as earth piled up on a fresh grave.

Laura shouted for Nown. Her shout echoed from The Pinnacles.

Nown came at a swift run. He saw that she wasn't in any danger and stopped beside her, anxiously searching her face till he noticed the direction of her gaze.

They contemplated the grave together.

"Why would anyone choose to be buried in the Place instead of being taken back to their family?" Laura asked, haunted and horrified. "To their family," she thought, "and trees, grass, rain, day and night, church bells and birdsong."

"This might not be choice, Laura."

"Do you mean that someone was murdered? But this isn't a secret grave. It's here in plain sight—even if only dream-hunters and rangers can see it."

"There's no marker."

"No." Laura's skin was clammy and her scalp tight. "Nown—could you see if there was someone *alive* in there? Could you see their . . . web of light, under the earth?"

"No. I can't see the gannets once they go into the water. I

couldn't see your body in the river, only your head, and your arms moving in and out as you swam."

Laura moaned.

"Are you thinking of your nightmare?"

Laura clenched her jaw and nodded once, sharply.

"Shall I dig it up for you?"

Laura grabbed her sandman's arm, though he'd made no move to start digging. She shook her head. She didn't want to see any corpses. Since grass didn't grow in the Place, there was no way to tell how long ago the earth had been piled up over whatever lay beneath it. "Let's just go," she said. She turned away to find somewhere else to make herself comfortable. She didn't look back. She didn't see Nown pause, long, his gaze apparently penetrating the disturbed earth as if, perhaps, he could see what lay there.

Who lay there.

3

✦ ✦ ✦

HE GATE TO THE PASS THROUGH THE PINNACLES WAS CLOSED. THERE WAS NO ONE BEYOND IT ON GUARD—NO ONE ANY-where around. The gate was made of black iron, a plain, workmanlike thing, bolted together and set into two short walls of mortared brick. The walls were pressed right up against the sides of the pass.

The Pinnacles themselves were perhaps only a hundred and fifty feet high, but steep and unstable. No one with any sense would think to set foot on their mealy gray slopes. There was no grass or scrub on them. It was as though they, like the grave, had come into existence after the grass had grown (and had stopped growing), as if they had bubbled up through the ground and set, a belt of brittle peaks.

A length of chain was wrapped around the joined sides of the gate. The chain was fastened with a padlock.

Laura put her face to a gap in the bars and looked along the pass at a road sprinkled here and there with hunks of fallen earth but otherwise swept smooth.

Behind her Nown said, "If you step out of the way, I'll break it open for you."

Laura took several steps back. Nown seized hold of the bars and began to shake the gate, pulling back and thrusting for-ward with his whole weight. At first he moved as if he were a

body with muscles; then he began to move faster than any human body could. The gate clanged and boomed. The noise set
off slides on the sides of the pass. It looked as if The Pinnacles were melting. Laura glanced around but saw no one. The
din the gates were making would be audible for miles.

Finally, in the racket, there came a sharp, metallic crack.
One of the hinges had broken, so that half of the gate sagged.
Nown said, "Can you climb that?"

She nodded.

He picked her up and boosted her into the gap. She scrambled, then lowered herself over the top of the gate, hung on
for a moment, and dropped. She backed away and waited for
Nown to join her. He tossed her the water skin, then
swarmed up the slope of the bars and tumbled over, landing
with a thump that shook the ground at Laura's feet. He got
up. They stood still for a moment, listening to pattering falls
of earth. Before them the surface of the road was no longer
smooth but blistered with debris.

Nown and Laura began along the path, she now and then
jumping and scuttling aside from small rushes of dislodged
pebbles. They walked softly for fear of shaking down the walls
above them. They didn't speak.

Laura thought it was reasonable to assume that the gate was
closed only for safety, when The Pinnacles Pass was in poor
repair, or when the Body was transporting materials for the
secret railway of Rose's theory. So, Laura realized that, because the gate was closed, she and Nown were likely to en-
counter other people—making repairs or carrying rails. At
any moment, they might round a corner and run into a party
of rangers hurrying back to see what had made all the awful
noise. She should have a plan in case someone appeared.
Things had been going badly—she'd lost her bedroll, her
food, one water skin; she'd missed the fruit; and Nown had

lost part of his feet—though the ones on which he was walking looked almost exactly the same, if a little smaller. She should decide what to do if she and Nown did run into rangers. She racked her brain. Eventually, she spoke. "Nown?" she asked.

"Yes, Laura?"

"If we meet any rangers, could you—um—render them unconscious?"

He was silent.

"Could you—?"

"Are you sure?"

"Unconscious. Yes." Laura was annoyed. Nown was acting like a responsible adult again. "Do you have any other suggestions?"

Nown was quiet for a long time, then he said, "You could shout at them: 'Run for your lives, my nightmare has gotten loose!'"

Laura laughed. It was silly but seemed less chancy than her plan.

Her sandman added, "I'm not sure that I know how hard to hit a man to make him unconscious. I could try putting a hand over his mouth, but then I could deal with only one man at a time." He sounded practical.

"All right. We'll try your idea. Maybe that should be a contingency plan if we meet another dreamhunter or ranger."

"Even your friend Sandy?"

Laura fell silent, thinking of her unanswered letters. She was going along with her head down and so missed the branch in the path. She stopped only when Nown called out to her. She looked up and saw that he was standing beside another closed and locked iron gate while she was paces along the open path.

The path they had already traveled had twisted and turned so much that Laura had lost her usual vague east-west orien-

tation (the feeling that, since she was on this border of the
Place, and facing In, Tricksie Bend lay somewhere west on
her right-hand side). Laura was sure that the path she was on
was the trail from the map she'd studied. A trail that led to
Sanctuary Valley, a spread of open grassland containing a handful of commercial dream sites, the only official destination
beyond The Pinnacles, and the only reason the Regulatory
Body maintained a pass through those dangerous peaks.
There'd been no sign on the map Laura looked at that the
trail branched anywhere beyond the gate. And yet Nown was
standing by another gate, which blocked the way onto another
trail.

This gate had a sign on it: DETOUR ROUTE. CLOSED APRIL
1905 BY ORDER OF EUGENE PARKER, CHIEF RANGER.

"Break it open," Laura said.

The second gate was far stronger than the first, and Nown
had to resort to rushing at it, crashing into it with his shoulder. The trail at this point was so narrow that even though
Laura stood in the middle of the intersection, the myriad
slides set off by her sandman's impacts on the gate spilled debris right to her feet. Every hillside was shivering and shedding stones and earth. The air filled with gray dust. Laura
closed her eyes, covered her mouth, and crouched down,
coughing. She felt the wind of Nown's swift passage again.
There was a louder crash, the squawk of iron tearing, the
singing rattle of a chain unraveling, a series of ringing clangs,
then nothing but the bubbling whisper of crumbling earth.

Laura staggered up and peered through the dust, her eyes
streaming.

Nown was extracting himself from the fallen gate. He
turned to her and held up the broken chain, which appeared
to be giving off a fine blue smoke, quite distinct in the dust-
filled air. "Smoke, without sparks," he said, apparently im-

pressed. "And the old saying has it that there is never smoke without fire."

Laura laughed, then coughed and pulled her shirt collar up over her mouth. She went to her sandman and pushed him forward. He stepped onto and across the fallen gate, then turned back to give her a hand.

The supposedly abandoned detour route was narrow, its sides so close together that they seemed to arch over the trail. It was gloomy in the winding pit of the pass. Because there was no direct sunlight in the Place, there were never any shadows, only degrees of bright, misty obscurity. But here, between the close walls of The Pinnacles, shadows seemed to have pooled, a thin stain of gloom.

Laura followed Nown, one hand against his back, which was warm, as if, in his recent furious activity, the grains of sand in his body, chafing together, had woken heat. He felt the same as he did when sun-warmed. It was reassuring and kept Laura from—from whatever it was that seemed to live along that squeezed trail.

The dread Laura felt seemed alive, and to come from outside her. She'd felt it earlier, when she'd stood looking at the grave on the border. She had thought then that her dread was only the memory of the nightmare Buried Alive, and of the howling, thumping, flower-covered grave in The Water Diviner, the dream she'd caught with Sandy. But the atmosphere in the abandoned detour trail was exactly like that of the grave. It had a sense of something stopped, and powerless, and profoundly miserable, but still *there*, like the afterlife of despair.

"I hate it here," Laura muttered to Nown.

He said, "I hope I won't have to break another gate. The walls are too close." Then he spun around, gathered her into

his arms, and carried her. She closed her eyes and pressed her
face into his neck.

After only another half hour, Nown came to a halt. He
stood so still that it was as though he'd become inanimate, a
real statue. Laura lifted her head and saw that he had stopped
before a platform built of timber and bolted steel, and topped
by some kind of apparatus. Laura wriggled, and Nown set her
down.

There was a cage on the platform, a chest-high box covered
in steel mesh. It had a gate at the front and rods rising from
its top corners. The rods joined in an apex above the box.
There was a hook attached to the apex, and the hook was
locked to a cable.

Laura tipped her head back to follow the cable up from the
platform to another identical platform, diminished and distant on the leveled summit of a high pinnacle.

The rangers had built themselves a cable car.

Lying around in the widening of the trail before the platform were chains, a small pile of rails bundled in thick straps,
large, heavy canvas sheets with steel-reinforced eyelets at all
four corners, and all sorts of other signs—an overlapping
melee of boot prints, greasy rags, dropped work gloves—that
rangers had been hard at work here lifting loads to that summit.

"The winch has two handles," Nown said, "with double
grips on each. Four men can work it at one time."

Laura saw that he was right. She stood quietly for a moment, thinking. The cable car looked very sturdy. Nown was
as strong as four men—at least—and could probably manage to
winch up the slope as much weight as the cable could bear.
She was slight. She'd be safe. She would only have to go to the
top and take a look. Then she could come right back down.

Although Laura was thinking of a quick trip and a little look, she said to Nown, "May I have the water skin please?" Her words came out with brittle politeness.

"No," he said.

"Nown!" Laura stamped her foot, sending up a small puff of dust that hovered around her ankles. "Look—there's probably no way down the far slope. Or, I mean, there is probably another cable car and no one to wind it for me. You don't need to worry."

"If there's no way down the far slope, you won't need water."

"You're supposed to do what I say!" Laura said.

Nown didn't reply to this.

"May I just have a drink then?"

Nown passed her the water skin. Laura screwed off its copper cap and took a long drink—more than she wanted or needed. She replaced the cap and wrapped her arms around the skin, cradling its sloshing, damp bulk. She knitted her brows at her sandman, then turned on her heel and went up the steps onto the platform. She opened the gate on the box cage, stepped in, and fastened it after her. "Now you will winch me up there," she said.

Nown followed her up onto the platform and studied the winding mechanism. He didn't touch it. He looked at her, waiting.

Laura glared at him. A minute went by, then she burst out, "This might be our only chance! I should go as far as I'm able!"

"Yes."

"Well—get winding then!"

"I can be made again, you can't. This is your only chance."

Nown was telling her that this was her only *life*. Laura lost her temper. "Let me make the decisions! I'm in charge!" she yelled.

Around them again came the rustling whisper of falling earth. Laura's knees gave way. She crouched down in the cage, her fingers gripping its mesh and the water skin pressed between her thighs and belly. She began to cry. She pressed her face against the grid of wire and sobbed. She cried because she was frustrated and tired, even of crying—she had spent a whole year in tears.

The cage quivered, then swung free. It was ascending. Laura stood up. Nown was winding the mechanism's great drum. The handles squeaked, and the greased cable wound in on itself with a sticky kissing noise. The sounds gradually receded. Then Laura could only hear the cage creaking as it swung. Nown and the platform grew small, and the cage slid up above the gray slope. The ground below Laura was as pockmarked as a glacier honeycombed by sun-heated dust and pebbles. It looked treacherous.

Laura felt no wind. The air temperature remained the same—warm and dry. The view opened up around and then below her, revealing a series of peaks back the way she and Nown had come, then all around, to the eastern and western horizons along the border—but not extending beyond the border into that visible but inaccessible hinterland that all dreamhunters looked into before crossing back into their own world. The Pinnacles were clearly a feature of the border itself. Laura could see the opening to Sanctuary Valley, several hours' walk along the branch of trail they hadn't taken. Flanking the valley, and stretching away Inland, was a forked tongue of gray pinnacles thrusting out from the main mass of peaks. The farthest fork was thick, a real barrier, like the main range. The other was slender, in places perhaps only three peaks wide. From ground level this fork might appear to be a real barrier, but from high on the cable car it showed as not much more than a fence or screen. For these peaks did screen the eastern hinterland from anyone on level ground.

As the cage swung gently up, Laura looked into the land beyond the narrow barrier. She saw grasslands with, here and there, stands of dry trees like clutches of stilled smoke. And, as the cage bumped against a wall at the back of the platform, Laura saw the rail line that ran, plumb straight, through the grasslands till it faded into the vaporous brightness of the In-land horizon.

Laura opened the cage door and got out onto the platform. She waved at Nown. He didn't acknowledge her gesture.

Laura went to the far end of the platform and looked down. There wasn't another cable car. Instead, there was an aerial cableway. The rangers could let gravity do the work of carrying down loads of rails and other goods bundled in the canvas slings. For themselves, however, they had built a steel tower that had many flights of steps. The tower stood out from the base of the pinnacle and could be reached from the summit by a twenty-something-foot span of bridge.

Laura went back to the cage and waved to Nown again, this time to say not "I'm all right" but "Goodbye, I'm going." She thought she saw him shake his head, then knew he had, because he raised a hand to wave her back. Laura held up her wrist and touched her watch face. She spread her fingers, counted them off with the pointing index finger of her other hand. "Give me five hours," she signed. She hoped he would know that she didn't mean five minutes. Laura waited for her sandman to react, then turned her back on him and struck out across the bridge to the tower.

4

✦ ✦ ✦

*S*INCE FIRST COMING TO THE PLACE, LAURA HAD SEEN SOME ROADS SO SMOOTHLY SURFACED THAT BICYCLES COULD be ridden on them. She'd seen rudimentary steps on slopes, latrines, well-leveled camping grounds, and even one stubby lookout tower. She had never seen anything that showed the purpose or industry of the cable car, tower, and rail line. All showed signs of heavy use, so that, looking at them, she knew somewhere, at the other end of the line, there would be a settlement of some kind, buildings and people—for the railway was a supply line.

When Laura reached the foot of the tower, she found a handcar, sitting on the rails and up against buffers. It was a simple contraption, a platform with plenty of room for freight and two seats set facing each other with a couple of levers between them. The levers, if pushed back and forth, would make the wheels turn. Once the handcar built up momentum, Laura imagined that it would go quite fast—perhaps as fast as a sprinting man.

She set out along the rail line. She didn't mean to go far. She was thinking she'd go just far enough to find herself even with some landmark, like a stand of trees, that she could later use as a sighting from the tower in order to make a rough estimate of the length of line she could see. If it took her an hour to reach—say—*that* stand of trees, the one that appeared to her novice dreamhunter's eye to be about an hour away, then later she might be able to make a rough estimate of how many hours were beyond that. Laura knew that the Regulatory Body would never have bothered to build a rail line for anything that rangers would regard as a reasonable walking distance. The line must be at least longer than a day's walk. Its final destination was, most likely, days away.

Laura ambled along, remembering the sorts of things that were at the ends of secret trails in books she'd read. "A diamond mine," she thought, "something precious that they don't want to share." After all, there was no reason to suppose that there weren't pockets of precious minerals in the Place, and that prospecting rangers might not have turned something up. She imagined Cas Doran and his friends with a growing reserve of undeclared wealth. She imagined a fortress and a vast army of soldier rangers training in maneuvers. A secret army. Then she remembered that guns wouldn't fire in the Place, so the soldiers of her imaginary army would have to be lying on their bellies, pointing rifles, and making gun noises with their mouths.

She giggled.

The stand of trees Laura had picked as a landmark was getting closer, but only very slowly. She sighed and picked up her pace. She was hungry, but that was no excuse for dragging her feet and daydreaming.

A while later, when she'd raised a sweat and her mind was just idling, the thought that had been trailing her for days— possibly since Rose first told her about the "surplus rails"— finally caught up with her. She remembered that the Grand Patriarch had asked her about the "Depot."

Laura raised her head and squinted up the line. The "Depot" wasn't the name of a dream—it was a destination, where something was stored.

What else had the Grand Patriarch said? There was something else, a name from a rumor, because hadn't the Grand Patriarch said that most of his intelligence came from rumors?

Contentment.

Laura stopped walking when the word came into her head. She stood still, shivering and short of breath. The world darkened around her as her pupils contracted. Dread had crept up and pounced on her. And, now that she was still, she understood that her footsteps had masked a vibration. A sound.

A steely rolling was coming from the line behind her.

Laura spun to face back along the line. She saw the handcar bearing down upon her, fast. Riding on it were six rangers.

Laura jumped down from the raised railbed and sprinted away across the meadow. She heard a shout, then the handcar braking. She looked back and saw four men pouring off it after her.

The rangers came tearing through the dry grass with a sound like a grass fire. They ran her down and grappled her. Laura fought them, punched and kicked. She was lifted up into the air and then dumped onto the ground. The wind was knocked out of her. For a moment her only thought was how to fill her lungs. They ached and struggled to expand again. She was making a sound like one of those enraged sea lions she and the lighthouse keeper's girls had disturbed sleeping on the sands of So Long Spit. She drew breath in a prolonged, barking howl, rocking with pain and effort. She wheezed, and tears poured down her cheeks and into her ears.

One of the rangers tore her shirt open and grabbed her license on its chain. He put his head down to read the copper tags.

"We haven't had anyone escape," another ranger was saying, "and look at what she's wearing."

"She's not one of ours," said the one who had hold of her license. "This is Tziga Hame's daughter."

5

✧ ✧ ✧

HEY TIED HER WRISTS AND ANKLES WITH THEIR BANDANNAS AND CARRIED HER BACK TO THE HANDCAR. THEY SET HER down among boxes and baskets and tall zinc milk cans that Laura guessed were full of water. She could smell oranges and apples and the sharp perfume of the cocoa and cinnamon in dreamhunters' strong bread.

An argument was conducted over her head. Someone poked her with a boot, not hard but carelessly. "Who broke the gates?"

Another said, not to her, "Whoever it was must have heard us coming and run off along the trail to Sanctuary Valley."

"That's only conjecture. Still, I guess someone should go back and track them. Look—I'll go. And you come with me, McIndoe. The rest of you go on and raise the alarm."

Again the boot prodded Laura. "Who are they? Your accomplices?"

Another man said, "How did they know what they were looking for? What have you got to say for yourself, girl?"

"Let her alone," another man said. "She'll tell us afterward anyway."

After what? Laura thought, and bunched herself up into a tight, defensive ball.

The handcar bounced as two men jumped off it. Laura

heard the sloshing of water skins being settled. One of the men who was leaving said, "Be as quick as you can. Those gates will have to be fixed as soon as possible."

Laura wondered where her sandman had hidden. The cage would have been on the summit when the rangers reached the cable car—after passing through two broken gates. Not just broken but exploded. Laura remembered the stretched-licorice look of the smoking chain. Nown would be burrowed in somewhere probably, with only his roughly made back exposed. He could look as natural as a big stone when he really needed to.

The four remaining rangers settled themselves on the handcar. Laura heard a spring squawk as someone sat on one of the seats, preparing to work the levers. She mustered her courage. She unclenched her body, rolled onto her back, and looked up at one of the men.

He met her eyes, and his face creased with worry. "You're really only a baby, aren't you?"

"How far is it if you go around the long way?" Laura asked him.

"How far to where?" one of the other men said, impatient.

The handcar was moving now. The landscape slid by, faster every second. None of the crankshafts or levers made a noise; all were too well greased. The only sound was the creak of springs in the seats as the rangers' weight shifted while they worked. That, and the ponderous rolling noise of steel wheel rims on steel rails.

The man who was looking at Laura said, "She means, is there another way around The Pinnacles? She's hoping her friends will be able to follow her on foot."

The other man laughed. "There's no long way, girlie," he said. "Only a wrong way."

✧ ✧ ✧

Laura never did learn how long the journey was. They removed her watch, so she couldn't tell the time. They didn't try
to talk to her anymore. She sat slumped against a basket.

The rangers worked the levers in shifts. The Pinnacles
faded into mistiness before they fell behind the horizon. The
plain across which the handcar moved was bald and seemed
to swell toward the sky as though showing the curve of the
planet. Hours went by, and Laura fell asleep. She ran through
some colored rags of dreams, too fast to take in anything from
them.

When she woke up, stiff, her face numb on one side and
printed with a pattern of basketwork, one ranger remarked,
"It would have been easier for you if you'd stayed asleep for
just another half hour." He pulled her to her feet. She stood
propped and teetering between the stacked baskets as the
handcar reduced speed and rolled in among some buildings.

The ground was dusty and lightly embossed all over by
footprints—boot prints and bare feet. The compound con-
sisted of a cluster of huts, several long, barrackslike buildings,
and shelters with canvas roofs and walls, the walls rolled up
like window blinds to reveal rows of pallet beds. Some of the
beds were occupied by people, either sleeping or reading.
They were all wearing yellow cotton pajamas. More yellow-
clad figures sat around on benches, or stood where the grass
began again, facing away from the buildings, or lay on their
backs gazing up into the unremarkable white sky. There was
even a group of pajama-clad young men playing a not very
energetic ball game, all barefoot and scuffling in the dust.

The handcar pulled up at a platform. More rangers ap-

peared and began unloading the supplies, carrying everything
into one of the huts. Laura was lifted like baggage and put
down on the platform. She waited as people went by her with
boxes and baskets. She ignored the rangers and tried to catch
the eye of one of the people in yellow. Most were men, but
Laura did see a few young women among them. They all
looked well fed, well rested, and reasonably clean. They were
not at all interested in Laura's appearance. Their eyes went
across her as though she were no more surprising than anything else they looked at.

Laura didn't like their yellow uniforms or their vulnerable,
unshod feet. But she could see that none of the people
seemed sedated. They were all active and coordinated and
clear-eyed, only strangely calm.

Several more rangers emerged from one of the barracks
and came over to Laura. The one wearing a white coat and
stethoscope frowned as he came up and said, "Untie her immediately."

When her hands were free, Laura pulled the gaping front
of her shirt together.

"There's no need to do that, young lady. I want to look at
your license," the doctor said.

"She's Tziga Hame's daughter, Laura," one of her captors
said.

The doctor gave Laura a careful, appraising look.

"She was walking Inland along the rail line about an hour
from the tower. The gate at the beginning of The Pinnacles
was hanging off its hinges. The detour gate was smashed to
bits. But the girl was on her own when we found her."

The doctor looked into her eyes. "Did you break the gates,
Laura?"

"They were already broken," she said. "I wondered

whether there was some emergency. I went in to see if I could be of any assistance." She lifted her chin and stared at him, cool and defiant.

One of the rangers snorted in disbelief. "Who worked the cable car, then?"

Laura said, "I was so determined to help, I went up the cable hand over hand."

The ranger hissed in anger and reached for her, but the doctor fended him off. "There's no need to press her. We'll know her story soon enough."

To Laura he said, "I'm sure you understand that you're in trouble. You've trespassed. And there's the matter of damage to property."

Laura didn't like to meet his eyes. There was a look in them, a cold, stripped-down look, that frightened her. Instead she turned her attention to the rail line, which, she saw, didn't end at the platform but went away, dead straight, Inland. She asked, "Is this the Depot?"

"Yes, it is. But where did you hear that name?"

"I don't remember. What's out there?" Laura pointed along the line.

"The railway is being extended solely in the interest of exploration. Believe me, the farther you go, the less memorable it is. But I suppose you are one of those dreamhunters with romantic ideas about the hinterland? About a dream like Koh-i-noor? A big, matchless diamond of a dream."

He was making fun of her. He was all scorn and cynicism; a fortress defended, but defending only emptiness. That was what she could see when she looked into his eyes. He knew he was doing wrong, and meant to go on doing it, but was still capable of feeling resentment when anything reminded him of it.

Laura remembered seeing a similar expression in Maze Plasir's face when she'd asked him about supplying night-mares to the Department of Corrections.

As these thoughts went through her mind, she began un-consciously pursing her lips and shaking her head.

"Are you about to *scold* us?" the doctor asked, sarcastic.

✦ ✦ ✦

The look she gave him. The doctor remembered it all his life. She met his eyes, her expression icy and knowing. It wasn't bravado. She didn't strike him as brave. She was still shivering and clutching her torn shirt closed over her tiny breasts. Fear was there in her body, frank fear in her tremors and whitened knuckles. But she looked like someone who couldn't feel her own fear, because it was being interfered with by faith. Faith was pouring out of her face at him, bigger and louder than anything. She looked like a saint.

It was very impressive. But being impressed only made this man feel spiteful. He leered at Laura Hame. He said, "I'm pleased to see you're not afraid. You have no reason to be, as you'll soon learn." He nodded to the rangers she'd come with, one of whom laid a hand on her shoulder while the other knelt to unlace and remove her boots. The doctor smiled more widely and added, "I know you'll be very happy here."

✦ ✦ ✦

The hut had a wooden floor, and white dust had gathered in its corners. It had a window with bars on it but without glass. There was no need for glass, no cold to combat, or wind to screen. A thin mattress was set square against one wall. There was a bucket: clean white enamel, with a lid. There was no other furniture.

An hour after Laura was put into the room, the door was unbolted and a tray delivered to her. On it were a mug of water and oatcakes topped with honey. There was also a bowl full of some kind of cold tomato concoction and an orange.

Laura sipped the water slowly. She wasn't so much planning an escape as just meaning to. Because she meant to escape, she would take every opportunity to store water in her body. She drank slowly with the idea that she, like an indoor plant, would absorb more water if watered gradually. As she sipped, she looked through the window at the people in yellow.

She saw one she recognized. It was Maze Plasir's apprentice, Gavin Pinkney. Oily, snide Gavin—who had passed in the Doorhandle Try last autumn, and who was licensed before Laura since he didn't catch dreams about convicts.

Gavin was sitting, holding his bare toes in either hand and rocking gently back and forth.

Laura put her face against the bars and called to him. "Gavin!"

He was slow to react to his name but turned to her smiling already, then beamed. He got up and came over wearing a goofy but completely genuine grin. "Hello," he said.

"Gavin, how long have you been here?"

He shrugged. "It's great here," he said. "Though I could *murder* for a bit of cooked meat."

"A while, then?" Laura said.

"I'm so glad you've come," he said. "You'll find you feel better almost immediately."

Laura nodded to encourage him, and he began to echo her nod, his eyes creased with smiling. "It's wonderful that we're together," he said.

"You and me?" Laura was astonished. He'd shown no sign of liking her before.

"All together," he said, in a singsong voice. "It was all worth it."

"What was?"

"The work, the chances I took. Time well spent, to end up with this—this full well of time." Gavin's voice was nasal—his usual quacking voice, but his tone was so serene he sounded mesmerizing. "And we have the whole day ahead of us," he said. "This beautiful day." He looked around, his face shining, as if illuminated by brilliant spring sunshine.

Laura covered her mouth with her hand. She retched, and some of the water came back up from her gullet tainted with bile. She swallowed and tried to control herself.

Gavin went on. "There's my mother waiting for us—still in the best of health. And my grown children, favored by fortune, he prosperous, she generous. How foolish I was to worry about them. And the grandchildren—here they come up from the beach, the girls practicing cartwheels and the boys carrying the canoe paddles—"

"It's a dream, Gavin," Laura said, to put a stop to his rapturous chanting.

"A dream . . ." His eyes flickered.

"Contentment," Laura said, guessing.

"Yes." His face cleared. Then he said, puzzled, "Don't you want to be happy?"

There was a clanging from one of the buildings. It sounded like a dinner bell. Gavin got up, dusted off his backside, and left without saying another word. Laura watched all the yellow-clad figures making their way, orderly and eager, toward the sound of the bell.

There was no fence around the compound. There was no need for one; the barefoot, captive dreamhunters wouldn't want to run away from decent food and the blessed company of the dream.

Before they had put her in the hut, the rangers had made Laura turn out her pockets. She'd said to them, sneering, "Do you suppose I'm carrying a lock pick? Or a knife?" But of course they'd been looking for Wakeful. Wakeful was what Laura wished she had now—the drug, or a lock pick, or a knife.

She knew that her captors had only to wait for her to sleep. Then they could ask her their questions. Once she had taken a print of the dream, and been drugged by its bliss, they would ask their questions and she'd answer them, trustingly. Nothing would matter. It would be a beautiful day, and she'd have the whole day ahead of her.

Before she could have second thoughts, Laura began to feed the oozy oatcakes through the bars; then she poured the tomato stuff out after them. As she did this, she whispered, "I don't want to be happy. I don't want to be happy." She didn't put the food in her slops bucket because the bucket was still empty and clean, and she might be tempted to take the food out again. Her captors might not be patient—she reasoned—they might drug her food to make her sleep sooner. Laura could still see how the smashed gates had looked. If they were *her* gates and she had found them and hadn't known how they'd been broken, she'd be very eager to find out as soon as possible.

Laura ate only the orange. She chose to believe that it was protected from tampering by its peel. She stopped whispering to herself as she ate but went on once she'd swallowed her last bite, in a slow-burning panic. "I don't want to be happy."

She moved to the window again to stare out into the grasslands. She imagined she saw a far-off figure, a dark speck.

But it was only a dust mote sliding down the surface of her eye.

Her mouth shaped his name.

✧ ✧ ✧

A ranger found the food. He picked up the oatcakes and went away. The doctor appeared a few minutes later at her door. "You're being very stupid," he said. "Unless you want to answer our rather pressing questions now."

Laura shook her head and backed away from him.

He signaled to the rangers waiting behind him. The men stepped into the hut and grabbed her. The doctor advanced on her. He pulled a square, black leather case from the pocket of his white coat. He snapped its lid open. Laura glimpsed the gleaming glass and steel of hypodermic needles. "No!" she shrieked.

"No?" The doctor hesitated, the case open. He tilted it back and forth so that bubbles slid in the glass barrels of clear chemical.

"I'll be good, I'll eat, I'll lie down." She was babbling. Then she burst into tears. She sobbed in rage and fear, her voice dropped a full octave, and she said, "I'll kill you," sobbing.

"You'll be good, and you'll kill me?" the doctor said, cold and sweet. But he must have made a silent command too, for the rangers released her. Laura cowered away from them against the wall. Through the distortion of tears, she saw the doctor point down, at the mattress she was standing on. She obeyed him, lowering herself to her knees.

"I'll send in more food. It isn't drugged, Miss Hame. You'll sleep better with something in your stomach."

"Yes," Laura said. "Yes, all right." She held her hands out, palms up, pushing them away.

They left. She heard the bolt on the outside of the door slide into place. Someone gave it a rattle for good measure. Then it was quiet. She could hear footsteps, their feet in the yard, the occasional murmuring voice. She thought she could hear the other captives having dinner, the clack of spoons on enamelware. She covered her ears and squeezed her eyes shut and tried to push back the panic that was threatening to annihilate her, prematurely, since Contentment was poised to wipe her out as soon as she slept. The dream would replace herself with itself, her desires with its self-satisfaction. It would replace her family with its family, its cartwheeling granddaughters.

Laura found herself singing. She sang to stay sane. She sang the school song of Founderston Girls' Academy, a song about striving and virtue and setting forth together. Then her voice trailed off, and she stared through the striped mattress cover in front of her.

She had come up with a plan.

✢ ✢ ✢

The ranger sent to look in on Laura Hame stopped by her cell window and took a quick peek. He didn't know quite what he expected—to surprise her at something perhaps, but what?

The girl had her back to the window and didn't notice him. She was kneeling in one corner and seemed to be busy sweeping up the dust gathered in the angle of floor and wall. She was using her hands and was in danger of picking up splinters from the rough planks flooring the hut. The ranger thought, "So—she's decided to keep herself awake by doing housework." She looked like a penitent, on her knees and grubbing away at the dirt.

"It's futile, you know," he said.

She stopped what she was doing, stiffened, but didn't turn around.

The ranger waited for a moment, then went away.

When, over an hour later, he came back to check, the Hame girl was sitting cross-legged in the center of the room, with her back to the window. She'd removed her jacket and spread it out before her. The dust she'd swept up was gathered in a tiny pile on the jacket. This was odd, but he was reassured to see that she had in her hand the small, seedy loaf from her second plate of food.

"Good girl," he said.

She turned around and gave him a cold look. "Don't gloat," she said. Then, "My clothes are uncomfortable. I'd sleep better in a pair of those yellow pajamas everyone is wearing."

He went away and found a clean pair, a little too big for her, but she could roll up the sleeves and ankles. He returned to the hut and found her standing at the window. Over her shoulder he could see her jacket, lying humped in the middle of the room. There was no sign of her housekeeping dust pile. The bread was gone, the water cup empty and on its side.

He pushed the pajamas through the bars. She thanked him, and he went away once more.

The ranger stayed away over an hour. The next time he looked in on the Hame girl, she was still up but was in the pajamas—their yellow highly visible in the gloom of the hut.

She was singing.

The ranger opened his mouth and drew breath to say something to startle her; then a familiar, lovely odor hit his palate. The scent seemed to come billowing out through the bars in the window. Ozone—summer rain on warm earth. The ranger shook his head and shouted, "Girl!"

Laura Hame broke off her singing with a cough like a sob. Her shoulders slumped.

"Do you want me to tell the doctor to come and pay you a visit?"

"Go away!" she yelled. She didn't jump up or twist herself around. She spoke vehemently but only turned her head to look back over her shoulder. "I want to sleep," she said. "I have a sore stomach. I'm waiting for it to pass."

"Better be soon," he threatened, then went away once more.

＋ ＋ ＋

Laura put her palms over her eyes to catch her tears. She rocked back and forth in her own darkness. There was only *this* to do. Either it would work or it wouldn't. She had to empty her mind of all fear and expectation. She had only to remember that it did work—that she, Laura, was already living in a world in which she'd succeeded at this already. The only rule was the spell. The only effort, faith.

She set her wet fingers on the drying surface of the little man she'd made out of dust and chewed bread. She made the surface of the mix tacky and pliable once more. She began to sing again, from the beginning: "The Measures," that chant made of Koine, demotic Greek; and nonsense sounds, glossolalia, the tongues of angels. Every word was different from the one before.

The power began to build and spin around her. She sang on in her tired, sweet, young voice, and, this time, no one came to interrupt her. When she finished singing, the room seemed to vibrate—it was so stuffed with energy. Laura picked up the second of two small, crescent-shaped slivers of fingernail, her own, and stooped over the tiny, tacky form of the bread-and-dust man. She scratched the letters onto the broadest part of his anatomy, his chest. The other bit of fingernail was already buried in that doughy chest, as a heart. Laura etched "N O W" but left off the final N. She didn't need him to speak to her, only to follow her orders.

For a second the tiny bread-and-dust figure lay inert. Then, suddenly, his stillness looked like surprise. He flexed his legs, got up, and turned his little, roughly formed face to hers.

Laura laughed and smiled down at him.

His attention was so focused and expectant that it pulled her out of her brief moment of rapt relief. "Look," she said. "I'll just go check the window to see how many people are out there. We need plenty of people in yellow, and fewer rangers. A while ago I heard a bell ringing at that building farther off— so perhaps the rangers are having *their* meal. I hope so." She bit her lip to stop talking. She didn't need to explain her whole situation. He was so tiny that she thought she'd better keep her instructions simple. "His brain can't be very big," she thought, nonsensically. Then she recalled that he didn't have a brain anyway, so maybe his size didn't determine his mental capacity.

Laura made herself stop thinking it all through. She went to the window, saw that there were now plenty of yellow-clad people around—as many as there had been when she first arrived, hours ago. Perhaps this was their daytime roster. The camp might very well run with a "day" and a "night" for the convenience of the rangers. So, it was "day," and there were people around. There were even a few wandering quite far from the camp—maybe as far as they'd ever want to go on the invisible leash of the dream.

Laura turned back to the room. She picked up her bread-and-dust man and put him on the windowsill between the

bars. "I want you to jump down, run around the hut, and figure out how to climb up and unbolt the door."

The tiny Nown didn't hesitate. He jumped out the window. Laura heard the pattering sound he made landing. She
didn't hear his footfalls.

She went to the door and waited. Eventually, she heard
noises, as if someone with sticky fingers was touching the
door. She put her ear to the wood and concentrated till she
could hear that the noises were progressing up the outside
surface. Then she was deafened by the rattle of the bolt. She
pulled her ear back, and the door swung in, the little man
riding it, his elbows locked around the loop of the bolt and
his legs braced against its sleeve.

Laura poked her head around the door. A few of the yellow-
clad people looked at her, some smiling but none with any
real interest. She put out her hand, and the bread-and-dust
man stepped onto her palm. She slipped him inside her shirt,
where he clung like a lizard.

Laura stepped out of the hut and bolted the door behind
her. Then she put her head down and ambled away, smiling
to herself and swinging her arms as though she was filled with
some private, sunny monologue. She imitated the other people. As she went past one of the tent dormitories, she petted
its canvas wall. She walked in a weaving, indirect way, in the
opposite direction from the isolated rangers' barracks. She
didn't attempt to keep the rail line in sight—she would have to
find it later.

She sat down for a time where the bare, beaten earth of the
compound began to sprout grass again. She kept her back to
the buildings and tried to look relaxed, drizzling dust through
her fingers and talking to herself. Now and then she glanced
back till—at one glance—she saw the buildings, the yellow-
clad bodies, but no rangers nearby or facing her.

Laura immediately ducked down and stripped off the yel-·
low pajama top and pants. She was still wearing her own
clothes underneath. She pushed the pajamas down the front
of her pants, then rolled and wriggled away into the thin
grass, headed for the scrub. As she went, she rubbed herself
in the dust—her face and hair, her dark pants and pale shirt—
till she was as dun-colored as the ground she crawled along.

For a long time she slid from bush to bush. Her bread-
and-dust man now nestled in the small of her back, holding
on to her belt. The heels of her hands, her fingertips, and the
skin on her feet dragged on the ground till they were scraped
and burning. Her palms filled with splinters of dead vegetation. She didn't dare put her head up until she could no
longer hear any noise from the Depot. Finally she got to her
feet and, stooped over, hurried away.

❖ ❖ ❖

It was hours before Laura let herself turn back toward the
rail line. She took a course only tending in the direction
where it lay. At every few steps she glanced around, looking
for rangers on foot or riding on a handcar. When the handcar
did appear, Laura was surprised how close it was. She threw
herself down on the ground and lay completely still. Her
bread-and-dust man tumbled off her back and lay still too, by
her ear, with his cracked and drying hand against her cheek.

When Laura looked again, the handcar had traveled out of
sight.

She went on, parallel to the railway. She just kept putting
one foot in front of the other, hour after hour. She walked,
straining her eyes, looking and looking for any sign, however
far off, of The Pinnacles and the tower.

She slept for a time, but badly. She was thirsty and fever-ish.

A nosebleed woke her. The blood only oozed, sluggish and tacky. While she held her nostrils closed, trying to stanch it, her bread-and-dust man leaned against her knee and watched her.

"He knows where I am. Wherever I am," Laura said to him, in a pinched, croaking voice she scarcely recognized as her own.

Eventually she got up and went on, not noticing that she'd left the small man behind till she felt him leap and cling to the leg of her trousers. She scooped him up and put him on her shoulder.

She walked. Nothing moved but her. Hours went by, trans-parent, emptied out, even of time.

Laura's lips cracked. Her tongue gradually grew a coat of some thick, salty stuff. Then it began to swell.

Many hours later her bladder began to cramp. She fum-bled at her trousers and squatted to urinate. It burned. There were only a few drops, and it went on burning deep inside her.

Laura sat down and cried—cried without producing tears.

The bread-and-dust man tugged on her hair.

She got up and went on.

Later—a long time later—Laura had a lucid moment. She thought: "I'll die unless I let the rangers find me." She lifted her head and took a good look around. She could see no sign of The Pinnacles, not even a smudge on the horizon. She turned and saw she had wandered close to the raised railbed. The steel lines were shining at her like water. She went to-ward them, clambered on all fours up the little slope and sat there, slumped.

Her bread-and-dust man scrambled off her and onto the railbed. He doubled up and pressed his whole little length against the steel.

Laura thought, "He's listening for a handcar." Then she lay down.

✦ ✦ ✦

Someone touched her. It hurt. A hard something rasped across the stinging fissures on her mouth.

Wet parted her lips. At first she could taste only water on her tongue, then, as she took more, its true taste came—musty warm, stale water.

It was taken away from her before she was full. She croaked a complaint and drooped, her head lolling against the yielding, creaking arm that held her.

With a ghost of decision, she whispered, "I don't want to be happy."

She was lifted up. She was gathered in her loose skin, in her own weakness; she was gathered in his strength. She was lifted, cradled, carried in safety.

And they went so fast there was wind to cool her skin.

6

✦ ✦ ✦

LAURA AND NOWN EMERGED FROM
THE PLACE JUST WEST OF THE
RAILWAY BRIDGE OVER THE SVA. IT WAS
dawn, but the air seemed to cool only Laura's skin, not to
reach the parched, burning core of her body. Her chilled skin
had formed a shell around her. She'd lost touch with the
world. She was being carried, but the movement seemed to
pantomime walking. Perhaps Nown was only pretending to
move. Yet, when Laura opened her eyes, she saw that they
were farther out on the tide-bared sands of the Inlet.

Nown sat her down by a channel of the river and slid her
forward so that her feet dangled in the stream. Its cold
burned her blistered skin. She cried out and tried to flex her
knees but was too weak to withdraw her legs from the water.
Nown held her in place until her feet went numb. Then he
picked her up again and carried her back to the train stop by
the bridge. He put her down on the gravel of the raised
railbed and lifted the metal flag that would signal the next
train to stop. He came back, hunkered down, and drew Laura
into his lap. "I have nothing with which to wrap your feet," he
said, then, "From now on I'm going to put things that might
be necessary to you into my body."

Laura puzzled over this remark but couldn't make any
sense of it. Minutes later he said, "I've filled the water skin.

The tide is going out and the stream flowing seaward, but its water might be tainted by salt. I wouldn't know. I can't taste it."

Laura tried to answer him but only croaked. It seemed to her in her fever that her sandman was brooding on his shortcomings. The water skin pushed against her. She fumbled for it with her hands and scabbed mouth, but it was too heavy for her to lift. Nown raised it and eased the nozzle into her mouth. The water was a little salty, but Laura liked its taste. Perhaps she needed salt.

"Not too much at once," Nown said, and they had a little tussle, she clinging to the skin and he trying to take it away without upsetting her. The water gushed out onto her face and shirt. Laura felt the cascading coolness, then the panicked scuttling motion of the creature who—all this time—had ridden clinging to the inside of her shirt. Laura's bread-and-dust man emerged, clambered up her, finding handholds on her collarbone, then the ends of her hair. For a moment he swung bumping against her jaw, then Nown closed a fist around him and plucked him from her.

The bread-and-dust man surveyed Laura, the rail line, and the Inlet from his perch in Nown's fist. His mittlike, fingerless hands were folded across the top of Nown's thumb. His flat and vestigial face looked mild and perhaps curious.

Nown stretched back the arm that held the little creature, then punched it into his own chest. Laura had one glimpse of a tiny, gaping mouth and kicking legs, then both Nown's fist and the bread-and-dust man vanished, buried in the sandman's chest.

"No!" Laura rasped. She was horrified.

"It is better if there are not too many of us around at one time," Nown said. His buried wrist began to separate itself

from the sand of his chest, and he withdrew his hand, whole
and empty.

"Is two too many?" Laura's eyes were stinging, but no tears
would come.

Nown didn't answer her.

"Why did you do that?" She knew he could hear her, however insubstantial her voice had become.

"There were too many of us."

"Is two too many?" she asked again, and again Nown didn't
answer her.

"Can you do that?" she said. "Destroy him? Don't *I* have to
do that?"

"It isn't destroyed; it is only swallowed."

Nown put his hand on the rail line. He announced that
there was a train on its way. He set Laura on her feet by the
train stop signal, then lifted her arm and hooked it around
the signal pole. "Stay there. Stay standing," he said, then he
left her. He picked his way down the embankment and strode
along a reed-lined beach beside one channel of the river.
Some distance from her he hunkered down and wrapped his
arms around his legs, dropped his face onto his knees, and
imitated a tide-worn stone.

✧ ✧ ✧

The train was a local headed toward Sisters Beach.

On a clear day the red painted steel flag of the stop signal
was visible to the engineer from the lowest turn of the Mount
Kahaugh spiral. He had miles to slow and stop. The Secretary
of the Interior had a house in the Awa Inlet—and it was Doran who most often used the train stop. There was never any
question that the train would pause, though stopping always
put at least ten minutes more on a journey.

It wasn't until he was going very slowly, and approaching the bridge, that the engineer spotted the small, ragged figure by the signal. As he pulled to a halt, he saw that it was a girl, her clothes torn at the knees and elbows and white with dust.

A conductor got out to inspect the prospective passenger. He took in her bedraggled appearance and lack of luggage. He went up to her ready to ask whether she even had the fare, but, when he reached her, he saw how young she was, and how she trembled, and how she was holding herself up against the signal pole. Instead of demanding money, the conductor placed his strong hand under one of her elbows. "What happened?"

Passengers were pushing down their windows and poking their heads out to take a look.

"Are you a dreamhunter?" the conductor asked.

"Yes. I got lost," the girl whispered.

"Can you walk?" the conductor said, then looked at her feet and gave a little yelp of sympathy. He put an arm around her and took some of her weight. They tottered together toward the nearest door. Another conductor leaned out and lifted her up. He said to the first, "The only house here is up beyond that border."

"Yes," the girl whispered. "I couldn't look for help there."

There was a clatter of stones behind them as someone came running along the track beside the train. It was a passenger, who had jumped from one of the second-class carriages. He was wearing a dreamhunter's long duster coat. The young man said, "I'll take her." He sprang onto the steps behind the girl and scooped her up.

The second conductor retreated into the carriage ahead of him. The first followed, leaning out only to wave all clear to the engineer.

The train exhaled and began to move.

"We have an empty compartment in first-class," the first conductor said to the young man. "She'll be more comfortable there."

The girl had her eyes closed and her head on the young man's shoulder. Perhaps she had fainted.

"I can't pay." The dreamhunter looked stricken and stiffly angry at the same time.

"Was anyone asking you to pay?" The first conductor was irritated. "If you'll please just carry your friend this way." He set off up the carriage. The young man followed.

The other conductor went to find towels and soap, bandages and ointment, food and drink.

✧ ✧ ✧

Laura woke up to see a man in a brass-buttoned uniform bandaging her blistered feet. Her head was in someone's lap. She looked up, said, "Sandy."

"Laura," said Sandy. Then, "Love." Then, "What have you been doing?"

"I got lost," she said, and closed her eyes again.

Laura didn't really come back
to herself till she and Sandy
were in a taxi taking them from Sisters
Beach Station up to Summerfort. The driver was sitting out
in the open air. They were in the back, and she was leaning
heavily on Sandy. He thought she was still faint and feverish;
then she started to speak.

As she talked, he realized that she'd postponed answering
his question, "What have you been doing?" and that what he
was now hearing was her answer.

"The Regulatory Body has built a rail line beyond The Pinnacles at Z minus 16." The map reference made her sound
lucid, despite her ravaged little voice. She said, "They run
handcars on it. They move supplies. There's a kind of camp
far Inland along the line. A camp they call the Depot. It's full
of dreamhunters, missing dreamhunters, and, I guess, a few
no one misses—like little Gavin Pinkney. Rose told me she
saw Gavin on St. Lazarus's Eve after the riot. And Aunt Grace
saw him before she went into quarantine in the forest near
Doorhandle. I bet if you asked Plasir where his apprentice
was, he'd say Gavin had suffered a breakdown and was under
treatment."

Sandy saw Laura's eyes glimmering at him in the gloom of
the cab. He saw her tears spill and how her skin grew instantly

red where the tears were running. She wasn't sunburned—no one ever got sunburned in the Place—but the skin of her face was so parched and damaged that it flared wherever salt touched it. Sandy drew his cuff up over his hand and dabbed gently at her cheeks.

Laura went on. "The camp is on the site of a dream, a master dream called Contentment, which makes people perfectly happy. Perfectly, slavishly happy." She shuddered.

Sandy put his arms around her.

"I didn't sleep," Laura said. "I got away."

"Good girl."

They had arrived at their destination. Sandy opened the door, dropped his pack onto the shell driveway. He pulled money out of his pocket and paid the driver. He said, "Keep the change," which felt as strange as anything else that was happening since it was something he'd never said, or been moved to say, before. He eased out and lifted her up—she was so light, so small.

Sandy watched the taxi backing around the corner of the drive, its tires kicking up clanking scallop shells. He asked Laura, "Is anyone here?" Then he turned to the house in time to see someone appear—a small man with graying black hair and a badly scarred face.

The man looked alarmed and hurried down off the veranda.

Laura croaked, urgently, "It's all right. *I'm* all right!" She sounded even more worried than the man looked.

The man reached Sandy and for a moment, despite his slightness and fragility, looked set to snatch Laura out of Sandy's arms.

"I can walk," Laura said. "Don't try lifting me, Da. It's only my feet that hurt."

Sandy finally recognized the man. He was Laura's father—

Tziga Hame—reported missing a year ago, declared dead shortly after that.

"Take her inside," said Tziga.

"I'm all right, Da," said Laura.

"Shhhh," said Sandy and Tziga together.

Sandy carried Laura indoors. Tziga went ahead. He led Sandy up to Laura's room and pulled back the covers on her bed. Sandy put her down, and Tziga shook out a down comforter and draped it over her, leaving her bandaged feet uncovered.

Laura lay looking at Sandy, then at her father. Her gaze went back and forth between their faces, and her eyes began to close. For a moment longer her eyes went on moving behind their shut, smooth lids. Then she was asleep.

Tziga said, "It's probably best just to let her rest. I'll sit with her. I have a nurse, who is out at the market. When she returns, could you please send her up to me? Laura's aunt Grace went In yesterday to catch something for The Beholder. Laura's cousin is in Founderston with her father for a dress fitting. I'll cable them tomorrow. You can help yourself to something to eat. The kitchen is on the right at the foot of the stairs. And, Sandy, if you can be so good as to not go off anywhere before I've had a chance to talk to you."

Sandy was puzzled that he was known to this man he'd never met, and by Tziga Hame's tone, which wasn't just gratitude but a kind of warm eagerness that Sandy knew he didn't deserve. "Um" was all he managed to say.

"Good," said Tziga, as though Sandy had said, "Yes, sir."

Sandy retreated from Laura's room, went downstairs, and wandered around examining everything. The house wasn't at all what he had imagined—what he had been imagining since the day the previous summer that the two beautiful, forward, tangle-haired girls had edged up to him when he was lying on a lounge chair on Sisters Beach in order to read over his shoulder. They had talked about their libraries, two libraries in two houses. They had talked about their town house in Founderston and their beach house, Summerfort. Sandy had spent the following few days looking up at the big house on the headland. And—more recently—he'd looked at it from the sea when he sailed into Tarry Cove on a coal barge. Sandy had thought Summerfort would be full of brocaded chairs and tasseled lamps and furniture darkened and gnarled with carving, with gilded mirrors and brass fire screens and Turkish rugs and crystal lamps. He wandered around looking at the bare floorboards—oiled timber—the few rugs, the faded, comfortable sofas, everything showing the wear of sun and sand. Everything except the books in the library, whose windows were shaded by white Roman blinds. The chairs in the library were studded leather, but so aged and scuffed by use that in some places the leather was pink, not red.

Sandy sat down and gazed up at the spines of the books. After a moment he heard the front door open and went to relay Mr. Hame's message to the nurse.

✦ ✦ ✦

Later, the sun went down and Sandy followed the light out onto the veranda in order to keep reading a book he'd discovered, a book with a title irresistible to him. Laura's father found him frowning over *The Seven Principles of Self-Reliance*. Tziga Hame sat in a chair opposite him.

"How is she now?" Sandy said.

"She's sleeping. Her feet have been lathered with some smelly ointment and properly, professionally bandaged. When the nurse left us, Laura told me about her ordeal."

"She told me too."

Tziga nodded. "I hope you'll stay, Sandy. I mean—you must."

Sandy bit his lip for a moment, then his irritation and the sense he had of himself being salt of the earth got the better of him. "I can't just hold my breath, even when someone I care about is convalescing," he said. "I have to earn a living."

"I wanted to talk to you about that. And about Laura."

Sandy was speechless. Was Laura's father trying to talk to him about his "prospects"—whether he could support his daughter? Laura's father didn't sound stern, or prying, he didn't seem embarrassed either, and if he was joking he was being remarkably deadpan.

Tziga went on. "There's a dream I'd like to have again. I doubt I can catch it myself. I don't have the strength anymore."

Sandy realized that he wasn't being asked about his intentions toward Laura. He also understood that Tziga Hame's scars and smashed-in cheekbone were signs of a more serious, invisible injury. "I must be kind to him," Sandy thought—though the notion of trying to be kind made Sandy feel he was trying to stuff his big feet into small shoes.

"Just listen." Tziga smiled, a sweet, fey smile. "Let me finish before I forget how I began," he said. Then, "Master dreams are all somehow brutal, even when they're beautiful. I couldn't manage The Gate now myself, but Laura certainly can. And Grace tells me you show great promise . . ."

V

The Gate

1

✦ ✦ ✦

*W*HEN LAURA WAS UP AND ABOUT AGAIN, AND CHORLEY, GRACE, AND ROSE WERE BACK AT SUMMERFORT, THERE was a family conference.

Sandy Mason sat in on it, looking at once embarrassed and pleased with himself. For a time they talked about the Regulatory Body's secret railway and the happy captives at the Depot. Laura hadn't told anyone but her father that she'd been caught, and held, and how she'd made her escape. She did tell them she'd been seen, and possibly recognized, but didn't say that Cas Doran and his cronies might be surprised to see her alive after she'd vanished from the remote and isolated compound. Laura and her father didn't discuss the possibility that she was in danger. And it crossed Laura's mind that her father—still sometimes muddleheaded with fits—hadn't even considered it. She didn't raise the subject, because she didn't want to have to hide again.

Laura's father was, himself, tired of hiding. At the meeting, Tziga said, "If I reappear in Founderston, the Regulatory Body will, no doubt, feel uncomfortable. But since I only want to visit medical specialists, and not darken the Body's doorways, they'll soon get over it."

"We should all return to Founderston," Chorley said. "You'll get better care. And Laura must talk to the Grand Patriarch about this Depot. We should put the problem in his hands—for now."

Grace frowned. She said, "I agree that Laura should go back. Late summer is a very good time for her to return to work. All the regular healing dreamers supplying the hospitals and nursing homes are out of the city enjoying their vacations. It makes sense for Laura to go back when there's less competition, and when she can do so in a kind of disguise." Grace looked at Sandy. "And this is where you can help. The best thing you can do for Laura is form a temporary partnership with her. You can catch the same dreams and sell yourselves together—two dreamers for the price of one. You can say you're boosting each other, and then maybe—with smaller houses, and less supervision—your performance won't strike anyone as *too* remarkable. Laura's Buried Alive pushed her penumbra out to about five hundred yards. I think it must have blown her wide open."

Tziga said, "At some point Laura's figures must become official."

"Yes," said Grace. "Just because we have to deal with Cas Doran and his bloody Depot and whatever the hell his plan is, that doesn't mean that Laura's future is finished. Or mine, or Sandy's. When the Regulatory Body is straightened out, there will still be—well—a Regulatory Body. We'll all still be dreamhunters. Laura will have to work according to the advantages and constraints of her power. What we need for now, so that nobody will suspect she acquired her big penumbra by catching Buried Alive, is a way for Laura to ease into work until she's recovered enough to catch The Gate—which, when I shared it twelve years ago, gave me another twenty-five yards."

"When you catch The Gate, you can offer it to the sanatorium at Fallow Hill," Tziga said. "I can make the arrangements for you."

Grace and Tziga had, it seemed, taken their cue from Laura. Sandy was now completely in their confidence. Chorley trusted him—up to a point—but resented the fact that his own fatherly authority had been usurped by Laura's actual father. Tziga seemed to think he was up to making decisions for his daughter despite the fact that he'd always been impractical, and was now confused and forgetful.

Chorley watched Grace and Tziga handling Sandy Mason and thought, "Grace is ambitious for Laura. She's so focused on Laura's future that she's overlooking present problems."

"So," said Grace to Sandy. "Will you work with Laura for a time? Does that suit you?"

Sandy blushed and nodded.

Laura looked at the floor and smiled. Then she got up. "If that's settled, can Sandy, Rose, and I go to Farry's? There's only *invalid* food here."

"Fine, fine," said Grace, and waved them off.

When the young people had gone, Grace said, "I'm so pleased Sandy's gotten over the business of the letter. Now that he's seen Tziga, he thinks he got it all wrong and she was writing to her father."

"Why do you say 'he thinks she was' instead of 'he knows she was'?" asked Chorley.

Grace looked irritated. "Fine—*knows* she was, if you like."

Tziga said, "The point is that Sandy isn't angry with Laura anymore and can be called on to help her."

Chorley did agree that Laura's well-being was important, and that the young man seemed to be important to her well-being. He would like to feel as settled as Grace seemed to feel about the subject of the letter Laura had asked Sandy to deliver. But, no matter which way he looked at it, some things refused to become clear. Sandy supposed now that Laura's letter must have been to Tziga. But the letter had come from the lighthouse, where Laura was staying *with* her father, so she would hardly have been writing to him.

Chorley had always supposed that Sandy Mason was the one who had helped Laura carry his movie camera from Y-17 in the Place back to Summerfort the previous winter. But, if so, why wasn't the boy *with* her when he and Rose arrived? Sandy Mason didn't strike Chorley as particularly well bred or bashful. Laura had been in the bath when Chorley and Rose arrived, and Chorley was convinced that if he arrived at Summerfort *now* to find Laura bathing, he might well find Sandy Mason in the damn tub with her!

So the question remained, who was Laura's letter to? And who had carried the camera? Apparently there was some shadowy agent whose existence no one but Chorley seemed ever to notice, as someone sensitive to drafts notices the least touch of cold moving air.

Grace got up and stretched. "I'm so glad that's all settled. It's time Laura got on with actually being a dreamhunter—instead of a spy for the Church." She gave her husband an indulgent smile. "And how *is* your investigation going?"

"Slow, puzzling, and possibly pointless," Chorley said. "I have one more person I want to talk to. Then—like the Commission of Inquiry—I'll ponder my findings. Such as they are."

2

✦ ✦ ✦

ON A WARM DAY IN EARLY FEBRUARY CHORLEY SAT IN A CAFÉ IN UNIVERSITY SQUARE. THE ESTABLISHMENT WAS surprisingly busy, since commencement was still over a month away. Chorley had an appointment with Dr. Michael King. He'd reached the stage in his investigations where what he wanted was to chew the fat with any intelligent person prepared to really *think* about the Place. He'd decided that the historian Dr. King was his man.

King arrived half an hour late. He bustled in, scanning the tables, spotted Chorley, and gave him a wave, his raised hand making a little wriggle as if to mime smoke going up a flue. Then he swerved and pounced on a table near the door, and one student at that table. "Mr. Jones! Where is that thesis you're supposed to have finished and turned in?" he said, in a loud, friendly tone.

The young man got up. "I came to see you about it—" he began.

"Yes—and a colleague of mine caught you putting curses on my closed door!"

"I wasn't cursing you, sir. I was just annoyed not to find you there, because I wanted to put my paper into your hands personally."

"Mr. Jones, did you, or did you not, wish a pox upon me?"

"No, sir. I only wished a pox upon your closed door."

King laughed. It was a silent, wheezy laugh, but his shoulders bobbed up and down. He put a hand on the young man's shoulder. "If you don't have your paper with you, why don't you run off and get it? I'll be here for the next hour talking to this gentleman." He pointed at Chorley.

The student hurried out. King came over to Chorley, beamed at him, and offered his hand. They shook hands. King called for more coffee. "That lad," he said, "wants to see his paper safely in my hands. He must think that he's done something astounding." He chuckled some more. "Now, before you tell me why you wanted to meet me, I must pass on a hello from Judge Seresin. He said that you were one of his cleverest students. And the laziest."

Chorley remembered his old professor Seresin, who was now a judge at the Supreme Court and, incidentally, the Head of the Commission of Inquiry into the Rainbow Opera riot. Chorley had disappointed Professor Seresin. "I didn't complete my degree," he said. "I fell out a third-floor window while drinking with some friends. I don't remember it at all. I wasn't hurt. Apparently I landed in a freshly turned flower bed and got up and wandered away. There were dozens of witnesses, and a fuss, and my father put me on a boat to Europe. And that was the end of my studies. I had a full year in parts foreign, then my father died and it turned out we didn't have any money."

The coffee came, a double order, since Chorley had ordered for himself shortly before King arrived. Chorley had also ordered a large savory scone. King eyed it. "Please help yourself," said Chorley, pressing the plate forward.

"No, no," said King and slid the plate back beside Chorley's elbow. "And so, when you discovered that your father hadn't left you anything, were you ever tempted to Try?"

"I arrived back during the first of the rush. It was like a gold rush, wasn't it?"

"Yes and no. So many people were stopped right away. It was as if they discovered that, despite there being gold in the ground, they weren't physically able to *dig*." King's fingers fluttered, then made a little foray toward Chorley's scone. They broke a piece off. The fingers conveyed the fragment to his mouth; he glanced down at it, apparently surprised, then opened his mouth to accept it.

Chorley said, "I thought then that the whole dreamhunting thing was a little vulgar. I mean—citizens were carrying blankets and pillows into the People's Park on summer nights. Founderston was my town, and it changed almost overnight. I felt somewhat resentful." He shrugged. "So I didn't go near the border till I went with my wife, shortly after we were married."

"And you found that you couldn't go In."

"That's right, I couldn't." Chorley piled three sugar lumps into his coffee. "I read your chapter on the Place in your *History of Southland*. It struck me as one of the most lucid things written about it."

"You flatter me. And surely there are dozens of even more lucid paragraphs buried among official twaddle and statistical stuff in the Dream Regulatory Body's records?"

"I'm not going to bother the Body."

"Why not?" King was giving Chorley a shrewd appraisal.

"The Grand Patriarch has given me this task. I'm supposed to think about the Place."

"That's fine. That's not a novelty," said King, and his hands pounced again on Chorley's scone. He broke off a big piece and continued to talk, gesturing with the fragment and scattering crumbs around the table like a priest scattering drops of holy water in blessing. "Plenty of people have *thought*

about the Place. But really intelligent debate hasn't been possible because feelings run so high. The Church preaches against
dreamhunting. Dreamhunters feel defensive. And the Regulatory Body tries to smooth things over by behaving like a
strict parent toward dreamhunters—in public, at least. All the
discussions are about whether the Place is good or bad, and
how it should be used."

"Yes," said Chorley, eager.

Dr. King seemed startled at the interruption. He slapped
the tabletop. "Exactly! We know how the Place can be used,
but not why it's there. Do you realize that that is opposite to
our views on human life? For instance, as a man who believes
in the material rather than the spiritual, I know that my fun-
damental *purpose* in life is to father children and teach them
the skills for survival. To, in short, do what a mother cat will
for her kittens. A human version of that. So—you and I must
continue the species—"

"Oh dear," said Chorley, "you and I?"

Dr. King patted Chorley's hand. "No, my dear man, you
with your charming wife, and I with mine. But that description of why we are here doesn't give any clues about how we
should actually live our lives—the *uses* of our lives. How many
times are we confronted with a thing for which we have a use,
but no knowledge of its nature? Its purpose? That's what the
Place is to us."

Again King made a raid on Chorley's scone. Chorley
didn't dare take a bite of it himself. Momentarily distracted by
this, he found, when his attention returned to what Dr. King
was saying, that the man was talking about Aristotle.

Chorley was bemused. Hadn't they agreed that there had
been enough theological and philosophical thinking about
the Place? And now King was bringing up a philosopher.

"You are familiar with Aristotle?"

Chorley, in his impatience, quoted part of a song he'd learned at the University—or rather in the bars and cafés around the University. "Aristotle, Aristotle, was a demon for the bottle."

Dr. King gave him a wry look. "Was 'demon' the word you learned?"

"No, I substituted 'demon' for the word I learned. Of course I know Aristotle. Greek philosopher. Taught Alexander the Great. Disapproved of plays, because he thought that, if people enjoyed the villains in plays, that would encourage them to behave badly. The Grand Patriarch would like him."

King laughed his vigorous, shoulder-shaking laugh and reached for some more scone. "Would you like your own?" Chorley said, and turned to seek a waiter.

"Oh no! No!" King desisted. "Now—why I mention Aristotle is that, with the Place, investigators are reduced to the same state of knowledge as the ancients. We really don't have any scientific methods we can apply. There are so few fruitful experiments. Yes, we have brought out bottled air and burned it. Yes, we've collected soil samples and performed chemical tests. But what of it? Chemistry won't do it.

"Aristotle invented an early system of classification, with a place for everything: animal, vegetable, and mineral. For instance, in Aristotle's system, put simply, man is a two-legged animal without wings. A chicken, on the other hand, is a two-legged animal with wings—"

Chorley, annoyed by this detour, said flippantly, "And Long John Silver, having only one leg, wouldn't be a man?"

"Well—yes—but do we count his parrot? Its legs and wings?" Dr. King chortled.

Chorley wondered whether he dared to call a waiter over and order himself another scone. He didn't want to embarrass King, whose trespasses were rather charming. In most situations Chorley was the one licensed to be less formal. But King was making him feel a little stiff and starchy. That was why he'd made his silly remark about Long John Silver—only to get a witty comeback.

King said, "Aristotle is useful in the case of the Place because we can use him to ask very simple questions about it. Shall we try?" He began, "What is the Place made of?"

"Land," said Chorley. "Plains, hills, riverbeds—land."

"Good! What does it contain?"

"Vegetation. Dead pasture, brush, and trees. There are no animal remains, which is very strange."

"No, no!" Dr. King waved his remnant scone back and forth, as if by sowing the tabletop with crumbs he might encourage a crop of little scones. "Let us ignore what the Place lacks. Aristotle would have you start with what a thing *has*, not what it lacks."

"So the missing leg doesn't count, but the parrot does?"

"Quite so! And therefore Long John Silver was a three-legged creature with wings. Now—let us say that the grass and trees in the Place are land too, shall we? We don't normally exclude grass and trees from any purchase of a property, do we?"

"All right. Then what the Place contains is dreams."

"And what are dreams?"

"They are like thoughts. An activity of our sleeping brains."

"Dreams are thoughts," Dr. King said, and made a coaxing motion at Chorley. "Thoughts suggest consciousness. So what do we have, so far, as a classification for the Place?"

"Land—with consciousness," said Chorley.

"Yes," said Dr. King, then, "Do you mind?" as he took the very last piece. It was the first time he'd asked. "The medieval scholars who were Aristotle's heirs had the whole of creation in ranks, with ideal examples at the top of each rank. So, in the category of animals there were noble animals, like lions, 'the king of the beasts,' man above that, and above man, angels. Even gems were ranked, not according to rarity but by all sorts of other ideas, mostly religious." King paused and then glanced guiltily at Chorley's empty plate.

Chorley had to struggle not to laugh.

King brightened again, and said, "So, in those old categories, the animal world rises into the spiritual through man. But the mineral world does not rise into the spiritual. So what is the Place? It's invisible to most people, like a spirit. It's land; so mineral. And it has dreams; so it's conscious."

"Conscious, and mineral," Chorley said. "Which leaves us none the wiser." Then, because he felt he owed it to Dr. King, Chorley told him what he knew so far. About the telegrams, and how some of the dreams seemed set in a time further on than now. He talked about the convicts in Laura's first dream, and the ones Tziga would edit from the end of Convalescent One. The newspapers hadn't printed Lazarus's letters—but Chorley knew what at least one letter had said, the one Cas Doran had shown Grace when he questioned her. The newspapers only claimed that a dreamhunter "assailant" calling himself Lazarus had sunk the audience at the Rainbow Opera in a nightmare as a protest against the use of convict labor. This claim had started all sorts of public discussions about, for instance, how miners' wages were low because some mines were worked by convicts. But no one was talking about the Department of Corrections' use of nightmares in prisons. Chorley told King about the letter Grace had seen in the hope of getting him talking to others. The man was a talker, and a lecture hall in the University may not have been as good as a newspaper at getting word out, but it was at least as good as the pulpits of Southland's churches.

When Chorley had finished, Dr. King shook his hand, and
said, "You will let me know how you get on with your investigation, won't you?"

"I will."

Dr. King signaled the waiter, paid the bill, then rearranged
his scarf, handkerchief, crumpled papers, wallet, and glasses
case in the distorted pockets of his white linen summer suit.
He shook Chorley's hand again, started away from the table,
swerved, came back, asked Chorley if he was intending "to
write it all up in a book," insisted that Chorley *must*, patted his
pockets again, shook Chorley's hand once more, and wandered out of the café—disappearing only a few minutes before his student returned, panting, with the essay he was so
proud of.

✦ ✦ ✦

Chorley left University Square and turned onto the riverbank, heading toward home. It was a sunny day, and the cafés
on the embankment were full. He found himself enchanted
by these sultry, underpopulated squares. It was years since
he'd spent any time in Founderston in summer. When he was
young, his parents and sister, Verity, would always go to a hotel at Sisters Beach, and he and his friends would have the
town house to themselves. They'd stay up all night and sleep
all day and roam around looking for adventure.

Chorley was ambling along in a mild fever of nostalgia
when he spotted his niece and Sandy Mason at a table outside
a café. They had pulled their chairs together. Laura was leaning on Sandy.

Chorley veered off his path and stood over them.

Mason straightened and said, "Good afternoon, Mr. Tiebold. Please join us." He jumped up to get a chair from an

adjacent table and placed it for Chorley. "Will you have something?" He reached for his wallet.

Chorley placed his palm on Sandy's breast pocket and patted him firmly and discouragingly. He wasn't about to let this boy buy him anything.

"We're flush, Uncle Chorley," Laura said.

"It's going well, then?" Chorley caught the eye of the waiter. He said to his niece and her friend, "What will you have?"

Sandy went red.

Laura, oblivious, asked for a scone and another pot of tea, then excused herself and dashed off to the bathroom.

Sandy waited for the waiter to go away and said, "Mr. Tiebold, please don't act as if you're paying for me to take care of Laura."

Chorley gave the boy a look of wounded innocence. "I don't mean to make you feel that," he said.

"My money is as good as yours," Sandy said. "You can enjoy my hospitality, can't you?"

Chorley raised an eyebrow.

"Laura's *father* approves of me. Who are you to disapprove?" Sandy seemed furious.

"Laura's father is brain-damaged," Chorley said.

When Laura returned to the table, she couldn't fail to notice that Sandy and her uncle were glaring at each other. "What's the matter?"

"Apparently my money isn't good enough for your uncle," Sandy said.

"Uncle Chorley always pays for everything," Laura said. She sat down and nestled up to Sandy again. "You'll just have to get used to it."

"I think it's very good for old dogs to learn new tricks," Sandy said.

Laura chuckled. "He's calling you an old dog," she said to her uncle.

"Woof," said Chorley.

The waiter brought tea and Laura's scone. "I'm still so hungry," she said. "My dressmaker keeps having to let out the seams of my ball gown—which is good, because it's quite close-fitting in places, and before I started filling out again there wasn't much difference between me and the cloth still on its bolt."

"We're going In again in three days to get The Gate," Sandy said. "Laura's ready." He put his arm around her waist.

"We have to go," Laura said. "It's not working out—performing together. We're just too big. I've been doing midnight at Pike Street, and Sandy's doing midday at St. Thomas's. We're booked at both places together and go along together, then I stay awake all day in my room next to his. They always supply separate rooms, did you know that?"

"No. And, good," Chorley said.

"Sandy has to stay awake all night, which is hard on him. The only problem I have is making sure I hang on to consciousness when Sandy goes down. He's a bit of a Soporif now."

Sandy said, "Buried Alive did that to me. Once I'd gotten over the patch where I couldn't catch dreams at all."

"That was emotional," Laura said, and swayed against him, bump, bump, bump, till she got a faint, conceding smile. Then she looked back at her uncle. "Anyway, the doctors at Pike Street, where I sleep, think they have two real talents, and a great bargain. St. Thomas's is happy enough to have two for the price of one, but one of the doctors said to Sandy, sadly, that while our Convalescent One is Hame quality—soothing and significant—even with Sandy helping me I seem to be getting only the sort of range that can be expected from any reasonably talented young dreamhunter."

Sandy said, "We can't go on with our ruse. Sooner or later the different hospitals will compare notes."

Laura said, "Sandy's very pleased that we've been able to work these day and night bookings, because we're earning twice what we would otherwise."

Chorley smirked at Sandy. "That must have been very gratifying for you," he said, and watched the young man suppressing objections.

"So, it's time for us to go and get The Gate," Laura said.

Chorley looked across the Sva at the dome of the Temple, perfect in actuality, wrinkled in its reflection on the river. He thought about The Gate, a dream Tziga had had twelve years before and claimed not to be able to find again, a dream other dreamhunters had looked for in vain.

Tziga had caught The Gate when his wife, Chorley's sister, Verity, was dying. Tziga had carried the dream back for her, only to find she had died while he was away, and without his, or *its*, help. Tziga had fought sleep for two days after the funeral. He'd gone down fighting, as thought he'd meant to die with the dream and take it to Verity. Tziga was a religious man and may well have been able to imagine meeting his wife in the afterlife. But he'd succumbed to exhaustion—and to his brother-in-law's tender determination to comfort him. He'd slept and dreamed, and a good portion of his neighbors had shared his dream.

Chorley remembered the dream as one of the most wonderful experiences of his life. He understood why Tziga had kept it hidden all these years. No matter how anyone else who shared it experienced The Gate, to the bereaved Tziga the

dream might have seemed only a beautiful lie, not an answered prayer.

Looking back on his memory of The Gate, with much
more life behind him, Chorley could see now that the dream
wasn't a lie—or not exactly. It didn't matter whether you believed in an afterlife (and Chorley didn't), or even whether
the *dream* believed in one, because The Gate wasn't a true vision. For a start it was different from every other dream. All
the Place's other dreams were based on natural laws, and possible facts. No one flew in a dream, or breathed underwater,
or met a minotaur. The Gate, however, was mystical, tran-
scendent, and unreal. It promised an afterlife.

"But it isn't either true or false," Chorley thought. "Because what it *is*, is a wish. And wishes aren't either true or
false."

"I'm looking forward to this dream," Laura said. "I remember the feelings it gave me when I had it when I was little. It'll help Da." She rested her head on Sandy Mason's
broad shoulder. "Besides, I want to fall asleep with Sandy. It's
perverse to keep resisting it."

Chorley knew she meant that it was hard to keep herself
awake and reading a book while Sandy dreamed Convalescent
One, but, when he glanced at Sandy, Chorley could see the
young man feeling the effects of her unintended double
meaning. Sandy flushed, clenched his jaw, and crossed his
legs. Laura had picked up his hand and was playing with the
soft flesh between his thumb and finger—childish and inti-
mate. Sandy was having trouble with this, and Chorley saw,
at last, that the young man was in love with Laura, not just
drawn and possessive. Sandy was trying to control his desire,
and having difficulty doing so. Chorley could see that the
young man too thought Laura wasn't ready for things to go
any further between them. She was in danger of getting in

too deep too young, not because Sandy was older and infatuated with her but because of her own behavior. Something—Chorley could not imagine what—seemed to have stripped away all the normal caution she should have about just touching another person, any other person. The attention she was lavishing on Sandy's hand was playful but intense. She stroked and pressed his hand as if in search of a secret mechanism that would make it open up, or turn into something other than a hand.

Chorley said, "If you don't mind, Sandy, I'd like a word in private with my niece."

Sandy retrieved his hand, nodded curtly, and got up. "I'll be in that bookshop on the corner," he said, and took off.

Laura dropped her hands into her lap and assumed a blank, wooden look.

Chorley cleared his throat. "Judging by your expression, I think perhaps you know what I'm about to say. You must be careful with that boy."

"I'll try not to *lose* him, Uncle Chorley, if that's what you mean."

"You know that isn't what I mean. He must be several years your senior."

"Three years. Which is nothing," Laura said. She sounded dry—not exactly impatient.

"At your age, that's a big difference."

Laura laughed.

"What?"

"I see difference differently," she said. Then she sighed, a sigh like a yawn, as if she was sleepy. "Sandy suits me."

It seemed a strange, cold thing for a girl to say, and Chorley shivered to hear it.

"I like to be with him," she added. "I'm safe with him."

"Yes, I think you probably are. And he does seem to sincerely care for you. But even if no one is mistaken in their feelings, feelings get hurt. And there are physical dangers of intimacy."

"Uncle Chorley, you're talking to someone who nearly died trying to see what was at the end of a rail line. Intimacy—as you put it—is safer than half of the things I've had to do."

"*Did* you nearly die?" Chorley knew she'd been sick—"depleted" Tziga had said—but Tziga had understated his own injuries too.

"We'll have some film soon of the Depot," Laura said.

"What?"

"Da and I arranged for someone to go In at The Pinnacles with one of your movie cameras, to film those buildings and people. We need documentary evidence."

Chorley supposed he shouldn't be surprised that Laura and Tziga were communicating independently with the Grand Patriarch, and calling on his help. Of course the Grand Patriarch must have had dreamhunters who would act as his agents.

"We'll show the film to the Commission of Inquiry," Laura said. "That's probably the quickest way to get questions asked, and to cut Cas Doran off at the knees."

Chorley reached across the table and waited for her to take his hand. She did—hers dry and callused, a smaller version of his wife's and Tziga's. "Dreamhunter," Chorley said, wonderingly, and squeezed her hand. "You changed the subject," he said. "Don't think I didn't notice."

"Yes, I did. But, back on that subject, Aunt Grace was only Sandy's age when you met her."

"Your Aunt Grace was a powerful woman."

"Uncle Chorley, *I'm* a powerful woman," Laura said.

"Or girl," Chorley said.

"Don't worry. Sandy is loyal and kind, and I think maybe I do love him."

Chorley sighed; he got up and helped her up too. He opened his wallet and dropped bills onto the table. "All right then, honey." He took her arm. "I'll deliver you to your destiny."

They set off toward the bookshop on the corner. As they went, Laura said quietly and fervently, "Oh—I wish he was."

3

❖ ❖ ❖

*L*AURA WAS LATE FOR HER FINAL BALL GOWN FITTING. GRACE AND ROSE HAD BEEN THERE FOR HALF AN HOUR. Rose had her dress on and was standing between two angled mirrors. Sunlight came in the high fitting-room windows, and there were electric lights on the walls, but Rose managed to look like candlelight and moonlight combined, like the central panel of some devotional altarpiece, haloed with radiance.

She had wanted a high-necked dress, and the design she'd chosen had a Chinese-style collar that circled her strong throat. The bodice was fitted, boned and tapered in at the waist, then followed the swelling curves of her hips. The fabric was heavy bone-white silk. The sleeves and bodice were sewn with a filigree of seed pearls. The dress had a train that Rose would have to fasten to one arm in order to dance. She was practicing this when her cousin came in.

"You'll do very nicely," Grace was saying. "And we must put your hair up."

Rose arched her back and neck and threw off light.

Grace grinned at Laura. "I think there will be displays of dumb admiration and the falling over of feet."

"It's not too tight?" Rose said.

"No," said everyone.

The dressmaker nodded to one of the seamstresses. "Please go and get Miss Hame's dress."

Laura had toyed with pale blues and greens, and Rose had nearly persuaded her to wear pink. But her aunt had insisted that, since Laura wasn't a debutante and didn't have to wear white, she should realize, for the purposes of fashion, she wasn't a young girl and could choose a strong color, one that would set off her tan and her dark hair. Laura's dress was also silk, of a vibrant coral red. It was sleeveless, with a low, square neck, fitted at the bust and flaring under it. It was a simple dress of a rich fabric, and Laura was going to wear it with long black gloves and her mother's jet choker.

Laura put her dress on and shared the mirror with Rose while her hem was pinned. They stood looking solemnly at each other.

"Do debutantes wear white so that men can imagine the brides they'll be?" Rose asked her mother.

"I'm not sure," Grace said. "I didn't have a coming out."

"It's for *you* to imagine the bride you'll be," said the dressmaker.

"I don't look like a dreamhunter," Laura said. She wished that Nown could see her in her ball gown—which was silly, since he couldn't see color anyway.

Her tall cousin walked out of the mirror's frame. "Can I take this off now?"

"Certainly. And we should look at your friend's dress. She's due in for a fitting tomorrow at three. Her mother has already given the dress provisional approval." The dressmaker looked worried.

Rose had finally taken it on herself to design Mamie's gown, after they had held every variation on white—icy, bone, cream, pearly peach, salmon, beige, fawn—up to Mamie's face, and every shade, without fail, had made Mamie's mauve, mottled skin look corpselike. Grace and Rose had found a pattern Mamie liked, a dress that would let her bare shoulders and the tops of her breasts rise out of it. A dress with a belted waist and a skirt that had two generous pleats at the back and two at the front. Rose's innovation was to make the shawl neck and sleeves of black silk—to add a black belt, and to make the recessed pleats black also. The silks were the same weight, the white brocaded, the black with a sheen rather than a gloss. The black made Mamie's skin look better—a lilac-tinted pallor rather than fishy.

When the dress was produced, Rose, Laura, Grace, and all the seamstresses gave it their full attention.

"Mamie's mother can't mind if we come to her next fitting," Rose said.

"I'm sure she won't," said the dressmaker.

"It's a big responsibility—making this ball less of an ordeal for Mamie," Laura said.

"She'll enjoy it," Rose said. "You wait and see. As for me, *I'm* going to have—a ball!"

4

✧ ✧ ✧

ANDY STOPPED IN AT MRS. LILLEY'S ONLY TO SMUGGLE SOME BLANKETS OFF HIS BED AND STUFF THEM INTO HIS pack. He hid the pack outside, then went back into the kitchen to get Laura, whom he'd told to keep Mrs. Lilley and her girls chatting.

The Lilley girls were scarcely responding to Laura's polite patter. They were cool and monosyllabic. The elder shot Sandy a wounded look and spun back to scrubbing the stove top.

"Well, ladies—good day," Sandy said. Then, "Come on, Laura." He put an arm around her shoulders and ushered her out the door. He picked up his pack.

"We're going In only for one night, so what's all that?" Laura said, then, "Do those girls hate me just because they had to keep airing out my room?"

Sandy grunted. He listened to Laura's patient silence. She put her hand in his. He felt that she was waiting for a confession. He said, "I took one of them to a dance held by the Wry Valley Young Farmers. The girls sat on one side of the room and the men on the other, like a school dance. And a good proportion of the men were out among the cars and carriages drinking whiskey."

"Which one did you take?"

"Patricia," he said. "The elder."

"I knew they liked you," Laura said.

On the way back from the dance, Pat had pushed Sandy against a tree trunk and put her hand down his trousers. He'd liked that too, rather helplessly, but the very next day he'd set out walking the border—the walk that finally took him to Debt River and the site of the dream Quake.

"One of them even said to me that you weren't really my type," Laura said.

"I'm not," Sandy replied, sulkily.

"I don't have a type. Do you think you do?" She sounded breezy. "What's she like then, your type of girl?"

Sandy thought it was best to be quiet.

"Taller, I suppose," Laura said, musing.

They walked hand in hand into the rangers' station and headed straight for the line before the big ledger of the intentions book. Several older dreamhunters smiled at them in an indulgent way.

"What are we going to write?" Laura whispered as they shuffled forward.

"That we're walking a short way east along the border."

"Is that what Da said?"

✧ ✧ ✧

Tziga Hame had given Sandy directions on the day Sandy delivered Laura to Summerfort. He told Sandy that The Gate was just inside the border, about two hours east of Doorhandle. "It's easy to find because it is right on a landmark rangers refer to as Foreigner's West."

"I've been to Foreigner's North," Sandy said. He wanted to impress Laura's father with what he knew, to tell him all about the supposed French explorer and his crazy attempt to

map the Place, and his odd compass bearings, "Nord" and
"Ouest"—North and West in French. It was interesting, Sandy
thought, the whole question of who the man had been and
how the hell he'd gotten himself so turned around, since
"Nord" may have been in the north but "Ouest" was more
south and east—east of Doorhandle anyway. But Sandy hadn't
launched into a dissertation on what he knew, because he'd
figured out that it wasn't a good idea to interrupt Tziga
Hame, whose concentration was ragged and who got upset
when he lost the thread of his thoughts.

"The Gate is in plain sight," Laura's father had said to
Sandy. "But scarcely anyone would think to bed down there,
because the ground is hard and uneven and cut up. The
dream is in a tightly confined spot, actually in the circle.
You'll find a circle on the ground. I knew the dream was there
when I first saw the site. I don't know how I knew, but my
need was so great I suppose that some instinct led me to it.
The confined site, the bad ground, and the rarity of dreamhunters who can catch master dreams, all have guaranteed
that The Gate has sat there untapped since I caught it."

✧ ✧ ✧

Nearly two hours after they went In, Sandy and Laura ran
into a ranger with paintbrushes in his pockets and carrying a
can of paint. He had been refreshing signs, he said.

"Are we anywhere near Foreigner's West?" Sandy asked.

The ranger laughed. "You young dreamhunters are so
funny, with your little alliances and your sightseeing." He
raised one brawny arm to point with the hand holding the
paint can.

"Is there a latrine near here?" Laura said. She didn't like to
squat behind bushes when she was with Sandy—and she knew

that dreamhunters and rangers disapproved of such behavior in the Place's more populated areas. She asked her question peering out at the ranger from behind the shelter of Sandy's shoulder. The Body employed at least a thousand rangers, so she knew she shouldn't expect that every one she met would know about the Depot, or that she'd escaped from it.

"The trail branches by those trees up there. The Inward branch leads to a latrine, then back to Foreigner's West. I've painted the latrine too, so be careful, it might still be wet."

"Thank you," Laura said.

"What are you planning to catch?"

"We're not dreamhunting. We're just sightseeing, as you divined," Sandy said.

"And spending time together." The ranger winked at them, and went on his way.

They walked on till they reached the branch in the trail. Sandy let go of Laura. "I've been watering the bushes along the way," he said.

"Yes, you have." Laura laughed. "You're nearly as bad as a dog."

"It's because we spend all our time in cafés drinking tea," Sandy said, resentfully. Then, apparently without any thought of the connection in ideas, he said, "I'll make a bed for us with these blankets. Your father warned me that the ground was bad."

Laura went on peering up into his face, waiting for some sign of self-consciousness, for him to relent and acknowledge what everyone else could see and was teasing them about. They *had* been spending all their time in cafés when they weren't shut up in separate rooms in hospitals. She never went home. He never used his key to his uncle's flat. They sat in cafés—together.

Sandy looked down at her. Laura noticed that his jaw was hastily shaven and scratchy in patches. She looked into his eyes, saw resentment and, behind that, baffled, patient misery. She put a hand on his arm and felt a sharp shiver pass over him.

And then he bent his head and kissed her.

They were kissing, wrapped together, upright, his hands on her face, her hands covering his. His lips were full and firm, his chin rasping and rough.

Laura's bladder gave her a stab.

She broke away from him. "I have to go," she said, waved her hand in the direction of the latrines, and sprinted off.

Her bladder was full but shy. She spent a long time in the fresh-paint-smelling box before anything came. She kept giggling and shivering. The little byway was quiet—as deadly silent as anywhere else in the Place, but Laura had the impression the shelter she was standing in was in the middle of a stampede.

When she'd finished, she uncapped her water bottle and spilled water over her hands, patted her cheeks with her wet palms, then ran back along the path to find Sandy.

He'd made a bed of his purloined blankets and emptied his pack of all the cans and hard-edged packages to make one pillow. He was sitting down, setting out a picnic, but he jumped up when she appeared. He grabbed her—or she collided with him—and they continued kissing, more involved with each passing second.

Laura thought, "Do people do this?" She'd never seen anyone kissing like this. Books said things like "He rained kisses on her face." But suddenly they seemed tied together, mouth to mouth. She felt his skin, the wiry hair on his chest. Her hands had gotten into his shirt. They seemed to have a mind of their own. No—she *agreed* with her hands. Sandy's skin was smooth, his muscles springy and supple. He was lovely to touch, warm and dewy.

He was saying her name, into her mouth.

"What should I do with your clothes?" Laura said. Her throat was so tight she wanted to cough.

Sandy caught her hands and held them away from him. "Laura. We shouldn't. We have to be careful."

"I don't care!" she said fiercely. "I love you." She began struggling with the buttons of her own shirt. She pulled its halves apart—sending one button spinning.

Sandy caught her hands again, then pulled her against him. Their bare skin came together, and Laura sighed. Sandy was saying yes, all right. "But go slower, Laura." He began to help her with her clothes. She attacked his belt buckle, then responded to his "slower" and let go, leaned into him, kissed his shoulders, as high as she could reach when his head was raised.

He took her face between his hands again. "I love you, Laura. I mean it. I don't want to be without you, ever. Can you—would you—do you think we might get married? Please say you will."

"Please, Sandy, let's lie down together."

"I don't really know what I'm doing," he said. "Neither do you. That's why we have to go slow. And I wish you'd *promise*." He sounded as though he might cry.

"Oh—look at you," she said. She'd uncovered some more of him and thought he was beautiful, and that made her tearful too.

Sandy gave a gasp and grabbed her, and they fell down together onto the ground, which was still impossibly lumpy, even under all the blankets. They writhed around, trying to get comfortable, and to get at each other, clumsy and hasty.

They slowed down and stared at each other, their eyes moving, and sometimes meeting, with bright, searching, softened
looks.

Inside Laura's great excitement, there was a kind of peaceful expectation. She had felt big and powerful before, and she
had felt small and lost. Being like this with Sandy seemed the
best way to discover what size she *really* was, and where she belonged, both in her body and in time and space.

*He found himself in what he supposed was the garden of one of the farms in the
valley. An ordinary garden, made glorious by his exhaustion and the glow of
final things.*

*He had somehow lost his shoes, and the grass was tender on the soles of his
bare feet. It was twilight, sometime in the half hour after sunset, when the sky
still fumes with the sun's power but the earth is drowsy. The garden was giving off
vapor, scents, ghosts of dewfall in the soft air.*

*He wasn't dreaming. No one could fall asleep while in flight, stumbling and
singing, every breath a phrase of the song. And why bother to fall asleep before a
thing you don't need to survive?*

*Ahead of him a path wound through rhododendrons. The bushes were not in
flower, because it was summer. Because it was summer there had been a bonfire
on the beach—three days ago, was it? Three days, when he still had his strength,
and shortly before he'd lost all hope.*

*He became aware that someone was ahead of him. A woman was winding
her way through the rhododendrons. He could see the pale streak of her skirt
disappearing around the curve in the path.*

*He followed her onto the clearing of a lawn. Around the lawn's dusky green
arena were citrus trees: lemons and limes, mandarins and kumquats, glowing
like lanterns among the glossy darkness of their leaves.*

*The woman glanced back and lingered, as though he were lagging behind and
she must wait for him.*

*There was a gate before her. It had white-painted posts and a peaked roof,
like the gate to a churchyard. Beyond the gate there was another green room.*

The woman waited, and he caught up with her; then she went ahead, and he fixed his eyes on her hand, the hand held back to him. He would know it anywhere. It looked like his mother's.

She beckoned, trailed her arm like a rope he could catch. She walked on, caressing the petals of flowers, the quilted foliage of a humble hydrangea, a tibouchina, its purple flowers haloed with cerise.

There was too much color to take in. His prison-ruined eyes watered and made afterimages, a halo around every object. The woman's pale skirt reflected the colors, as though she stood in the light of a stained-glass window.

She stopped at the gate and waited. He could see a little of the garden beyond her—its piled flower-colors and flower-lights.

It seemed to him that the fierce currents of heat had been only momentarily calmed. The sun had gone, but something had electrified the atmosphere. Something impossible was about to happen to the twilight.

The woman who might be his mother smiled at him, as if to say, "Wait till you see this."

The sun had gone, and the birds had settled and roosted, shadows nestled into shadows. But suddenly they began again to make expectant noises, like dawn birdcalls.

The sun was coming back.

Because the sun was coming back, the day would return and take him through it again. Not his real yesterday but something better. Every hour would brighten back to noon, and then on toward morning. With every hour he would be cleaner and fresher and more full of the certainty that is health and youth. There was no hurry. It was the first time for everything. That was her promise, that was where she meant to take him—through the gate, into all that was sweet, and easeful, and good in the green fathoms of a garden.

Then the sun came back and covered them both, and carried them off to the first time for everything.

5

✢ ✢ ✢

CAS DORAN WAS STILL IN HIS OFFICE, HIS BACK TO HIS OVAL WINDOW WITH ITS VIEW OF THE ISLE OF THE TEMPLE AND its three domes. Nearest was the green copper-clad dome at the top of the offices of the Dream Regulatory Body. In the middle distance was the scintillating skin of the Rainbow Opera. Farthest off the Temple shone, so pale that the sky seemed to show through it, as the bruise of a slight tumble will show on a petal of fallen plum blossom.

Doran had for some minutes been peering out from under a steeple made of his hands at a telegram on his otherwise clean and empty desktop. He looked as if he was developing a headache.

"Are you going to tell me what it says?" Maze Plasir was sitting across the desk from the Secretary and sipping wine.

"Laura Hame has finally signed in at Doorhandle in the intentions book. I've already had reports from St. Thomas's and Pike Street. I knew she was back in Founderston, dream-hunting, peddling Convalescent One with her friend the Mason boy."

"Why is her signing in worse than her continuing to hide?"

"She's mad," Doran said. "She escaped from the Depot— God knows how. She was threatened, deprived of liberty, and she simply comes back to Founderston and picks up where she left off late last winter. She's insane. Or she's very simple."

"I'd love to talk to her," said Plasir.

"Why?" Doran looked up, sharp.

"To sound her out. She's not simple, Cas, though she may be mad."

"Is she trying to draw me out somehow? Is this the advice they've give her?"

"*They*, Cas?"

"Them—my opponents."

"Do you mean 'Lazarus'?"

"I mean the Grand Patriarch," Doran said.

Plasir nodded. He twirled his glass, looked at the lozenge of light spinning in the wine. "How did the Hame girl escape?"

"Incompetence," Doran said. "My allies are incompetent."

"Not all," Plasir said, mildly.

Doran scowled. He thought of Rose Tiebold in the library at his summerhouse, tearful but cool underneath. Rose asking him about the surplus rails in the Awa Inlet. Rose after the riot, saying of her cousin, "She didn't sleep. We were talking."

"Courage isn't cleverness," he said, thinking aloud. "They can't outwit me." He opened one of his desk drawers and produced the rolled map of Founderston. He spread it open and peered at the circles that represented the penumbras of dreamhunters—dreamhunters loaded with Contentment. None of them were in place yet, but soon could be.

Plasir said, musing, "I remember how I would sometimes see people stop Tziga Hame in the street, to kiss his hands. Do people like Hame ever need to resort to anything as vulgar as cunning?"

Doran studied his map and thought of the fortress that was

the Temple—how he hadn't been able to buy, or rent, any property in its vicinity, so couldn't get one of his dosed dream-hunters near it. "What I need is a Soporif," he said.

"Then we must acquire one, by all means," Plasir said, and sipped, then smacked his lips. "Perhaps we should separate Miss Hame from her friend the Mason boy. The reports from St. Thomas's seem to suggest he is one, like his uncle. What do you say to that, eh, Cas?"

6

✦ ✦ ✦

FTER THE DREAM LAURA AND SANDY WERE STILL IN ITS DEEPS, WAITING TO SLEEP AGAIN. THEY TALKED AND KISSED; they rested and slept and went back to The Gate. After a time, hard to measure how long with no night and day, they exhausted their food supply and their ability to sleep. They got up, groggy, and began stuffing their rubbish of wrappers and empty cans into their packs. Laura stepped off the muddled blankets, and Sandy began picking them up, one by one, to shake them. Together they folded each blanket. When the last one was lifted, Laura looked down on the bared earth. At that moment it seemed to her the most significant things that had ever happened to her—The Gate, and Sandy—had happened in this uncomfortable spot. She stood looking reverently at the ground, her face soft with serenity and bodily tiredness.

There was a circle carved in the dirt. Much of their discomfort had been because of this deeply scored mark. Laura frowned at it. "What's this?"

"Foreigner's West," Sandy said. He was busy fastening a belt around the bundle of blankets so they'd be easier to carry.

"Pardon?"

"You know how rangers have their own legends, like we dreamhunters do? Theirs are about exploration rather than dreams." Sandy got up. His knees creaked. "Rangers talk about the Foreigner as though he's a good story rather than a historical fact—a pioneering ranger who didn't make maps but left compass marks."

"I don't get it," Laura said.

"Does it matter? All it means for us, Laura, is that no one tries sleeping here because it's too uncomfortable. And since The Gate is on just this confined site, no one else has ever caught it. Your father said he only found it because he was always able to sense where healing dreams were. When he walked by Foreigner's West, he knew the dream was here."

Laura began to twist her hair. Her curls were matted at the back, she had been lying down for so long. "But this isn't a compass mark," she said. She spoke so softly Sandy had to lean forward to hear her. Finding himself near, he kissed her on her earlobe. He said, "The idea that these are compass marks is the only reason rangers suppose the pioneer was a foreigner. *French*. They think the marks stand for north and west in French. The dream Quake is right on top of Foreigner's North. Foreigner's North is an N carved in the ground. 'Nord.' This is an O, for 'Ouest.' "

Sandy went on with what he was doing, lengthening one shoulder strap of Laura's pack so that he could carry it for her. It took him a moment to notice how still and silent she had become. He looked up at her.

"It's a Nown," Laura said. "The Place is a Nown." Her voice was almost inaudible.

Sandy tried to figure out why she had chosen this moment to correct his grammar. He reviewed what he'd been telling her and couldn't recall having mentioned the Place at all.

Laura still stood as if entranced. The color had drained out of her face.

Sandy put his hand under her elbow. He was afraid that

she was about faint. But she didn't sway or crumple, she simply stood frozen in place.

Nerves made Sandy giggle. He said, "Love, you are looking like Lot's wife, white and fixed to the spot."

✧ ✧ ✧

Laura could hear Sandy only as a murmur through a wall, one of those sounds that wakes you—a late-night conversation, or muffled crying. She was lost in the past.

She remembered the day she had made Nown. He had stood up out of the dry streambed and shown her his true face, a face she had longed to see. He had gotten onto his knees before her and made his pledge and introduction: "Laura Hame, I am your servant." She had been exhausted after making him and had slept for a time. When she woke up, she had lain admiring him. He'd stood, surveying the grasslands Inland, engrossed. When she'd asked him what he was doing, he had answered, "Listening." When she'd asked what he was listening to, he'd said, "I can hear now." And she had stupidly, wooden-headedly, imagined that, just as she'd made a more handsome sandman, she had also managed to make one with better hearing. He had even repeated himself in an effort to explain what must have bewildered him. "I can hear now," he'd said. "I am here with myself."

I can hear Now. I am here with myself.

They were *all* his selves—the Nowns, and speechless Nows. He'd come alive again and discovered he was standing *inside* himself—another self—a speechless Now, a Nown who hadn't had its final letter added, the letter that, in the spell, "gives speech." He'd tried to tell her, but she hadn't heard him. She hadn't heard his name when he used it. "Now" was only a word, and Sandy had just heard her say that "the Place" was a noun. It was an easy mistake, an obvious mistake. One word for another: "noun" for "Nown."

And to invent some surveying French ranger to explain an N and an O carved on the ground was an irresistible mistake. Because whatever logic such mistakes lacked, they still made some kind of daft sense.

What was the alternative? That someone had walked in a long loop around miles and miles of ground, singing "The Measures" and stopping occasionally to inscribe the letters of the spell: N O W. Someone had brought the land itself to life and tried to make a slave of it.

✢ ✢ ✢

Sandy found himself holding Laura up. She was overcome, by exhaustion or the elixirlike power of the dream, or with trepidation about how far they had gone. Sandy couldn't tell exactly what it was that had thrown her into a state of shock. He didn't know what he could do to help.

She clung to him. Her skin was cold, and she was shivering. Sandy coaxed her to sit back down, and she all but collapsed on him. But then she was asking questions again, and her voice sounded rational. "The N on the site of Quake—is it in one piece?" she asked.

"Never mind that now," Sandy said, soothing.

"Please tell me."

"No, it isn't. The letter is cracked straight across. There really was a quake there at some point."

✢ ✢ ✢

"It's free then," Laura thought. "Its first N has been erased, as I erased Nown's in the early hours of St. Lazarus's

Day. It's its own. And I've always felt it was talking to me because it *was*, or was *trying* to. It knows me. The dreams are set in the future, so it must once have known me. My father's sandman was the eighth Nown, mine is the ninth. The Place must be a later one."

Then she thought of the angry demands from the bad telegrams: "Rise up and shake them all off! Rise up and crush them!" She didn't understand it at all. What did it want?

✤ ✤ ✤

"Laura, please stop crying," Sandy begged.

She held her breath, hiccuped, struggled.

Agonized, Sandy burst out, "You should be happy!" But he was asking too much for himself, and that scared him. "Because of The Gate," he added. "How can you be unhappy with *that* inside you?"

Laura shook her head, choked. "This is just a reaction. Don't mind me."

He put an arm around her waist. "Can you walk? Let's go home. Let's go do your father some good, and start making our fortunes."

Laura nodded. She let him help her up. They stepped out of the circle and went slowly away from that place.

7

✦ ✦ ✦

FIVE DAYS BEFORE FOUNDERSTON'S
PRESENTATION BALL, THE DIRECTOR
OF THE CITY'S LARGEST SANATORIUM, FAL-
low Hill, was shocked by the sudden visit of a man he'd
thought was dead. Called to his office, the director found
Tziga Hame sitting in front of his desk.

For nearly twenty years Hame had had a contract with Fallow Hill. When the dreamhunter disappeared, it had been a
great loss to the sanatorium. The director was surprised and
delighted to see Hame. Then, looking harder, he wondered
whether the man had come seeking treatment. In the minute
it took the director to process these impressions, he noticed
his office was full of Hame's relatives. He shook hands with all
of them, then sat down to hear what Hame had to say about
his injuries.

Hame and his sister-in-law were sitting. Grace Tiebold's
husband, her daughter, and Hame's daughter stood at the
back of the room, with a dreamhunter unknown to the director, a young man with tired eyes and several days' stubble on
his jaw.

The director leaned forward and focused on Hame, or
tried to, because his eyes kept wandering, and he found himself counting them, *one, two, three, four*—four dreamhunters in
the room. He imagined he could feel them, like storm pres-

sure, an inaudible roar coming off them, and an invisible fire raging around them.

"As you know," Tziga Hame began, "it isn't often that any dreamhunter catches anything new. The almanac gains perhaps fifteen to twenty dreams in any year, and most aren't of any great consequence."

The director nodded, then was distracted by Rose Tiebold, who was making a quizzical face, touching her own chin, then pointing at her cousin's, miming a question about the grazes on Laura Hame's cheeks and chin and top lip. The marks were nothing much, gorse prickle scuffs. Laura Hame touched her own face, looked away from her cousin, and kept her fingers pressed against her mouth. The young man glanced at her; then his hand found hers, and the director saw them move their arms to conceal their entwined fingers behind their backs.

Tziga Hame was saying, "If we go straight to the Body with this, it will be classed as 'a dream for the public good.' But I think it should be tested before it's classified. I think it needs expert witnesses. You and your doctors are experts on dreams, long-term illness, and palliative care."

The director sat up straight. "Good God!" he said. He had realized that it was the *dream* he could feel, in the room, an endless cascade of high emotion. He looked into all the dreamhunters' faces. He should be able to *see* it.

"My daughter, Laura, and Alexander Mason here have a dream the like of which has never been felt," Tziga said.

Grace Tiebold coughed. She covered her mouth with her gloved hand.

The director said to her, "You've sampled it already?"

"Yes. We both have," Hame said. "And I'd very much like to have it again. So, if you could include my board in their six-night contract?"

"The Presentation Ball is in five nights," Laura Hame added, as though to explain something vital.

"Laura wants to stay till the very end of the ball," the young man said. He blushed and looked around nervously, as though he had no right to speak. Then he squared his shoulders. "But I will sign up to play the night of the ball, and for however long the dream lasts after that."

"I can come back too, and sleep with Sandy—only not on the night of the ball," Laura said. Her chafed cheeks dimpled.

Alexander Mason looked stony.

Grace Tiebold turned around in her chair to look at the young dreamhunters. She froze, staring, then said, "You should shave, Alexander." She sounded wrathful. The director couldn't imagine what the boy had done to offend her, or what his position was among this talented and high-handed family.

Grace turned back to the director. "These young people should wait outside while Tziga and I settle details."

"It's been a pleasure to meet you, Miss Hame, Miss Tiebold, Mr. Mason," the director said.

The young people left, the girls whispering fiercely. The director busied himself with the paperwork.

✧ ✧ ✧

Rose said to her cousin, "I hope you can get rid of that rash by Saturday night."

"What rash?"

"On your chin."

Laura touched her chin. She gave a secretive smile, then she looked at Sandy. "Aunt Grace is right, you should shave," she said.

"Oh—it's a *kissing* rash," Rose said. "I've heard about those."

8

✧ ✧ ✧

ROSE STOOD IN THE LOWER HALLWAY OF THE FOUNDERSTON HOUSE, READY MINUTES BEFORE EVERYONE ELSE, THOUGH hers had been by far the most involved preparations. Her hair had been washed and loosely curled in the morning, then pinned into seemingly artless whorls and tendrils shortly after lunch. After dinner it was decorated with real pearls, both fixed pins and drops that shimmered and shimmied every time she moved her head. Rose had been sponged down, powdered, and perfumed by eight o'clock and had gotten into her stockings and slip, then finally her dress. She'd had a maid to help her, hired especially for the occasion, since the household ordinarily had no need of ladies' maids. The maid had worn cotton gloves to protect the lustrous silk of Rose's ball gown from her hands. Rose was gloved now too, in one of the five pairs she had gotten for the season. She had covered herself with her white velvet cape. She was ready—ready to be presented to society, and to make a spectacle of herself. It was nine p.m. The ball was to begin at nine-thirty.

Where was everyone?

Rose tapped her foot. She didn't touch anything. She began to imagine that dust and cobwebs would jump off the walls, that fingerprints would float off the banisters beside her and drop greasily onto her clothes like soot from a ship's funnel.

Rose heard a door latch. It was the back door. Laura pushed through from the kitchen, walking backward, her brilliant skirt bunched in one hand. In the other she had a large canister of film. She had her gloves on, but her hands were poking out from the unbuttoned openings at her wrists. There was a small spray of dark mud on the back of her skirt.

"This is it!" Laura said, panting. She opened the door under the stairs and went into Chorley's darkroom. Rose followed her, stopping in the doorway when she caught a whiff of all the chemicals.

Laura put the film canister on the table and opened the drawer where Chorley kept his pasteboard labels. She uncapped a bottle of ink, dipped her pen.

"Be careful," Rose said.

Laura stopped, pen poised. "You're right. What should I put? I can hardly write 'Damning Evidence,' can I?"

"I meant don't get ink on your gloves."

Laura laughed, overexcited. She'd been like this all week. At times she was deliriously happy, at other times she seemed paralyzed by gloom. The dream alone couldn't explain it. Rose supposed that it was whatever Laura and Sandy were up to—more than kissing maybe. She felt left out, and left behind. It wasn't that she saw herself as less grownup than Laura, because Laura wasn't acting particularly grownup—she wasn't acting like anything, except perhaps a string of firecrackers lit at both ends and dropped in the street. It was just that Rose found she couldn't imagine what it took to generate this crazy pitch of feeling.

"I've come home every day just to watch for his sign," Laura said.

She meant her monster's sign, his five stones in a line. Rose said, "There I was thinking you'd come home to bathe in buttermilk, like me."

Laura hadn't spent the last days washing her hair in chamomile (or rosemary in her case) to brighten it, or having manicures and pedicures. Instead, she would come back from Fallow Hill midmorning, with Sandy Mason in tow, and they'd sit in the library or parlor alone together. Chorley had pointedly opened the door the one time they'd closed it.

"I came downstairs about fifteen minutes ago and heard a knock on the door, then someone tormenting the pump in the yard. He'd come in the back and left the film on the steps. With a note." Laura pulled a paper out of the top of one glove and passed it to Rose.

The handwriting was in smudgy charcoal, the letters evenly sized and backward sloping. The note read: "I am under Market Bridge." Rose turned the paper over and saw that it was a paste-scabbed strip from some bill advertising a dream.

"I have a bone to pick with him," Laura said. "It's almost as if he knows and is avoiding me." Then, "Damn ball."

"Damn inconvenient Presentation Ball," Rose said. "Damn untimely debut." Then, waspishly, "Our big milestones are very different these days, aren't they?"

"Yes." Laura was blunt. "But you want this film to see the light of day just as much as I do."

"True," said Rose. She came all the way into the darkroom, forgetting her fear of the contaminating chemicals. She took the canister from her cousin and stowed it in a drawer. "We'll hand it over to Da tomorrow. He can deliver it to the Grand Patriarch. Or straight to the Commission of Inquiry. His decision."

From the hallway Grace called, "Rose! Laura! Where are you?"

Rose swept out of the darkroom, clutching her cape around her. Laura followed, struggling to stuff her hands back into her tight kid gloves. Grace started fussing. "Where's your wrap, Laura?"

Laura dashed into the kitchen to retrieve it. When she returned to the hall, her father had appeared. He kissed her on the forehead and said, "Have fun." He kissed Rose too and wished her the very best of luck. "I wanted to go, but I don't think I can manage the excitement."

Grace was flustered. "Rose—are you all together under that cape? I didn't get to inspect you."

"Ma, I'm a work of art," Rose said.

Grace hustled her family down the front steps.

Rose was muttering mutinously that it was silly to take the car when the People's Palace was only five minutes' walk away.

"You must be delivered to your debut, Rose. You can't walk there," her mother said.

"Here, let me help you with that," Chorley said to Laura. He'd been watching her attempts to fasten the buttons on her right wrist with her left hand. He helped her into the car, sat beside her, and bent over her hand. She felt his fingertips on the inside of her wrist and said, dreamily, "Sandy will be there."

Everyone laughed. "Yes, we *know* Sandy will be there," chorused Rose and Grace.

✧ ✧ ✧

At the People's Palace there was a separate entrance for the debutantes and their mothers. This took Grace and Rose straight up the building's secondary staircase to the debutantes' dressing room. It was, in fact, a series of rooms, one where they left their coats, then a large, mirror-lined room with love seats and ottomans, then an innermost room, with attendants in black-and-white uniforms, and lavender-sprinkled towels, big bottles of cologne, and a seamstress—should one be required. Rose looked at all these elaborate comforts and mused on the value Founderston put on the female offspring of its first families. It all made her feel rather like a prize racehorse being transported to an important fair.

The rooms were crowded with slender girls in white and their generally more substantial mothers, in every conceivable color. Grace, accustomed to dream palace finery, had welcomed the chance to get into something plain. When Grace removed her daughter's white velvet cape, she felt that she was indeed unveiling a work of art. She stood beside Rose and basked in her daughter's glow. Rose shone, she scintillated, and she towered over most of her peers, even in her flat-heeled dancing slippers. Grace saw various mothers bridle at the sight—the shock—of Rose's beauty. Rose's friends' reaction was quite different. As soon as they caught sight of her through the crowd, they squealed and rushed over to Rose, who collapsed into their cluster, hugging and bouncing around, a giggly girl again. Grace blinked away tears. She was glad Rose couldn't hold her composure—it was just too much, too soon, and could serve only to isolate her, to set her apart, among older male admirers. Grace could imagine it already, the sterile triumph that was waiting for her daughter, who, she judged, was too young to escape the traps of flattery.

✣ ✣ ✣

Mamie's mother was determined to make the best of the ball, to put on a brave face, and to show her daughter how to do it. As she said to Mamie when she was making her final, short-tempered motherly adjustments to her hair and wrap,

"There are some things that are simply expected of ladies, and that is that." Mrs. Doran wasn't blessed with docile children, but Mamie could usually be relied on to be calm, if only as a result of being chronically unimpressed. However, for the past week, Mamie had been stuffing herself shamefully, and for the last twenty-four hours, on and off, she'd been vomiting. Mrs. Doran was determined that her daughter wasn't actually ill but was only giving way to nerves.

Everything necessary had been done for the girl's debut. She had a double strand of pearls—a gift from her father. She'd had five hair appointments till they found a style that suited her. And she had gotten her way about her deviant black-and-white gown. She had her black gloves, her crown of flowers. Mamie's interests had been served with the best possible care, attention, and expense. And now, her mother thought, it was time for Mamie to show that she could make the best of her lot.

What Mamie's mother couldn't see was that, while the ball had been still far off, Mamie had been happily scornful about it and anyone who hoped to enjoy it. She'd gone along with plans, scoffing at all the fuss. Then, one night, a week before the event, she woke up with a heart full of dread. *This was it,* the first occasion in her life on which it would matter that no one much liked her. She wouldn't fit in, wouldn't be just one more goose in the gaggle of girls. She was too serious, too ponderous. She wouldn't be sought out. Her dance card had a number of names on it—friends of Ru, who understood what was expected of them—but no one would actually want to dance with her, or sit with her.

Mamie knew Rose had done her best for her. She also knew Rose understood that Mamie was unattractive—and it seemed to matter to Rose, though perhaps only as a *problem* with possible, partial solutions. Rose had served her friend;

Mamie knew that. But now Mamie was on her own, with her transformed classmates, and all the people who knew how to behave, how to enjoy themselves, how to rise to occasions.

The Doran family was half an hour late. Cas Doran let his wife, son, and daughter sit in the car for minutes before he joined them. He left the house flanked by officials passing him telegrams and taking dictation. Then, when the family got to the People's Palace, Mrs. Doran spotted *more* officials in black bowler hats. "Cas, this is impossible," she said as she eased her wide self, and wider skirts, across the seat. "Why must the government be in crisis on the night of the Presentation Ball?"

Her husband's fingers closed like claws around her wrist, crushing the links of her diamond bracelet into her flesh. "The government is not in crisis, my dear. You must not say such things. And have you forgotten that you and Mamie do not get out here? That the car will take you around to the north door, and that it is only for reasons of security that I have been delivered before you?"

"I hadn't forgotten." Mrs. Doran settled herself again and rubbed her wrist. She heard Mamie whisper, "Stop it. Just stop it."

Cas and Ru got out. Ru stood waiting for his father at the foot of the staircase. He kept adjusting his uniform tunic, pulling at its hem, twitching its collar. Mrs. Doran wanted to shout at him. The car wasn't moving. It was in a line. And, for all his nonsense about security, Cas was standing on the steps holding court—with no one of any consequence, only his bowler-hatted underlings. She heard him say, "I have no use for another report. I want to see the man. Bring him to me." Then he summoned his son to his side and went up the carpeted steps, pulling on his gloves.

✧ ✧ ✧

Up in the dressing room, the society matrons presiding over the ceremony of the presentation were marshaling the girls.

Grace kissed her splendid daughter on the little patch of bare arm between her sleeve and the top of her glove. Then she let Rose go.

A matron said, "You young ladies all know which row you'll be in. Please remember that the order of your presentation will be determined by the alphabet, not by any sentiments of friendship."

Grace heard her daughter from among the white, glistening throng. "Yes, girls, we can put friendship in our glory boxes and get it out again after we're married."

There was laughter. One of the other mothers—perhaps someone young enough to remember the society dragons herding her—applauded.

Another mother sidled up to Grace and whispered, "This is all very strange." As they followed their daughters down what seemed like endless hallways and staircases to the ballroom, Grace and this woman, whom she'd never met before, talked about their very different comings of age—Grace at twelve in an apron behind the counter of her father's shop, and the other woman as a governess at seventeen.

The debutantes and their escorts bustled into the Great Hall before the ballroom. As they passed under the forty-foot lintel carved with the names of the founders, the woman beside Grace touched her hand and pointed out the name at the center of the shallow arch—*Tiebold*.

✧ ✧ ✧

Mamie and her mother caught up with the cavalcade of debutantes at the entrance to the Great Hall. The matrons were lining up the girls—one hundred and five of them, in fifteen rows, seven abreast. The girls had practiced, and the maneuver was quickly accomplished. Mamie was in the fourth row, Rose the thirteenth. Mamie craned over her shoulder to see her friend, highly visible because of her height and radiance. Inadvertently, Mamie caught Patty's eye. Patty was babbling to any of her neighbors who would listen that she shouldn't be nervous, she'd been to all sorts of assemblies all summer in the South. "Fancy dress balls, cricket club balls, the Masonic Ball in Canning. Girls who know how to dance don't have to wait to come out. And all the married ladies dance because women are still so outnumbered by the men in our town . . ."

"Shhhh . . . ," said someone.

"Mamie, you're wearing *black*," someone hissed.

"Perhaps she hopes to start a fashion."

Simpering.

A matron clapped her hands. "Girls!"

"Bloodstock. Brood mares," Mamie muttered at her feet.

"Oh, God, I need to *go* again!" squeaked the girl behind her.

From the ballroom came the sound of trumpets and drums, cymbals and violins—their processional music.

✢ ✢ ✢

Cas Doran left his son in the company of several young naval cadets. (Ru had a commission and was now at the naval academy in Westport.) He joined the throng around the President. There was a flurry of hand shaking among the powerful men of the government. Doran watched the master of ceremonies at the far end of the room conferring with Mamie's grandmother Eugenia Chambers—a woman like some imposing public building that has been flounced, frilled, tucked, and draped with lace.

Doran had the sense of some threat looming behind him and turned to see a long, black slab of a body—the Grand Patriarch in his robes, his beard combed and oiled and glistening golden-white.

"Secretary Doran," said Erasmus Tiebold. "Are you and your family back in Founderston for the entire season?"

"Yes. My daughter, Mamie, is out this year."

"Congratulations."

There was a silence, then Doran, pricked by curiosity and a catlike delight in hunting, tried to continue the conversation. "Were you able to get out of the city yourself over the summer? New Year's was very uncomfortable, I hear."

"Alas, no. I must always look forward to the ball season— when the churches are full."

"Indeed? The theaters and dream palaces too, I gather."

Erasmus Tiebold shot Doran a look of scarcely veiled contempt. Doran, inspired by this, went on. "And can you manage to have a quiet season by stocking yourself with sermons well ahead of time?"

"Sermonizing is the least of my work."

Cas Doran nodded, a polite, understanding nod. "And yet I hope you may discover some leisure in the coming weeks. As I say, I predict a peaceful season. And, surely, if the flock is contented, the shepherd is also?"

The Grand Patriarch was silent for a moment, then he replied, "With too much rest I fear I should not know myself."

Doran had to turn away from the old man's cool, keen scrutiny. He thought, "How much can he know? And what

can he prove?" Then he recalled the telegrams and secondhand news, the wild reports he'd had all evening, and he
shivered. He shivered, but his skin went hot and his muscles
hardened and he was filled with a wish for combat and the
bodily joy that always came with that.

The master of ceremonies drummed his staff on the floor.
The crowd drew back toward the walls of the ballroom, and
the orchestra struck up a processional tune.

Cas Doran was surprised how taken up he was by the ceremony. He had always thought the whole idea of the presentation of girls to society relied on the society being more
limited than that of the Republic of Southland. Families rose
and fell in the Republic. People made fortunes, and their
daughters were presented—by now often only to other fortune
makers. It was a transplanted tradition, and Doran took it
only as seriously as his wife's insistence that the family dress
for dinner. The ball was just another silly social exercise that
it was pointless to resist. Yet, as he watched the As, Bs, and
Cs, Doran was gradually overcome by a sense of suspense.
Something important *was* about to happen. Then came Lil-
lian Danvers, and Rebecca Deal, and Penelope Dische, and,
finally, Mamie Doran, who didn't stumble or falter, passing
from one state to another—schoolgirl to Society—with no visible embarrassment.

Doran relaxed. His mind idled for a time. He refused to
think about the mad, fragmentary reports that had come in
from the rangers who had arrived in Founderston shortly before he left for the ball. One of these rangers—whichever his
officials judged would be the most coherent—would be delivered to him here at the People's Palace. They would find a
quiet room, he'd get the stories straight, and he'd make
plans. In a short while, he'd make plans.

✧ ✧ ✧

The entire population of the room held its breath, then sighed collectively as Rose Tiebold dropped into her curtsy and came up again, graceful and glistening, holding up her coiled golden hair like a heavy crown on her slender neck.

Several young men thought to themselves sadly that Miss Tiebold's dance card was bound to be full already.

Minutes later, when the first chords of the first dance had sounded and all the debutantes had taken to the floor, some with their fathers, some with brothers, some with suitors already, one of Maze Plasir's best clients caught him on his way to the refreshment room. The man clutched Plasir's sleeve and stood close to whisper in his ear. "Rose Tiebold," he whispered, his breath wet on Plasir's earlobe.

"No," Plasir said. "I'm terribly sorry, but no."

"Surely, Maze, you can't suddenly have developed scruples?" the client said, bunching his round face so that it looked like a deformed apple that has grown pressed between branches.

"Get away from me!" Plasir hissed.

✧ ✧ ✧

In the breather after the second dance—a maxina—Rose went back to her mother and showed her card, full except for one space. "I'm about to meet twenty new people," she said. "But if I like any of them, I won't be able to get a second look."

Grace threw up her hands. "I don't have any advice."

Mamie's grandmother, the formidable Mrs. Chambers, leaned across Grace and told Rose that tomorrow the calling cards would come in. "And a parade of young men's mothers. Next Wednesday there is the President's Ball, then after that Founders Day Ball, the Naval Ball, the Grand Social, and the Carnival Social—and a dozen other private functions. Anyone you like you are bound to see more than enough in the coming weeks."

"That's why you have five pairs of gloves, Rose. And another gown coming," Grace said.

"The girl has only *two* gowns?" exclaimed Mrs. Chambers.

"Oh, dear," said Grace, and laughed. "I'm no good at this."

Rose's next partner came to claim her. She gathered up the hem of her dress; he took her hand and led her onto the floor and into a crisscrossing, lively contra dance. It was fun, and all Rose's hours of practice came back to her. No one on the floor seemed lost or clumsy. The girls were all weaving their way deftly backward past their partners, their hair bouncing, their heads turned back over their shoulders. Rose saw Mamie, wearing a look of determination and concentration but doing fine. She saw Laura, who was dancing not with Sandy but with a tall, fair-haired army lieutenant. Laura was easy to spot, in her vivid dress, flying, light on her feet.

The next dance was a waltz. And Laura danced with Sandy, scooped against him so that he seemed to support half her slight weight. Rose's partner was a proficient dancer, but so shy and formal that Rose had a hard time not laughing her way through the whole thing. He talked about the weather, and the heat of the room. She wished he hadn't mentioned the heat. Her close-fitting, pearl-encrusted gown was proving hot and heavy. She was going to be cooking before the night was through.

✧ ✧ ✧

One of the ushers delivered a note to Cas Doran and pointed out the men, bowler hats in hand and standing partly concealed by pillars in the entranceway. Doran made his way around the edge of the dance floor.

His daughter galloped past, part of a group of couples skipping counterclockwise within the clockwise movement of a greater circle of dancers. Mamie looked at him as though he was guilty of some terrible treachery to her. He slowed down and stared after her as she was swept away. He was annoyed—his wife had promised and assured him that, *ultimately*, Mamie would enjoy this ball. It didn't appear to him as though she was enjoying herself.

The Regulatory Body officials had delivered one of the rangers who were the source of the reports that, all evening, had been aggravating the Secretary of the Interior. They had secured a quiet room in the Palace. Their chief closed that room's door, and they all gathered around the tired man.

"I want you to explain these reports," Doran said, and produced two of the telegrams. "I know you've been told to be careful in your communications. But in this instance you've been so careful that you've left us in the dark."

He placed the telegrams in front of the ranger. The top one read: AGENT SEEN FILMING THE DEPOT STOP GAVE CHASE BUT LOST INLAND STOP.

"How is it possible that your people pursued this cameraman but didn't manage to catch him?" Doran said. "You were, after all, selected for your strength and stamina as well as your discretion."

Every ranger had once hoped to be a dreamhunter. All had enjoyed moments of elation at their Tries. They had crossed the border! Each one of them had imagined being rich and famous, but all had found themselves unable to catch dreams. There were no famous rangers, and all were wageworkers for the Dream Regulatory Body. Some did a little better in private deals they made with various dreamhunters, but none were rich. Rangers did tend to suffer from a sense of thwarted ambition, so it had been no trouble for Secretary Doran to recruit men eager to take on extra risks—and vows of secrecy.

"The man was faster than we were, even carrying his camera," the ranger said. Then he straightened in his chair. "I want to give a report, Mr. Secretary, not offer excuses." He began: "At five-thirty p.m. on February the twenty-eighth, rangers McIndoe and Butler first spotted a man standing around one hundred and fifty yards from the outbuildings of the Depot and cranking the handle of a movie camera. As we watched, he came closer. Rangers McIndoe, Butler, Carter, Hollander, and myself—"

Cas Doran looked at one of his officials, who supplied the ranger's name, "McIntyre."

"We approached him," said McIntyre, then paused and passed his hand across his face, pressing hard, as though to wipe something off. "Secretary Doran," the man said, "the cameraman seemed to be wearing some kind of suit."

"A uniform?"

"No." The ranger seemed reluctant to say what he'd seen.

"Please go on," Doran said.

"He was wearing an all-over, skintight, glistening gray suit of some kind."

"Knitted," one of the officials added; he had obviously heard the story earlier.

"I didn't say knitted," the ranger snapped.

Doran knew that the navy was trying to develop garments to keep bodies warm in cold water, and he supposed it was possible that someone enterprising might have invented a protective, water-conserving suit to be worn deep Inland.

"Not knitted, not rubber, not any of those things you've speculated about," the ranger said, glaring at the Body officials. "I want to say that it—" He broke off and scoured his face with his hand again. Then he finished, very softly, "—that it wasn't even a suit."

"Wait," said Doran, though no one had spoken. He walked around the room a few times.

After the riot at the Rainbow Opera, several members of the fire watch had claimed that a "glistening, gray, monstrous man" had shorted out the power board and smashed all the doors on the private balconies. Cas Doran paced and thought. He thought that Arthur Conan Doyle's Hound of the Baskervilles was only a dog daubed with luminescent paint and howling with pain. He didn't believe in monsters, he *traded* in them, at least in monstrous dreams. He knew that impressionable people could be made to believe things that weren't true, could be tapped for fear of the unknown—as if dread was the groundwater of humanity and all any intelligent master of men had to do was sink a well.

Doran rounded on the ranger. "You've been manipulated. You're a superstitious lot—you rangers and dreamhunters. You make myths faster than you make money."

"All right," said the ranger, then added, "sir."

"Perhaps you couldn't catch him because you were afraid of him," Doran said, insinuating.

"We ran after him. He slung the camera over his shoulder and took off—like a horse."

"Oh—not like a flying horse?" Cas Doran's voice dripped sarcasm.

The ranger went red. "He went Inland, west, at a forty-degree angle to the rail line. He didn't have any water with him. Or none we could see. He may well have had a cache of supplies somewhere. But we immediately posted guards at the tower, and over the cable car. He can't possibly have gotten his film out again. There's no danger of that."

"Laura Hame is out there in the ballroom, dancing, a picture of health. And yet I was assured that she couldn't have used the cable car either." Doran swooped on the ranger, slapped his hands down on the arms of the man's chair, and leaned over him.

The man cowered back into his seat.

Doran shouted, "There is obviously another pass through The Pinnacles that you lazy incompetents couldn't find! A route that wouldn't have required years of work and thousands of dollars of engineering to open!" He snapped upright again, releasing the arms of the chair so quickly that it teetered and the man flailed for balance before the chair came down again on all four legs. His voice quiet again, Doran asked one of the officials to fetch Maze Plasir. "As for you," he said to the ranger, "you can get back to the Depot, immediately. And I will arrange for you to supervise several months' worth of supplies on your journey."

"Are we to be under siege, then?" the ranger asked, and flinched when Doran looked at him.

"There you go again," said the Secretary. "Imagining yourself surrounded by monsters." He signaled to several officials, who helped the man up and led him out.

Maze Plasir appeared, fanning himself with a lady's ivory-and-rice-paper fan. He took one look at Doran's face, sat himself down, and waited.

Doran said to his men, "I want that Soporif you've been promising me."

One replied, "We've had him under constant observation since he began performing at Fallow Hill. But he's never on his own. He's even been sleeping in the same bed as the Hame girl."

"Ah, young love," said Plasir. "How inconvenient."

"He dressed for the ball tonight at his uncle's apartment. His uncle was there."

"You could always have taken his uncle too," Doran said.

"We didn't have the manpower, Mr. Secretary."

"Tell your detail to be a little more daring," Doran said. He dismissed them. When the door closed, Plasir said, "Are you about to put your plan into action?"

"Yes."

"And you will tell me when you need me to go In and catch a master dream to provide your household with some shelter?"

"My house and the houses of my allies are safe. Out of range. I'll need you to have some strong dream as a safety measure. In case some dreamhunter actually thinks to go on the offensive. I imagine that a small capsule of one of your master dreams could withstand the wide sweep of Laura Hame's?"

"Yes. If you keep me close, I can keep you safe," Plasir said. "But, Cas, I'd much rather we made a slow start and experimented with the dosage of Contentment. This has all been so long in the planning that you should act only on *your* timetable." Plasir's posture and tone were casual, but he was trying to warn his friend.

"I don't have time."

"This isn't about Tziga Hame's return, is it?"

"No. I've made inquiries. He's under treatment for epilepsy. There are no epileptic dreamhunters."

"True."

"The Tiebolds and the Hame girl are out there dancing,

bending their knees to the seasonal social rituals. The Grand Patriarch is bestowing blessings on debutantes. Whatever measures they are taking against me, they must suppose they'll work. They must suppose they have me somehow. The Hame girl may be simple. She might not have had the imagination to see what the dream at the Depot could be used to do. She might just have run back home wiping her brow with relief that she'd avoided charges of trespassing. She might believe she's a naughty girl and be thinking nothing much about Contentment and what it can do. But I can't count on that, can I?"

"No."

"They've forced my hand."

9

✦ ✦ ✦

SHORTLY BEFORE MIDNIGHT, THE OR-
CHESTRA STOPPED FOR A SUPPER
BREAK. THE DEBUTANTES CAME OFF THE
dance floor, and some found their mothers waiting for them
with plates. Grace beamed at Rose and handed her one on
which cold meats and salads were heaped in a perilous pile.

"Ma!" Rose passed the plate to her father. "I have to go upstairs and cool off. This dress is magnificent, but it's killing
me."

Grace looked crestfallen. "We didn't really think it
through, did we?"

"Never mind." Rose squeezed her mother's hand and
smiled at her father, who was foraging through the green salad
with a fork, chasing chunks of meat and potato.

Rose left her parents. She spotted Mamie in the slow line
making its way into the supper room. Mamie was with Ru, but
Rose still went up and asked her friend whether she was enjoying herself.

"I'm hungry," Mamie said.

"You stood up for nearly every dance," Rose said, congratulating her.

"That would explain why I'm hungry, wouldn't it?"

Rose glanced at Ru and saw that he had his back to them.
She relaxed a little.

Mamie said, "I know you want me to say it's not so bad after all, and I'm having a fine time because, really, Rose, it's you who persuaded me into all this." Mamie gestured around her at the crowd in their finery.

"You always intended to come out this year."

Mamie screwed up her face. Her cheeks began to show webs of red—her skin never flushed evenly. "Who says I intended to come out at all? Why would I want to? This ball is nothing but a way for a girl to declare that she expects to get married."

"Can't it just be fun?"

"It could be fun if it *was* fun," Mamie hissed.

Rose lost her temper. "Why do you always have to be above everything? You're acting as though this whole occasion exists as a slight to you. You're not enjoying it, so it must be no good!"

"It's easy for you, Rose," Mamie said, with quiet contempt.

"Yes, it's true, some things are easy for me," Rose said. Her voice was cool, but Mamie stepped back from her stare. "Nature has been kind to me. But I'll be damned if I'm going to let my friends act like checks and balances to nature, when really they are only the social law of *averages*."

Mamie was on the defensive, and breathing hard, but she held her ground. "I don't need your charity," she said to Rose.

"It was just help, Mamie. It's what friends do."

Someone touched Rose's shoulder, and she jerked, knocking whoever it was back.

"Ow!" said Laura.

"Watch it, Rose," said Sandy.

"Do you want me to go up to the powder room with you?" Laura asked her cousin.

Rose looked at Laura sheepishly, and all the fight left her. "Yes. Thanks," she said.

"I'll be down again to say good night before you go," Laura

said to Sandy. He was going to dream The Gate in the early morning hours at Fallow Hill. She had opted to stay for the whole ball. ("Rose will want to talk about it," she'd explained to Sandy. "It's a big thing. And I'd like to be there in the morning to see the first calling cards come in.")

The cousins strolled away, arm in arm.

Mamie turned her face to her brother's back, her lips pressed together hard.

Sandy joined the line and shuffled along. He pretended he hadn't heard a thing. He expected Ru to comfort his sister, but Ru kept on chatting to his new naval academy friends. Those young men were peering at Mamie, some embarrassed, some concerned, some spitefully amused—but no one uttered a word. Sandy tried to think of something to say. Something kindly. His mind was blank. If he meant to stay, he could ask her to dance, but he didn't mean to stay.

Chorley Tiebold went past, gave Sandy a friendly nod, then glanced at Mamie and stopped in his tracks. He came over. "You shouldn't have to stand in line," he said. "You girls are supposed to have plates waiting for you. And trainers who can toss a blanket over you so you won't cool off too quickly while they walk you around."

Mamie snorted.

"What can I get you?" Chorley said. "I've eaten. There're plates all over the seats in there." He jerked his thumb at the ballroom. "I managed to balance mine on the bust of President Broughton, with the help of his laurel wreath." He drew a circle around the top of his own head, then mimed balancing something.

"I'd like some trifle and cheesecake," said Mamie. "My mother has had me on lemon and barley water for two days."

"Time for a mutiny," Chorley declared.

"Yes."

"You stay there, I'll be right back," Chorley said, and sailed off to the head of the line.

"Mr. Irresistible," Mamie muttered. But she was prepared to accept charity, so long as it came with cake.

✤ ✤ ✤

Laura unfastened the hundred small pearl buttons at the back of Rose's dress. Rose sat slumped in front of one of the dressing room mirrors while Laura and an attendant fanned her face and bare back. Rose's head felt impossibly heavy, weighed down by her high coif of humid hair. A drop of sweat trickled down behind one ear, and the attendant dabbed it away with a towel. Someone brought her an iced tea.

Debutantes were in and out to make themselves comfortable and repair their looks. Some appeared with their mothers, girls who were already being debriefed about whom they had met, whom they had liked, and who had seemed to like them. Several sat miserably and listened to anxious motherly advice. Most didn't stay long. By the end of suppertime, the powder room and cloakroom were almost empty. The attendants were gathering discarded towels and dropped hairbrushes. One senior from the Academy was lying on a sofa, her mother in attendance, overcome after dancing every dance. Another girl had a blistered foot. She had spent the supper hour soaking it in briny water. Her mother had bandaged the blister, and the seamstress was now busily unpicking a seam on the girl's dancing slipper so that she could stuff her bandaged foot back into it.

Rose told Laura she wasn't yet ready to go. She'd wash herself a bit and splash on some witch hazel.

"I'll just go down and say good night to Sandy," Laura said. "And be back to help button you up."

Laura hurried out to the second staircase and down one floor—where there was access to the main staircase and she could find her way back to the ballroom. Sandy was waiting for her in the entranceway. She grinned at him, grabbed his hand, and dragged him back to the stairs. "Surely I'm not allowed up there?" he said, but he went with her.

She scampered ahead of him, sometimes going backward and holding him with both hands. They got to the second floor, and she took him along a hall and onto the secondary staircase. She led him down to the low-ceilinged hallway that all the debutantes had entered by earlier. Laura whispered, "Rose told me it might be quiet here, but it's even better, there's nobody at all!"

The gas lamps on the stairs had been lit, but the ones near the street doors were out. Neither Sandy nor Laura wondered about this unguarded entrance; they only embraced it as an opportunity to be alone. They stopped to kiss, Laura with her back to the wall. They broke apart when they heard running footsteps on the stairs, but then, when no one appeared, they melted together again.

"I wish I'd known more of the dances," Sandy said.

"But Captain Goodnough's *Useful Guide to Ballroom Dances* says that good taste forbids a lady to dance too frequently with one partner."

Sandy stroked Laura's curls. "You like dancing. I didn't know that."

For minutes more they leaned together, sharing breath and not speaking, then Sandy said, "I'm late already."

"And I've left Rose all unbuttoned."

Sandy pushed her gently away. "Good night," he said.

Laura left him, skipped into the light, and, turning every few steps, went back to the stairs, then vanished up them.

Sandy straightened his tie and checked that his shirt was

tucked in—Laura had the habit of pulling its tails out of his trousers.

He heard faint music, the orchestra striking up again.

Light appeared on the dark street beyond the door, lamps carried low and making a grid of shadows on the cobblestones. Then there were men in the doorway, who held their lamps so that their faces were concealed and only their shapes could be seen, their suits and bowler hats.

"Alexander Mason," said one of the men.

Sandy began to back away.

"You are to come with us." They advanced into the hallway. Their kerosene lamps reflected off the lustrous oiled-silk wallpaper and revealed their faces and shrewd, stony expressions.

Sandy turned to flee and heard the men break into a run behind him. They caught him at the foot of the stairs. He struggled and yelled. The bar of an arm closed on his throat and silenced him. He grappled with it but couldn't get his fingers under it. Someone hissed "Be still!" in his ear.

But Sandy continued to fight; he kicked and threw his weight forward. He was wrenched upright by the arm pressing on his windpipe.

"Subdue him!" a man ordered in a fierce whisper.

"*No!*" said another—the only man among them with any sense or foresight.

Sandy couldn't breathe. He was blacking out. He clawed at the arm. His fingers fizzed, then went numb. Everything went white—like sheet lightning without a thunderclap to follow it.

✧ ✧ ✧

The man who'd remained at the door to watch the street wasn't the one who had foreseen what would happen. He saw what *did* happen but, for several long moments, didn't understand what he was seeing. The dreamhunter was putting up a fight. Five men were clustered around him, grunting. The man in charge was issuing orders. Finally the dreamhunter slumped—

—and all the men around him dropped to the floor, like marionettes whose strings had been severed. The man at the door felt a stunning blow, violent lassitude that seemed to come from the core of his own body, a warm explosion of sleep. It struck him onto his knees. Nearer the floor, the air seemed full of the smell of flowers and freshly fallen dew.

The man shook his head to clear it. When he looked up, he saw that two of the dropped lamps had shattered and spilled kerosene, and that the floor was on fire. A liquid fire crept toward either side of the corridor. It didn't look dangerous. It looked like the flames over a pool of brandy-cradling crêpes suzette. Nothing bad could happen. Not in a world that smelled like a beautiful garden.

The man shook his head again and staggered up. He could see a heap of inert bodies beyond the pool of fire. The flame reached the walls, licked at the oiled-silk wallpaper, then streaked upward and spread, flowing onto the ceiling.

The man hurried toward the fire, his arms over his face. The corridor had become a squared tube of flame. The flames were bright, but black at their bases, consuming their smoke before it fumed from them.

The man jumped over the fire. He fumbled at the fallen bodies, got hold of one by an arm and a thigh, hoisted it onto his shoulders, and stood up. He turned back to the exit and ran through the fire. The kerosene coated the soles of his shoes, so that he left fiery footprints behind him.

10

✧ ✧ ✧

When Laura arrived back in the powder room, she found Rose sitting straight while one of the attendants closed her back into her pearly carapace of dress with the help of a button hook. Rose was relieved to see her cousin. She opened her dance card and found the name of her next partner. She showed it to Laura. "Could you find him and give him my apologies? I'll be down shortly."

Laura took note, nodded, and rushed out again. She was enjoying this dashing around. She wasn't hot, she was very fit, and she liked the way the gilded panels and mirrors and her own vivid reflection flashed past her as she ran. She liked leaping soundlessly down the carpeted stairs.

Laura sprinted down one flight of the lesser stairs, then along the hall that came out onto the main staircase. She loped down the wide steps of its outer curve, raced through Founders Hall and into the ballroom. She slowed down and looked around for the young man, saw him between the rows of a Scottish dance. The expression on his face suggested indigestion to Laura. She worked her way around the dance floor to him and touched his arm. "Rose says sorry. She's still upstairs. It's the heat."

"Oh," he said.

For a moment they stood awkwardly side by side, then it finally occurred to him that he could dance with this girl. "If you're not engaged?"

"No. I'd love to." Laura beamed and held out her hand.

For the next few minutes, whenever the open weaving figures of the Scottish brought them together, he'd babble about his university studies, the horse his father had in the Founders Day Cup, and so on. Then he remembered to introduce himself. Then he lost his tongue when he realized he was dancing with Tziga Hame's dreamhunter daughter. Laura flew through the dance smiling at everyone, aglow with happiness.

She had just come off the dance floor and caught her breath when another young man introduced himself and engaged her for the mazurka. During it Laura looked around for Rose, but it seemed her cousin had missed another dance and again left someone standing.

Then the music faltered, a horn sounded a farting note, a violin swooped into discord. The dancers slowed and turned to the orchestra. Someone had hold of the conductor's arm. The conductor's baton was pointed at the floor. The musicians were setting aside their instruments, and some—those nearest the conductor, who could hear what was being said to him—were on their feet.

The master of ceremonies released the conductor and turned to the crowd. "Ladies and gentlemen. I must ask you to leave the building immediately. Could you please make your way in an orderly fashion through the Founders Hall, down the stairs, and depart by the main doors. Would you then please assemble on the west side of People's Plaza. Do not collect your belongings. Do not look for your family members. They will find you—this message is being repeated in every other room. Now go at once, and peacefully."

The crowd began to move, with more speed and elbows

than had been suggested. The murmur of questions became a rising buzz of alarm, then someone yelled, "There's a fire!"

Laura and her partner had come together when the music stopped. They went along together, turning slowly in an eddy of pressing bodies. "My mother is in the supper room," he said. He began to push his way against the current, aiming at the high door of the supper room, visible over all the flower-decked and brilliantined heads.

People were shouting the names of relatives and receiving answering shouts. The hall was ringing with calls and throbbing with a clamor of fright. But everyone stayed on their feet, and the room was clearing. Laura went with the flow. She wanted to locate her uncle and aunt, and was sure the quickest way to do that was to get out of the building and into the plaza. She was simply too short to see over the heads of the crowd.

Laura was in Founders Hall when she smelled smoke. Somewhere in the building someone had opened an external door and let in a breeze, the air pressure changed, then the scent of smoke swept across the crowd. The people started and shuddered and, as one, shied away from the smell.

An elbow collided with Laura's head. She saw stars. When she managed to get her bearings again, she found she was facing backward. Her feet weren't touching the ground. She was being carried along by the crowd. It was terrifying, and she began to cry out for help.

She caught a glimpse of a bunch of bodies in black formal wear on a dais at one end of the hall. Men, who had fought their way free from the crowd and were now scanning it, looking for their own people. She saw her uncle among them, taller than most. His head was swiveling back and forth—he had heard her screaming but wasn't able to find her. She lifted an arm and waved to him, and he launched himself off

the dais and into the thick of the people. He shoved and swam
his way toward her. He picked her up and lifted her over his
head, then let the crowd carry him onto the sweeping curves
of the wide staircase and down into the street.

Chorley put Laura down. He hurried her clear of the main
doors. Once free from danger, the crowd seemed to collect
itself and begin to cooperate—for the most part. People hovered, waiting to see who came out, while the police tried to
get them to move out of the path of the clanging fire trucks
and horse-drawn water tenders.

"Rose was still up in the powder room," Laura said to her
uncle.

He said, "Can you see your aunt?"

They kept hold of each other and turned this way and that
searching for the little figure in the gray silk dress. Then
Chorley snapped upright and cried out. He pointed. Laura
followed his finger and saw that her aunt was on the terrace
outside the ballroom, with dozens of other people, all clustered at the stone balustrade and calling down to the crowd.
None of them seemed terribly worried, and, as far as Laura
was able to tell, they were asking for news, not help.

Chorley gripped Laura's arms and fixed her with his
sternest look. "You stay right there," he said. "Grace should
be fine. It'll be possible to reach all those people with ladders.
I'm going back in to get Rose."

Laura hung on to him.

"Laura!" he yelled in exasperation, broke out of her grip,
and ran back to the still choked exit, dodging firemen unraveling hoses and opening fire nets. He found his way up the
steps and through the main doors and vanished from Laura's
sight.

Laura looked up at the People's Palace. Streetlight caught
on the woolly underside of a pall of smoke that didn't seem to

have come from any exterior part of the building. Perhaps it was oozing through the roof, or up an internal air shaft. The smoke hung, quite still and colored only by the lights from the plaza. It looked so innocent, so anticlimactic after the crush of escape. The sounds of human frenzy were dying down. People still called out to loved ones, and there were orders, from police and firemen, and the pounding of pumps and rattle of hose reels and extension ladders.

Then came a deep, bright smash from the building, and flames burst out of an exploded window on the second floor. The crowd shrieked, then moaned. Arms went up, pointing. The innocent fleece of smoke above the building now had the light of fire at its heart.

✦ ✦ ✦

It was one of the attendants in the dressing room who first noticed the smoke. She supposed it was the smell of scorching and went to check that the two irons had been returned to the stove top. The irons were where they should be, the kettle was still half full, its base in no danger of burning through. For a few moments the woman stood frowning at the stove and sniffing.

Somewhere in the large building a door opened to the outer air, and the faint whiff shifted and became a strong odor. Then, in the cloakroom—the room nearest the hallway—an attendant shrieked as a wisp of smoke coiled in and spread thinly across the ceiling. She ran into the powder room, screaming, "Fire! Fire!"

"Be quiet, child!" her superior commanded.

Rose was before one of the full-length mirrors giving herself a final check. Her face was still too pink, and she was very uncomfortable. She heard the shouting, and, at the same time, the lights wavered as a film of smoke covered them.

Rose picked up her train and hurried out toward the hallway. Everyone else followed her.

They found the hallway filled with a haze of gray-white smoke. But halfway down its length, pouring along the ceiling, as though gravity had reversed itself, was a brown pall, oily and thick.

It was Rose's instinct to move away from the sight. But she didn't know what lay the other way. There were no signs pointing to exits—as in the Rainbow Opera. This was a much older building. It still had gaslight on its upper floors, and Rose couldn't remember ever having noticed fire escapes bolted to the heavy carving of its stone exterior. She pulled her train up, pressed it against her mouth, and, with a quick glance at the woman beside her, set off into the smoke.

After she'd gone a short way, she realized that only three other young women had come with her. Her eyes were streaming. She began to cough through the cloth muffling her mouth. She, and the women who had followed her, turned around and retreated.

✧ ✧ ✧

Chorley ran up the steps of the building at the same moment that some shift in the air inside the building—a window breaking, a door opening—gave the conflagration a breath of fresh air. He was in the entranceway, pushing through firemen toward the stairs, when the main staircase seemed to open like a dragon's throat and vomit fire. The flames spat down the stairs and sailed free from their bases, touching curtains and carpet, the beautiful oiled-silk wallpaper, and the deadly, glistening cellophane decorations. Everything flammable caught fire. The firemen staggered back. Chorley was knocked over, and the back of his head hit the marble floor.

✧ ✧ ✧

Grace was waiting to one side of the jostling group of people who had gathered at the balustrade of the terrace where, they judged, the first ladder would touch down. The people were craning over, watching the ladder swivel and expand as men on the back of a fire truck cranked it into place.

Grace wasn't in any great hurry. She thought it would be safer to hang back than to join the shoving bunch. Besides, from where she was, she had a better view of People's Plaza.

Her eyes hadn't yet found Rose. She'd spotted Chorley and Laura as soon as they appeared. Chorley's graying gold hair and height made him easy to find in a crowd, and Laura's dress was highly visible. A moment ago she'd seen Chorley leave Laura and run back to the Palace, passing out of sight under her, where the main entrance was. She knew he was looking for their daughter. Rose wasn't in the plaza.

Grace's eyes went back and forth, back and forth.

There was Mamie, standing with her mother, grandmother, and brother. Cas Doran was on the steps of the State Library, with the President and other ministers and dozens of bodyguards and police. It made Grace furious to see all those able bodies in uniforms forming a fence around dignitaries instead of doing something.

Grace looked over her shoulder and into the ballroom, the far end of which was on fire. Only a few moments before, fire had come, following the smoke. It had climbed the vines of cellophane streamers that festooned the entrance to the ball-

room. The cellophane went up like a fuse and dissolved into
drips of flame. The velvet hangings behind the orchestra ig-
nited.

The fire was more than sixty yards from where Grace
stood, but she could hear it. The sound it made was solid and
soft, like a huge audience clapping with gloved hands.

Grace tilted her head back and looked up at the façade of
the People's Palace. She saw smoke wafting through only one
window on the third floor, a few threads straining into the air
above the window's deep molding, then dissipating. It looked
so innocent. It looked like smoke coming from the window of
a busy workingmen's bar.

Grace walked along to the corner of the terrace. She joined
a young man who stood with his coat held up over his head as
if it could protect him from anything that fell from above. He
seemed to sense her approach. He turned and said, "Careful," and pointed at the tiles beneath her. Smoke seeped between the slabs, and Grace could feel heat through the thin
soles of her dancing slippers. The man turned back to the
balustrade, dropped his coat, and pointed. Grace looked and
saw what he'd been watching.

In the side street facing the State Library, the whole wall of
the People's Palace was ablaze. Smoke poured through every
window, and fire through a good half dozen of them. A fire
truck and a water tender were in the street, and the cobbles
were already submerged. The stream from one hose played in
spurts on the building but reached only as far as the second
story. The other hose was trained into the side entrance of the
Palace. As Grace and the man watched, something moved or
collapsed inside the building, and a gout of fire spat out the
entrance. It swallowed the men holding the hose, then retreated again, leaving them rolling on the street, their uniforms and skin smoking.

Grace put her hand over her mouth.

The man shouted to her that his mother and sister were up in the third-floor dressing room. "I'm sure of it!" he shouted.

"I think maybe my daughter is too," Grace said, then burst into tears. She gripped the hair at her temples and held on to it as though it were her only handhold and she was hanging over an abyss. She could see the man had begun to cry too. He was saying, over and over, "That's where they went in," about the red maw of the side entrance. "That's where I left them."

Some of Grace's hair came away in her hands. It hurt. She looked at the smoke seeping through the tiles and said, "We should move. The fire is under us." She took his arm and led him away, back to the balustrade but not into the crowd. A window exploded over their heads and showered them with glass. The crowd on the terrace howled, and a number of people scrambled up and knelt balancing on the stone coping of the balustrade.

✦ ✦ ✦

After her uncle left her, Laura stood for a few moments watching her aunt, a little isolated figure, head turning back and forth, back and forth. Laura knew that if Rose was any-where to be seen, Grace would see her. Laura watched. She held her breath, let it go, held it again. But no matter how long or hard she stared, she didn't see her aunt seeing Rose.

Laura came back to herself. She couldn't obey her uncle—just stay put and do nothing. Not when she had someone to turn to for help. She looked around for a gap in the crowd and went through it, away from the burning Palace. When she reached the street that led to the river, she began to run. She

ran alongside a hose not yet fattened by water. She burst out
onto the west embankment and swerved to avoid the firemen
and their big pumping truck. They had a hose in the river.

Laura set off toward Market Bridge.

None of the busy firemen noticed as the fleet little figure
in coral red silk sprinted by them.

✧ ✧ ✧

The women shut the cloakroom against the smoke. They
retreated from the outside door. Rose ran into the powder
room and pulled open the curtains covering one window. She
threw up the sash—ignoring the sudden shrieking behind
her—and thrust her head out. The window opened onto an
air shaft. The air shaft had a jumble of rubbish at its bottom
and was already full of smoke.

Someone hauled Rose back and slammed the window shut.
It was the head attendant. The woman was more stern than
frightened. Rose saw that there was more smoke in the room
than before she'd opened the window and instantly understood that, by opening it, she had offered the smoke free passage into their sanctuary. "Sorry," Rose said.

"The only windows on an outer wall are those above the
toilets," the attendant said. "And they only open a gap."

Rose ran to look. She made sure she shut the two doors between the dressing rooms and bathrooms. Her caution was
unnecessary. The toilet windows were already ajar. They were
frosted glass, about fifteen inches high and twenty-five
across. Metal catches were firmly screwed into the frames on
either side of each window, allowing them to open at an angle, with a gap of perhaps seven inches at their tops.

Rose lowered a toilet seat and climbed onto it. She reached
around the tank and gripped the top of the frame with both

her hands. Then she lifted her feet and hung her whole weight from the frame, which creaked and buckled. The glass cracked, and most of it dropped out. A large piece scored a cut in Rose's cheek as it fell. She released the frame and dropped back onto the toilet seat, then tumbled to the floor of the stall. She pressed the back of her gloved hand to the cut and looked up at the angled window frame—still firmly in place, though empty of glass. She picked herself up, shook glass from her gown, and left the toilets.

In the dressing room, the head attendant and the one mother were soaking hand towels in a basin and handing them around.

The head attendant passed Rose another basin and told her to fill it with water in the bathroom and, before she did that, to wet her own gown and hair thoroughly.

Rose went into the bathroom and turned on a tap. Water came in a dribble, then stopped altogether.

The gaslights in the room flared, then dimmed and were extinguished. Rose dropped the basin, and it shattered with a sound like the single stroke of a big bell.

. The room in which Rose stood was now dark, except for a fluttering, sullen glow and the rectangles of faint light from the high windows over the toilets.

"Rose!" the attendant shouted. "Come back!"

Rose wasn't surprised to be known. But it did seem strange and lonely to hear herself summoned out of the dark by a stranger's voice.

✧ ✧ ✧

"Nown!" Laura's shout reverberated in the hollow of the first arch of Market Bridge. She had come only partway down

the steps from the embankment. The light from the nearest
streetlamp reached no farther.

A shadow appeared out of the blackness and resolved into
her sandman. He mounted the steps. She held out her arms,
and he picked her up. His limbs felt coarse and very cold. She
realized that she was making a comparison between the feeling of being held by Nown, and by the warm and pliant
Sandy. "Run," she said, and held on tight.

Nown bounded up onto the embankment, and Laura let go
one arm to point at the pall of red-lit smoke several blocks
away above and beyond the buildings. "Faster," she said.
She was out of breath after her run. She wanted to say, "Why
didn't you tell me that the Place was a Nown?" and "You said
you were with yourself, but you never said what you meant."
But Nown had picked up his pace so much that his running
jolted her and she had to press her head against his shoulder
so she wouldn't suffer whiplash. His body began to heat up
and smell like rain on hot stones.

He ran in the shadows of buildings backlit by fire. He bore
down on the firemen with the hose in the river, went by
them, and turned to follow their hose, turned so fast that a
snap of white sparks outlined one of his flexed feet. Laura's
stomach lurched.

He slowed as the street opened out onto the People's Plaza.
He came to a stop and set Laura down.

"Rose is on the third floor," Laura said. "North side. But
you'll have to shout for her."

Nown looked at her, and Laura saw the black band of iron
sand drain away from his eyes, like dampness seeping through
him. The black settled beneath his cheekbones and over his
mouth and jaw. She didn't know what it meant, the shadow
passing down his face, but it made her think of sorrow. Then

he jumped away from her and plunged through the crowd, straight at the building. He scattered people—all of whom had their backs to him and their faces toward the fire. The people left reeling in his wake were perhaps able to get a look at the missile of his body only when he was yards beyond them. He sprinted in a straight line and with inhuman speed to the main steps of the building, among the firemen, who at this distance were only strokes of black against a maw of flame. Some of the firemen took a step or two after this mad figure, but they stopped when he ran straight into the flames on the blazing staircase.

✛ ✛ ✛

Grace saw Chorley carried out of the People's Palace. She saw him placed on a stretcher and borne away through the crowd. She had lost sight of Laura. She could see the debutantes. Many were draped in borrowed coats, but still all their lustrous white dresses reflected the fire as faithfully as polished silver.

The air between the terrace and the plaza was distorted with heat. Grace could no longer recognize any of the faces below her. She stood, frozen in place, till someone took her arm, drew her to the balustrade, lifted her up, and lowered her onto the ladder. Her feet and hands found its rungs. She looked over her shoulder, saw others well below her making their way down. She began to follow them.

Grace was fit and nimble, and her skirt was a manageable length. She soon caught up to the person below her. Then someone pulled her off the ladder, and for a moment she stood on the vibrating back deck of a fire truck. The air smelled of steam and hot steel. A fireman took her arm and showed her where she could climb down. The cobblestones were drenched. Another fireman drew her back from the truck. She was in the way.

Suddenly Laura was standing beside her. Grace put her arms around her niece, and together they walked away from the Palace, the pounding engines, the torrents of cold and warm water. They stopped at the edge of the crowd and stood, clinging to each other. Grace was drenched and shivering, but her feet smarted, as though they'd been sunburned.

✧ ✧ ✧

When Rose returned to the others, she found the head attendant had finished passing out wet towels. "There's no more water in the taps," Rose said.

"There's no time," the other woman replied, and passed Rose a towel. Then she walked out of the only illumination— smoke-bruised firelight—and fumbled her way across the room. Her workmates began to bleat at her. "Come back!"

She returned carrying scissors. She squatted and began to hack at the train of Rose's gown. She made a sizable hole, then wrapped the cloth around her hands and ripped the train away from the skirt. Then she picked up her own towel, went to the cloakroom door, and opened it.

For a moment all they could see was smoke—they'd made way for it, and it came toward them, twisting and black, as solid and supple as kelp in a fast-moving tide. The women and girls instinctively ducked, cowered on the carpet in the hallway, where they found that the air was clearer.

The head attendant choked out, "Hold on to one another's skirts." She began to crawl toward the staircase. The others followed her. Rose came last and reached back to pull the cloakroom door closed behind her. She wasn't sure why she did it, but she had the sense that the fire was behind the

smoke, pushing it, hungry for drafts, like those coming
through the high windows in the bathroom.

The women crawled quickly along the hallway to the head
of the secondary staircase. The smoke there was like black
mud, obscuring everything. The women stopped, coughing
through their muffling towels. Then there was a flurry among
them, a galvanizing panic as the head attendant rolled away
into the muck, without a word or sign. The girls behind
swayed with indecision, then followed, one after another.
Rose hesitated a little longer. She hadn't seen the head attendant go—she'd been too far back. If she had, she might have
thought—wrongly—that the woman had fainted and fallen. As
it was, she followed the others into the smoke-filled stairway.
She followed them because it simply seemed better than being
alone.

Rose tumbled down; she knocked against the walls and
against something soft. She kept her eyes closed but felt
sparks touch her face when she reached the bottom.

She found herself on a flat surface. She'd gotten turned
around and wasn't quite sure where she was. The head attendant seemed to know, though, because she was gathering
them together, crawling in a circle around the entire group.
Rose was relieved to be able to see again. Here the smoke
poured blackly only along the top half of the hallway and was
transparent below that. The clearest air was near the floor. It
was as though the smoke was sediment and had settled on the
ceiling because the ceiling had its own gravity.

Rose felt the head attendant pulling at her, driving the
decorative seed pearls on her gown into the flesh of her arm.
It hurt, but when Rose turned back to detach the hand, she
saw she was being hauled away from a drop.

The lower flights of the secondary staircase were entirely
gone. The women were on a landing that ended in hanging

strips of smoldering carpet and charred floorboards. Below that was a shaft full of fumes and sparks and rags of floating fire.

Now that she'd shown them what to avoid—and where they couldn't go to escape—the head attendant continued to crawl the other way, along the corridor that, Rose recalled, should join the main staircase.

Rose paused to fold her skirt up and stuff its hem under the boning of her waistband. She bared her knees, then picked up her wet towel and followed the others. She'd gone only a little way when a sensation brought her up short. A *memory* of a sensation she'd felt just a few moments before and hadn't fully registered. On her tumble down the stairs, she had struck something soft. Now she knew that it was a body in a dress and petticoats—a girl like her.

Rose dropped her towel, turned around, steadied herself, and plunged past the open shaft and back up the stairs. She ran up five, eight, ten steps, her arms out wide, touching the top of each step. She held her breath. Then she felt silky cloth, and a solid body under it. She followed the shape of the limb and closed both her hands on one of the girl's ankles. She threw her weight backward and dragged the girl down the stairs.

Once Rose had the girl out in clearer air, she saw it was another debutante, a girl from the class a year ahead of hers at the Academy. Rose found her towel and slapped the girl's face with it. She shouted her name. The girl didn't stir; her face was a terrible color, waxy, her lips tinged black, as though the smoke had been kissing her. Rose shook the girl, who flopped, her head banging on the carpet.

Then, through her own hoarse shouting, Rose heard her name, "Rose!"

Rose dropped the girl—the *dead* girl—and retreated. She

scuttled along the hallway in the direction she'd seen the others go. The smoke seemed to be thinning, streaming away faster behind her and sucked into something ahead of her. It was as if where she was—perhaps halfway along the hallway that joined the two staircases—was at a tipping point, a summit with solid avalanches of smoke breaking loose on either side of her.

"Rose!" The call came again. It was a deep voice, like an echo out of a dark cave. It wasn't the voice of the head attendant.

Suddenly Rose saw the others. They were a distance away, their faces and figures brightly lit and stripped of their individuality by the color of fire. The head attendant was signaling to her, Rose was sure. Then, the next moment, she was equally sure the woman was trying to call another one of their number back to her. Rose recognized the mother of the girl who had been left behind on the stairs. She recognized her by her finery—all the other women were attendants, not guests at the ball. And Rose recognized her too by the expression on her face—one of horror and despair.

Rose lurched up and ran toward the woman. She didn't want the mother to see her daughter. She knew that if the woman went back, she wouldn't stir again, she wouldn't make any further efforts to escape. Rose saw all this at once, her mind making calculations full of people instead of figures. The face and name of this woman's younger daughter, a cheeky junior at the Academy, came instantly to Rose. Her memory of the existence of this girl seemed to jump right into her body and drive her forward so that she collided with the woman and sent her hurtling back across the landing and into the others, who were crammed in the doorway of a room—a room that was dark, though only with night, not smoke.

Rose struck so hard that she rebounded. Her weight shifted. And then the whole landing moved too, under her. It tilted and tipped her toward—

—*heat*. Rose flung out a hand and caught hold of the edge of a decorative shield, part of the high-relief carvings on the wall panels of every one of the Palace's main chambers. The shield was only gilded plaster; it crumbled under her touch but helped her regain her balance.

Rose saw that, below her, the whole main staircase was on fire. Fire had climbed its sweeping curves, consuming every atom of carpet and curtaining. Flame flowed over all the carvings, a film of fire like some spirituous liquid. All the shapes of shields and crossed swords, wheat sheaves, grape bunches, lions, griffins, cherubs, ribbons and bows—everything retained its shape beneath its fiery double. It was as if the fire meant to make a mold of all the baroque glories of the Palace so that it could be formed afresh again one day.

Rose saw all this in flashes, her eyes squeezed down to their narrowest and pouring tears.

The other women were shouting at her. She couldn't make out their words. The fire was too loud, as loud as the engine of an express train blasting through a country station, but a roar without rhythm.

Rose heard her name once more. The sound came from below her. Shielding her face with her hand, she looked first at the women—they were signaling her to come to them, to dare to run across the tilting landing. And then she squinted down into the maelstrom of fire.

Laura's sandman was below her, pressed against the wall on the curve of the staircase. He hadn't been there a moment ago. The fire was licking the panels, and the timber runners of the great stairs, but it shunned his body, finding nothing of interest to it. Laura's monster had always appeared to Rose as a shadow, a shapely, shadowy body; now he shimmered in the light of the flames, as though his skin was covered in frost. He moved another two steps up, in one bound.

The landing jolted and tilted further. Rose fell to her knees and dug her fingers into the crumbling plaster. Her cousin's sandman stopped and stood still. Rose imagined that his eyes were directed not at her but at the underside of the landing visible to him. He dared another step, but it was *his* weight disturbing the fragile equilibrium of the staircase. He stepped, and it shuddered and gave more.

Above the roar and sharp crackling of the fire, Rose caught the thread of a call. She looked at the women again and saw that the dark room beyond them had opened up. From where she hung, Rose could see a long series of rooms, through several doors, to a window. The window was open, and one of the women—the head attendant, Rose thought—was standing before it. Beyond her was the façade of another building. Rose recognized its arched windows as those of the State Library. There was a window directly opposite the one where the woman stood. It too was open. There were men at it, leaning out and slowly feeding a ladder across from one building to the other. Rose could see that the ladder had wheels on the end pointing her way. It was a library ladder. The head attendant reached for it, pulled it toward her, then flipped it over so that the wheels locked on the edge of the windowsill. She turned Rose's way—Rose saw her face flash orange in the firelight. The head attendant began to call and signal to the clustered women. They had been facing Rose, but they all turned away and ran toward the window and ladder—without a backward glance.

Rose slid her hands along the wall and edged a foot along the sloping floor. It shuddered. She glanced at Laura's sandman. He was motionless. Then he slowly raised an arm and pointed toward Rose's avenue of escape. He was encouraging her to go, to try it.

She edged forward. The landing quivered again as something beneath it wrenched and dropped. Then the floor suddenly bucked and pitched Rose forward. She caught herself on stiff, extended arms. The floor had turned into a flat chute pointing Rose down at the fire. The heat blasted her face. She smelled burning hair and scorching fabric and scrabbled backward. Then her hands were on her slippery skirt, and she lost her grip on the slope. She slid forward, crying out, the hot air slamming into her mouth. Her fingers found carpet and again dug in. She spun around and went up the slope, her eyes wide open. She saw handholds, whatever would give her purchase. The floor was moving, but not one of her lunges missed its mark. She seized every safe hold just an instant before it gave way, just long enough to propel herself upward.

Finally she found herself suspended, her hips and legs hanging over a drop, her arms, head, and shoulders on the firm floor of the hall beyond the landing. She heaved herself all the way onto the landing, then beat out the fire on her skirt with her hands in the remnants of her ripped gloves. Her dancing slippers were smoking, her stockings were a web of shriveled silk through which showed utterly hairless, pink skin.

Rose swarmed back from the drop, but the floor was firm. A series of supporting walls beneath her had held up (and, in fact, would still be standing more than a day later, when the fire had finally burned itself out).

Rose looked across the gap at that faraway window. She could see two women waiting to cross, and another hunched shape crawling slowly along the ladder. She could see the urgent faces and beckoning hands of the librarian rescuers.

Rose looked away. She turned her eyes down to Laura's sand-man, who stood, his face turned up to her. As she watched, he set his hands back against the wall behind him. He flexed his knees. He was preparing to jump—to try to join her.

For a moment Rose went weak with hope and relief. She wasn't going to be left alone and have to save herself.

Nown leapt. The steps came loose from the wall and dropped away behind him, robbing his leap of any impetus. He arched out and up toward the edge of the landing, his body stretched as though each particle could provide propulsion to the one above it and force him upward. He hung in the air. Then his snatching hands fell short, and he went down. His lower body fell first, his arms and head and blank face followed. Far below, and still falling, he condensed back into a proper human shape against the fire. Then the fire swallowed him, and he was gone.

✦ ✦ ✦

Rose got to her feet and fled, back along the hallway to what remained of the secondary staircase. There was less smoke in the hall now—the fire below had finished burning carpets, curtains, paintwork, whatever would produce a lot of smoke. It had moved on to consuming the dry and seasoned timbers of the Palace's interior. The heat funneled through the hall behind Rose and propelled her along. She hesitated at the sight of the black-lipped body of her schoolmate, then averted her gaze and ran up the stairs.

The third floor was hot and full of smoke. The air wasn't moving, the fire wasn't being pulled that way. But as soon as Rose threw open the cloakroom door, she felt, behind her, the fire belch and take hold and vault forward, moving up toward her.

The marble tiles of the bathroom were warm but not smoking. The toilet seat she'd stood on perhaps only ten minutes earlier was still down. Rose lifted it and dipped her scorched feet in the bowl, but she was still too inhibited by years of habit to cool her hands in the water. She kept her tattered gloves on, dropped the lid once more, and stepped up onto it.

She was going to try to squeeze through the empty window frame. She thought perhaps she'd fit, but she'd done a lot of growing over the past two years, and her sense of her true size was with her only sometimes. At this moment she felt small, like a child who should be able, seeking safety, to cram itself into little spaces or escape through tiny gaps.

She found she needed something else to stand on. She thought of the dark dressing room and cloakroom behind her. She examined her memory and rejected the footstool—its legs were set too wide, the chairs (same problem), the basins (they broke too easily; she'd broken one). Then she remembered the seamstress's wicker sewing basket.

Rose ran out and felt her way around the side of the room where she knew the basket must be. She touched the stove—it was still hot. As she snatched her hand back, she knocked over the poker. If only she dared to open the door to the hall, there would be more light—from the fire, the fire she mustn't let find her.

A moment passed when nothing happened. Rose coughed and didn't think. The clang of the falling poker echoed in her brain. Then she bent over, felt for it, and picked it up. Holding the poker, she continued in her search for the sewing basket—round, wickerwork, sturdy enough to stand on. Then she felt the texture of braided willow beneath her tattered glove. She put her arms around the basket and hurried back to the toilets. She placed the basket on the toilet seat and stepped up onto it. It creaked and rustled but held her weight. The window was right in front of her now. She measured the empty frame with her eyes, saw how the light caught in a few jagged bits of glass sticking up out of the cracked putty like teeth from gums. Rose thought, "Laura could fit through this." A silly thought, but Laura was the person with whom Rose had shared every moment of wriggling through places only children could wriggle through—the ventilation grille in the Academy cellars, sometime in their junior year; and the wood box at Laura's aunt Marta's.

Rose pulled the empty frame down till it stopped against its catches. She shoved the poker into the gap and wrenched it back and forth. The frame let go suddenly, splintered at one corner. Rose began to work on the right angle that had remained firm. She demolished the frame till it was a disjointed mess of splintered timber hanging from its hinges.

Rose dropped the poker and pushed her head and shoulders out through the window.

She found herself high above the graveled back lots of several small buildings. There were signs of fire there—or of people's attempts to combat it. The back doors of all the buildings were open, and the empty yards were full of dropped buckets and big puddles near the pumps. Even from where she was, Rose could see that all the walls were drenched.

She called out—her voice hoarse from smoke.

No one appeared.

She wriggled and writhed to get her hips out through the window. Her dress caught and tore as she moved. It scattered pearls. The window was too small for her to perch in it without a handhold. But it wasn't until she was almost all the way out that Rose found one—the gutter above her.

She stopped to catch her breath, and cough, her legs still inside, her back to the drop. Without her grip on the gutter, she would have fallen. Next, she knew, she would have to heave herself up over the lip of the gutter and onto the roof. She would need to keep her legs straight to get her knees out the window.

Somewhere in the Palace, something caved in with a series of crashes. The whole building shook. Far away, a crowd of people screamed together.

Rose sucked in the fresh air. She inched one hand forward, feeling for a handhold beyond the gutter. It was a big, square gutter with a high lip on its inner edge. Rose hooked her fingers over that and then began to pull herself simultaneously out of the window and onto the roof. Her shoulders and elbows popped, the muscles in her back stretched to snapping. Then her knees came out of the window and she was able to get her feet onto the sill, not to balance—there was no possibility of a pause to find her balance—but only to push up. She moved her other hand to the back lip of the gutter and, painfully scraping her breasts, forced her head and shoulders and chest onto the roof.

After that it was easy. She swung a knee up and was suddenly kneeling in the gutter set into the stonework. Ahead of her was a flat expanse of roof sealed with tar and set with several skylights. The big skylight over the central staircase was like a greenhouse in which fire was growing and running riot. Around it the roof tar bubbled and smoked.

Rose got to her feet and made a long circuit around the big skylight. She went gingerly, because the tar was hot and soft, and because she was afraid the roof might collapse under her, sending her down—like Laura's sandman—into the heart of the fire.

❖ ❖ ❖

Laura and Grace stood in the crowd and watched fire rise to fill every window of the front façade of the People's Palace. During those minutes someone came and draped a blanket over Grace's shoulders. She said "Thank you," but her eyes never strayed from her watching. The engine and tender backed out of the side street north of the building—retreating—the firemen hauling the heavy hoses with them. More fire trucks had arrived, and hoses were working over the whole front of the building. The smoke flowed straight up now, pushed by superheated air.

Someone put a hand on Laura's shoulder, and she looked around and saw that it was her uncle. Chorley stood behind them, almost supporting himself on them. There was a bandage wound around his head. He caught Laura's look of horror and said, "It's nothing. A bump." He bit his lips. He didn't say, "Where's Rose?"

Grace was weeping and trembling from head to foot.

Some stranger first spotted Rose. He shouted and pointed at the figure in white, glimpsed through the smoke streaming from the plumes of fire that belched from every window. Then the whole crowd saw her and made a sound, a rumble of anxiety that gained volume and turned into urgent yelling. The firemen moved almost as one, turning their hoses on the windows directly beneath where Rose was standing.

Chorley and Grace ran into the confusion of water, shouting their daughter's name. The firemen rushed to hold the couple back. A truck was being moved. The fire nets had been laid aside, unused. Now a group of firemen converged on one net. They spread it out, pulled it taut, lifted it, and hurried across the plaza to stand beneath the corner of the building, the only place without windows, and so also without fountains of fire.

Laura could see that Rose was watching the firemen. She'd

seen the net. She came nearer to the edge and picked up her skirt to climb out onto a jutting cornice.

It was then that the big skylight exploded. It sprayed glass in every direction. The crowd howled in terror, but the girl on the roof only dropped into a crouch and covered her head. Then she got up again, slowly. Her hair had come loose and was floating straight up from her head like a bright flag. She stood looking down at the net, a slender figure in white, apparently utterly composed.

✧ ✧ ✧

It was a long way down. The circle of the fire net seemed a small hope. A twisting column of flame had erupted from the gap where a skylight had been. Rose could hear tar sizzling, she could see where the roof was sagging. The heat behind her was terrible. In a moment she'd be on fire.

Rose took a couple of steps back. She wanted to be sure she could jump far enough to clear all the masonry below her. Only two steps should do it. She kept her eyes on the circle of the net. She lined it up with her gaze as she'd line up the deepest water when she was jumping at high tide from the rocks below Summerfort.

The crowd saw her retreat and howled. Rose heard her parents' voices rise above the cacophony of the fire, the roar and splash of hoses, and all the other voices. Their despair made them audible; those cries could be heard through anything, it seemed, even through the rules of the universe.

Rose ran forward and jumped. The air rushed past her. Her feet flew up over her head so that she slapped, shoulders and back first, into the canvas. Her breath was knocked out of her. She bounced up once, then the canvas caught her and she lay tumbled on it, her elbows smarting.

Through the faces bent over her and the hands reaching for her, Rose looked up at the roof, which didn't seem so far away now. It really wasn't any surprise that she'd made it.

Then her ma and da and Laura appeared. The firemen laid the net down, so Rose was on solid ground. Her father scooped her up. He was crying. Her mother was crying. Laura was crying. But why on earth were all the other people crying, even the firemen? Weeping and touching her as though she was a holy relic.

VI

Epidemic Contentment

1

✢ ✢ ✢

THE FIRE BURNED FOR A NIGHT AND A
DAY, FUELED BY COAL STORED IN THE
PALACE CELLAR. WHEN IT WAS OUT, THE
smell of it hung, horrible, over much of the central city.
There were no calling cards, no parade of mothers, no preparations for later balls. For a day Rose lay upstairs and
coughed, then her cough quieted. Laura went out and called
for Nown under the dark arch of Market Bridge, looked for
him among the broken glass, rags, and human waste. Then,
when Rose was able to tell her story, she told Laura she'd seen
Nown fall.

Laura lost track of time but did wonder why Sandy hadn't
come. Then, on the afternoon of the second day after the
fire, George Mason arrived with red-rimmed eyes and his bad
news. He stood in the library and showed the family what
he had—wrapped in his handkerchief in a nest of soot—the
broken chain and charred copper tags of his nephew's
dreamhunter's license.

The next day, when Laura was sitting at the dinner table
and her father was trying to persuade her to eat, even cutting
up her food for her, Rose saw that Laura had a look like the
façade of the People's Palace, stony, and still standing, but
burned out inside.

✢ ✢ ✢

Rose went to visit Mamie. She waited in the entrance hall and overheard Mrs. Doran say to her daughter, "Really, Mamie, it's so *common* of your friend just to turn up unannounced. It's to be discouraged."

Rose heard Mrs. Doran coming and darted away from the door. Mamie's mother emerged, gave Rose a smile with no buoyancy whatsoever, and said, "Mamie is waiting for you, please go in."

"Thank you," Rose said. She opened the door a crack and flitted through it, trying not to touch anything as she went.

Mamie didn't get up but did begin to fidget. She said, "What's under the scarf?"

Rose touched her silk bandanna. "My hair is frizzy at the front. I'll have to let it grow a bit before it can be repaired."

"You look sphinxlike," Mamie said.

"You mean I don't have any eyebrows. Frankly, being a sphinx stinks."

Mamie said. "Do you want tea?"

"No, thanks. Do you want to play hostess?"

"Not really."

"Aren't you pleased to see me?" Rose said, being blunt.

"Yes." Mamie straightened her spine, sat as a lady should. She looked like her grandmother, without that woman's corsets. "I saw you jump. There was even a picture of it in the papers."

"I'm sorry that you felt I bossed you about the ball," Rose said.

"Don't think about it. You meant well. And I couldn't have resisted Mother anyway."

Rose wriggled forward on her seat. "Just because everyone

imagines that coming out means we're advertising ourselves as available for marriage, that doesn't mean we have to experience it all that way. We don't have to take any of it seriously."

Mamie shrugged. "But have you thought what you're going to do with your life apart from getting married?"

"No. I've only thought what I might do for the next year or so. Have a final year at school, then travel around the country staying with all my classmates and distant relatives—really get to know the whole country, not just resorts like Sisters Beach and the spa in Spring Valley. Then, when I'm twenty-one, I can go to university."

"To study what? And why?"

"Something for its own sake. Or law—for justice."

Mamie gave Rose a slow smile. "I'm going to eat until I'm so fat that everyone will leave me alone."

"No, you're not," Rose said, impatient. "Da is going to teach me to drive. He can teach you too, if you'd like."

"What on earth for?"

"Independence. Get-up-and-go. Honestly, Mamie, complaining doesn't make you a rebel, only action makes anyone a rebel. We girls have to do what we can. Take whatever opportunities we're offered."

"Tea?" Mamie offered again. "There's some lovely almond cake."

Rose laughed.

Mamie continued. "What you have to realize, Rose, is that I'm not adventurous. Laura is your natural companion for adventures. You can't charm me into joining you. It's not that I'm timid, it's just that I hate failure, and hate to be uncomfortable, and I don't particularly enjoy effort. I'm a lost cause."

Rose looked at the floor. She thought, "Whereas Laura is just lost."

The day before, Laura had gone with Grace to see George
Mason off at the station. Mason was taking Sandy's remains—
a collection of carbonized bones—back to his family. Afterward Laura had talked to Rose, in a wispy voice. She told Rose
what she knew about Sandy's home—his six brothers and sisters. One brother was the head of the night shift at the
sawmill. Another was an engineer in a railway workshop. His
father was a shop steward at the carpet factory. Laura talked
about the year Sandy had spent working in that factory, about
his school, with its tattered books and sour hallways. Sandy's
mother was a teacher at a similar girls' school. The family had
tenuous respectability—all of them had stayed in school till
fifteen.

Rose said to Mamie, "Laura has had adventures I can't even
imagine. She's even been in love. Her heart is broken."

"Laura hasn't been lucky, has she?"

"No. Sandy. Her mother . . ." Rose looked hard at Mamie.
"I suppose you've heard that her father's back?"

"I've heard that he's ill."

"Yes. That's what's finally roused Laura. In a couple of
days she is going In to get The Gate."

"The miracle dream."

"I've had it three times now." Rose could feel her face soft-
ening. "It's extraordinarily beautiful. It is proving a little
controversial, though. At Fallow Hill it carried off any of
their patients who were close to death, or ready to die. It can't
be dreamed near anyone critically ill or injured who has any
chance of recovery. What it does is tell whoever dreams it that
there's something beautiful to go on to after death. It tells it
with such conviction that very sick people just let go of life.
But it's excellent for chronic illness, pain, madness, and misery. I'm glad Laura's father has persuaded her to get it for
him. Of course he's hoping it'll help _her_."

"Is your mother planning to catch it too?"

"No. Ma is going farther In to get Drought's End. She's going to perform it at the Rainbow Opera. What Founderston needs after the fire is a balm of rain—and the dream's sloppy romance, and little white horses."

"You forget I haven't had any of these dreams."

"Oh," said Rose, feeling awkward. She did keep forgetting that Mamie's mother hadn't let her daughter go to a dream palace.

Mamie was looking sly and thoughtful. "Is Drought's End a master dream?"

"I didn't know you knew anything about that."

"I know *all* about it, despite my lack of firsthand experience."

"I don't think it is a master dream."

Mamie rearranged herself and seemed to change the subject. "Well," she said, "I'm getting on a train tomorrow night. My father is sending me off to our summerhouse."

"Alone?"

"The servants will be there."

"Does your father think you need a holiday?"

"No." Mamie stared into Rose's eyes.

Rose searched her friend's face. Mamie was looking sphinx-like, though she still had her eyebrows. She was trying to tell Rose something, to tell without actually saying.

"Or," said Rose, "does he just think you'll be better off out of Founderston?"

And Mamie said, "That must be it."

✦ ✦ ✦

It was Rose who remembered the film, five days after the fire. Chorley developed it, and they all sat down to watch it.

Laura saw that Nown had cranked the camera a little too slowly, so that the film's action was fast, the captives and rangers jerky and insectile in their movements. There was shutter flicker, as though the camera were peering through eyes that were blinking away tears. But there were the huts, the barracks, the canvas-walled rooms of the Depot.

"How did you get this?" Chorley said.

"I didn't," Laura said. "I was here."

"We sent someone," said Tziga.

When Nown had been shooting the footage, Laura had been lying in Sandy's arms within the circle of Foreigner's West. They got up and folded the blankets, and she gave up one life for another. Nown had betrayed her. He was heartless. He should have told her what he must have known. He'd always carried her, but—in a way—he'd made her walk. Her long, hard journey might have been simple and short if only he'd said: "The Place is the same thing I am, a Nown—that's something you need to know."

Chorley said, "I'll take this to the Grand Patriarch. I imagine he'll want to present it to the Commission."

"Make a copy first," Tziga said.

Grace said, "I hate having to rely on that old man to get things straightened out."

"We're not relying on him, we are consulting with him," Chorley snapped.

Laura thought how strange it was that her aunt was still able to imagine things being "straightened out," as though all that had to happen was that Cas Doran be exposed and the Regulatory Body encouraged to mind their own business. Grace seemed to think that if those things were accomplished, then dreamhunters would be able to get back to their prospecting and performing in peace. Rose and Chorley and Tziga wanted Doran stopped and punished. They wanted to weed out corruption. Was Laura's aunt right to look to a time beyond that, to order and everyday life?

Laura thought nothing could be mended. And she was sure she was thinking just as straight as her aunt Grace. So which of them was right?

✢ ✢ ✢

The family agreed that Laura shouldn't be left alone. But only Rose understood what that meant. As soon as her cough eased, Rose had taken to climbing into Laura's bed. She didn't try to watch with Laura, to stay awake and stare into the dark—she slept, but she was there.

The night they screened the film, Rose fell asleep almost the moment she put her head on her pillow. She woke after an hour or two, from a dream in which she wandered along red-painted hallways, unable to open any of the doors because their handles burned her hands.

"Nightmare?" said Laura, from the other side of the bed.

"Yes. There's never any fire in my nightmares. Just heat."

"I still have nightmares where I'm thirsty."

Rose turned over and tried to see her cousin. There was a little light coming in the window from the street, enough so that the shadows of the flowers on the frosted-glass lamp on the nightstand were visible. Rose could see the lumpy shadow that was her cousin, and the glimmer of Laura's eyes. Because it was dark, Rose felt a little daring. She said, "Have you thought that you could make your sandman again?"

"He let me down," Laura said, her voice flat.

"He couldn't help it."

"Not in the fire. Before that."

"So you won't make him again because you're mad at him?"

"I won't make him again because I can't make Sandy."

Rose thought about the logic of Laura's statement. Of
course it was flawless. It made perfect sense. Rose knew that
her cousin had loved both of them, Sandy and the monster.
Laura wouldn't resurrect one if she couldn't resurrect the
other.

"It's not just a decision," Laura said. "I think it's prohib-
ited. My need is great, but I can't feel the song. When I found
Da's sandman, but before I knew 'The Measures,' I could feel
this storm of music around me. Now I don't feel anything."

Rose found one of Laura's hands under the covers and
held it.

"I'm just going to be good and do what I'm asked. Then
maybe I'll stop feeling so sick and tired. Sandy felt like my
family and my future."

Rose squeezed Laura's hand.

Laura said, "Wouldn't it be terrible if none of us had fu-
tures, only fates?"

"I don't believe in fate," Rose said. It was true; Rose believed in the poker, the sewing basket, the broken window,
the rooftop, the fire net, the way out. She believed in reprieve. And she was sure that, sooner or later, she would
think of some way to help Laura. Something would come to
her—it was only a matter of time.

2

✢ ✢ ✢

*S*ATURDAY EVENING. TWO MEN, ONE TALL, THE OTHER SMALL, WALKED SLOWLY BACK ACROSS MARKET BRIDGE FROM the Isle of the Temple. The evening was autumnal, and there was a white mist rising from the surface of the river.

Other pedestrians they passed glanced, then turned to stare after them.

"It's taking a while for the word to get around Founderston that you're not dead," Chorley said.

"I've been sequestered at home, or at Fallow Hill."

"After Monday we'll be able to deal with the reports of your death. We can bring up the matter of the forged signature in the Doorhandle intentions book."

"After Monday that will be an even smaller matter than it is already."

Chorley and Tziga had shown the film of the Depot to the Grand Patriarch. On Monday afternoon the Commission of Inquiry was due to convene again. Their report would be published soon. All submissions had been read, all witnesses questioned, all arguments heard. But the seven men of the Commission were due to meet again to discuss their findings—and the Grand Patriarch intended to deliver the film to them, with Laura and her testimony.

"I wouldn't like to be in Doran's shoes after Monday,"

Chorley said. "Though he must have been forewarned. Your cameraman was spotted. In the final seconds of the film, a ranger points at him." Chorley was quiet for a moment, then added, "He'll have to testify too, I expect."

Tziga was silent.

"Tziga? Why did Erasmus ask you how you got the film? I thought the cameraman was his agent."

Tziga looked vague and baffled, and Chorley was once again overcome by nervous tenderness toward his damaged brother-in-law. "Never mind," he said. "Don't worry about it." They came off the bridge onto the west embankment. The air was still but nevertheless carried the smell of damp, burned timber.

When they arrived home, they were met by a one-girl whirlwind. Rose was wrapped in a thick shawl. She said the house was cold. She said there were fires laid already, kindling and coal under a summer's worth of dust. "Could someone else please put a match to them? I'm allergic to matches. Temporarily, I hope." She followed her father into the parlor, and, as he knelt to light the fire, she stood behind him, ranting. "I'm sick of salad and eggs and bread," she said. "Now that Uncle Tziga's no longer a big secret, could we *please* get back our cook and maids?"

"Cook left last year. She retired to nurse her sick sister. Remember?" Chorley said.

"Why would I remember? I wasn't here. I was boarding at school, and eating boiled bacon and boiled broccoli and boiled bloody potatoes."

"We can summon the maid back any time. She's only on leave. Paid leave."

"This family is hopeless!" Rose raved. "Renting rooms they don't use. Paying maids to take holidays. Throwing money at problems!"

Chorley got up and stared at his daughter with wide eyes. "What on earth has gotten into you?"

"The Doran house is packed with servants. Mamie and her mother can sit around being ornamental. What would we have done if gentlemen *had* come calling for me? Fed them dried fruit and boiled eggs with their black tea?"

"Sorry," said Chorley. "I'll place an advertisement for a cook on Monday. After Monday everything will be different. We'll sit down and talk about the future. You and I. We'll make some plans."

"Fine," said Rose. She came to stand beside her father and leaned against him, not to be friendly but to edge him aside so that she stood directly in front of the fire's warmth. She said, "So it's to be Monday, then?"

"That's when the Commission reconvenes. Would you like to go with us—me and Laura and Tziga, and the Grand Patriarch and his people?"

"No. I don't want Mamie to hear I was in on the kill. She'll probably never speak to me again anyway, no matter what I do."

Chorley put an arm around his daughter. "Are you warmer now, dear?"

"Yes."

"I'd better go see what Tziga is up to. Partway through your tirade he headed for the kitchen."

"Oh no!" Rose rushed off to rescue the food from her uncle's absentminded efforts.

✢ ✢ ✢

Chorley was in bed by eleven, but it took him a long time to go to sleep. He would be drifting off but would wake up with his heart pounding, startled by the memory of his daughter's plunge from the roof of the People's Palace, or by panic at all the little things he'd left undone. He hadn't talked to Rose about what she wanted to do this year. And what was Laura going through now? Just how involved with that Mason boy had she allowed herself to be? Was Tziga any better? Would Grace be safe walking Inland alone?

Taken together, all these little worries and serious frights kept rousing Chorley till around three in the morning, when he fell asleep in the midst of a memory of the Depot film—the pajama-clad figures in flickering black-and-white—an agitated picture of serene sleepwalkers.

The man was with his family. They were trailing up from the beach after an early-morning swim. The blond sandstone of his house caught the light of the lifting sun. In the high tide, the forest seemed to come right down to the water, so that the headland spilled over its reduced shoreline like a gem bulging with light above a gold setting. In the scoop of the bay, two sails were visible, and one far-off smudge of smoke from a steamer's funnel. The man gazed at the horizon and had a sense of the world beyond his peaceful property, going on, industrious, and in good order.

As he strolled and looked around him, the man was filled with satisfaction at everything he saw. He realized that this was one of those moments when it seemed the world itself stopped him and clasped his hand and gave him its congratulations.

He stopped walking. He took a cigar from the pocket of his robe. He trimmed the cigar to his satisfaction, then lit it and blew out smoke of a creamy texture and bluish tinge, the taste of which reminded him of other pleasures he'd had— meals eaten, deals struck, rivals beaten. He planted his legs and stood in his orchard, his bearded chin tilted up, blowing smoke into the branches above him.

Wasps had burrowed in the hanging shells of the last apricots of the season. The smoke dislodged them, and the man watched, delighted, as the insects kept on seeking the lost sweetness through the smoke, dogged and stupid.

"It was all worth it," thought the man. "All the risks I took, all the sacrifices

I made." Before him, yesterday, today, tomorrow, was the proof of the good he'd done himself—his beautiful house and happy family.

He could see his mother on the terrace, with her silver tea service and old-worldly shawl. She was ninety years of age and still straight-backed and sound of mind. With her was his second wife. She'd seen him. She was coming down the terrace steps. In a moment she'd join him, and he'd put his hand in the small of her slender back.

His son and daughter passed him in friendly conversation. He watched them with gratification. He'd been wrong ever to worry about them since, true to their mother's habitual saying, they were the cream that had risen to the top of society. His son looked every inch the prosperous businessman he was—a major stock-holder in the nation's largest utilities company.

The man detected that advice was being offered, brother to sister, and that it was a happy exchange. His daughter had mellowed, had grown up generous and grateful and good. He had been foolish to worry about her too—though he could always say to himself now that worrying about her was part of doing well by her.

One of his granddaughters stopped beside him. "Look, Grandfather!" she said, and did a cartwheel.

"Very good," said the man, then, "Watch out for the wasps."

She did. She was careful. She called out the same advice to her younger sister. There were no mishaps. He could hear them, their laughter broken up by grunts of effort as they practiced all the way to the house.

The eels the boys had caught yesterday would be smoked and boned and ready for breakfast. The man had a good appetite. He ground out his cigar on the trunk of the apricot tree.

The girls had gone indoors, and the Inlet became for a moment a silent arena in which the future—his future—breathed like an expectant audience. Yes, it had all been worth it, the brinkmanship, the qualms of conscience. He had taken things on himself, had made hard decisions for others, and had been rewarded by this peace—and by being right. He was the architect of the prosperity of his nation. It had all turned out for the best. And he knew that he was, in the balance of time, a better man than most.

The orchard grew warmer, and the wasps took themselves off to their bush nests.

His grandsons came last, walking gingerly barefoot by him. They were strong boys, sun-browned, carrying their canoe paddles.

For another moment the man was by himself in the warm morning. He was utterly content. Whatever wrongs he'd committed were only, in the end, part of this loveliness, this life he'd made, this nation he'd shaped, this whole beautiful day ahead of him.

3

✧ ✧ ✧

On that same Saturday, Grace drove Laura to Doorhandle, their bones shaken by the bad early autumn roads. Before either of them went In, they asked for a claim form at the Chief Ranger's office and filled it out. Laura staked her claim on The Gate. They made a note of where they were going in the intentions book, then walked In.

They went together to Foreigner's West, and Grace sat beside Laura as she slept. Then Grace kept Laura company again to the coach stop at Doorhandle before heading back In herself on a three-day round trip to the site of Drought's End.

✧ ✧ ✧

Laura was in the waiting room by the stagecoach stop when she heard the announcement that, because of a cracked wheel rim, the departure of the Sunday coach would be delayed an hour. She looked at her watch and then went out. She wasn't hungry, so she wandered up and down the short boardwalks, browsing shop windows. She was doing this when she saw from a distance one of the Misses Lilley coming her way and decided that she couldn't face *any* Lilleys.

Laura ducked into an alley between the draper's and

butcher's and came out on the slope down to the banks of the Rifleman. There was a bridle path by the river. Laura walked along it, away from the border, until only Doorhandle's church steeple was visible over the riverside trees.

Most of the flowers had gone to seed, but the Queen Anne's lace had lasted and stood waist high. There were big dragonflies zooming back and forth across the path, and, whenever one passed close, Laura would warily stop to see what it was going to do. They had always liked to fly into Rose's hair, and Laura was worried that, since Rose and her hair weren't present, the insects might find *her* attractive instead. But the dragonflies swerved around her as if she were protected by an invisible barrier.

It was very quiet on the path. The native birds had, for the most part, gone back into the forest—everything they liked to eat was gone. With the bullying parson birds gone, the thrushes were back and singing. Laura stopped to listen to one, its song a flow of joy so sure it was almost matter-of-fact.

The breeze dropped altogether, and the sun seemed to kiss the tops of Laura's ears.

Then there came a vibration—footfalls on the path behind her. Laura remembered that she wasn't supposed to be alone. That there were reasons other than her bereavement that her family was sticking so close to her. She turned—and threw up her hands. She was dazzled. The low sun shone, magnified, through a volume of glass. The sun melted as the glass moved.

Laura closed her eyes and cried out.

Someone spoke, said her name in a deep, melodious voice—a voice she didn't know.

Laura opened her eyes again and looked to where the voice had come from. The patch of magnified, blinding sunlight had gone. The thing between her and the sun had moved. She could get a better look at it now. What she saw was a human-shaped volume of glass. She could see trees and grass and the river through the body, distorted, twisted like the petals of color at the heart of a glass marble.

Laura backed into the cloud layer of Queen Anne's lace and didn't stop till she met the trunk of a tree.

He approached her slowly, the glass Nown, and as he came she saw a smear of dirty bread dough in his abdomen, all that remained of her little bread-and-dust man. She saw the solid lump of dark matter in his chest, a rust-stained rock from the railbed. She saw that he wasn't completely, limpidly transparent but had, in his human-shaped volume, here and there, bubbles hanging like frog spawn in pond water. She saw that the different thicknesses of his different parts made shadows within him, and that these weren't shadow-colored but bronze and indigo and blue-black. The shadows and distorted world melted in him as he came toward her—*moved*, a glass statue that was flexible, as if still molten.

As he came close, Laura saw that the soles of his feet were frosted by the wear of walking. Up close his hand was white too or, because he put his hand up to touch her face, the white may only have been her breath misting the glass of his palm.

Nown stooped. He brought his head down to hers so that their foreheads were pressed together. Laura didn't say anything. She only rubbed her face against his. Her cheeks were wet with tears and squawked against his smooth glass skin.

He put an arm around her to support her. She could scarcely stand and couldn't speak. His skin was warm from the sun but unyielding. Her hand against his jaw felt a fake sinew, like a seam of some harder mineral in a sea-worn stone. His jaw moved but stayed as hard as any stone. He said, "Rose?"

Laura cried harder.

"I called," he said. "And I was lucky, she was near. It didn't take me too long to find her in the fire. But the staircase was eaten away by then, and I did more harm than good. I'm sorry. I promise in the future to do more, to do—*I know not what*—to save whoever you love."

Laura clung to him. She had the feeling that something blocked had burst open and she was being swept toward the future she had thought she'd lost. She choked out "Rose saved herself" and felt him relax—as much as anything unyielding could be said to relax.

"Sit down," Nown said, and lowered her to the ground. He knelt before her. His body became the yellow-green of grass and flower stalks, his head milky with flowers—filled, and surrounded, and crowned with flowers. Laura touched his face again. It was a little unclear where he began and ended. He was there, and not there. And it was more difficult than ever to read any expression on his face.

After a long time, when the light was turning gold and midges had gathered under the tree, Laura was calm enough to tell Nown what had happened. She told him about Sandy. "Men must have been lying in wait for him," she said. "The Gate had turned him into an even more formidable Soporif than his uncle George. His uncle thinks he was knocked out in a struggle and took everyone down with him. The men who attacked him were carrying lamps. None of them would have been conscious when the fire started."

Nown sat still and seemed to be thinking. Laura watched him and considered how she'd felt betrayed by him. How she'd given him up in her heart and wrapped herself in Sandy, Sandy's warm flesh, her sense that Sandy was a real life, a true future. She considered that some of her willingness to fall into all that—love, and promising her life—was made up of fury at Nown. She had felt spiteful and righteous.

Now she didn't know what she felt. Her feelings were so strange, beyond relief, or reprieve, or gratitude.

She took a deep breath. "The site of The Gate is on the border, inside a big O that someone has inscribed on the ground. For years rangers have supposed that the O stands for 'ouest'—the French word for west. They think that because there's also a big N on the ground in the north. N for 'nord.' But when I saw the O, and Sandy told me about the N, I knew what it really was. What the Place really *is*. Why didn't you tell me that it's a Nown?"

"You didn't ask."

"That isn't an answer. Once I'd freed you, why didn't you tell me? You must have understood that it was something I needed to know."

"Yes."

"Why didn't you, then?"

"I didn't know what would happen."

Laura reached out, put her knuckles against his rock-hard shoulder, and gave him a hard shove. He didn't stir.

"I couldn't foresee the consequences for you and me if I told you."

"Couldn't you just act in good faith?"

"My freedom isn't like yours, Laura. I think that whenever I have to choose what to do, I have to know what will happen. My free will has laws, it seems. Because I cannot lose my soul, my free will must have laws."

This somehow all made sense to Laura. It made her feel terribly tired, but better. She'd been wrong to resent him— she was always wrong when she expected him to act like a human. She sighed—she had just realized that she'd missed the coach. She asked Nown, "Why didn't you come to find me in Founderston?"

"It was only yesterday that I was able to dig myself out. They had finally moved enough of the debris to make the ash loose around me."

"I thought you'd been destroyed."

"I fell into a pit of coal. It was burning. There were hours when I thought I might not be able to go on. To go on distinguishing myself from the burning coal. We were the same temperature, and I became confused about where the coal ended and I began. Then I felt myself melting, and as I melted I reduced and found myself, my limits. I drew some air into me so I wouldn't shrink too much. I didn't want to be small. And, as I took that breath, I remembered that Laura had made me, and that I'd promised to watch Laura, and never to hurt her. I kept myself together and cooled. And then I had to wait."

Laura looked at him. The sun was bristling through him now, broken by the shadows of the trees across the river. "All right," she thought, "this is my life." What she said was, "Father needs me. I have The Gate for him. Can you get me to Founderston before midnight?"

"Yes."

She studied him. He wouldn't be too visible in the dark, but by daylight he was conspicuous. He could no longer pretend to be a stone. She was sure that, although he could move, he could no longer stretch or flatten, or make a comfortable sling of his arms to carry her in. Then she had an idea. She knew where she could find clothes he could wear. She had a moment of confusion about her plan—it was practical, but it made her a little queasy. "You stay here," she said. "I'll be right back."

Laura left him. She hurried back to the village and to Mrs. Lilley's boardinghouse.

She asked her landlady about the trunk she was storing.

George Mason had asked Grace to tell Mrs. Lilley that he would drop by in a day or two to collect his nephew's belongings. Laura said to the landlady that George Mason had told her she could have one or two of Sandy's things. Conveniently, tears filled her eyes as she spoke.

Mrs. Lilley patted Laura's shoulder, took her to the trunk room, and gave her the key to Sandy's trunk.

Half an hour later, Nown was clothed in trousers, a knitted hat, and Sandy's long dreamhunter's duster coat. Laura saw that her sandman hadn't totally managed to combat the shrinkage of his change from river sand to glass, despite the frog spawn skeins of bubbles he'd drawn into his body. He was nearer to Sandy's size now—a little over six feet and as slender as a young man. He'd kept all his proportions, but there was less of him.

As Laura stood gazing at Nown and wondering about the change, he finished buttoning the coat and slipped his glass hands into his pockets, to see how much bright surface he could hide. Something in the pocket rustled, and Nown drew out a piece of paper. He gave it to Laura.

It was a yellowing newspaper clipping. It was a photograph of her, looking fearfully through the veil of her new hat, into the blast of a photographer's magnesium flash, on the day of her Try, a year ago.

Laura folded the picture and put it in her own pocket. Then she held her arms out, and Nown picked her up and began to run with her, upriver, away from Doorhandle.

4

✦ ✦ ✦

*L*AURA DIDN'T GET TO FALLOW HILL TILL AFTER MIDNIGHT, SO MISSED SPEAKING TO HER FATHER. IT WAS NOWN who held her up at the end of their journey, by arguing about leaving her. She had to insist that she'd be all right, she'd be with her father. Nown had finally let himself be persuaded and taken himself off to Market Bridge.

Laura settled into the room beside the one she'd always shared with Sandy. They'd liked the room whose single bed was against a wall, so that they could share it with less danger of tumbling out. Laura chose to sleep in the adjacent room, in a narrow iron bed. She dreamed The Gate and woke to find sunlight filling the room, because she'd forgotten to close the curtains. She got up and went to find her father, who, it turned out, *hadn't* checked in the night before.

Laura was alarmed. She said no thank you to breakfast and set off for home.

She caught a streetcar. It was early, but the usually packed Monday morning coach was as empty as a Sunday evening one. Laura got off in the market. The farmers' stalls were full, but the market wasn't. Laura didn't notice the anxious vendors; she was intent on getting to her favorite pastry shop, on a corner near her house.

But when she arrived at the shop, she was disappointed to find the trays under the counter almost empty.

"Do you have any pinwheels?" she asked the woman behind the counter.

"I have cream cornets, almond puffs, and lemon tarts. All the ones *I* like best," the woman said, and beamed.

"All right, I'll have eight almond puffs."

The woman slipped them into a bag. She passed them to Laura and left Laura's money lying on the counter, though a little change was due.

"What a beautiful day," the woman said.

Laura said, "Mmmm," and waited a moment longer for the woman to ring up the sale and give her change. Then she blushed, and left.

The awnings were still closed on the news kiosk opposite Market Bridge. Bundles of the *Founderston Herald* lay beside it, the strings fastening them still uncut. Laura steered around the bundles and dashed down the steps by the bridge. Before she got to the first arch, she saw a pile of clothes lying in the bottom of a boat tethered to a ring by the steps. She recognized the knitted hat on top of the pile. Then she saw, against the submerged steps below her, a clear patch in the river, like raw egg white dropped in milky tea. The patch stirred and unfolded, and water rose up out of the water, shedding water. Nown walked up the steps.

"It can't matter to you that your clothes stay dry," Laura said, pointing at the bundle in the boat.

"They're not my clothes," said Nown.

Laura went back up onto the embankment and looked around, both ways. She could hear traffic on the bridge, but there was no one in sight. She told Nown to put his clothes—*the* clothes—back on.

She took him home and into the backyard. She planned to smuggle him up to her room later. "I can always run a bath and hide you in it," she said. Then, "Can you *see* water now?"

"No. And I can't see through it either. I felt you on the steps by the river. I can always feel you as you come toward me."

Laura stood with him, thinking about what he'd said. She knew she should go in. She needed to know what had happened to keep her father from his appointment at Fallow Hill. But the yard was quiet and familiar and private—and she wasn't unhappy. She laid her palm against her servant's side. His shirt—Sandy's shirt—was damp, having blotted the river water from his surface. He felt like stone under the cloth. "And what do I feel like as I come toward you?"

"Laura," he said.

She removed her hand and went toward the back door.

"Laura," he said again, and she turned back to him. But he was only finishing his answer. "Laura, who is life," he said, "But not *just* Laura."

"I should hope not. There's life everywhere," Laura said, somewhat primly. She lifted the latch, pushed the door, and went inside.

"Laura and someone else now," Nown finished, speaking to the closed door.

✢ ✢ ✢

Laura found boiled eggs broken and mashed into the flag-stones of the kitchen floor. She stopped and stared at them, then hurried on into the hall. She called, "Hello!"

"Hello, darling!" Rose called back.

Rose was lying on the window seat in the morning room, in her robe. She was playing with the tassel of the curtain, catching it and tweaking it with her toes.

"Are you all right?" Laura asked.

"Yes. Isn't it a lovely day?" Rose stretched, arched her back, relaxed again, continued to pluck at the cord.

"Have an almond puff."

Rose sat up and took one. She bit into it and gave a little grunt of happiness.

"Where's Da?"

"Don't know," Rose said, muffled and scattering flakes of pastry.

"Isn't he up yet?"

"He was up for breakfast," Rose answered. Then she giggled. "We forgot the eggs, and they almost boiled dry. They were bouncy."

Laura went to look for her father upstairs. His door was open, and he was asleep in a tangle of bedclothes. He looked peaceful, so she left him.

Chorley was in the library listening to his gramophone. He too was in his pajamas and robe. He had little purple dots of spilled jam on his front. The top of his desk was clear except for a row of gramophone cylinders lined up across it. All his papers, notebooks, even his inkstand had been pushed to the floor.

"Laura, listen to this!" Chorley said. He raised a hand to conduct the tenor's squeezed voice for a few bars of the song. "This music reminds me of eating dinner outdoors," he said. "*Alfresco*. Surrounded by family. How wonderful it is to be surrounded by family."

"Well—yes," Laura said. She couldn't believe she was looking at her uncle wearing food stains. She didn't think she'd ever seen him drop food on himself. He could even eat ice cream in a stiff wind without mishap.

He kept his hand up, conducting, his arm moving just a little off the beat. "It was all worth it," he said, dreamily. "I put in the time and ended up with this—all the time in the world," he said.

Laura backed out of the room and into the hall. She leaned on the wall, her legs watery.

✢ ✢ ✢

A few minutes later Laura was back in the yard. She was carrying a pair of her uncle's slippers and a long scarf and gloves. She gave them to Nown. He sat down to put the slippers on. She had to help him with the gloves.

"Your hands are shaking," he said.

"My family have had that dream. Contentment. They're all blissful and silly," she said. Her voice had a tremor too. "This is my fault. I was afraid to tell them all how bad it was at the Depot. I didn't want to upset Da. And I kept hoping that Gavin Pinkney was so hopeless because he'd had the dream over and over, and because he was so soggy to begin with."

Nown didn't respond to this. He wound the scarf to mask his lower face. He was overdressed for the weather, which was still warm. He looked a little sinister—or as sinister as anyone in slippers could. Yet no one would imagine his bundled figure was anything but human.

Laura walked out of the yard. Nown followed her. He didn't ask where they were going, or what they'd do.

As Laura walked, she saw all the things she hadn't noticed before, like how quiet the streets were—a Monday like Sunday. And that none of the people who were out and about were in a hurry, and all looked friendly and happy.

The motorists on Market Bridge were the same as ever, jostling and impatient. Most were from outlying suburbs.

They were going about their business and perhaps felt just as baffled as Laura by a choice of only three pastries in their favorite pastry shop, and the *Founderston Herald* printed, packaged, but not on sale.

Laura and Nown crossed the river to the Isle of the Temple. They made their way to Temple Square. Laura told Nown to wait for her in St. Anthony's Chapel, which was in the northwest corner of the nave and always full of shadows in the morning.

Laura went to the Grand Patriarch's palace and told one of the caped guards at the gate that she wanted to see His Eminence.

✧ ✧ ✧

After a long time, over an hour, Laura rejoined her glass man in St. Anthony's Chapel. It was gloomy and uninviting, but Nown wasn't the only one there. There were two women at the altar, silhouetted, heads bowed, in the light of the candles they'd lit.

It turned out that Nown could no longer whisper. His voice had been a deep, dry rasp. It was deep still, but now clear and melodious, and even when he spoke quietly it was like listening to water falling into a stone basin in a still garden. "St. Anthony is the patron saint of the lost," he said, informatively.

"We should say a prayer then," said Laura. "I couldn't get anywhere near the Grand Patriarch or Father Roy. Apparently they are either out or terribly busy. The people I spoke to wouldn't disturb them just to say a little dreamhunter had come to see them. I'm a person of no consequence, and I've been snubbed by pompous functionaries. I did get to leave a note for Father Roy. I hope he jumps out of his skin when he reads it."

"It's because you're a girl," Nown said, matter-of-fact.

"Yes," said Laura. She put a coin in the donation box, took a candle, lit it, and said a short and not terribly coherent prayer. Then she took her glass man by his gloved hand and left the Temple.

5

✧ ✧ ✧

MINUTES AFTER LAURA HAD LEFT HER HOUSE, A CAR PULLED UP IN FRONT OF IT. THREE MEN GOT OUT. TWO were in pinstripes and bowler hats, and had heavy, swinging bulges in their jacket pockets. The third was the red-haired, waxy-skinned Maze Plasir.

Plasir tugged on the bell chain for several minutes before Chorley opened the door. "Hello!" Chorley said, cheery. "Visitors! Isn't it a lovely day, visitors?"

Plasir took Chorley's arm and propelled him back indoors. The other men crowded in after them.

"Shall we sit down?" Chorley said. "My papers are all over the place in the library. Let's go in here." He threw open the parlor doors and swept into the room ahead of them. He flopped into a chair, draped his legs over one of its arms, and let his slippers drop off his feet to the floor.

The Regulatory Body officials perched together on the edge of a sofa, ramrod straight and ready for action.

"I must go out and buy some more music," Chorley said. "I've listened to everything I have here."

Plasir nodded sympathetically. "This afternoon, perhaps," he suggested.

"Isn't it afternoon yet? I'm looking forward to a nice nap later," Chorley said.

"An excellent idea," said Plasir.

One of the burly officials sniggered.

"I've come to ask about one of your films, Mr. Tiebold," Plasir said.

Chorley's face lit up. "That's something else I could do later. Watch my films. That would be fun. Those films are certainly one thing I've done that was worthwhile. I've been thinking a lot about that lately—what was worthwhile."

"Yes. Taking stock. Very healthy," said Plasir.

"That's right, humor him," said an official.

Plasir gave the man a cold, quelling look. "There's one film in particular that interests me," Plasir said to Chorley. "A film of the Place."

"I have two of those," Chorley said. "No one in the world but me has a film of the Place." He looked thoughtful. "Except Cousin Erasmus, I suppose."

"Cousin Erasmus has a film of the Place?"

"Yes." Chorley swung his legs down, and when his bare feet touched the floor, he looked at them and laughed. "Why *do* people bother with shoes indoors?"

"He's full of opinions. True to his character," said one of the officials.

"Be quiet," Plasir said. "Mr. Tiebold, where do you keep that film?"

"It's in my darkroom."

"Would you get it for me?"

"Do you want the other one too?"

"Cousin Erasmus's copy?"

"No. *He* has that. I mean the one Tziga took, it's only two or three minutes long, but it's very beautiful in its way."

The officials were nodding, so Plasir said, "Yes, I think we'd better have both of them."

One of the officials got up. "I'll help you, Mr. Tiebold."

The other said, "Is Mr. Hame at home?"

"Yes, is he?" said Plasir. "And when do you expect your wife back?"

"Tziga was here at breakfast," Chorley said, vague. He left his slippers and wandered to the door. "I can't remember what Grace said about when she'd be back. Does it matter? We have the whole day ahead of us. This beautiful day."

Plasir frowned and shook himself. This dream of Cas's was horrible—incomparably horrible. Cas was making adjustments, moving his loaded dreamhunters around, and making sure that the capital kept on running, that its civil servants and politicians were soothed and full of generosity, but not as lost as *this*—or as desperately lost as the dosed dreamhunters themselves. The Hame-Tiebold house had been two nights at the intersection of overlapping penumbras, under the spell of no fewer than three vivid dreamhunters. And this was the result. Chorley Tiebold had always sneered at and snubbed Plasir, and yet here he was being good-natured and cooperative without giving his actions a moment's thought.

When Chorley disappeared into his darkroom, Plasir went looking for the house's other inhabitants. He found Tziga upstairs asleep, and smiling. He found Rose in the morning room, playing with one of those toys where a clown climbs a ladder and does flips. She had an empty cookie tin before her, and her robe was speckled with crumbs. She looked up at Plasir and gave a shriek of laughter. "I wasn't thinking about *you*," she said. "I was daydreaming. I thought my daydream might conjure someone. But not you. Yuck!"

"I'm wounded, Miss Tiebold," said Plasir. Then, "Your cousin didn't stay for breakfast at Fallow Hill. Where do you think she is?"

"Um," said Rose. She squeezed her toy so hard that the little clown flew right off it.

"On such a beautiful day, where might Laura have gotten to?" Plasir coaxed, since Rose was a little more feisty than he had expected.

"She was here shortly after breakfast," the girl said. Then she grinned. "Uncle Tziga and I bounced boiled eggs."

"That sounds like wonderful fun," said Plasir. "But where is Laura?"

"Laura is alone," Rose said, blankly. "Alone. All alone."

"Do you have any idea *where* she is alone?"

"Everywhere. She doesn't have to be, though. She could make herself another monster. She's being stubborn about it." Rose looked up at Plasir, and a little frown marred her smooth brow. "Doesn't she want to be happy?"

Maze Plasir shook his head in sympathy. He went out to check on the search for the film and found both of the men he'd come with in the library. One was pushing together a pile of paper under the bottom of a long damask curtain. The other had a reel of film tucked under his arm and was holding a box of matches.

"What the hell are you doing?" Plasir demanded.

"What we were told to do, Mr. Plasir. We have the film. We are meant to take care of everyone who has seen the film."

"Doran told you to 'take care of them'?"

"Yes, Mr. Plasir."

Plasir was stunned. "No! Stop!"

The man who was standing put his hand up, in warning.

"At least let me take the girl. Doran can't possibly want Rose Tiebold killed. She's a friend of his daughter."

"Nothing was said about that."

Plasir pushed forward, and there was a scuffle. He was shoved from the room. He heard Chorley calling in a plaintive voice from the darkroom, "Hello? I seem to be locked in."

Plasir hurried in to Rose, grabbed her, and pulled her to her feet. "Come with me," he said.

At that moment there was a knock on the front door. Plasir froze. Rose wriggled her shoulders and got out of his grasp. "Don't be so rough," she said.

The officials ran out into the hall. Both men were carrying revolvers.

The person on the front step called, "Rose! Why is this door locked?"

"It's Laura Hame," said Plasir.

"Good," said an official. He rushed at the door. But just before he yanked it open, the shadow of the girl left the glass. She had bolted. He chased her out into the street.

Plasir saw his chance. He made his choice. He'd leave Laura Hame to her fate—but he'd save Rose Tiebold. He hustled her out the front door. He was in time to see the Body official sprinting through the side gate and into the alley that led to the backyard of the house. It seemed the Hame girl had boxed herself into a dead end.

Plasir gripped Rose's arm and dragged her along the embankment.

✢ ✢ ✢

Laura skidded into the yard and pushed past Nown. She yelled, "Look out!" She didn't even look back, just rushed to her family's rescue. She banged through the back door, stumbled across the kitchen, skidding on mashed eggs, and fell through the kitchen doorway.

A man with a revolver jumped forward and seized her. He thrust the gun's muzzle into her ribs. She twisted, and then a gap appeared beside her—the darkroom door had opened. The gunman's grip loosened momentarily, and Laura flung herself through the door, crashing into her uncle, who was saying, "I remembered where I put the spare key." Then, *"Ouch"* as she trampled him, though he didn't sound very perturbed.

Laura crashed into the worktable and turned to see what was coming. For an instant the doorway was full of the Body man, his gun raised and pointed right at her, then a shadow slammed into the man, snapping him in the middle so that his knees bashed his head. The doorway was empty.

Laura emerged to find Nown standing over the felled man. Nown was still, erect and calm, not like a combatant but like a ceremonial sentry. He said, "I have rendered them unconscious." He'd clearly dealt the same way with her pursuer.

From the street Laura heard an unmistakable noise—the squeal Rose used to make as a child when she was angry about not getting her own way. Laura looked for the revolver. She picked it up and went to the door. She peered out.

Plasir was struggling with Rose, who'd sat down like a stubborn toddler and was kicking her legs.

There was a barge out on the Sva. The man at its wheel was watching the struggle. Laura heard him shout, "Hey! You there!"

Laura ran down the front steps, hurried up to Plasir, and pointed the gun at him.

Rose stopped struggling and stared at Laura with big eyes. "He's a nasty little thing, but I don't think you should shoot him, Laura," she said.

"She won't," said Plasir. His eyes were darting about, between the gun, the barge, and the door to Laura's house. "What did you do with those Body men?"

"I shot them," Laura said, and eased the hammer back a little.

Plasir released Rose and backed away, his hands raised. "I didn't hear any shooting," he said, but looked uncertain.

"Don't go another step," Laura said. "You are to come with me."

"You won't shoot me." Plasir continued to edge away. "There are too few of you," he said. "You can't win. You'd better just leave the city."

Laura raised her voice, and called, "Nown!"

Rose said, "Oh—your monster! Do you have him again?" She cackled and shook her finger at Plasir, then gaily began to call too, "Nown!" Nown!"

Nown came along the embankment. He noticed the agitated barge man, gave him a wave with his gloved hand, then advanced on Rose, Laura, and Plasir. Laura kept her eye on Plasir, who saw that the reinforcement she'd summoned was a man bigger than he was. He turned to run.

Nown went by Laura, gently relieved her of the gun, then closed on Plasir, caught him in a few swift bounds, pinned him, picked him up, and carried him back to the house.

Laura put her arm around her cousin, helped her up, and followed.

Plasir had gone completely limp. Nown carried him to the darkroom, took the key from Chorley, and put Plasir inside. Laura saw that Plasir was shocked and passive. He was staring at Nown, trying to penetrate all the wrappings to see why the body that had grappled him had been so unnaturally hard. He peered but seemed to wince away too, as though, much as he wanted to know what was under the wrappings, he was also afraid of knowing.

Nown picked up the unconscious official and put him in the darkroom too. He closed the door and locked it.

"Who is this?" Chorley said to Laura. "Why is he wearing

all that? Is it snowing?" Then, distracted, "Rose, your robe is torn."

Laura took her uncle's arm. "Let's get something to eat and drink. My friend here will check on Da and bring Rose a clean robe."

"All right," said Chorley, and contentedly went with his daughter and niece into the kitchen.

A few minutes later Nown came through the room, handed Rose a robe, and said, "No, thank you, I'm a little busy," to Chorley's friendly offer of a cup of tea. Then he went out into the yard, returning with the other unconscious man. He disappeared with his bundle into the hallway, this time to stay out of range of Chorley's happiness-hampered but still too lively curiosity.

✧ ✧ ✧

At three in the afternoon, Father Roy turned up with several cars as an escort. Laura let him in and showed him her father, Rose, and Chorley, who had opened every can and jar of preserves and were at the kitchen table enjoying a long, large, messy lunch. She told Roy about Plasir and the two unconscious officials locked in her uncle's darkroom. She handed over the revolvers. "I'm putting all this in your hands," she said. "I have a dream that will clear space in Doran's grid of Contentment. I only want to get my family back. Please, can you tell someone to meet Aunt Grace when she comes out of the Place? Can you bring her to me so that she can be safe too? The dream she's gone to catch isn't a master dream."

Father Roy sat down at the kitchen table and spoke in a very gentle voice to Chorley, Tziga, and Rose. "Come on, we're all going for a ride."

"If I'm going out, I should get dressed," Chorley said.

"Naturally. Let's see how quick you can be," Father Roy said.

"Race you!" shouted Rose to her father. They jumped up, jostled each other into the hall, and thumped up the stairs.

"I'm an invalid," Laura's father said, and drew his robe protectively around himself. "I'm excused from making efforts."

Laura closed her eyes and rubbed the bridge of her nose.

Father Roy summoned his escort, unlocked Chorley's darkroom, and manhandled Plasir and the one limp and one groggy official to the cars outside. He then went back to the darkroom and gathered up an armload of film canisters, including the one the Body officials had located. "I'm taking all these in case we need decoys at some stage," Father Roy said.

Laura was alarmed. "Didn't the Commission reconvene today? Isn't this almost *over*?" Her throat began to hurt. She was going to cry again.

"No. That's why we missed you when you came to find us. His Eminence and I were cooling our heels at the Palace of Justice. When your uncle and father didn't turn up with you, we simply imagined you'd gotten word."

"Word of what?"

"Word that the meeting was postponed because the convening judge, Seresin, was 'unavailable.' "

"*No*," said Laura. "No. This can't go on. Someone has to put a stop to it."

Chorley and Rose came downstairs. He looked very spruce, as usual, but reeked of cologne. Laura could see that his jacket was dewed with it. Rose had her shirt buttoned up wrong and was wearing all her favorite necklaces—amber, coral, carved ivory, crystals, jet, pearls—together. She said, "I ate so much I had to be sick." She spoke in a loud whisper, perhaps meaning to speak only to Laura.

Chorley looked at the stack of films in Father Roy's arms. "Are we having a screening?"

Laura went to get her father, and while she was in the kitchen she poked her head around the back door and told Nown to follow her. "There are steps down to the river around three sides of the Temple. You'll be able to find a place to hide. My task now is to sleep and take care of Da and Uncle Chorley and Rose." She spoke to the space between his hat and the top fold of his scarf. His glassy surface was in shadow, and, without reflected light, the visible segment of his head was just an absence, something watery rather than airy on which the hat seemed to float.

"There were weapons," Nown said. "When there are weapons, I should stay at your side."

"I don't feel safe without you, true. But I think I *am* safe at the Grand Patriarch's Palace. And his people need my protection."

"Yes," said Nown.

Behind Laura, Father Roy said, "Miss Hame, we should go."

Laura gave Nown a beseeching look, then pushed the door shut.

She helped Father Roy get her father up. Tziga walked, slow and shaky, leaning on both of them. As they went along, he said to Laura, "The thing about this dream, darling, is that even though the man is blissfully pleased with himself, it's the wasps eating the apricots that are most *present*. Those wet shells of fruit still hanging on the branches. It's as though the dream uses the man's eyes like a camera to show us something more real than the story he's telling himself about what a fine person he is."

"Da!" Laura was floored by surprise and admiration. "You're yourself."

"Not really. But I am a dreamhunter."

Laura kissed her father's hand.

"Also—when Rose and I were bouncing the eggs, I had a seizure. Didn't she tell you?"

"She didn't."

"She and Chorley must have carried me up to bed. The fit seemed to shake the dream loose a little."

Father Roy helped Tziga into his car. Laura climbed in beside her father and cuddled up to him. She whispered, "The dreams *are* memories, Da, like Uncle Chorley always thought. Human memories from a time in the future. But the Place itself uses them to try to talk. It shows us what *it* finds meaningful."

Laura's father peered at her, puzzled.

"The Place is a Nown, Da."

Tziga opened his mouth but didn't say anything for a long moment. Finally he said, "Whose?"

"I don't know."

6

✧ ✧ ✧

ON TUESDAY MORNING LAURA WOKE
FROM A LONG, REPEATED CYCLE OF
THE GATE. SHE OPENED HER EYES. SHE FELT
her whole body breathe in and exhale the dream's radiance.
Then the person beside her in bed said, "Am I where I think
I am?"

Laura sat up and studied Rose. Her cousin looked af-
fronted. She lifted the covers and said, "You let me get into
bed wearing shoes."

"Sorry," said Laura. "It was an emergency. *You* were an
emergency."

"I certainly was," Rose said, with feeling. Then, "Who can
I sue? Who can I kill? Show me my enemies and I will burn
them to the ground!" She propelled herself out of bed, then
had to throw the blankets over her head and burrow in the
covers for a shoe.

Someone knocked on the tall double doors of the gloomy
bedchamber. A nun put her head around the door and said if
they would wash and dress she would see them in to breakfast.

Rose began to straighten herself out. She ran her fingers
through her tangled hair. She rubbed her mouth, which was
still crusted with food. She found a mirror and inspected the
crocodile skin on her neck, the indentations of all the beads

she was wearing. Then she stood stock-still. "You pointed a gun at Maze Plasir!" she said. And then, in an elated squawk, "You have your monster back! He was dressed like a cabbie on a cold night. He *scragged* Plasir!" She laughed.

"Come on," Laura said. "I want to hear what the adults are planning. Dear God—let them have a plan."

✧ ✧ ✧

The adults looked grim. But they were all there—everyone Laura could have hoped to see. Her father, in pajamas and a knitted gray shawl. Uncle Chorley, his jaw set and nostrils white. Grace, who looked frightened.

Laura's aunt Marta was there, and her Mrs. Bridges was taking plates from servants at the door and carrying them to the table.

George Mason was there too. The car sent to meet Grace at the Doorhandle border had passed him in the village. He had been on his way to Mrs. Lilley's for Sandy's trunk. Grace had persuaded him to come along with her. He was sitting beside Laura, and, as he passed her a plate of muffins, he said, "The Regulatory Body stalked Sandy—I know it. I don't care what it takes; I'll see Doran pay."

The rest of a crowded table was taken up by Erasmus Tiebold, Father Roy, and a half dozen other priests.

Maze Plasir was at the breakfast too, though Chorley had pointedly removed his butter knife from beside his plate.

Plasir wasn't eating.

Erasmus Tiebold was asking Plasir questions. "I imagine Doran has himself, his allies, and the Founderston Barracks at least out of the range of this dream, or covered by other dreams. But how long does he mean to keep it up? My cousin

Chorley's household had it very strongly—were they targeted? Or are all Founderston's citizens lying around gathering moss and gorging themselves?"

Plasir leaned back in his chair and looked at his hands. He said, "You can't win."

"If the whole city is in the same shambles that my cousin's house was, then I can't see what Doran hopes to gain, or how he hopes to get away with it."

"Can't you? For a start, the film and the girl can be kept from the Commission. You might still have the evidence in your possession, but who will be interested in it?"

Father Roy had a lightweight edition of the *Founderston Herald* open before him. He also had yesterday's papers from Westport and Canning and other smaller towns in the south. He said, "It is reported here that Congress voted to abolish the two-term limit on the presidency."

"And then there's *that*." Plasir gloated. "You're in the Temple, and the dreams you need to catch to keep people safe are in the Place—two localities far apart. You have only four dreamhunters in this room, and one of them is an epileptic."

Rose put down the muffin she was picking at and pushed aside her teacup too.

Plasir looked around the table, his eyes glittering. He said to Erasmus Tiebold, "And, unless I'm mistaken, Your Eminence, you have been chewing Wakeful. Why? Are you so reluctant to share *any* dream that you're drugging yourself to save yourself from Miss Hame's charming specialty?"

Laura gazed at Plasir with amazement. He could make anything sound corrupt. The Gate was her "charming specialty."

"Please remove him," Chorley said.

The Grand Patriarch nodded to one of the priests, who called on some of the Temple guards. Plasir got up and gave them a nasty smile. He said, "Face it—you're finished." He was led out.

When the door had closed, Grace said, "He's right about some things. All they have to do is get *us*—me, George, Laura. Then we're finished. You can't go on chewing Wakeful forever."

"I thought that Wakeful could give me eighty sleepless hours," Erasmus Tiebold said.

"Not safely," said Tziga. "With a dream inside you it can. Without a dream you'll become gloomy, angry, and possibly dangerous within sixty hours."

"Then you'll develop an irregular heartbeat," Chorley said. "It's hearts that need sleep."

The Grand Patriarch looked disturbed. It was his first sign of worry.

"Drought's End is useless," Grace said. "I have to catch a master dream. Laura's The Gate will be good for another four days, possibly more. I have to catch something to spell her, and buy us some more time."

"My penumbra won't go anywhere near protecting the whole palace," George Mason said. His face creased with unhappiness.

Chorley said, "We have to focus on the film."

"The Commission is—out of commission!" Grace shouted. "What good is your bloody film?"

The Grand Patriarch winced. "Please, Mrs. Tiebold." There was something about his expression that made Laura think he was scolding her aunt for a lack of refinement.

Laura put her hands over her ears. She sat for a moment and listened to her blood roar. She concentrated on not being sick. All the food on the table smelled awful, the eggs sulfurous, the muffins soapy with baking powder, the milk fatty.

Food had been tasting funny to her for days, but now it was as if it were poisonous.

"Hey!" said Rose suddenly, very loud, and interrupting everyone. She leapt up and put her fists on the table, leaned across it and over the newspaper Father Roy was reading. She grabbed the paper and turned it—she had been reading it upside down. "Listen," she said, and read out a death notice. "Seresin, Kathryn (née Kralls). March 14, 1907, at the age of fifty-five, after a short illness. Beloved wife of Judge Mitchell Seresin." Rose looked around the table. "The Commission didn't reconvene because its head wasn't in town. He would have been at his wife's deathbed. And he'll be at her funeral, in Castlereagh, this coming Friday. We can take the film to him!"

There was a short, electrified pause. Then everyone started talking.

7

✢ ✢ ✢

No one who saw the large party that arrived at Founderston Central Station the following day would have thought that they were engaged in a desperate plan. The group stood under the great clock suspended from the cavernous ceiling of the main concourse. They were well-dressed and well-equipped, with bags and picnic baskets and travel rugs. Among them they had a number of large film canisters, fastened in buckled carrying straps.

As they waited, they were met by men who, it seemed, had been sent ahead to buy train tickets. The men approached the group, tickets were produced, words exchanged—but no money, no tips. The party stood watching the clock; then they moved as one out onto the platform and, after a quick round of farewells, dispersed to different trains.

George Mason wasn't with them. He had left in the early hours by car. He was to travel by the back roads of Wry Valley to the border west of Doorhandle, where he planned to go In and catch Plasir's specialty dream, Secret Room—a master dream.

Marta and Tziga got on a train going south. Their tickets would take them to the spa in Spring Valley, where invalids often went to bathe and drink from the mineral springs. With the Hames were a priest, one of the Grand Patriarch's most trusted men, and a stolid Temple guard. Marta carried a copy of the film, the long strip of nitrate removed from its reel and wound in a figure eight into the false bottom of her narrow valise—a bag of a shape that no one would suppose could store a reel of film. Marta and Tziga intended to check into the spa, where Tziga—another decoy—would stay. Marta would take a boat—supposedly for a day trip across the lake—escorted only by the Temple guard. On the opposite side of the lake was a small but picturesque mountain village, from which a road wound down fifty-five rough miles to the far side of the mountains that divided Southland. A weekly coach service ran on that road, delivering mail and other goods to farms and settlements along the way. Marta and the Temple guard would catch that coach, then the train again from a small station south of The Corridor. The train would get them to Castlereagh by Friday evening.

Two priests carrying a reel each boarded the express to Westport. Both reels were unexposed film—decoys.

Chorley and Grace got on the Westport local. They too carried films. One was of the sand-sculpting competition, the other of a pod of blackfish stranded on So Long Spit. The couple would leave the train at the small stop near Marta Hame's house, where they would be met by Marta's Mr. Bridges, with a car. They would take the car, skirt the capital on country roads, and meet the border to the Place just east of Doorhandle. Grace would go In and try to catch The Gate. Chorley meant to drive on through the Rifleman Pass to Sisters Beach, where he would stay with his daughter and wait for news.

Rose represented the group's backup plan. She left the concourse of Founderston Central Station and boarded a local for Sisters Beach—alone. She carried an overnight bag and a hatbox containing a wide-brimmed, flower-trimmed hat.

She was in first class, as usual, and as soon as she got on the train she locked the door of her compartment.

Laura was to stay in Founderston, at the Temple, to dream The Gate and hold the fort till Grace—or George Mason if Grace was unable to make it back in time—relieved her.

That was the plan.

Laura was allowed to accompany the others to the station to see them off. When they got to the divider between platforms 5 and 6, she hurriedly kissed her cousin, then turned to plead with Father Roy. "Could I please, *please*, see my father onto the train and settled in?"

"Very well," said the priest. "But be quick."

✛ ✛ ✛

Laura unfolded a travel rug and tucked it around her father's knees. She gave her aunt Marta some hasty instructions on how to mix elder-flower cordial to his taste.

"Yes, yes, child," Marta said. She gestured at the priests waiting for Laura on the platform. "You should go. You must understand that, if this were a game of chess, you would be the king."

"I don't play chess."

"Don't draw it out," her father warned. "It only makes saying goodbye more difficult." He caught her eye. She was still fussing around him, rearranging his pillows. Their heads were together. He said, "What's on your mind, Laura?"

Marta said, musing, "Founderston must be full of dream-hunters wondering why business is falling off. If Erasmus could only gain their confidence . . ."

"Contentment will have erased any dream that isn't its near equal," Tziga said to his sister. Then, to his daughter, "What is it, love?"

She kissed his cheek. "I should go." She kissed her aunt too and wished them both good luck. Then she said again, to her father, "I must go."

Laura left the compartment and turned away from the door she'd come in by. She hurried up the train, into the second-class compartments, which were full. She went along, peering into the compartments and through their windows, which looked out onto the train on the track beside theirs— the Sisters Beach local. Finally Laura saw what she was looking for, her cousin, a solitary figure clutching a candy-striped hatbox. Laura pushed into a compartment. She said, "Excuse me," to its occupants, then stretched over them to haul down the window. She leaned out and waved.

Rose got up and opened her window.

The people behind Laura were protesting and pulling at her clothes.

"Wider," Laura said to Rose.

Rose leaned her weight on the window and forced it open. Laura gripped the luggage rack above her, stepped onto the windowsill, and climbed out the window of the train she was on. She straddled the gap. Rose leaned out and helped her through. They tumbled together into Rose's compartment. The hatbox fell off the seat, lost its lid, hat, loose satin lining, and reel of film. Rose got up and slammed the window shut to cut off the sounds of indignation: "Well I never!" and "Of all the nerve!"

The train beside the local began to move, the annoyed faces slid out of sight, then the dining car with its SPRING VALLEY legend. Laura pushed Rose back into her seat. She said, "Don't look," and ducked down herself as one of her father and aunt's escorts hurried along the hallway of the moving train, looking and looking, no doubt alerted by the people Laura had left behind on the platform.

Then the windows were empty, the train gone. Rose pulled down the window blind. A minute later their train jerked and began to move. It slid out of Central Station, jostling through switches in the rail yard before finding its way onto the north line.

Laura got up off the floor. She gathered the hatbox and its contents.

"I thought there was a fishy lack of ceremony in your leave-taking," Rose said.

"The Grand Patriarch will have to make do with Plasir and his Secret Room," said Laura. "He can pack everyone he really needs into a few rooms with Plasir, and they'll be safe from Contentment."

"He'll have them all chewing Wakeful, Laura, before he ever shares one of Plasir's sleazy dreams."

Laura grinned at the thought. "Well, a sleazy dream might offend him, but so would The Gate. It's blasphemous. It says that paradise is only time running backward. And someone's mother guards the gate instead of St. Peter."

Rose gave her cousin a careful look. "The woman in The Gate isn't 'someone's mother,' Laura—she's you."

"Yes, I know."

"And all those years ago, your da must have mistaken her for *your* mother. He'd have thought that the dream really was meant for Verity, to ease her dying."

Laura nodded. "I thought it was Sandy's doing that she looked like me. Then I caught it without Sandy, and she still looked like me."

Rose put up the window blind again, in time to see the birch-lined playing fields of Founderston Girls' Academy slide by. She said, "Do you think Uncle Tziga and your aunt Marta have a chance?"

"Not much of one, not if they're followed."

Rose plucked at her skirt, patted its lace-edged pockets. "I hope you have a plan then."

"No."

"You climbed between trains without a plan?"

Laura did know where she was going. And she knew that Nown would feel her leaving Founderston and would follow her, as fast as he was able. There was a place she would go, and he would join her there—then they would see. She said, "I have this much of a plan. You should go out and find a conductor and pay my fare. And you should tell him that we want to get off at the train stop in the Awa Inlet."

"We're visiting Mamie? That's the plan?"

"You are."

Rose nodded and got up to do as she was told.

✢ ✢ ✢

It was dark at the train stop. The tide was out, and the only light came from the breakers, a mile away at the mouth of the Inlet. Gulls roosting on the sandbar made a warm clucking out in the dark. At intervals the lighthouse on So Long Spit blinked its warning at them.

Laura and Rose sat on the stony bank. They didn't dare go on till there was more light. Rose had her bag and hatbox. Laura had Rose's coat, and in its pockets a bottle of lemonade and some wafers from the train's dining car.

"I can't think what you're planning," Rose said to the patch of solid darkness that was her cousin.

"Neither can I. I don't mean I don't know—I mean I can't think about it."

"Don't do anything self-sacrificing."

"I think I have to, Rose. But it's not that bad. I promise you'll see me soon."

"There's only that rail line and the Depot over the border here. Do you mean to make your monster wreck the cable car?"

"I hadn't thought of that."

"It would be a pretty desperate measure. The people at the Depot might starve."

"Yes. That's a good argument against it."

Rose scooted next to Laura and put her arm around her. She was seeing certain things very clearly now. She saw that there were decisions people had to make, alone, for other people. And that sometimes there was no substituting for whoever had to decide. There were torches that couldn't be passed on. Laura's light would go out in Rose's hands. Rose saw it now—and it made her feel very old and lonely.

A band of light the shade of a ripening lemon outlined the eastern headland. The world came back, bit by bit, till the girls could see water glimmering in the channels of the reedbeds, and the white streak of crushed shell that was the path to the Doran summerhouse.

✧ ✧ ✧

Mamie woke when a maid knocked on her door, came in, opened the curtains, and started talking. "Miss," she said, "your friend Rose Tiebold is here. She must have arrived on the five o'clock train. She was waiting on the terrace when the boy went out to get milk from the springhouse."

Mamie got up and found her robe and slippers. She stumped downstairs scratching her scalp.

Rose was at the breakfast table. A maid and the butler were bustling around her as though she was in danger of dying in the next several minutes for lack of jam, honey, and hot rolls.

Mamie sat down too and waited for the servants to leave.

When they had gone, she said, "Did you have some kind of disagreement with someone, Rose?"

Rose hesitated, then looked amused. "Yes."

"And you came here to me?"

"Yes."

Mamie was pleased. She nearly told Rose she was honored, only that wasn't quite right. She'd been so bored. Now she felt useful. Then she frowned. "I'm not any good at drying tears and so forth."

"You won't have to do that. We can sit on the terrace drinking cider, and playing cards, and reading books all day. That will fix me."

Mamie pushed the plate of rolls toward her friend. "My perfect day," she said. She missed seeing Rose's pained expression.

For much of the day they did sit on the terrace, sipping cider cooled by luxurious ice. They read mostly, for Mamie hated cards and every other game of chance.

In the late afternoon, alertness pulled Mamie out of her book. She looked up.

Rose put her own book down and stood. She walked on the edge of the terrace and slowly, tentatively, raised her arm.

There was a man striding up the avenue of plane trees. When he passed through the bands of sunlight, Mamie saw that he was wrapped, head to toe, in an odd assortment of garments.

The man saw Rose, broke stride, and raised a hand to return her greeting. Then he strode on and vanished into the air.

Mamie said, "Do you know that dreamhunter?"

"No. I don't know him at all," Rose replied.

8

✦ ✦ ✦

OWN WAS TWELVE HOURS BEHIND
LAURA. HE TRAVELED BY DAY-
LIGHT AND NIGHT, AND MANY PEOPLE SAW
him—the motley, bundled man who ran as fast as a horse. He
was a sign and a wonder to many, who were able to say there-
after: "Only the day before, I saw . . ."

✦ ✦ ✦

Laura, waiting, was afraid of being seen. She was out in the
open. She hid herself as best she could by lying down beside
the low mound of earth. Her wait was long, and she fell
asleep.

It was late in the epidemic, and the boy knew what to expect. He'd seen things at
other houses along the country road on which they lived. He'd seen how the
mailboxes at the breaks in poplar hedges would have white tea towels tied to
them. That was what people were told to do if they needed help. The Boy Scouts
would come by to deliver cooked meals and clean linen.

During the sickness, the boy's mother had said that he was allowed to go out
for exercise but shouldn't go near anyone. He'd sometimes lie in wait in the cul-
vert by the crossroads, and would emerge when the Boy Scouts went by. He'd follow them, fishing for news. From them he heard of the houses—two neighboring

—where only silence greeted the visitor's knock and everyone inside was discovered dead. "With their faces and fingers turned black," one Scout said.

When his mother became ill and banned him from her sight, the boy would sit outside her bedroom door and listen to her cough. And at night he'd wake up in his own bed and listen for silence—the silence he imagined coming, as eloquent as speech, from a blackened face. Then he'd hear her cough again.

The third night he woke up because the cough was dragging itself along the hall. The boy lay straight in his bed, like a body in a coffin. He was cold because he didn't have enough blankets on his bed. He was cold because he was feeding himself and had let the stove go out. And he was cold within himself, all the way through, as though he were an orphan already and had to think first what he could do for himself.

He got out of bed and followed his mother into the kitchen. She had carried her writing box from her bedroom to the table. It was open, and the boy saw her many packets of letters, bundled with ribbons that had faded over the years and grown brittle.

His mother's face was white. Her hair was plastered to her neck by sweat. She knelt on the floor pushing handfuls of wood chips through the stove door. Then she got a match and lit the stove. Tendrils of smoke came out the door, then were sucked back into the stove as the fire began to draw.

The boy was practical. Since there was a fire, he filled the kettle and put it on the stove. He reached over his mother to set it down, and she pushed him back, her hand hot on his leg.

The boy sat on the other side of the kitchen and kept his eyes fixed on the spout of the kettle, waiting for steam. He'd make some beef tea. While he waited he picked up his violin and tuned it. He didn't watch his mother burn her letters, or glanced only once and saw the fire turn one packet into a black-striped brick, then a kind of paper chaff, flakes of soot circling in the stove.

She burned all of them—the letters from her cousin who lived in another country. One letter a week for eight years. She had never read any of the letters to the boy, and so it didn't matter, nothing was different, the cousin in another country knew all about him and he knew nothing about her. But his mother was burning the letters, and that mattered. And then she didn't want beef tea, and *she wouldn't let him touch her or help her as she dragged herself back to bed.*

He washed his few dishes, because there was hot water. Then he returned to his bed, where he tried to stay awake and listen, as though his attention was a rope—a rope that keeps a boat tethered to a jetty as the river rises. His waiting turned into a dream. In his dream the rope wasn't long enough to keep the boat afloat when the river rose. It was the rope that drowned the boat.

In the morning the house was silent, so silent that, as he strained to hear, the boy heard a plum fall from the tree in the yard—landing with a soft thump on the neglected lawn.

After the dream, Laura didn't go back to sleep. She stayed down, her cheek turned away from the bulk of the grave and her eyes on the bleak, ashy peaks of The Pinnacles, so near but hazy, standing in a white ground mist of dead grass.

Time went by. Then the ground vibrated, and Nown said, "Laura," in his low, musical voice.

Laura sat up. Nown pulled off his hat, as if removing it out of good manners. Then he began to undress. He stripped off and abandoned all the clothes but handed her Sandy's coat and told her to put it on.

She didn't argue with him, even though the request was strange. She had a coat on already. And she somehow knew he didn't mean for her to take off the one she was wearing. Laura simply put Sandy's coat on over hers. It was hot and heavy, and she knew she wouldn't be able to walk anywhere dressed like that. But she obeyed Nown because it was the first time he'd ever given her instructions.

She rummaged in her now blanketing clothes for the apples Rose had picked for her in the Dorans' orchard. And for her bottle of lemonade. She pulled on the wire that loosened its china stopper and took a mouthful. "I wish we could sit down and share a meal," she said to Nown.

"With this grave as a table?"

Nown was easier to look at in the light of the Place. The light was even, and his skin threw off no dazzling reflections. He did kneel by her, kept quiet as she ate an apple and the crack of each bite echoed off The Pinnacles.

Once the apple was gone, Laura licked its juice from her fingers and touched Nown's chest. She saw her fingers suspended only inches from his heart. She could recall distinctly the velvety feel of the rust-stained lump of gravel she had picked up from between the rail lines at Sisters Beach Station. "Nown," she said. "This grave is the heart of the Place. Its unhappy, horrible heart."

"My heart isn't me," Nown said. "It's only what you put into me."

Laura closed the space between them and leaned on him. He held her tight. After a time he started to speak, in his beautiful new voice, as clear as he was. It was like hearing fresh air speak.

"Laura, this Now—the Place—is so immense and powerful, what must it have as its heart?"

Laura shivered.

"A person," Nown said.

Laura pressed her face against his shoulder and opened her eyes wide. She saw her own arm through his body, her bone bent as though she'd suffered poor nutrition in childhood.

"Someone is buried here," Nown said.

Laura whispered, "I knew it." Though her nose was pressed against him, he had no smell. When he was sand, he'd sometimes smelled of heat and moisture; now the air near him was empty of odor. She said, "I hated this grave when I first saw it. I thought of the grave in The Water Diviner—rustling and moaning."

"Yes. What is buried here isn't a body, it's a living person."

"Buried alive!" Laura said, and began to cry. "But I don't hear anything." She mashed her mouth and nose into Nown's hard, impossibly flexible shoulder. He didn't taste of anything either, left neither flavor nor matter on her tongue. "You're not *there*," she grieved. "And I can't change you."

"My own," he said. "My sweet—you must try to be calm." He said, "Listen—leaves don't fall from the trees here unless someone walking by them brushes them off. Nothing is alive, and nothing is dead."

Laura pushed herself away from Nown. She propelled herself backward and knelt, her arms wrapped around her stomach, stooped so that the crown of her head touched the dirt of the graveside. "I can't bear this," she said. Then, a moment later, "What will happen?"

"What will happen when you ask me to dig up this grave?"

Laura laughed, wildly. "You'll refuse me, because you can't *know* what will happen. Isn't that the rule for you?"

Nown was silent.

"Your free will has laws. That's what you told me."

Nown said, "I think this Now is keeping promises I made to you."

Laura clenched her body into a tighter ball. She cried out as though he had struck her. Above her head, dulcet, clear, the glass Nown kept on with his pitiless reasoning. "I promised to do everything to save whoever you loved."

Laura gasped for air between sobs. The pressure of tears behind her eyes was so great she thought she might literally cry them out. She shouted at Nown, "*Who* is being saved? *Who* do I love?"

She had often imagined Nown sighing, but this time he did and she heard it. "You know that it is difficult for me not to answer your questions, Laura. It is in my nature to answer whatever I can. So I will give relief to my nature and answer you—though I'm tired of it, tired of my routine obedience."

Laura looked up and saw through her boiling blur of tears that Nown was counting off the fingers on one of his hands. "Who do you love?" he said. "You love your father and your cousin, your uncle and your aunt. And you love me."

"I do love you!" Laura said, in the voice of someone begging for mercy.

And still he went on, and she heard him say, "And you *will* love that child you're carrying."

Laura bent over again. She howled like an animal. She thought, "God, let me die now. God," she thought, "if it was God at the beginning and end of all this, in the tomb at Bethany opening Lazarus's ears when they were stuffed with the silence of death, and, somewhere, not too long, please God, when this music finally falls silent for my cursed family. God," Laura begged, "let me not have to choose."

Because Laura did feel she was being asked to choose between her friend and her future.

Nown gathered her up again and held her while she cried, and while the jagged remnants of sobbing shook her, and when she was worn out and looking listlessly through her swollen eyelids at the blue shadows inside his body.

Close to an hour passed that way. Finally Laura stirred and sat up and looked into her servant's face. "When I ask you to dig up this grave, I'm afraid the world will end."

"But, Laura, we already know that it doesn't."

It was true. They knew that an invalid would ride on the roof of a train, and convicts fleeing through a forest would look down on a bonfire on the beach like the beacon of a better world. They knew a girl would get a beautiful horse, friends would ride together down a wild river, a boy would find a spring pushing through a seam of coal on his father's property, a drought would end, and a mother would shelter her child while an earthquake shook the scent of honeysuckle down over them. And they knew that some lost, grown child would wish so hard for salvation that he'd have a vision of his mother waiting for him at the gate to Paradise.

"Laura," Nown said, "you came here and waited for me so that you could ask me to dig up the grave. You didn't need me to tell you any of this."

Laura nodded. He set her away from him and began to delve in the dry earth of the mound, digging quickly with his hard, transparent hands.

"Wait," she said. There was more to say. She had said it already, but it was one of those things that couldn't ever be said enough. "I love you."

"Yes." Nown waited, reasonable, peaceable, his dust-gloved hands poised above the crumbling rent he'd made in the piled earth. Then he set to digging again.

✢ ✢ ✢

The man lying in the shallow hollow in the earth looked dead, his face gray with dust over black grime, coal dust in the pores of his skin. His face was familiar. Curiosity made Laura daring. She licked her palm and ran a lock of his hair through her wet hand. His hair was grimy too but showed a trace of a true, bright red.

"I've seen him before," she said to Nown. "He was building a wall in a dream. He crept over to me and pulled a paper from his mouth. It was the bottom part of the letter Cas Doran wrote asking the ranger to follow Da. He was also the man who stopped to help that crippled convict up when they were being hunted by dogs through the forest. And I think he's one of the convicts working on the stone bridge in The Water Diviner. And he's one of the convicts in Convalescent One, in leg irons, standing on the causeway."

Nown seemed unmoved by Laura's wonder. He only said, "Remember what I told you about the final N? You cannot end this Nown until you have first given it its voice."

"Have pity," Laura said.

"I will."

Everything she asked her servant to do trapped her further in what had already been done. Nown's pity was a promise fulfilling itself over time—a long, inhuman time.

"Here, I'll help you," Nown said. He took her hands and assisted her down into the shallow trench so that she perched above the body. She kicked toeholds in the wall of the grave, steadied herself, and stooped over.

The man had his hand on the wall, his index finger curled to make a mark. Laura glimpsed the wings of the letter W beneath the hand. She turned her eyes up to her servant, tried to find his eyes in the glowing, glassy nothingness of his face. She said, "What will happen?"

"Ask him," Nown said.

Laura bent to her task. She scratched an N into the wall beside the man's hand.

Nothing happened. No one spoke. The Place was as still as ever, a silent desert.

Laura thought of her family, separated, trying desperately to fix things.

She took the man's thin wrist in her hand. It was like touching a fresh corpse. The temperature of his skin was tepid, too cool for life. She moved his hand away from the wall, so that the W was exposed. Then she used his fingertips to wipe the letter away.

✧ ✧ ✧

Far Inland, the compound of the Depot imploded. The buildings rushed together like matter in water pouring toward a drain. The timbers of the huts and barracks split as a slope thrust up under them, and all their bolted doors burst open.

Greenery—ferns, trees, vines—burst like fireworks amid the splinters and billowing dust. Fireworks that froze into permanence, startled trees above gouged, wet earth. Forest birds fled shrieking from the mess and circled up over a towering tangle of metal—fifty miles of narrow-gauge rail line concertinaed into fifty yards of mangled mountain forest.

And yet, by some miracle, this violence spared the few people there. A miracle of care and intention. When the barracks dormitories exploded, the yellow-clad bodies were momentarily cradled in huge fists of dust—dust as soft as talcum powder—then released and spilled into the tree ferns on the forest floor.

✧ ✧ ✧

Grace lay in the circle of Foreigner's West, a dusty blanket thrown over her for camouflage. She was asleep, despite the lumpy ground jabbing into her hip bones.

. . . the woman waited for him at the gate. He saw that her eyes were red, ruined by weeping. She stretched out a hand to him and clasped his wrist. He remembered that he was dreaming. He knew that the twilight was a landslide, and its silence his deafness.

The woman, small, young, strong for her size, tightened her grip and hauled him toward her through the arch of flowers, through the gate—to where it was cold and someone was whistling, and someone else was angry, slamming a teacup down into its saucer.

A fly made a tickling six-point landing on his face . . .

Grace touched her face. The blowfly took off, bounced from her arm like an electrified thistledown and zoomed away. When its buzzing had faded, Grace heard a parson bird whistling above her, spitting and clanking in its characteristic mix of music and disharmony. She opened her eyes on green leaves, and the blue sky between them.

VII

Lazarus Hame

1

✧ ✧ ✧

ROSE AND MAMIE WERE HAVING BREAK-
FAST WHEN THE FIRST FIGURE CAME
OUT OF THE FOREST. A MAN IN YELLOW PA-
jamas made his weaving way through the stream below the
springhouse where the valley narrowed.

Mamie got up and opened the door to get a better look.

Another man came out of the trees. This one seemed eager. He blundered through the stream and raised his arms as
if rushing to embrace someone.

"What do you make of this?" Mamie said.

Rose had watched the film and listened to Laura's description of the captive dreamhunters. But these men had come
from the forested foothills of the Riflemans, not appeared at
the border on the avenue.

Mamie flicked Rose an anxious look. More figures were
walking down the valley. They were mostly men, but a few
were women. They all seemed disoriented, then very excited.
They saw the house and hurried toward it.

"They don't seem to be together, as such," Mamie said.

Rose joined her friend at the door. They waited. Several
servants joined them, two footmen, one carrying a cricket
bat, and a maid with a feather duster, who had seen the men
from an upstairs window and now looked as though she
wished she'd remained upstairs.

There were more yellow-clad people arriving all the time.

"I don't like this," Mamie said. She drew Rose inside and shut the French doors. She shot the bolts.

As they came upon the house, the people began to babble. At first they were speaking only to themselves, rapt with relief. "This is my house," Rose heard one cry. "I'm home!"

"My beautiful house!"

"It was all worth it, for this!"

Several paused on the terrace, puffed out their chests, and gazed around them with proprietary satisfaction. Others headed straight for the front door. The footmen repelled two—then retreated inside and slammed the door. "Miss Doran! What shall we do?"

"Don't let them in!" Mamie looked terrified. She and Rose joined the servants gathered in the entrance hall. They listened to the voices beyond the door. Raised, contending voices. It didn't sound like an argument; it sounded like a group of children all clamoring for attention.

"This is *my* house."

"No. It's mine. I built this house twenty-eight years ago."

"Both of my children were married out of this house. My grandchildren visit me here."

"What should we do?" Mamie asked the butler.

He looked desperate.

Rose grabbed her friend. "Let's leave. We can get out by the back door."

Mamie moved immediately to do this, but Rose detained her. "I mean, we should grab what is necessary, then set off."

"What?" Mamie wrung her hands. "What is necessary?" She jumped when the door knocker sounded.

"Wife?" said a voice, outside. "Is that you?"

"Where is everyone?" said another.

And, "Why don't you come out? It's such a lovely day."

Rose dragged Mamie upstairs. She pushed the hatbox that held the film to the back of the wardrobe in the guest bedroom. She found a sunhat, a coat, her good walking shoes. She went through Mamie's wardrobe. She tossed a heavy coat onto the bed, and a soft bag. "Change your shoes."

Mamie sat down to swap her slippers for her school shoes. "Shall I take my jewelery?"

"I don't think they're here to loot the house. Only to live in it."

"Why?" Mamie was in an agony of incomprehension.

Rose heaved a sigh. "Your father has been dosing kidnapped dreamhunters with a dream that makes people happy and compliant. He's filled half of Founderston with it. That's why I'm here. Mamie, you *knew* something like this was going on."

Mamie began to cry. "But why do they think that this is their house?"

Rose considered. "Well—I've had Contentment and, come to think of it, this *is* the house in the dream." It was so strange. Rose realized she had seen Mamie as a middle-aged woman, and Ru as a middle-aged man. She had seen their children—either his or hers or a mix of both—turning cartwheels and carrying canoe paddles and hurrying indoors for a breakfast of eels they'd caught the day before.

"Please pull yourself together," Rose said to her friend. "This is frightening, I agree, but I've been living with alarms for some time now, and do you see me carrying on?"

Mamie made an effort. She picked up her coat and bag and followed Rose to the kitchen, where Rose rifled the cupboards and drawers for cans of fruit, a can opener, cookies, ginger beer, candy, matches. She stuffed their bags and lifted them to test their weight.

Mamie jumped and cowered at every noise. But the noise

was only voices and the door knocker. The dreamhunters were puzzled at not being let into their own house, but they were in too good a mood to force doors or break windows.

Rose checked the servants' entrance. There was no one in sight. She went back to Mamie, gave her a bag to carry, and led her away from the house.

2

✦ ✦ ✦

*L*AURA AND THE BURIED MAN WERE
IN A FOREST OF TEA TREES. THE
SEA WAS VISIBLE AS BRIGHTNESS DOWNHILL
through the tangled black trunks. As the minutes passed, a
bird dared to speak up again. "Peep?" it said—perhaps asking
some other bird, "Did you notice that? What was that?"
"Peep?" it went, each time a little bolder, till it was answered
and the whole hillside began to gossip.

The man sat with dry dust smoking away from his hair and
clothes in the slight breeze. He turned his head slowly to face
Laura, moving like someone half frozen and very depleted.
He whispered, "Why are you just sitting there?" Then, "Why
aren't you running away?"

Laura searched her pockets, found her remaining apple,
and offered it to him. His hand came out, tentative, then
snatched. He hunched and bit into the fruit, then gave a little
grunt which seemed to say that, although the food pleased
him, he'd rather not let himself in for the possibility of being
pleased again. He gobbled the apple and wiped his fingers on
his shirt.

"I don't know any way over the Rifleman," Laura said. "Except the rail bridge. It's best crossed in daylight. So we should
set out now."

He raised his head again and peered at her, suspicious.

"After that we can follow the coast. We can be at Sisters Beach in a day and a half." Laura got up and removed Sandy's coat, which Nown had asked her to put on over her own. He'd been right to do that. The slippers and trousers and scarf and knitted hat had all vanished with the Place. So had Nown. Nothing cataclysmic had happened at the grave. Nown had only gone more transparent, till he wasn't there. The beige grasslands and ashy barrier of The Pinnacles vanished, and the tea trees came, in a close crowd, and stood like dark spirits around them, not quite still, a sea breeze sieving through their aromatic leaves.

Laura gave the man Sandy's coat.

He got up, with difficulty, and put it on.

Laura saw that his feet were wrapped with strips of cloth torn from the bottoms of his trousers. His shirt was blue cotton, a work shirt, but the ragged trousers were printed with prison arrows. He covered himself up with the coat.

Laura pulled out a lemonade bottle and let him have the last of its contents. "We'll need the bottle for water," she said. "You can carry it."

She set off toward the sea, without waiting to see whether he'd follow her.

3

✧ ✧ ✧

HORTLY AFTER LEAVING THE VILLAGE OF DOORHANDLE, THE SISTERS BEACH COACH PULLED UP FOR SOMEONE WHO STOOD in the road, both arms raised, a fan of ten-dollar bills flourished in one fist. Naturally the driver let the woman on.

It was not quite the low season, but still the coach had plenty of room to take on another passenger. The other travelers made a few rearrangements to accommodate the woman. She crammed herself into a corner and sat biting her fist and staring out the window as the coach went on up the Rifleman Pass.

There was mist on the summit. Dark, lumpish shapes loomed at the roadside, the stumps of trees from a forest burned off years before, and limestone outcrops.

The woman, though at first despondent, eventually seemed to be taking a great interest in the view.

Finally one of her fellow travelers asked her, "Is this the first time you've been through the Pass?"

"Yes."

"Are you—forgive me if I'm wrong, and I must be—the dreamhunter Grace Tiebold? You do look like her."

"I am Grace Tiebold."

The passengers exchanged looks. "But how?" one said, for they all knew that any dreamhunters attempting to cross the

Rifleman Pass on the Sisters Beach stagecoach would find themselves falling from a suddenly immaterial coach onto the border trail of the Place.

"How can you be here, Mrs. Tiebold? We're beyond the border."

"The Place has gone," Grace Tiebold said. "It just went."

4

✦ ✦ ✦

LAURA DIDN'T RELAX UNTIL THEY HAD CROSSED THE RAIL BRIDGE OVER THE RIFLEMAN AND CLIMBED THE slope to the tunnel mouth. It wasn't a long tunnel. When she looked through it, the far opening appeared the size of one of her own fists. Still, she didn't like to venture into it. She turned to the man, who was limping behind her. He stopped and stood at some distance from her.

She called out to him. "I don't think either of us is in a fit state to have to run." She wanted to complain that this did concern him too, and why should she have to be the leader? She gestured at him to join her.

He came up, reluctantly, and peered into the tunnel.

Laura saw that he was as pale as ever, and slick with sweat. His shirt was open, and she could have counted all his ribs.

"We can go over the headland," she said. "It takes longer, but we can just creep along."

"This is your stamping ground," he said. "Lead on."

"I'll need a leg up," she said, and went to the side of the buttressed tunnel mouth to show him where they'd have to climb.

It was a struggle, but eventually they both managed the steep part and got into the scrub. From the top of the headland, Laura pointed out the beach where there was a fresh stream. "No more than two hours," she promised. "We'll rest there."

The man looked back at the Awa Inlet. His slack, exhausted face registered surprise.

"What?" Laura said.

"The causeway," he said. "It's not there." He was terribly puzzled. He rubbed his eyes and squinted. "I'm shortsighted, but even I couldn't miss a strip of black across the Inlet. That *is* the Awa Inlet?"

"Yes."

"I don't understand. I helped build that bloody thing."

Laura put out a hand and touched his forearm. He flinched and snatched it away. She said, "Tell me your story."

He glared at her. "And I don't understand why you're not running away from me."

"Tell me your story," Laura said again. She kept her gaze level and calm. She stared into his eyes—eyes the color of oil and hot with hatred and suspicion and hurt. She said, "We're going to have to help each other all the way down the slope. So, as we go, you can tell me your story."

He put a finger in the outer corner of one of his eyes and pressed the eye into a slit. Laura had seen one of her glasses-wearing school friends do that when she'd put her own pair down somewhere and was looking around for them. "How old are you?" he asked, trying to get a good look at her.

"Five months ago I turned sixteen."

"You're just a kid."

"A *kid*?" She was unfamiliar with the usage.

"A kid."

✦ ✦ ✦

"I suppose you think I just flaked out in the forest?" said the man. "I guess I must have. I was trying to do something. Something incredible. Of course it didn't work. It wasn't ever going to work. I must have been crazy. I had strange ideas in my head that I guess I resorted to in a time of need. I should be dead. I should have keeled over dead and deluded. Gone off in a happy fantasy."

Laura interrupted him. "No. I wish you'd start at the beginning."

"I was starting at the point where I'm dead and discover there's no heaven." He sounded as though he hated his story—and himself.

"Please," Laura said. She held the branch of a bush so that it wouldn't flick back into his face. When he took it, she saw his tattered nails and bloody nail beds. He must have dug his grave using only his hands.

"All right," he said, and began again. "You can see by my trousers what I am."

"No," said Laura.

"Do you mean no, you can't see that I'm a convict, or no, don't start there? Maybe you want me to start with my birth?" He was sarcastic.

"Yes. Start there."

"Well—how is your history, girl?" he asked. Then, without waiting for an answer, he just began.

✢ ✢ ✢

"My mother was a dreamhunter, but the Place disappeared before I was born. I didn't have a father. I lived with Mother and Grandfather, who wasn't ever a well man. He taught me to play the violin. We lived on a small trust fund my mother had. She'd had a famous uncle. Her uncle made films. But when I was still an infant, he went to the Ross Sea with one of those expeditions, and he died there. His daughter, my mother's cousin—they were very close, they wrote each other letters every week for years. This cousin had married a man no one in the family much liked, and she went with him to live in another country. It was a kind of exile, I think. After the Ross Sea, my mother's aunt joined her daughter. I can just remember her—the widow—she used to bring me expensive chocolates whenever she visited.

"Grandfather passed away when I was eight. After that we lived quietly. I went to a little country school. My mother died in the Influenza when I was ten. When she was dying, she burned all her cousin's letters. I was left to suppose that she hadn't wanted me to know them—her cousin, and her cousin's husband.

"After she died I went to live with her father's sister, who sent me to school and gave me more music lessons. Even after its lonely beginning, my life should have been not too bad, but I got into trouble because people did, in the years when things were at their worst, with the bread lines and men walking the roads looking for work. You see, even with all those men out of work, and willing to work for the price of food, the bloody government still had its Prosperity Measures—the penal code."

He broke off. "I don't expect you to agree with me about this. You're a well-dressed girl with rounded vowels."

"I'm glad I've got something rounded," Laura said.

They had stopped in a patch of shade. Flies had found them—or him, for he was rank with filth. They were too tired to go on right away.

He said, "How do you like my story so far?"

"I hate it."

"Not enough romance?" he said, acid.

Laura burst out laughing. He sounded so like Sandy. Her laugh was affectionate, and he was rather thrown by it. "Oh—just go on," she said, wiping her eyes.

"If you stepped over the line, back then," he said, "you'd end up contributing to the economy in some involuntary way—believe me. I got into trouble during the worst years of the Depression, the very worst. My violin was my means of making money—but no one was hiring musicians. I pawned my violin to buy food. But I couldn't bear not having it. I'd patrol the pawnshop window looking at it. And one evening, I just broke the glass and took it.

"I got caught and sent to prison. I had a light sentence, I was with the chicken chokers and the disgruntled men who set fire to their employers' wheat fields. The work they gave men on light sentences wasn't exactly hard labor, and I was young and fit. But the wardens were sadists. One day I witnessed something very cruel. Impossibly cruel. I lost my temper, attacked the guard, and injured him badly. After that I was in for twenty years. I was very young, and at first I didn't understand twenty years. What young person understands twenty years?

"I worked building the causeway, and on the Howe Peninsula digging bird shit for the nitrate trade. I worked in the coal mine at Westport. Over time I lost all hope, except of escape, which isn't much of a hope on an island, even a big island like Southland.

"Then came the riot in the prison, and the fire. I escaped with a couple dozen other men. We took a sloop from the wharves, but none of us were sailors and we foundered off Pillar Point on the west coast of So Long Spit. The search party and their dogs caught up with us on the Spit, and, at some point, I left the others and took to the sea. I was lucky. I was carried by the rising tide back along the shore of Coal Bay to Debt River.

"And this is where my story will become incoherent to you—or very interesting possibly, because you're a bit of a strange girl, aren't you?"

"Yes," Laura said. Then, "Let's go on and find that stream and get a drink."

Telling his story seemed to have calmed the man and helped him regain some sense of consideration. As they went on, he stopped now and then to see how she was—though he was in far worse condition than she. Nothing further was said between them till they reached the stream.

It was a quick, small stream that came onto the beach and cut a sharp-edged channel on the sand. The man lay down on his stomach and sucked at the water. Laura scooped out a hollow in the sand, waited for the grains to settle, then dipped the lemonade bottle into the pool she'd made.

The sun was setting over the mountains on the far side of Coal Bay. The dark was coming, so when they finished drinking, they crawled up the beach and flopped in the fringe of salt-burned scrub. Without consultation, they had decided together not to try to traverse the beach of boulders in the dark.

"After this stretch it's all easy going," Laura said. She dropped her head and closed her eyes. She heard him say, "Why are you doing this?"

She shook her head, her hair rasped on the sand. She nestled into its cold softness.

"Strange girl," he said. Then he went on with his story.

✧ ✧ ✧

"The search party wouldn't have expended any energy mopping up one stray convict. They only had to wait for me to turn up somewhere I couldn't give a good account of myself. They only had to wait for someone to turn me in. But I decided they were still in pursuit. It was because I felt special. Especially hated and feared. Even when I was a free man, I felt that some people I met would act as though I were a tiger pretending to be a schoolboy or a musician. It was my name, you see."

"Hame," Laura said.

There was a long silence. Finally he said, testing, wary, "But you're not chasing me, are you?"

"No," Laura said.

Another long silence. Laura broke it. "You're someone I've just met. Someone I feel for." She thought, *"Family."*

"You don't think I'm mad?"

"No."

"You wait," he said. "We're not there yet. Wait till I tell you what I did—what I tried.

"Some guards had been killed in the riot, and the prison was razed. I imagined they would kill us when they caught us. It seemed to me that just running wasn't enough. I wanted to defend myself. And later, once I'd lost my mind, I just wanted revenge. I should have gone to a farm family and trusted someone to have pity. But I was in a bad way in my head—wet, and cold, and hungry. I didn't feel human, or entitled to fellow feeling. I hated everyone free. It seemed to me that whoever was free had let us convicts be beaten and broken, and driven into the river to drown. They'd stood by and let it happen.

"Something came into my head at Debt River. A story I'd heard my great-aunt tell, between music lessons, about magic. She'd taught me a song, though I was only interested in tunes I could play on the violin. The song was supposed to be a spell that would make a little portion of the earth come to life—be alive and *obedient*. At Debt River I remembered the song, and I remembered an earthquake that had frightened me when I was little. No one we knew was hurt in the earthquake, but I remembered going into the city afterward, once they'd replaced all the sections of wriggly rail line. I remembered seeing heaps of tumbled stone in the street. There were little aftershocks. I'd wake up crying, and my mother would sing to me. She, too, had sung that song. To comfort me she told me that she and I—if we *wished* hard enough—could make the earth itself listen. Listen and lie still.

"At Debt River I was hiding near the mining camp, eating fern shoots—stripping off the black fur and eating them raw. After a short time I'd exhausted the food supply; I'd found every freshwater crayfish in the stream and had gouged out the heart of every tree fern. The sounds from the camp made me sad rather than kept me company, and so I just *began*. I began without thinking. It was as if something in my head had more use for me than I did for it. I took the first steps of the spell I'd been taught and had thought was only a quaint folk ritual. Or, rather, I began the spell but adapted it to my purposes.

"I'd decided to show everyone. The men hunting me, the oblivious miners, the families on the farms I didn't dare go to. I'd show them, I thought. I started to sing and made a mark on the ground and began to run again. I traveled up Debt River and into the mountains, then I crossed over into Wry Valley.

"I traveled like that for more than a day. Then I slept, and dreamed the song, woke up, and kept on singing. That's how I went along. And at one place I slept I made another mark on the ground. The song seemed to be consuming me—and I dreamed impossible things. I dreamed of being saved and starting over."

The man fell quiet.

Laura waited. She was too afraid to prompt him or comfort him. She did want to know his story, and she wanted to help him, but she didn't know what to do.

When the man spoke again, his voice had changed; it was remote and resigned. "I did die," he said. "But there wasn't another garden beyond the gate, there was a whole world, the same again. More thirst and cold and hunger. Here. Here with you—you strange girl."

"You dreamed something impossible," Laura said. "But that isn't the end of your story."

"No. I woke up." He stirred. Then he sounded faintly amused. "You know, that's what is comforting—that parts of what I recall, even after I lost my mind, still seemed logical and real and practical. I remember wrapping my feet in strips of cloth after I lost my shoes. I remember singing and walking many more miles, mending my makeshift shoes as I went. I remember how my last meal wasn't much, because wasps had spoiled the apricots left hanging in the orchard by a grand mansion. I remember deciding that it was altogether too big a gesture to dig my own grave with my hands, and spending some time finding a flat stone to serve as a spade."

"You dug your own grave?"

"After days, and miles—and the same thought in my head for days and miles. I didn't have to survive it. All I had to do was keep singing, and come to a place where I'd feel that I'd closed a circle. When I did come to that place, I scratched out a hole in the ground, a hole big enough to lie in. I lay down in it. I was finished. I wanted time to stop, and to let *me* stop with it. And I wanted revenge.

"I made the final mark that finished the spell—a W—and

then said to the land, 'Bury me, and rise up. Rise up and crush them all.'

"And then I felt you brush the earth from my face."

The outdoor, nighttime quiet had a stealthy quality, as though it was listening to both of them, stalking them with its attention. Laura thought of Nown and could almost feel him, far, far away, reaching for her, his wish to touch so strong that she felt touched.

This man's vast servant had obeyed him. The earth of his excavation had fallen in to cover him and had piled up over him to make what he'd imagined for himself, a low grave mound. His servant took him to its heart, as its heart. And then it rose up. There was an earthquake—and back along the miles of its master's journey the ground moved and cracked and *broke* the N that came to be known as Foreigner's North. By its master's own actions, the first letter of that Nown's name was erased. It was its Own, it was free, and it remembered an earlier promise it had made: "I promise in the future to do more, to do—*I know not what*—to save whoever you love."

Laura knew she would love her as yet unborn son. She *had* loved him—she, the woman who had lived a quiet life caring for him and her invalid father. Laura's servant, the Ninth Nown, had loved her, and so the giant, immobile, speechless Tenth, the Place, remembered having loved her and went looking for her to ask for help. To say, "Here is one you love who has asked me to stifle him. What should I do?" It moved its territory of stopped time back in time. It went too far, went on until it found the first someone it felt it knew— Laura's father, who had taught its heart music. It tried to tell him. It showed him his grandson, standing in chains beside a rail line. It tried by the only means available to it—the memories of the lives its territory had encompassed—to tell anyone who would listen. To show them not just the injustices but the beauty of human life that injustice is a blasphemy against—the joy of the boy on the shore racing the schooner, the happiness of the sing-along around the beach bonfire; dancers, banquets, desires, balloon rides, the miracle of rivers. *Life.* It said, though not in words, "There is something underneath all this, someone buried alive." It was like a person talking in his sleep—speaking urgent nonsense. It waited, and it felt Laura as she came toward it, through time, being born, growing up, reaching the age of her Try. And sometimes it would rap out its faith and rapture on the Founderston–Sisters Beach telegraph line, singing: "She is coming, my own, my sweet . . ." Singing a song she had taught it.

"Why the hell are you crying?" the man asked. He seemed offended. "It wasn't my intention to make you cry, girl. Look—if I was crazy, it's passed now."

"Shut up!" Laura said. And cried.

He got up and shuffled down the dark beach to drink some more. When he came back, she said, "I'm glad it's so dark. It's easier to talk to you without seeing you."

"I guess I am a pretty pitiful sight—especially for anyone in prime condition."

"I'm not feeling guilty because I'm healthy and you're half-dead!" Laura shouted. "You idiot! And the condition I'm in is *pregnant!*"

"You've run away from home because you're pregnant?"

"Shut up!"

He did, and she knew that was perhaps because he felt sympathetic—if exasperated—and that he wasn't at all the hard and heartless person he made himself out to be. She couldn't help but feel for him—he was so like Sandy, and he had her father's beautiful black eyes.

After a time she said, "Do you think you can stay awake long enough for me to tell you *my* story?"

"I think I should hear your story. And I'm not sleepy, only hungry and weary. I feel as if I've slept for ages."

"Well—you have," she said. And then she told him her story.

5

✦ ✦ ✦

HERE WAS A ROUGH TRACK FROM THE
AWA INLET ACROSS THE SADDLE. IT
WASN'T ONE DREAMHUNTERS KNEW, OF
course, since it was within the section of the map they couldn't
enter. Mamie was familiar with a few miles of her end of it.
Her family sometimes went along it to have picnics at the
lookout. Beyond the lookout, sparse foot traffic meant the
track was overgrown. Gorse shoots grew out of the path, and
the bare patches were stippled by holes cicada nymphs had
tunneled out of. It was rough going, and the girls stopped
walking when it got dark. They curled up in their coats, back
to back, and Mamie shed more tears about her "stupid situation" and Rose's "exaggerated ideas" about her father's schem-
ing. Rose let her friend cry and complain, and they were both
soon asleep.

The following morning they were walking along the spine
of a hill over the sea when they spotted two figures far below,
making their way around a cove, stepping from boulder to
boulder.

Rose stopped and shaded her eyes. Then she cupped her
hands around her mouth and shouted, "Laura!" She saw her
cousin hesitate and look around, then wave to her. "Stay right
there!" Rose shouted. "Come on," she said to Mamie. "We're
going down there."

Mamie moaned, but when Rose set off downhill, she hurried after her.

✧ ✧ ✧

The man Laura was with had filthy red hair and was wearing Sandy Mason's coat—Rose was sure of it. The coat was wet. The strips of cloth wrapping the man's feet were oozing blood-tinged seawater. He'd been pulling mussels off the rocks at the tide line and was smashing them open and eating them raw.

"I told him you'd have some food," Laura said. "But he has a somewhat independent disposition."

Rose put her arms around her cousin and held her close. Mamie began to burble, more excited than complaining, about the dreamhunters who had swarmed the Doran summerhouse. "Rose thought it best to run off. But I'm beginning to suspect there's a strong streak in your family of fleeing the scene."

"Huh!" said the man smashing mussels.

"Who is he?" Rose asked Laura. She could see that he was wearing arrow-printed trousers and that his ankles bore the marbled purple scarring caused by years of wearing leg irons.

"This is my cousin, Rose," Laura said to the man.

Rose was intrigued by how gentle and respectful Laura sounded when she spoke to him. The man looked up at Rose with great interest. It made her blush. Then he dropped the shell-and-meat-flecked stone and, looking decisive, said to Laura, "How many people are there who need to know?"

Laura said, "There's Da, Uncle Chorley, Aunt Grace, and Rose."

"But not this girl," he said, and pointed his chin at Mamie.

"No," said Laura.

"Well, I'll wait till they're all in one place. I'm only going to tell my story once more. Then, if I'm going to have any kind of life, I have to keep my mouth shut. I'm sure you agree."

"Hell—you're a bit forceful," Rose said to him. She had a very strong urge to pick a fight with him. It made her feel like a blowfly trapped under a glass.

"Do you have food?" he said, and gave Rose an up-from-under-the-brows look like the kind of dog who nips your fingers while snatching meat.

"Only if you tell me your name," Rose said.

"Lazarus Hame."

Rose looked at Laura, who said, "Yes—it turns out there was a Lazarus, after all."

6

✢ ✢ ✢

IN ONE OF THE FASHIONABLE TERRACES ABOVE THE BAY AT CASTLEREAGH THERE WAS A HOUSE WHERE ALL THE MIRRORS had been covered, and where, in the late afternoon following the funeral, only a few family members and close friends remained. The servants were gathering glasses and plates from under the chairs, on the windowsills, and from the top of the piano. No one expected a caller, given the time, and the funeral wreath on the front door.

One of the dead woman's daughters went to answer the knocking. It was something to do. Something to distract her from her nagging misery.

On the steps stood a small, severe-looking woman, and a man in a long cape, who had his arms folded under it in a way that made an imposing triangle of his upper body.

The dead woman's daughter stood aside and let the two in. She took them to her father, who was tucked in the house's smallest downstairs room, drinking whiskey with his best friend. Then, because the room was so small, the daughter went out and closed the door.

"Judge Seresin," said Marta Hame, "I'm very sorry for your loss. I hate to disturb you at this time, but I've come a long way and on desperate business."

"Mitch, this is Marta Hame!" Dr. King said to his friend the Judge.

The caped man took a pace back and leaned against the door. He let his hidden rifle dangle, so that its muzzle appeared from under his cape, pointed at the floor.

"With a Temple guard!" said Dr. King. He was intrigued.

Marta Hame put her valise on the table, opened it, and lifted out her folded clothes balanced on the flat false bottom. She put the pile down, then produced the figure eight of film. "We'll need to put this film back on a reel. It's footage of the Depot, a prison camp in the hinterland of the Place, reached by a secret rail line. Cas Doran and his Regulatory Body have been loading captive dreamhunters with a dream that makes anyone who has it stupid and incautious with happiness. Doran has begun to use this dream to control people in the capital."

The two men stared at her, mouths open.

"So far he's contrived to have a dream-narcotized Congress pass legislation to extend the presidential term. And he is hunting down and trying to eliminate, or permanently dream-drug, anyone he thinks will spoil his plans."

"I told you that vote was rigged," Dr. King said to his friend. "And I'm sure the earlier appointment of the Speaker of the House was somehow rigged too."

Marta said, "My niece, Laura, has been to that camp and can testify to its use. And anyone who has had a strong dose of the dream can testify to the fact that it is a gross abuse."

"But, Miss Hame . . ." Judge Seresin said.

Marta blinked at him in surprise. She was already worried that he hadn't leapt into action of some kind. Didn't he believe her?

"Have you not heard?" he said.

"Haven't you seen the newspaper?" Dr. King said.

Marta's hand crept to her throat and clutched her crucifix. "I've been traveling by back roads and in locked train compartments. I've had no news."

"The Place has gone," said Seresin. "It just melted away. Any plan of Doran's that requires dreams is doomed. Finished. Doran's empire has fallen."

"Poor sod," said Dr. King, then chuckled.

Then the Judge jumped up and stuffed a chair under Marta Hame's sagging legs. Dr. King poured her a stiff whiskey.

Marta knocked back the whole glass, grimaced, and said, "God be praised."

They refilled her glass and shook the decanter at the Temple guard, who set his gun against the door and joined them.

"I'll cable Wilkinson—who will quickly work out which side he's on," said Seresin.

"I'll cable the Grand Patriarch, and my brother at Spring Valley," Marta said, her voice already faintly slurred—she wasn't a drinker. "And could you issue a warrant for Doran's arrest?"

"I shall certainly be doing that," said the Judge. "But perhaps we should all get on the next train to the capital?" For a moment he looked defeated and exhausted.

Dr. King said, "Yes, Mitch. That would be best." He put his glass down and touched his friend's hand.

The Judge nodded. He looked at Marta with solemn dignity. "I think I should see to this myself," he said.

7

✦ ✦ ✦

THE PRESIDENT, GARTH WILKINSON, REGARDED THE MEN IN HIS OUTER OFFICE—THE GRAND PATRIARCH AND HIS secretary, Father Roy; Supreme Court Judge Seresin; Dr. King; and the resurrected dreamhunter Tziga Hame. He straightened his vest over his trim stomach, said, "I will be with you shortly, gentlemen," and walked back into his own office, his inner sanctum, where his friend the Secretary of Labor was waiting for him.

"Karl," said Wilkinson. "There's one thing I think we should do right away, and that is get Doran's name off the Prosperity Measures Bill. We don't need to lose the ground we've made there."

"So—you're letting them have him?"

"I don't have any choice."

"And what about the repeal of the presidential term limits?"

Wilkinson sighed. "Well—we've landed on a snake there. But it doesn't need to be a long snake, it might take us back only twenty spaces, since only the last vote will be discounted. The vote under the influence of that dream—about which you and I know nothing whatsoever."

"What if Doran's Colorist talks?"

"If Plasir keeps quiet about the coloring, then he's guilty of nothing but having a criminal friend. Or having misplaced his trust—as we have, Karl. We trusted Doran. How were we to have known he was such a villain?" Wilkinson put his hand over his heart and practiced a look of great disappointment. "And I doubt we're in danger from Doran himself. Cas won't say anything to further jeopardize his achievements."

"What makes you think that?"

"He's a patriot," said Wilkinson.

✧ ✧ ✧

They left the Presidential Offices in a cavalcade of motor-cars and men on horseback.

Dr. King and Judge Seresin rode in the President's own car. It was a five-minute drive to the Palace of Governance, where the Secretary of the Interior had his offices.

Wilkinson said to the two men opposite him, "I do not relish this task. Cas Doran is a personal friend."

The car turned onto the embankment. Across the Sva, on the upstream end of the Isle, the tower of the Regulatory Body seemed to be throwing off seed. Paper was being tossed from at least two of its top windows. Sheaves of paper that fanned as they fell into the swampy garden below, or blew out over the river to lie, white, on the water.

"I wish someone would put a stop to that," Dr. King said mildly. "That's history."

"The real tragedy is that thousands of people will be out of work," Seresin said. "Everyone in those offices, and dream-hunters, rangers, the staff of dream palaces, and proprietors of dream parlors. All will be ruined."

"Indeed. The social consequences are dreadful to contemplate," said President Wilkinson.

The cavalcade pulled up at the Palace of Governance, and

they went into its lobby, which was already full of police. Garth Wilkinson and his bodyguard got into the first elevator. The Grand Patriarch, Father Roy, the Judge, and Tziga Hame all waited patiently. King rocked back and forth on the balls of his feet saying, "Oh—to be a fly on the wall!"

✢ ✢ ✢

Doran was alone in his office. When the door opened and he saw Wilkie, he was pleased—and he was even more pleased when the President stepped into the room and shut the door on his escort, the police, and the handful of pallid and pop-eyed officials who were helping the police put Doran's papers into crates.

"His Eminence and Judge Seresin will be here soon," said Wilkie. "I'm very sorry, Cas."

Doran opened his mouth to speak, but his friend held up a hand. "We have only a moment," Wilkie said. "And I want you to know that I regard this failure as bad luck. Who could have guessed that the Place would choose this moment to vanish?"

Doran kept quiet but went on nursing the murky suspicions he had, because he didn't believe in coincidences, only in hidden influence.

"Very bad luck," Wilkie said, sounding like someone consoling a gambler after his favorite horse has taken a tumble at the Founders Day Cup. Then he said, "Oh—and that Hame is with them. I thought I should warn you since I know you regard him rather superstitiously."

"He's nothing now," Cas Doran said through clenched teeth. "He's a cripple, a fiddler from the old town. Curse him and his family."

And then the door opened and that man came in with the other men. The Grand Patriarch was all dignity, and so were his secretary and the Judge. The historian King was present too, which was something of a surprise to Doran. King—the bumptious twit—was so excited he was having to suck his lips in to keep from smiling. Tziga Hame had his eyes cast down as though he was embarrassed or ashamed.

Wilkinson said to them, "Secretary Doran was just saying that he has hopes of house arrest."

Doran flushed. He wanted house arrest even less than he wanted to be shut up in a cell in Founderston Barracks. At home he'd have to endure his wife's tears and recriminations. He didn't want that. He didn't want *her*. So—Wilkie was going to act sympathetic in private, then subject him to indignities. Like the indignity of having Seresin say to him, "Your charges will include abduction and conspiracy to abduct. They are too serious for house arrest."

Doran gave the Judge a polite nod.

"How did you hope to get away with it?" the Grand Patriarch said.

Doran thought for a few moments about a possible defense—and saw it was impossible. He thought about making Wilkie's life uncomfortable—of all the people he could take down with him. But he liked what he'd achieved too much to undo it all just because he couldn't enjoy it. Knowledge was enjoyment. Knowledge of a few lasting successes. And, since he didn't plan to defend himself, he at least had the satisfaction of being able to answer the Grand Patriarch. "I would have succeeded had the Place not disappeared."

"The Place is not the whole story. There will be other changes," said the Grand Patriarch in the tones of a crusader. "This society cannot continue in its callous willingness to base its wealth on suffering."

Doran laughed. "Oh, yes, Your Eminence? And what are *you* going to give up?"

Garth Wilkinson smiled ever so slightly and inspected the fingernails on one hand.

"Do you think I might be taken off to jail now?" said Doran. "My lawyer is here already and wants to go along with me." He touched the solitary paper on his desk and looked at Wilkinson. "This is my resignation—though I don't know why I imagined it was required."

"Thank you, Cas," said the President.

Father Roy opened the door and stood aside. Doran came around his desk and walked past them. He stopped beside Tziga Hame and tried to catch the man's shy gaze. He asked, "Do you know why the Place disappeared?"

"I know nothing," said Tziga Hame.

"And you *are* nothing now," said Doran. "You and your famous family."

Tziga Hame gave Doran a beautiful smile. "Yes, please God," he said. "Let us be nothing—for a time, at least."

Doran stared into that wavering black gaze and sought understanding. Understanding didn't come to him. "What I tried to do *had* to work," he said to Hame, very quietly, and with desperate puzzlement, "because there I was, twenty-six years later, congratulating myself on my successes. The dreams were the future."

"Oh—you knew that?" said Tziga Hame.

Doran nodded, then walked out to the waiting police.

8

✧ ✧ ✧

*W*HEN THEY FINALLY REACHED SUM-
MERFORT, LAURA DRANK A LARGE
GLASS OF MILK AND WENT STRAIGHT TO BED,
not worrying that her hair was tangled, or that her feet would
make her sheets filthy. She left any explanation to Rose, who
didn't know much but did explain why Laura was so tired.

For days Grace had alternated between silence, weeping,
and clinging to Chorley saying, "What will we do now? What
can I do with my life?" Rose's bit of news gave Grace something to think about. "Laura's *pregnant!*" she said. "How far
along?"

"Well—it must have been before Sandy—"

"Oh, the poor girl," Grace said. She jumped up. Rose
grabbed her. "No, Ma. Let her sleep. She told me that's all
she wants for now. I'll go and make up a bed for Mamie."

Mamie had remained outside. She'd picked up one of the
folded rugs from the wingback wicker chairs and was sitting,
cocooned, gazing out at the view.

"And then I'll run a bath for that man," Rose said, and
jerked her thumb at Lazarus.

Lazarus waited in the doorway. He stood very still, and his
extreme exhaustion only added to his presence. His face was
cadaverously thin and pale, and Chorley, looking at him, was

tempted to make some joke about Poe's raven—because the man really did look like he might start croaking "Nevermore!" at them.

✧ ✧ ✧

Rose took Lazarus to the upstairs bathroom. She put the plug in the tub drain and turned on the taps. The water splashed, then began to chime as the tub filled. "I don't think I've ever seen Laura so sad," Rose said.

"Laura is sad because she believes in fate," he said.

Rose was trying to figure him out. She kept staring at him, and the longer she stared the longer she wanted to stare. He was grimy and abrupt and, she thought, violent in some way she couldn't quite work out, but he was mesmerizing to her—the mysterious *fact* of him.

He said, with a kind of exhausted eagerness, "But I think what happens is that when anyone does anything absolutely extraordinary—great or terrible—then, when they change the world, they make *another* world. When God separated light from darkness and made the world, perhaps he left the dark world behind him. And, because the dark world is still there—"

"You really are a Hame, aren't you?"

A little color came into his cheeks, rosy gray under the dirt. "Meaning?"

"Quaintly religious."

"Who are you calling quaint, you old-fashioned girl?" he said.

Rose turned off the taps and tested the water. She couldn't tell whether it was a comfortable temperature. Her hands still felt warm as hot and hot as burning. But this man wasn't an infant and could look after himself. "Throw your clothes outside the bathroom door and I'll bring you something to wear," she said, and bustled out.

❖ ❖ ❖

Mamie was in the guest room, sorting through some of Rose's clothes to see what she could fit into. Chorley had gone out to send a telegram to Mamie's mother, saying she was safe and staying at Summerfort. Laura was still asleep.

Rose had taken up the task of listening to her mother's lamentations, which were a little less intense now and interspersed with thoughts about Laura's baby. "If I wasn't so worried about how we're going to make a living, I'd be happier about it. Your father and I always wanted another baby, but it didn't happen. I do love babies."

"Ma, we don't owe anyone money. And we have two properties. Everything is mortgage free, and there's money in the bank. We're not going to be poor."

"But I don't know who I am if I can't catch dreams," Grace said.

"Then you'll find out, Ma."

"Hello!" Chorley called from the front door.

"He has good news," Rose said. "He sounds really happy."

A moment later Chorley appeared, his arm clasped protectively around the waist of a figure in yellow pajamas.

"*Sandy!*" Grace and Rose shouted together. They rushed him and hugged him. Grace cupped his whiskery, grinning face and cried. Rose held his hand, noticing as she did the shiny, red, hairless patches that matched her own scorch marks.

"He was limping barefoot along the promenade," Chorley said.

"I'm all right," Sandy said. "I only walked from the Awa Inlet to Sisters Beach."

"Forty-five miles," said Grace. "Nothing for a dream-hunter."

"Are you all Contented?" Rose said.

"A little. I feel much less serious than I know I should. I *should* feel like tearing off Secretary Doran's head."

Chorley gave a gleeful laugh and pulled a telegram from his pocket. He gave it to Rose. It was from her uncle, Tziga. It said that Cas Doran was under arrest on charges of abduction.

"That's a start," Rose said. She felt only grim relief. She knew that she'd have to carry this news to Mamie, and that Mamie might feel she should go back to Founderston at once, to stand by her mother. And Rose knew that sometime in the near future there would be a trial, and that her family would be called to give evidence against her friend's father. Mamie already had difficulties with the world and its expectations, and this could only make it all worse. Remembering how she'd said to Mamie, proudly, that she would go to university to study "Law—for justice," Rose thought that it was all right for *her*, she had committed herself to a struggle, had spied, plotted, carried a copy of the damning film. But Mamie hadn't made any choices, yet she would have to suffer for those her father had made.

Rose touched Sandy's arm. "Laura is in bed," she said. "You know where her bedroom is, don't you?"

"Um, yes," Sandy said.

Chorley poked Sandy in the arm with a stiff finger. He said, with a prod for every word, "She. Is. With. Child."

Sandy opened his mouth, swallowed, then shut it again.

"Precisely," said Chorley, and pointed to the stairs. "Go," he said.

✥ ✥ ✥

Laura woke up, still tired, with the heavy, sickening feeling that comes when you know something terrible has happened. Then she remembered that the terrible things were still ahead of her—her whole future mapped out already in the story Lazarus had told her. She longed to speak to Nown. She badly wanted to tell him what it was like to *know* what would happen. To know, and to have to choose to be alone in knowing.

She opened her eyes—and looked straight into Sandy's. He had been lying with his head beside hers, waiting for her to wake up. He smiled and touched her cheek.

And in that moment everything changed for Laura. The world became world-sized again, and full of surprise.

Sandy said, "There's a strange man in the upstairs bathroom. A strange man who looked at me strangely."

"Well, he would," Laura said.

"I wasn't dead," Sandy said. He gathered her in his arms.

Laura took a deep breath of Sandy's own odor—with its overlay of dust and sea salt. "It's not *true*, then," she said, through her tears. "Here you are, my baby's father. I thought I was going to have to go through with it all—do all the lonely things. Say bon voyage to Uncle Chorley. Let Rose go away and live in another country. Nurse Father. Live quietly. Wait to die. I thought I had to do what fate dictates. Follow its laws as my poor Nown had to follow my orders."

"Shh, darling," Sandy said, and stroked her hair. "It's all right."

"Yes," she cried. "It *is* all right. Here you are. That poor man out there must come from a different world than this one. God is merciful. God has given us a new world to live in—like The Gate. There *is* a first time for everything."

Sandy smiled at Laura, moved by how moved she was but completely bewildered. "I have no idea what you're talking about, love."

She laughed, and her last two tears were squeezed out of her eyes by a smile. "I'll tell you," she said.

✧ ✧ ✧

When Lazarus came downstairs, wearing some of Chorley's clothes, he found Grace, Chorley, and Rose waiting for him. He seemed unable to look at any of them for long. His gaze flitted away around the room and finally lighted on Tziga's violin, sitting on its stand and covered in a peach fuzz of dust. Lazarus crossed the room—so thin in his borrowed clothes that he seemed to drift, bodiless. He picked up the violin and put it to one ear. He plucked at its strings with his scabbed thumb, then began adjusting it—plucking, listening, twisting its pegs. "This is mine," he said, softly, lovingly. "The last time I saw it, it was 'produced in evidence.'"

"*Excuse* me?" Chorley said, outraged.

Rose said to Lazarus, "I know this isn't everybody, but I promise I'll pass on faithfully anything you say if you don't feel like saying it again."

Lazarus nodded. Then he said, "My name is Lazarus Hame."

Chorley narrowed his eyes. "Explain," he said.

"Give me a moment," said Lazarus.

And it was amazing what Lazarus could do, given a moment.

9

✦ ✦ ✦

THE CITY WAS BIGGER, AND SO WERE ALL THE OTHER SETTLEMENTS. THERE WERE MORE ROADS, BETTER ROADS, WITH many more cars on them.

But Nown kept away from the roads. He traveled cross-country, and often by night. He walked so far that his feet turned as white as old ice.

Laura had been his compass—she was North, South, East, and West to him. He couldn't find her, but he kept on looking in all the places he'd found her before.

His pilgrimage finally took him along So Long Spit. He walked on past the lighthouse, then farther, beyond where he'd been that day with Laura.

At the end of the Spit, a sandbar pointing out into a thousand miles of empty ocean, Nown found the gannet colony. He stopped at the edge of the throng of black-and-white birds and gazed at the pattern they made, a glow going away into nothing. He thought, "Laura," her name like a prayer. "Laura, I am not in the same world as you."

He started forward and moved delicately in among the roosting gannets. The birds weren't at all afraid of him. They shuffled aside, clucking peevishly.

Eventually Nown stopped and stood surrounded by the

warmth of the colony. He looked out over the sea, gazed into nothingness, and waited. He began his waiting.

The setting sun shone though his glass body and showed up the dark matter at its heart—his heart, a rust-stained rock from the railbed.

Epilogue

(1912)

*I*T WAS THREE DAYS BEFORE CHRISTMAS, AND THE FAMILY WAS AT SUMMERFORT. CHORLEY HAD JUST FINISHED SHOOTING A film, his first two-reeler, and was shut up in his darkroom, editing it. His three jacks-of-all-trades—Sandy, Sandy's brother the engineer, and Lazarus—were kneeling on the lawn around a newspaper, on which rested a dismantled camera. The camera had been responsible for some edge fog on the film, and they were trying to work out where the light had leaked in.

The newspaper, disregarded by the men, carried a headline that, three days before, had made everyone in the family very happy: PRISON REFORM BILL PASSES—HARD LABOR ABOLISHED.

Grace was upstairs, getting her granddaughter off to sleep so that her daughter could study.

The afternoon was still and humid, the air filled with the abrasive music of hundreds of cicadas, and one violin. The violin belonged to a four-year-old boy, who stood, shoulders back, his instrument tucked under his chin, playing. He was practicing legato, his bow moving smoothly and never leaving the strings. His performance was watched by his grandfather, who sat on a stone seat at the edge of the lawn, back to the hazy, hot blue of the bay.

The cousins, Laura Mason and Rose Hame, were on the veranda. Between them was a table covered in books and papers.

Laura was using her cousin to test the wording of title cards for the finished film. Chorley liked to have as few title cards as possible. That morning he and she had watched a rough cut and worked out where it was absolutely necessary to add those six or so seconds of darkness and white words.

Laura hunched, chewing on the end of her big, flat builder's pencil. Then she pounced, scrawled for a moment, and raised the sheet of paper to flash it at her cousin.

Rose read: "Pat Slocum—General of the Heroes of Dog Alley."

"That's not bad. But is it worth interrupting the action for?" Rose said.

"He's a dumpy little dandy who swaggers, so we know 'General' and 'Heroes' are ironic," Laura said. She frowned at what she'd written, chewed her pencil some more, then had another inspiration. She scrawled more words and held them up.

Rose read: "The Commander in Chief of the mighty forces of Dog Alley—General Pat Slocum."

"Change his name to Pat Potts or something," Rose said. "Unless Da's done the cast credits already."

Laura was about to answer when Rose lifted her book and flashed its title—*Southland Constitutional Law*. She said, "I'm having enough trouble with this without the Dog Alley Gang."

Laura gathered up her sheets of paper. She went in search of another victim. She stood behind her son and flashed title cards at her father.

"I've forgotten the film's plot, darling," Tziga said, "so I'm not much use. But I like 'mighty forces.' "

And, at that moment, the ground began to shake.

Laura dropped into a crouch and put her arms around her son. She watched her father's slow realization that this violent noise and vertigo wasn't the beginning of one of his fits but was external to him. Tziga didn't try to stand up. He clamped one hand on the edge of the stone seat and rode it as it rocked and shuddered.

Laura could hear glass breaking. She looked back at the house.

The panes in the dining room windows were exploding, one by one. The windows had jammed in their warped frames and were bent and bowed. Laura saw that Rose was trying to crawl to the front entrance. Trying to get into the house and upstairs to her baby. But Laura could see Grace already had the baby. Grace was sheltering in an open door on the upstairs balcony, her back against the doorframe, her head and shoulders curved protectively over the lace-swathed bundle of her granddaughter.

Chorley staggered out the front door and pulled Rose back in under its solid frame.

The ground between Laura and the house cracked, the fissures only inches wide but showing stretched fibers of grass roots. The gravel on the new driveway jumped like popcorn in a hot pan.

And then the shaking stopped. Sound seemed to ebb all the way out of the world. The silence that followed the quake was like a presence—some vast, demonstrative, living thing.

In the Sisters Beach firehouse, a siren wound up into a long, wobbling shriek.

Laura saw that her father had held on to his seat with only one hand; he still had the book he'd been reading in the other, his finger shut into it as a place marker.

Sandy ran up to her. They both took a good look at their boy, Sandy squeezing his arms as if to check for injuries, she brushing his fine, red hair back from his face and peering into his black eyes.

Rose was already up on the balcony. Grace gave her the baby, who was howling louder than the fire siren.

Lazarus called, "Is she all right?"

"She's fine," Grace shouted down. "She was fast asleep. She's only angry because I woke her." Then, "Where's Chorley?"

Lazarus and Sandy's brother pointed at Chorley, who came out where his wife could see him and waved to her. "I'm going to go down into town and take a look around," he said.

"Take your camera," Grace and Rose said together.

Laura's son was trembling. She rubbed his arms. "Wasn't that strange?" she said in a bright voice, hoping to reassure him.

"It's all over now, son," said Sandy.

The boy looked from one parent to the other, his eyes round and bright. He said, "Was the ground angry? Was it trying to get up?"

Glossary

✦ ✦ ✦

claim Whenever a DREAMHUNTER finds a new dream, he or she must register it with the DREAM REGULATORY BODY and stake a claim on it. A claim will give a dreamhunter one-year exclusive rights to perform the dream. However, any dream that the Dream Regulatory Body chooses to classify as a DREAM FOR THE PUBLIC GOOD cannot be claimed.

Colorist A Colorist is a secret persuader who will insert into another DREAMHUNTER's performance some impressions at the dream's beginning or end, when the audience is less fully absorbed in the performance. The audience absorbs the Colorist's impressions and thinks these are their own thoughts or feelings. A Colorist's dream is usually a print of a dream taken from a GIFTER, who has altered it to deliver a desired message. Coloring is illegal.

dream for the public good A dream deemed too valuable for commercial use alone, usually a healing dream, will be classified as a dream for the public good by the DREAM REGULATORY BODY. The Department of Corrections also classes THINK AGAIN DREAMS as dreams for the public good. Any DREAMHUNTER may catch a dream for the public good and can perform it in a DREAM PARLOR or a DREAM PALACE. But each time the dream is caught, the dreamhunter's contract with the Dream Regulatory Body rules that the dreamer must spend several nights dreaming it in a hospital. Exceptions to this are dreams such as Convalescent One and Starry Beach, discovered before the formation of the Dream Regulatory Body; anyone can catch them and negotiate their sale at market prices.

dream palace A larger building, often purpose-built, in which dreams are performed is a dream palace. According to DREAM REGULATORY BODY regulations, to qualify as a dream palace the building must have over fifty beds. Dream palaces are often round or ovoid and consist of several tiers, balconies with bedrooms opening off them. In the center of the palace auditorium is the dais, where the dreamer sleeps. Only DREAMHUNTERs with large PENUMBRAs perform in dream palaces. Dream palaces are a vital part of the life of Southland; attendance of dreams is a social occasion, and most fashionable people own formal nightwear. The Rainbow Opera is Southland's largest and most magnificent dream palace. It was built for Grace Tiebold.

dream parlor Any place with fewer than fifty beds dedicated to the performance of dreams is a dream parlor. Many of the hotels and hostels on Founderston's Isle of the Temple became dream parlors during the early years of the industry. Dream parlors can have as few as five beds. Tickets to attend general exhibition dream parlors are much less expensive than those to DREAM PALACE performances, though there are specialist dream parlors with prices dependent on the market for their dreams. Maze Plasir, a GIFTER, is the proprietor of an expensive and exclusive dream parlor on the Isle of the Temple.

Dream Regulatory Body Established in 1896 under the Intangible Resources Act, the Dream Regulatory Body (also known as the Regulatory Body or just the Body) is a department of the Secretariat of the Interior, and the responsibility of the Secretary of the Interior, Cas Doran, who was the main author of the Intangible Resources Act. The Regulatory Body employs RANGERS to patrol THE PLACE. The Regulatory Body also holds Tries to identify new DREAMHUNTERs and undertakes the testing and training of successful candidates of each TRY. All dreamhunters, DREAM PALACEs, and DREAM PARLORs must be licensed by the Body. The Body also has contracts with other government entities to supply dreams for health care and for programs of education and rehabilitation in Southland's prisons.

dream sites Dreams are sometimes found in general areas in THE PLACE and can be caught by a group of people. This is the case with Wild River and is one of the reasons that it is used to test the successful candidates of each TRY. But some dream sites are very confined; their dreams are hard to discover, and can often be caught by only a particular kind of DREAMHUNTER. Maze Plasir's Secret Room is a confined-site dream. So is Tziga Hame's The Gate. That dream's site was so confined that Hame could claim never to be able to find it again.

dream trails Roads, paths, and scratchy routes in THE PLACE, dream trails usually lead to popular, tried and tested dreams.

dreamhunter Anyone able to enter THE PLACE, catch one of the dreams to be found there, carry it back into the world, and share it with others is a dreamhunter. Dreamhunting has been an industry in Southland for twenty years and is a major form of entertainment and therapy.

Gifter (or **Grafter**) A Gifter is a DREAMHUNTER who can take his own memories of a real person's face and manners and graft them onto the characters in the dreams he catches. Gifters are usually employed by people who want what they can't have, or who have lost someone they love.

healer Any DREAMHUNTER who can catch and convey vividly the great healing dreams is a healer.

Hame Any DREAMHUNTER with a big PENUMBRA is known as a Hame. The name comes from Tziga Hame, possibly the greatest dreamhunter.

loaded A DREAMHUNTER with a freshly caught dream is sometimes said to be loaded. Each dream is like a charge, discharged over a number of sleeps.

map references in the Place On maps of THE PLACE, the main references are bands and sections. Because the Place is vast, and its interior unexplored, it is mapped in bands from either end. Each band represents a three- to five-hour journey on foot, depending on the terrain. From Doorhandle the Place has been mapped from bands A to I. The Tricksie Bend end is less thoroughly explored, and has been mapped only from Z to U. From the Doorhandle border one enters Band A; from Tricksie Bend one enters Band Z. Each band is divided perpendicularly into sections. The sections are a kind of longitude to the latitude of the bands. The sections begin with I to the west of Doorhandle and minus I to the east, and the same at the Tricksie Bend end, so that the map will work if its references *were* ever to join in the as yet unpenetrated interior. Grace Tiebold's first dream, Pursuit, is at A minus I, In and a little east of Doorhandle.

master dream A dream that can erase other dreams, a master dream is particularly powerful and vivid. Examples are Buried Alive, Secret Room, and Contentment.

mounter Any DREAMHUNTER who can OVERDREAM another and erase the dream he or she is carrying is a mounter.

Novelist Any DREAMHUNTER who can catch a SPLIT DREAM is a Novelist. The people who share a Novelist's dream will sometimes pick up one point of view and sometimes another, or switch back and forth all night between the two. Split dreams are richer and more complex than other dreams. Grace Tiebold is the most celebrated Novelist dreamhunter.

overdream When a powerful and fully loaded DREAMHUNTER, especially one having a MASTER DREAM, erases another dreamhunter's performance, this is known as overdreaming.

penumbra A DREAMHUNTER's projection zone is known as his or her penumbra, a term borrowed from astronomy, where it describes the partial shadow the moon casts on the face of the earth during a total eclipse. (The "umbra," or totality, is the dreamhunter himself or herself, asleep and haloed by the shade of a dream.) An average public performance-sized penumbra is around eighty yards. Some dreamhunters, such as Maze Plasir, have small penumbras and still have good careers because they have other specialties, and their projection zones deliver hypnotically intense dream experiences. Grace Tiebold has a three-hundred-yard penumbra. Tziga Hame's, at four hundred, is the largest on record. Grace Tiebold and Tziga Hame cannot sleep just anywhere when LOADED with a dream.

the Place The territory where the dreams come from is called the Place. It is infinitely more vast than the hundred or so square miles of the mountain range it encompasses. Only a very few people can enter the Place. Of these, some become RANGERS and some DREAMHUNTERs who can make their fortunes from dreams caught, carried out, and shared with others.

No one has established how long the Place was there before being discovered. Protected by its own remoteness, and the sparse population of the Rifleman Mountains, the Place had its first verifiable appearance on a day in November 1886 when a young violinist named Tziga Hame disappeared from a coach traveling between the village of Doorhandle and Sisters Beach.

rangers Employees of the DREAM REGULATORY BODY, rangers patrol THE PLACE, maintain its trails, and perform search and rescue when necessary. Rangers are those who find that, although they can enter the Place, they can't catch dreams.

Soporif Anyone who is close to a Soporif DREAMHUNTER when he falls asleep will fall asleep with him. Soporifs often work in hospitals, enhancing the effects of anesthetics. For example, Soporifs can be helpful by entering the operating room before the surgeons and their assistants and lying down near the prepared patient. George Mason is Southland's best Soporif.

split dream   A dream that has two points of view is a split dream. Only a NOVELIST will be able to catch both points of view at the same time and deliver them to the audience. Examples of split dreams are Homecoming, the Second Sentence / Sunken, and Grace Tiebold's famous first split dream, Pursuit.

Think Again dream   A dream classified by the Department of Corrections as a DREAM FOR THE PUBLIC GOOD and used for educating and rehabilitating prisoners is a Think Again dream.

Try   Twice a year, in the fall and spring, the DREAM REGULATORY BODY holds Tries, at which people, the majority of them teenagers, attempt to enter THE PLACE. Only one person in three hundred will cross over into the Place.

Wakeful   A purple-red fibrous paste, Wakeful is a powerful stimulant with a pleasant perfume. It is dangerous if used for too long or in large doses. DREAMHUNTERs often chew Wakeful to stay awake when they have walked days into THE PLACE to catch a dream they don't want to waste before they have an audience.

GO FISH

ELIZABETH KNOX

What did you want to be when you grew up?

When I was about six I announced to my parents that I wanted to be a jockey—not that I'd ever been on a horse! Not wanting to let me know too soon what the world was like (then) my father said, "But darling, you'll grow too big!" So I put it out of my mind. I never did get too big, and by the time I was fifteen New Zealand had its first female jockey. Of course by then my plans had changed.

When did you realize you wanted to be a writer?

When I was sixteen. I'd started writing letters between the characters in an imaginary game I played with my sisters and friends. I remember lifting my pen from the page and thinking, "This is what I want to do with my life."

What's your first childhood memory?

I was eighteen months old. It was night, and I was buttoned into my father's coat with my head poking out of his collar. We were on the deck of the Lyttelton ferry. I remember looking at the lights of Seatoun and Breaker Bay as the ferry sailed out of Wellington Harbour.

What's your most embarrassing childhood memory?

I was eleven. It was the end-of-year school performance. The girls of my class and the class above ours were doing a fashion show of the clothes we'd made in what they used to call "Manual Training" (the girls did cooking and sewing and the boys did woodwork and all made taiaha—Maori spears—and caused one another injuries). I was the announcer of the show. My friend Denise hadn't given me her notes so, when she came on stage, I said, "Denise is wearing . . . " then, hissing, *"Denise, what are you wearing?!"*

As a young person, who did you look up to most?
My father. He was vivid, flamboyant, opinionated, and very handsome.

What was your worst subject in school?
Math.

What was your first job?
I had a holiday job with my father, who was the editor of a New Zealand encyclopedia. I had to make a photo library. I mischievously filed photos of the Prime Minister of the day under "Disasters."

How did you celebrate publishing your first book?
I bought a pair of boots.

When you finish a book, who reads it first?
My husband, Fergus, who is also my New Zealand editor and publisher (though only of my adult books).

Are you a morning person or a night owl?
Hoot!

What's your idea of the best meal ever?
Fresh mozzarella and sliced tomatoes drizzled with some grass green olive oil and followed by black Otago cherries.

Which do you like better: cats or dogs?
I have three cats—a ginger boy, a beige boy, and a black girl. They are from the same litter and still sleep in a warm, furry pile.

What do you value most in your friends?
Warmth and optimism.

Where do you go for peace and quiet?
The Wellington Botanical Gardens are at the bottom of the street where I live, so I go there.